"I'll take care of everything." His gaze never wavered.

Her stomach lurched. "What does that mean?"

"We'll be married." He said it without a pause, without the slightest hesitation.

And she wanted to cry again—partly from another, stronger, wave of relief. And partly because, really, it was all wrong.

Once, she'd dreamed of marrying his brother. It had to be beyond inappropriate simply to switch brothers. And since those four magnificent days two months ago, Rafe had made something of an art form of avoiding her. A man you marry shouldn't spend weeks dodging you—and then, at the mention of a baby, drop right to his knees and propose.

* * *

The Bravo Royales:
When it comes to love, Bravos rule!

THE EARL'S PREGNANT BRIDE

BY
CHRISTINE RIMMER

Published in Great Britain 2014
by Mills & Boon, an imprint of Harlequin (UK) Limited,
Eton House, 18-24 Paradise Road, Richmond, Surrey, TW9 1SR

© 2014 Christine Rimmer

ISBN: 978-0-263-91324-8

23-1014

Harlequin (UK) Limited's policy is to use papers that are natural, renewable and recyclable products and made from wood grown in sustainable forests. The logging and manufacturing processes conform to the legal environmental regulations of the country of origin.

Printed and bound in Spain
by Blackprint CPI, Barcelona

Christine Rimmer came to her profession the long way around. Before settling down to write about the magic of romance, she'd been everything from an actress to a salesclerk to a waitress. Now that she's finally found work that suits her perfectly, she insists she never had a problem keeping a job—she was merely gaining "life experience" for her future as a novelist. Christine is grateful not only for the joy she finds in writing, but for what waits when the day's work is through: a man she loves who loves her right back, and the privilege of watching their children grow and change day to day. She lives with her family in Oregon. Visit Christine at www.christinerimmer.com.

For Tom and Ed.
I miss you both so much.

Chapter One

Genevra Bravo-Calabretti, princess of Montedoro, heaved the lightweight ladder upright and braced it against the high stone wall.

The ladder instantly tilted and slid to the side, making way too much racket as it scraped along the rough old stones. Genny winced and glanced around nervously, but no trusty retainer popped up to ask her what she thought she was doing. So she grabbed the ladder firmly, righted it and lifted it, bringing it down sharply to plant it more solidly in the uneven ground.

Breathing hard, she braced her fists on her hips and glared at it, daring it to topple sideways again. The ladder didn't move. Good. All ready to go.

But Genny wasn't ready. Not really. She didn't know if she'd ever be ready.

With a very unprincesslike "Oof," she dropped to her bottom in the dry scrub grass at the base of the wall. Still panting hard, she wrapped her arms loosely around her spread knees and let her head droop.

Once her breathing evened out, she leaned back on her hands and stared up at the clear night sky. The crescent moon seemed to shine extrabright, though the lights from the harbor below obscured most of the stars. It was a beautiful May night in Montedoro. She could smell roses, faintly, on the air.

A low moan escaped her. It wasn't right. Wasn't fair. She ought to be out with friends in a busy café or enjoying an evening stroll on her favorite beach. Not dressed all in black like a lady cat burglar, preparing to scale the wall around Villa Santorno.

Useless tears clogged her throat. She willed them away. She'd been doing that a lot lately, pulling herself back from the brink of a crying jag. The worry and frustration were getting to her. Not to mention the hormones.

She didn't want to do this. She felt ridiculous and pushy, in addition to needy and unwanted and more than a little pathetic.

But seriously, what choice had he given her?

"I am not going to cry," she whispered fiercely as another wave of emotion cascaded through her. "Absolutely not." With the back of her hand, she dashed the moisture from her eyes.

Enough. She was stalling and she knew it. She'd dragged that damn ladder all the way up the hill. She wasn't quitting now. Time to get this over with.

Gathering her legs under her, she stood and brushed the bits of dry grass and dirt from the seat of her black jeans. The ladder was waiting. It reached about two-thirds of the way up the wall, not quite as far as she might have hoped.

But too bad. No way was she turning back now.

She put her foot on the first rung and started to climb.

A minute later, with another low moan and a whimpery sigh, she curled her fingers around the ladder's highest rung. The top of the wall seemed miles above her.

But she made herself take the next step. And the next. Until she was plastered against the wall, her hands on the broader, flatter top stones, her black Chuck Taylor All Stars perched precariously on that final rung.

"Bad idea," she whispered to the rough stones, though there was no one but the night to hear her. "Bad, bad idea...." Right at that moment, she wished with all her heart for the superior upper body strength of a man.

Her wish was not granted. And there was nothing to do but go for it or go back. She was not going back.

With a desperate animal grunt of pure effort, she boosted herself up.

It didn't go all that well. Her feet left the ladder and the ladder swayed sideways again, skittering along the stones, this time with no one to catch it before it fell. It landed with a clatter at the base of the wall.

Could her heart pound any harder? It bounced around madly inside her chest.

Had they heard the ladder fall in the villa? Would someone come to help her? Or would she hang here until her strength failed and she fell and broke her silly neck? Rafe would have to come and collect her limp body. Serve him right. She grunted and moaned, praying her quivering arms would hold out, the rubber soles of her shoes scrabbling for purchase against the wall.

And then, miracle of miracles, she figured it out. The trick was to simply hold on with her wimpy woman arms and use the sturdy muscles in her legs to walk up the wall. She swung her left leg up and over with way too much undignified grunting and groaning—and then, there she was, lying on top of the wall, legs dangling to either side.

Safe.

For the moment anyway. She rested her cheek on the gritty stone and took a minute to catch her breath again.

Through the night-dark branches of olive and palm trees, she could see the villa. The lights were on. But apparently, no one had heard the racket she'd made. The garden surrounding the house was quiet. She lifted up enough to peer at the softer-looking grassy ground on the garden side. It seemed a very long way down there.

She probably should have thought this through a little more carefully.

Maybe the thing to do now was to start shouting, just scream her head off until Rafe or the housekeeper or *someone* came outside and helped her down.

But no. She just couldn't do that, couldn't call for help and have to be rescued. She refused to be that pitiful and ineffectual. She'd gotten up here on her own. She'd get down the same way.

Dear Lord, have mercy. Please, please be kind....

She eased her left leg lower, swung the right one over and down. Now she was dangling on the garden side of the wall, holding on for dear life.

She squeezed her eyes shut. *Let go, Genevra. You have to let go....*

Not that she had much choice at that point. Her instincts had her trying to hold on, but her strength was used up.

She dropped like a rock and hit the ground hard. Pain shot up her right heel, sang through her ankle and stabbed along her calf. A strangled scream escaped her, along with several very bad words.

"Ugh!" She crumpled to her side and grabbed her ankle. "Ow, ow, ow!" It throbbed in time to her racing heart. "Ow, ow, ow..." She rubbed and moaned, rocking back and forth, wondering if there was any way she was going to be able to stand.

"Gen." The deep familiar voice came from just beyond the hedge to her left. "I might have known."

She whipped her head around. "Rafe?"

Rafael Michael DeValery, earl of Hartmore, stepped forward through a break in the hedge. And her silly heart leapt with hopeless joy at the sight of him, huge and imposing and as still as a statue, standing in the shadows a few feet away. "Have you hurt yourself?"

She shot him a glare and kept rubbing her poor ankle. "I'll survive. And you could have simply let me in the gate the times I came knocking—or maybe, oh, I don't know, taken one of my calls?"

For a moment, he didn't answer. Even in the darkness, she could feel his black eyes on her. Finally, he spoke in a rueful tone. "It seemed wiser to keep the agreement we made in March."

Those humiliating tears rose again, thickening her throat, burning behind her eyes. She blinked them away. "What if I needed you? What if I need you right now?"

He was silent again, a breath-held kind of quiet. Then, finally, "*Do* you need me?"

She couldn't quite bring herself to say it. Yet.

And he spoke again, chidingly. "You never said so in the messages you left. Or when you came to the gate."

She had the tears under control for the moment. But still, her pulse galloped along, refusing to slow. Her cheeks were burning red. Memories of their four-day love affair seemed to swirl in the night air between them, dizzying. Glorious. Yet awful, too, in the sense of loss and hopelessness that dragged at her. "Yes, well, I do have some pride. I'm not telling your housekeeper I need you. I'm not putting it in a text or leaving it on your voice mail."

He took a step closer. "Gen…" What was it she heard in his voice? Longing? Pain? Or only her own wishful thinking? She couldn't tell, not with just that one syllable to judge by. Whatever emotion might have gripped him, he instantly banished it and added with his customary quiet control, "Come inside."

"Fine." She braced her hand against the wall, put most of her weight on her good foot and staggered upright. Her bad ankle didn't give out, but it wobbled beneath her. She winced and let out a moan.

He was at her side in an instant. "Let me help." Eerie, the way he could move, that magical swift grace that so completely belied his size. One of his legs had been broken in the accident six months before. Two months ago, he'd still had a slight limp. The limp was gone now.

But when the moonlight fell across the right side of his face, the scar was still there, puckered and angry, though not as red as before. It started at the corner of his eye, curving around his cheek in a shape that echoed the crescent moon above them, the end of it seeming to tug at the side of his mouth, as though trying to force him to smile—and failing. Rafe rarely smiled. Two months ago, she'd asked if he'd checked into the possibilities of plastic surgery. He'd said no, he hadn't. And he didn't intend to.

"Here." He took her hand. His touch slammed into her, making him suddenly so real to her again, so warm and solid. And why did he have to smell so good? It wasn't the least fair. He'd always smelled good to her, even when she thought of him strictly as a friend—so clean, so healthy, like new grass and fresh air and sweet, just-turned earth.

And please. What did it matter that he smelled good? She had to put all her concentration on the task before her, on telling him what he needed to know.

He guided her arm around his huge, hard shoulders. His

heat and strength seared along her side. Together, with her leaning on him to keep her weight off her right foot, they turned to go in, taking the stone path through the hedge and across a stretch of lawn to the wide patio shaded by jacaranda and carob trees and through the open French doors into the combination kitchen and family room.

"Here..." He led her to a wide white chair.

"Maybe not," she warned. "I've got bits of grass and dirt all over my jeans."

"It's all right. Sit down."

"Your call," she said resignedly, easing her arm from across his shoulders and sinking onto the soft cushion. "It hardly looks like the same place." The large room had been redecorated and updated, the living area with light-colored fabrics and modern oversize furniture. The kitchen now had chef-quality appliances and granite and wood countertops.

"Tourists with fat billfolds don't appreciate heavy draperies and an ancient fridge. They want comfort and openness to go with the view." He gestured toward the terrace opposite the French doors. On that side, the villa needed no garden walls. It touched the edge of the cliff. From where she sat, she could see the crowns of palm trees and farther out, the harbor and the blue Mediterranean. The DeValerys were English, of Norman descent, but Montedoran blood also ran in their veins. Villa Santorno had come down through the generations from a Montedoran-born DeValery bride.

"So." She tried not to sound wistful. "You really do plan to make it a rental?"

"I do." He towered above her, the scar pulling at his mouth, his eyes endlessly dark and way too somber. Two months ago, he'd come to Montedoro to make arrangements for the villa's renovation. At that time, it had been four months since the accident that took his older brother Edward's life and gave Rafe the earldom as well as his crescent scar. Genny had essentially run him to ground then—just as she was doing now.

Two months ago...

They'd made love in this very room. But then the curtains had been heavy, layered, ornate velvets over floral damask, the sofas and other furniture a gorgeous mash-up of baroque, rococo and neoclassical.

He asked low and a little gruffly, "Do you have to look so sad?"

"I liked it the way it was, that's all." Now and then during her childhood, various members of his family would come and stay at the villa to enjoy the Montedoran nightlife, or attend some event at the palace. Occasionally during those visits, her family had been invited to dine or have tea here. She could still remember her ten-year-old self perched on a velvet-seated straight chair beside the French doors to the garden, holding a Sevres teacup and saucer, scheming to get his grandmother, Eloise, aside and wrangle herself another invitation to Hartmore, the De-Valery estate in Derbyshire. To Genny, Hartmore had always been the most beautiful place in the world.

He knelt at her feet and her breath caught at the suddenness of the movement. "I'll have a look, shall I?" Before she could decide whether or not to object, he had her foot in one big, gentle hand and was untying the shoelace with the other. He slid the shoe off, set it aside and then began probing at her ankle, his touch warm and sure, making her heart hurt. Making her body yearn. "It doesn't seem to be broken. Maybe a slight sprain."

"It's fine, really. It's already stopped hurting."

He glanced up, caught her eye. "Just to be safe, I think we ought to wrap it."

Harsh, angry accusations pushed at the back of her throat, but she only said firmly, "Leave it, Rafe. It's fine."

"Fair enough." He lowered her foot to the floor and rose to his considerable height.

She tracked the movement, and found herself staring up the broad, strong, wonderful length of him. Struck again with longing, her breath got caught and tangled somewhere in the center of her chest. How strange. She'd always loved him as a person, but found him hulking and coarse, unattractive as a man.

What a blind, childish fool she'd been.

"Tell me what's brought you here," he said, his eyes so deep and dark, seeing everything, giving nothing away. The man was like a human wall, always quiet and watchful and careful, as though wary of his own strength among mere mortals. "Tell me, Gen. Please. Whatever it is."

"All right, then." She drew in a fortifying breath—and suddenly, contrarily, she ached to delay the inevitable. But what was the point in that? He needed to know and she'd almost broken her neck climbing the garden wall to get to him and tell him. "I'm pregnant. It's yours."

Did he flinch?

She wasn't sure. Most likely he hadn't. He never flinched. That for a moment it had seemed so was probably only her imagination working overtime.

"My God, Gen." He said it softly, almost reverently. "How? We were careful."

"Not careful enough, evidently—and if you want a paternity test, I'll be happy to—"

"No test is necessary. I believe you."

I believe you. The soft-spoken, calm words echoed in her head.

And she knew relief, just a hint of it, like a slight breeze in a close room. So, then. She had told him at last. And he hadn't denied her, hadn't turned away from her. He was still standing there right in front of her, still watching her patiently without a hint of rancor or accusation.

Letting her head drop against the soft back of the white chair, she closed her eyes and released a long sigh. "Well. There. It's out at last."

"Are you well?" His voice came from down at her level again.

She opened her eyes to find he had dropped to his knees in front of her once more. "Perfectly," she told him.

"Have you been to your doctor?"

"Not yet. But I took four home tests. They were all positive. And the instructions on the box promised that the test was completely dependable."

"You should see a doctor."

"I know. I'll do that soon—but I'm perfectly healthy." She frowned. "Or maybe you somehow think I'm not pregnant after all."

"I told you, I believe you. But I think a visit to the doctor is in order."

"I… Yes. Of course. All right."

"I'll take care of everything." His gaze never wavered.

Her stomach lurched. "What does that mean?"

"We'll be married." He said it without a pause, without the slightest hesitation.

And she wanted to cry again—partly from another, stronger wave of relief. And partly because, really, it was all wrong.

Once she'd dreamed of marrying his brother. It had to be beyond inappropriate simply to switch brothers. And since those four magnificent days two months ago, Rafe had made something of an art form of avoiding her. A man you marry shouldn't spend weeks dodging you—

and then at the mention of a baby drop right to his knees and propose.

"Rafe. Honestly. I don't know if…"

"Of course you know. It's the right thing."

She should be stronger. Prouder. And seriously. Nobody married just because there was a baby coming, not anymore— well, except maybe for her brother Alex. And possibly her sister Rhia.

And come to think of it, both of those marriages were turning out just fine.

And she had such a *thing* for him now. Plus, their baby had a right to be the Hartmore heir, and to be the heir required legitimacy—or at least, it would all go much more smoothly, if the baby was legitimate. There would be absolutely no question then of who should inherit.

And then there was Hartmore itself. Her beloved Hartmore…

Mistress of Hartmore, temptation whispered in her ear. She could have her dream come true after all, though she'd been so certain it was lost to her forever with Edward's death.

Edward.

Just thinking his name made her heart heavy with guilt and confusion. She really had thought that she loved him, that she was only waiting for him to make a move toward her so they could begin to forge the life they were born to have together.

Now, feeling as she did about Rafe, she wasn't so sure about Edward, about all those plans she'd had to be Edward's bride. She wasn't sure about *anything* anymore.

"Say yes," the giant, seductive stranger who was once her dear friend commanded in a tone both tender and merciless.

She stared at him, trembling. "Are you sure?"

"I am. Say yes."

The word was there, inside her, waiting. She simply pushed her guilt and confusion aside and let that word get free. "Yes."

Chapter Two

Before Genny left the villa that night, they agreed to be married at Hartmore on the following Saturday. He said he would call his grandmother first thing in the morning; Eloise would make all the arrangements. He also got her to promise that they would face her mother and father, the sovereign princess and prince consort, right away.

"And we will face them together," he added, dark eyes determined, that wonderful soft mouth of his set.

It really wasn't necessary and she tried to tell him so. "Rafe, you know how my parents are. They're not going to disown me or anything. They'll be on our side and they'll just want to be sure we're making the right choice."

"We *are* making the right choice." He said it flatly.

"I'm only saying that you really don't have to——"

He put up his big hand. "Yes, I do."

As he seemed so inflexible on the subject, she agreed—after which he called a car and sent her home.

Home for Genny was the Prince's Palace, perched high on Cap Royale, overlooking the Mediterranean, where she had her own apartment. She was up half the night worrying, second-guessing her decision to marry Rafe, feeling guilty and confused. Very late, she finally drifted off.

The phone rang at eight, jarring her from much-needed sleep. It was Rafe, calling to remind her to set up the talk with her parents. "And don't tell them about the baby, or that we'll be married, until I'm there with you."

She grumbled at his bossiness. "I already said I wouldn't."

"Excellent." He made the single word sound almost affectionate. And that made her feel a little better about everything.

"Did you call Eloise yet?"

"I'm doing that next."

"Oh, I don't know. Maybe you should wait. We should tell her together."

A pause on his end of the line, then, "Gen, the wedding will be Saturday. I'm sure your parents will want to be there. Someone has to make the arrangements." He was right, of course. And his grandmother was a rock. She would take care of everything.

Genny answered with a sigh. "All right."

He instructed, "Call me as soon as you've set up the meeting."

"I will, yes."

They hung up and she showered, ate a light breakfast and was waiting in the reception area of her mother's office at the palace when her mother arrived at nine.

Her Sovereign Highness Adrienne, looking ageless and elegant as always in one of her classic Chanel suits, smiled at her fondly, agreed to the meeting with her and Rafe and then asked, "Darling, what is this meeting to be about?"

Genny knew that her mother would understand. She longed to just get it over with, to tell all. But she'd told Rafe that she would wait. He would soon be her husband. She wanted him to feel he could trust her to keep her agreements with him.

Rafe. Her husband...

Dear Lord. Was this really happening?

Her mother touched her arm. "Darling? Are you all right?"

"Yes. Absolutely. I'm fine. And we'll explain everything when Rafe is here, I promise." She asked that her father be there, too.

And her mother asked again what exactly was going on.

Genny hugged her and whispered, "Two o'clock. We'll tell you all of it then." And she escaped before her mother could ask any more questions.

Back in her apartment, she called Rafe and told him when to be there. He arrived at one-thirty and came straight to her rooms as she'd asked him to do.

She gestured him in. "It's good you're here early. We'll have a little time to plan."

"There's more to plan?" He sounded doubtful.

She stepped back to get a good look at him. "You look... terrific." She felt oddly breathless suddenly. Because he did look wonderful in a fine lightweight jacket and trousers. Wonderful in a completely feral, un-English way, with his thick black curls, full lips, black velvet eyes and huge, hard body. A savage in a suit. The scar only added to the impression of otherness.

"And you are beautiful," he said in that carefully controlled, formal way he had.

She wasn't, not really. Her mother was beautiful. And her four sisters, too. Genny was the most ordinary looking of all of them. With wispy blond hair and brown eyes, she was pretty enough, but nothing spectacular. She smoothed her hair and adjusted her fitted white jacket, which she'd worn over a simple jewel-blue shirtwaist dress, an outfit she'd deemed demure and appropriate for this particular meeting. "Thank you—did you reach Eloise?"

"I did."

"Did you tell her there will be a baby?"

"Yes."

Genny gulped. "How did she take it?"

"She was pleased on all counts."

"She wasn't surprised…you know, that you and I were, um, lovers?"

He looked at her with infinite patience. "Nothing surprises my grandmother. You should know that."

"I…" She started to say something vague and dishonest. But why lie about it? "Yes. I suppose I do." Eloise had never made a secret of her desire to have Genny join the DeValery family and had openly encouraged a union between Genny and the lost Edward.

Not only did Genny adore the DeValerys and Hartmore, she had money. Pots of it—and giant old places like Hartmore needed serious infusions of cash on a regular basis. The lion's share of Genny's money came down to her from her godmother and namesake, Genevra DeVries. Aunt Genevra had never married. She'd had no children of her own and had always considered Genny the daughter of her heart.

Now that Edward was gone, the supremely practical Eloise would see nothing wrong with Genny marrying her other grandson, the new heir. Genny only wished that she could be half as indomitable as Eloise.

"Grandmother loves you," Rafe said. "Never doubt that."

"I don't. Of course I don't.…"

He watched her steadily. She had that feeling she too often had with him. That he could see not only through her clothes to her naked body beneath, but even deeper, right into her heart and mind. And then he said, "Now. What are these 'plans' you need to discuss with me?"

She stared at him, chewing her lip, trying to decide how to begin.

He shook his head. "You had better just tell me."

"Ahem."

"I'm listening."

"Well, I've...I've been thinking that we shouldn't actually come right out today and tell my parents that I'm pregnant." He arched a thick black brow, but said nothing. She added airily, "I'm thinking we can do that later."

"When is later?"

"Oh, well. You know, after we've settled in at Hartmore. One thing at a time, I was thinking..."

He gave her one of his deep and oh-so-patient looks. "You don't think they'll wonder why the rush to the altar? Why you're suddenly marrying me, of all people?"

"What do you mean, 'of all people?'" she demanded sourly, as though she didn't know exactly what he meant. *Edward.* She was supposed to have married Edward.

Rafe regarded her solemnly. "You know exactly what I mean."

She could almost become annoyed with him. After all, he was the one who'd asked her to wait until he was with her to speak of the baby. If she'd just gone ahead and told her mother that morning, it would all be out in the open now. Her mother would have told her father and it wouldn't really be necessary to say much more about it.

Now Rafe would be there for the big reveal. And her father, too. Dear Lord. She should have thought this through earlier. Because she realized now that she just wasn't ready to sit in her mother's office and look in her father's face and tell him about the baby.

He was a wonderful man, her father. He was the best. She couldn't bear to think he might be disappointed in her.

Rafe caught her arm and she realized she'd been swaying on her feet the tiniest bit. "Gen. Do you need to sit down?"

She blinked up at him, all too aware of his touch, of the heat of him so close, of his tempting scent. Of the velvet darkness of his eyes. Carefully, she eased her arm from his grip. "Really, I'm fine."

"You're sure?"

"Yes. I'm fine. I just want you to let me do the talking, let me handle it with my parents."

He studied her from under the heavy shelf of his brow. Evidently, he believed that she wasn't going to faint, because he didn't try to steady hear again, but only lifted one huge shoulder in a shrug. "You don't want me to ask for your hand?" He was teasing.

Or was he?

She really couldn't tell. "I... No, of course not. It's already decided. We're just sharing our plans." For that, she got another unreadable look, one that had her waving a nervous hand. "More or less. Can we not overthink it, please?"

He captured her hand as it fluttered between them and pressed his lips to the back of it. A warm, delicious shiver danced up her arm. For such a giant rock of a man, he did have the softest, supplest mouth. "As you wish, love," he said.

Love. He'd been calling her that forever—at least since she was thirteen or so. She'd always liked it when he called her that, and felt as cherished as a dear friend.

Now, though, it only reminded her that she *wasn't* his love in the way that she ought to be as his bride.

She cleared her throat. "Ready?" He offered his arm. She took it. "All right, then. Let's get this over with."

In her mother's private office, there was tea served in the sitting area with its long velvet sofa and priceless old wing chairs.

At first, they endured the obligatory small talk—gentle condolences from her mother about the lost Edward, questions about Rafe's injuries, inquiries about the health of Rafe's family. He told them that his nephew, Geoffrey, whom Genny adored, had been sent up to boarding school in London "under protest." Geoffrey's mother, Rafe's sister, Brooke, was getting along fine. His grandmother, he said, was in good health and as busy as always about the house and the gardens.

Too soon, it seemed to Genny, the small talk ran out. Her parents looked at her expectantly.

And she realized she had absolutely no idea how to go about this. She'd purposely *not* planned what she would say, telling herself not to make a big deal of it, that the right thing to say would come to her naturally.

Wrong.

All that came was a frantic tightness in her throat, a rapid pounding of her pulse and a scary generalized tingly feeling all over, a full-body shiver of dread. And her stomach lurched and churned, making her wonder if she was about to experience her first bout of morning sickness.

"Gen." Rafe said it so gently. His big, hot, strong hand covered hers.

She looked at him, pleading with her eyes. "I…"

And he took over, turning to face her parents, giving a slow, solemn dip of his large dark head. "Ma'am. Sir. I know this may come as a bit of a surprise. But I love your daughter with all my heart."

Loved her with all of his heart? Had he actually said that? Her throat clutched. She swallowed, hard, to relax it, and tried to paste on a smile.

Rafe continued, so calmly and clearly, still clasping her hand, engulfing it in his heat and steadiness. "And Genevra has done me the honor of consenting to be my wife. We're here today to ask for your blessing."

Genny stared across the coffee table at her parents. They both looked surprised. But not in a bad way, really—or was that just desperate wishful thinking on her part? The two of them shared a long, speaking glance. What exactly that glance said, well, she just couldn't tell.

And her mother said, "We had no idea."

Rafe squeezed her hand. She knew she really *had* to say something. But she couldn't for the life of her think what. Once again, poor Rafe had to answer for her. "It's sudden, I know. And we're..." He seemed to seek the right word. "We're eager to get on with our lives together. So eager that we're planning to marry in Saint Ann's Chapel at Hartmore on Saturday."

Her father frowned. "Saturday is four days away."

"Um, five if you count today," Genny put in helpfully.

"So quickly," said her mother, drawing her slim hand to her throat. She looked at her father again.

Her father didn't catch that glance. He was busy watching Genny, frowning. "Genevra, are you ill?"

And Genny knew she couldn't just keep sitting there like a lump, trying not to throw up and letting poor Rafe lie for her. It wasn't right, wasn't fair. So she opened her mouth—and the truth fell out. "We were together for four days in March, when Rafe came to arrange renovations at Villa Santorno. I, um, well, I'm pregnant. And, er, Rafe insists on doing the right thing and marrying me."

Rafe corrected stiffly, "We *both* feel it's the right thing. And of course, I *want* to marry your daughter."

There was a silence then. An endless one.

Finally, her mother said softly, "Oh. I see."

Her father turned his gaze on Rafe and said in a carefully controlled tone, "You know we think the world of you, Rafael." He went on, with growing heat, "But what in the hell were you—?"

Her mother cut him off by gently murmuring his name. "Evan."

Her father shot her mother a furious glance—and then sighed. "Yes. Fine."

Genny just ached for them—all three of them. Her mother and father because they'd already been through this with two of her siblings. Genny hated that she was putting them through it again. It really shouldn't be that difficult to practice proper contraception in this day and age.

And she *had* practiced it. They'd used a condom every time.

But then, there had been a *lot* of times....

And poor Rafe. He thought so highly of her parents. It had to be awful for him, to have to face them with this news.

"Of course, you're both adults and this is your decision, between the two of you," said her mother, and went on to add exactly what Genny had known she would say. "We only want you to be sure this is the right choice for you."

"It is," Rafe said in low growl, not missing a beat.

Her mother's legendary dark eyes were focused solely on Genny. "Darling? Is it the right choice for *you*?"

The right choice...

Genny went through her list of reasons in her mind again: the baby, who deserved the right to claim his inheritance. And her fondness for Rafe. Surely they should have a good chance to make a successful marriage together, with friendship as a basis. And being intimate with him wouldn't be a hardship—oh, who was she kidding? Sex with Rafe was amazing.

And Hartmore.

Yes. She would have Hartmore. And, fair enough, she was a little ashamed that Hartmore mattered so much.

But the plain fact was that it did.

"Genevra?" her father prompted gruffly.

She wove her fingers more tightly with Rafe's. "Yes," she said. It came out firm and wonderfully sure sounding. "Marrying Rafe is the right choice for me."

After three days jam-packed with shopping and preparations and endless visits with lawyers to hammer out all the legal and financial agreements, they flew to East Midlands Airport on Friday. There was Genny, Rafe, her mother and father and Aurora, whom they all called Rory. The wedding would be very small and private, only family members, just the bride and groom in the wedding party, with Genny's father to give her away.

Rory would be taking the pictures. She was the baby of the family, a year younger than Genny—and everything Genny wasn't.

There was nothing ordinary about Rory. Rory loved the great outdoors. She thrived on adventure. She had a bachelor of fine arts in photography from the School of the Arts Institute of Chicago and she'd already had her pictures published in *National Geographic, Country Digest* and *Birds & Blooms.* Genny found her baby sister a little intimidating.

But then, Genny found all of her siblings intimidating. They seemed larger than life to her, somehow, each of them not only knowing what they wanted, but also going after it with passion and grace. True, Genny had always known what she wanted: to be a DeValery and mistress of Hartmore. But her sisters' ambitions were so much grander than hers. Compared to them, Genny sometimes felt like a plain gray pigeon raised in a family of swans.

At East Midlands, two cars were waiting to take them to Hartmore. Genny, Rafe and Rory rode together. Genny's and Rory's bodyguards sat in front, one of them at the wheel. The ride took about an hour. Rafe was mostly silent and Genny didn't feel much like talking, either. Rory, always full of energy and plans, tried to keep the conversation going, but eventually gave up. They rode in silence through the English countryside and Genny drifted off to sleep.

She woke suddenly, her head on Rafe's shoulder, as they pulled to a stop at Hartmore, the North Entrance, so stark and spectacular. Open parkland, designed two hundred years before by Capability Brown, rolled away into the distance dotted with giant old oaks and beeches. A masterpiece of Georgian perfection in its day, the house was composed of a central block joined by single-story links to three-story wings on either side. Six Corinthian columns supported the central pediment.

The façade remained magnificent. But inside, Genny knew, more than a few of the two hundred rooms had been water damaged due to roof leaks. So much needed doing in the months and years to come. But right now, all she could think of was the first time she'd seen the house. Her mother had brought her and her four sisters, Arabella, Rhiannon, Alice and Rory, for a visit when Genny was five.

For Genny, that visit had been a revelation; at the tender age of five, she'd suddenly known what she wanted, known where she fit in. Now, twenty years later, she felt exactly the same. She was coming home—home to stay, at last.

"We're home," said Rafe so softly, echoing her thoughts. She smoothed her sleep-flattened hair and gave him a smile that only trembled a little.

An hour later, after her mother, her father and Rory had been properly greeted and shown to their rooms, Genny and Rafe met privately in one of the East Wing drawing rooms with Rafe's grandmother, the dowager countess, Eloise.

Tall, with the proud posture of a much younger woman, Eloise had a long, heavily lined face, pale blue eyes and wiry, almost-white hair that she braided and pinned close to her head. She lived in old trousers and wellies, her tri-color rough collies, Moe and Mable, trailing in her wake.

Genny loved Eloise—absolutely and uncondition-ally. An amateur botanist, Rafe's grandmother ruled the grounds and gardens. And she ruled well. Overall, the estate lands were in much better shape than the house— especially the West Wing, where roof leaks had necessi-tated the removal of many of the furnishings.

"Moe. Mable. Go." Eloise pointed to a spot by the fire-place and the collies trotted right over there. "Sit." They sat. She lowered her hand, palm down, toward the floor. "Down." The dogs stretched out obediently. Then she turned a glowing smile on Genny. "My dearest girl."

With a low cry, Genny ran to her.

Chuckling, Eloise gathered her up in those long, ca-pable arms. She smelled of lavender and lemons. Genny took comfort from the beloved, familiar scents. "So. We shall have you as our own after all."

Genny hugged the old woman closer. "It's so good to see you."

"Let me have a look at you." Eloise took Genny by the shoulders and held her away. "A little pale, perhaps."

"I'm fine. Really."

"That's the spirit. We'll soon put pink in those cheeks and fatten you up." She pressed a rough, heavily veined hand to Genny's cheek. "I'm deeply gratified that you will be my own granddaughter at last."

Genny bit her lip and nodded and didn't really know what to say. "It's all a little overwhelming...."

There was a noise in the hallway. The dogs perked up their ears and the door flew open. "Genny!" Dressed in his school uniform, complete with blue vest and striped tie, eight-year-old Geoffrey came flying into the room. "You're here! You're really here!"

"Slow down, young man," Eloise commanded, hiding a grin.

Genny held out her arms.

He landed against her and hugged her good and hard. "They let me come from school because of the wedding," he said. "And Great-Granny says you will be my aunt Genny."

"Oh, yes, I will."

Then he scowled. "Mum's sending me back on Sunday."

Genny smoothed his tousled sandy hair. "I'm so glad you could make it."

He beamed her a big smile and she saw that he'd lost two baby teeth in front. "I'm so glad to be home." Then he turned and flung himself at Rafe. "Uncle Rafe!" Rafe chuckled and lifted him high.

"Put him down, Rafe." Brooke DeValery Landers, Rafe's sister and Geoffrey's mother, stood in the open doorway looking stunning as always in turquoise silk leggings, a big-collared white tunic, ballet flats and a look of disapproval. "He's way too excited, behaving like a savage. No manners at all." She raked her long sable hair back from her forehead and turned her angry sapphire eyes on

Genny. "Lovely to see you, Genevra." Her tone said it wasn't lovely at all. Brooke was divorced from an American, Derrick Landers. Her ex lived in the States. He'd remarried and had two more children.

"Hello, Brooke." Genny and Brooke had never really gotten along. The best they ever did together was a kind of cool civility. Genny put on a smile and went to her. They air-kissed each other's cheeks. "You look well."

Brooke stared past her at Rafe. "I understand congratulations are in order."

"It's true," Rafe answered without missing a beat. "Gen has made me the happiest man on earth."

"Genny." Geoffrey tugged on her hand. "Samson had kittens, did you know?" He gave her his jack-o'-lantern grin.

Genny widened her eyes. "But how is that possible?"

"Because Samson turned out to be a *girl!*" He chortled with glee.

"Geoffrey, come along now," Brooke cut in sharply. She held out her hand, snapping her fingers. "I want you out of that uniform before you get something on it."

His laughter died. He slumped his small shoulders. "But I want to take Genny out to the stables and show her—"

"Geoffrey. Now."

Dragging his feet, he went to his mother. Herding him out ahead of her, she pulled the door closed as she went.

Genny stared at the shut door and promised herself that she'd steal a little time with Geoffrey before he had to return to school on Sunday.

They had dinner at eight in the State Dining Room, with its Chippendale sideboards and urn-topped pedestals and the glorious old table that could seat forty.

Geoffrey didn't join them. Brooke said he was over-tired and already in his room. The conversation was, for the most part, innocuous. Rory whipped out a camera and took several pictures right there at the table before the meal was served. She said she was headed to Colorado on Monday, to the town of Justice Creek and a long visit with Clara, her favorite Bravo cousin. Eloise spoke of her bedding plants and the vegetable border in the walled garden, which she couldn't wait to show Genny. Genny's mother and father were charming and agreeable.

And Rafe was his usual silent, watchful self. He ate slowly, with never a clink or a clatter. When he set down his delicate crystal water goblet after taking a sip, the water within hardly stirred. Genny tried not to stare at him, not to get lost in inappropriate fantasies of those four days two months ago.

Or in distant memories of the feral boy he'd been once, roaming the gardens and grounds, unkempt and unsupervised. His mother, Sabrina, had doted on him and refused to rein him in. His father, Edward II, had little to do with him, except to punish him for what the earl considered Rafe's uncivilized behavior, punishments which were frequent and severe.

Genny had met Rafe during her first glorious visit to Hartmore, when she was five and he was thirteen. He was still running wild then. He'd dropped out of an oak tree practically on her head and she'd run off screaming. The next day, when he'd popped out from behind a topiary hedge into her path, she'd somehow managed to hold her ground. Before the end of that visit, they were unlikely friends: the earl's big, wild second son and the five-year-old Montedoran princess. Her mother, who had always encouraged her children to get out and explore the world, had allowed her to roam all over the estate as long as Rafe was there to look after her. He'd told her that he hated his father. And she'd admitted that she wished she could stay at Hartmore forever.

That fall, strings were pulled and Rafe went away to St Paul's in London. He shocked everyone by doing well there. After St Paul's he attended Emmanuel College at Cambridge, where he'd finished at the top of his class. More than once in recent years, Eloise had confided in Genny that Rafe had a brain to match his giant body and an aptitude for money management. He'd taken a modest inheritance from a great-uncle and made some excellent investments with it. Now he was doing well for himself. Before Edward's death, Eloise had even once let drop that Hartmore would be better off had Rafe been the heir.

Across the table next to Rafe, Brooke let loose with a brittle laugh. "Genevra, what *are* you staring at?" Of course she knew. She even turned a mean little smile on Rafe to drive home her point.

Genny ordered her cheeks not to blush and spoke up fast, so Rafe wouldn't feel he had to step in and defend her. "Why, at you, of course, Brooke. Love that dress."

Brooke made a scoffing sound and lifted her wineglass high. "To marital bliss, everyone. Though God knows in my experience it's not all it's cracked up to be."

Chapter Three

The State Rooms at Hartmore were open to the public Thursday through Sunday from noon to four in the afternoon, April through October. One small-budget film of Jane Austen's *Emma,* as well as a couple of BBC specials, had been shot there.

Hartmore was also available for weddings. There were two wedding parties scheduled for the next day, the first at one in the afternoon and the second at four, both in Saint Ann's Chapel, with receptions to follow in the State Dining Room and on the grand terrace, respectively.

By five-thirty, the second party had left the chapel. Hartmore staff got right to work switching out the flowers and hanging a fresh set of lace and floral swags from the ends of the gorgeous old mahogany pews.

At a quarter past six, Genny walked down the red-carpeted aisle in the six-hundred-year-old sandstone church on her father's arm. She wore a sleeveless white-lace creation bought three days before in Montedoro and carried pink roses from Hartmore's rose garden. Rafe waited for her at the altar dressed beautifully in a charcoal morning coat, buff waistcoat and gray trousers. To her, the whole experience had an air of unreality.

She was on her father's arm and then, as if by magic, she stood at the altar with Rafe, beneath the stained glass window depicting the crucifixion and ascension of Christ. There were vows and she said them, obediently and a little bit breathlessly.

Rafe kissed her, his soft lips brushing hers for the first time since he'd kissed her goodbye after their brief time together two months before. She shivered a little at the contact and her body ached. For him.

So strange, really. She'd been at his side constantly in the five days since she'd climbed the villa wall to tell him she was having his baby. But they hadn't really talked, not about anything beyond their plans to marry and what had to be done next.

And they hadn't made love. He'd been distant and carefully gentle with her. Attentive, but in no way intimate.

Right after the ceremony, as she posed with Rafe and the family and Rory flitted about snapping picture after picture, she wondered if, just possibly, she might have lost her mind. Pregnant. Marrying Rafe, her dearest friend, who was now like a stranger. Mistress of Hartmore.

It didn't seem real. It was all like some weird, impossible dream.

They had dinner, just the family, in the small dining room in the East Wing, where the family lived. For the occasion, Genny would have liked to have used the State Dining Room again. But it wasn't to be. The paying wedding parties were still going on in the heart of the house. After the meal, they moved to the East Solarium. There was wedding cake, as well as champagne that she pretended to sip while Rory took more pictures.

At eleven, she found herself in Rafe's bedroom, the East Bedroom, as it had always been called, though there were many more bedrooms in that wing of the house. The East Bedroom had its own sitting room, a dressing room and bath—and a second bedroom beyond the dressing room. The East Bedroom had been part of the original design of the house, back before the turn of the eighteenth century, and was revolutionary in its day. An en suite bath was rare at the time. Even the very wealthy went down the hall—or even out the back door—to the loo.

The bedroom itself was furnished with Chippendale lacquer furniture and an enormous, ornately draped canopy bed. Wearing the white satin, low-backed bit of silky nothing she'd bought the same day she bought her wedding gown, Genny sat at the lacquer dressing table and stared at her wide-eyed reflection in the slightly streaky antique mirror. She worried that he might not be coming to join her.

She started to chew her lower lip over it, but made herself stop. And then she leaned close to the glass to whisper furiously at her own reflection, "If he doesn't come, you are not going just sit here and wish that he would. You are getting up and going to find him."

And when she found him, she would insist that they sleep together as man and wife.

Because they had to start somewhere to build a real marriage. And since the sex had been so good with them, she couldn't help hoping that lovemaking might be a way to break through the wall of emotional reserve he seemed to have erected around himself.

"No need for that, Gen. I'm right here."

She gasped and whirled to find him standing there, not

six feet away. "Rafe! You scared me to death." Frantically, she tried to remember just how much of what she'd been thinking she'd actually said out loud.

He stood absolutely still, the crescent scar pulling at the side of his mouth in that perpetual false hint of a smile, his black eyes watchful. "Forgive me."

She thought of the wild boy he'd been once, tormented by his own father, wary of everyone—except her. And nowadays, he was wary of her, too. She had no idea what he might be thinking.

His thick brows drew together. "Are you all right?"

"Of course. Yes, fine." Dear Lord, this was awful. They really were like strangers, with the long, awkward silences followed by stammered-out reassurances. She rose and faced him, feeling way too uncovered in the revealing nightgown.

He blinked and announced gruffly, "Good, then. I'll just be a few minutes." He went through the door to the dressing room and bath, closing it behind him.

She realized she'd been holding her breath. Releasing it in one hard gust, she let her head droop and stared down at her bare feet on the gorgeous old Aubusson carpet. Would he actually come back? He'd said that he would. But there was that other bedroom in the suite accessible through the dressing area. Great lords and ladies, after all, shouldn't have to actually share a bed if they didn't wish to. Should she follow him, make sure that he...?

No. Time enough for that later if he failed to return. She drew her shoulders back, spun on her heel and turned off the lights, all but the one at his side of the bed. Then she climbed in between the heavy bed curtains, got in under the covers and sat up against the pillows to wait for him.

She pressed her hand to her chest. Her poor heart pounded away in there with a sick sort of dread. She feared that he wouldn't come and she would either have to go after him—or know herself for the coward she was.

But then the door opened and there he was, huge and muscular and marvelous, really, in a pair of dark silk boxers—and nothing else. He strode right for her. Her heart pounded hard, but with excitement now rather than dread.

He turned off that last light before climbing in next to her. She sat there in the dark against the pillows, acutely aware of his presence beside her, of his size, his heat. And his silence.

About then, it became too ridiculous. The unreality of it all was too much for her. A silly, hysterical little laugh bubbled up in her chest. She tried to swallow it down.

But it wouldn't be swallowed. It burst out of her, a breathless, absurd, trilling sort of sound. She slapped her hand over her mouth, but it wouldn't stop.

"You think it's funny, do you?" he asked from the darkness beside her.

She laughed some more. "I... Oh, God, I..."

And then she heard it, a low, rusty rumble. It took her a moment to realize that the sound was coming from him. He was laughing, too.

They laughed together, there in the dark, and she remembered...

How they used to laugh together often, over the simplest things—the antics of Moe and Mable when they were pups, or the way he would pop up out of nowhere, bringing a shriek of surprise from her. In the old days, they could laugh together at anything, really. She'd always felt so proud that he would laugh with her. He never did with anyone else. With her, he didn't feel the need to be constantly on his guard, to hold himself in check.

In recent years, though, he'd become more distant, more

careful with her. And she'd missed the playful times they used to share.

The laughter faded. The room was too quiet. Still, she realized she felt marginally better about everything.

And then he shifted beside her, moving closer and even wrapping his big arm around her. He pulled her against him.

She sighed in sudden, lovely contentment and leaned her head on his rock of a shoulder. "I think I've become hysterical."

"Must be the hormones." His wonderful huge hand moved on her bare arm, a tender stroking motion.

This was more like it. She snuggled in closer. "That's the advantage to being pregnant. Anytime I behave badly, I can just blame it on the hormones."

"You haven't."

"What?"

"Behaved badly." His lips brushed her hair.

She rubbed her cheek against the hot, smooth flesh of his shoulder and wished it might be like this between them always. "Have you forgotten what happened when we told my parents we'd decided to get married? The way I made you promise not to tell them about the baby—and then went right ahead and blurted out the truth when you were trying so hard to keep the secret for me?"

"That wasn't behaving badly. That's just how you are."

"Unable to stick with a plan of action?"

"No. Not wanting to disappoint your parents—and yet never quite able to hide the truth."

"I'm honest to the core, am I?"

"Yes." He said it so firmly, without even having to stop and think about it. His belief in her cheered her.

But then she thought about their marriage, which wouldn't have happened except for the baby. Now, because of the baby, she had achieved her lifelong dream: to be countess of Hartmore. "But I'm not," she said miserably. "Not honest at all."

"Shh."

She dared to lift her head. "Rafe, I—"

"Shh," he said again. And then his hand was there, at her throat, caressing, brushing upward to lift her chin. "Gen." His breath warmed her cheek. She drank in the familiar, exciting scent of him.

And then, light and questioning and heartbreakingly tender, his mouth touched hers.

A real kiss. At last.

She sank into it, parting her lips for him, welcoming him in.

He accepted her invitation, dipping his tongue in, making her whimper low in her throat as he pulled her closer, turning his big body toward her. She moaned in pleasure at the glorious feel of her breasts pressing into his broad, hard chest. Clasping his giant shoulder, she melted into him.

They sank down into the bed, still kissing. She pushed at his shoulder then, urging him over. He gave to her will, stretching out on his back so that she could ease her leg across him.

Her nightgown had slithered up. It was a crumpled knot at her waist. She didn't care. She was lying on top of him, her body pressed along the length of his.

His big hands were on her hips, pulling her closer. She could feel the hard, wonderful ridge of his arousal through the thin silk of his boxers.

He wanted her.

And she wanted him. Surely they could make things good and right between them, now, tonight, on their wedding night.

She reached up to caress his face and felt the curving,

puckered shape of the scar. And she moaned deep in her throat, in excitement. In pleasure. And also in sympathy for all he had suffered.

And then, out of nowhere, he froze. She made a soft, soothing sound. She stroked his shoulder, urging him to relax, to stay with her, to keep kissing her, touching her...

But he only shifted stiffly beneath her, tugging on her nightgown, smoothing it down to cover her. He eased her off him and gained the top position once more.

"Rafe, what—?"

He put a finger against her lips. She stared up at him through the darkness, waiting for him to explain himself, to tell her what had gone wrong.

But he didn't explain a thing. After a moment, he stretched out beside her, pulling her close again, settling her head on his shoulder. "Let it alone for tonight," he said quietly. "It will be all right."

She wanted to believe him. But she didn't, not really. And that had her thinking of Edward, for some reason.

Edward, slim and tall, with blue eyes and golden-brown hair. Edward was always so elegant, as sophisticated and charming as Rafe was stoic and tender. Edward had been the hero of her earliest fantasies. He used to flirt with her shamelessly. And she had thoroughly enjoyed every teasing glance and clever compliment.

Edward...

Maybe what they needed, she and Rafe, was to talk about the hardest things—like Edward's death, which he seemed to have a real aversion to discussing. Two months ago, at Villa Santorno, when she'd tried repeatedly to bring it up, he'd only refused over and over to go into it.

She went for it. "Is this about Edward somehow?"

"Go to sleep, Gen."

"I touched the scar on your cheek...and it all went bad."

"No."

"Rafe, I think we really need to talk about it."

"Leave it alone."

"No. No, I'm not going to do that. I know what happened that night, the facts of the situation. Eloise told me. She said that you were driving home from a party at Fiona's." Fiona Bryce-Pemberton was a longtime friend of Brooke's; they'd met as children, Brooke and Fiona, at St Anselm's prep school in nearby Bakewell. At the age of nineteen, Fiona had married a wealthy banker. The banker had bought her Tillworth, a country house not far from Hartmore. "I know that it was two in the morning and Edward was driving. Brooke had stayed the night at Fiona's. There was only you and Edward in the car when he drove off the road and into an oak tree. Eloise said that the investigation absolved you of any wrongdoing, that it was simply an accident, one of those terrible things that can happen now and then."

Rafe lay very still. At first. And then, with slow, deliberate care, he eased away from her. They still lay side by side, but their bodies were no longer touching. "So, then. You know what happened. There's nothing to talk about."

She sat up, switched on the lamp by her side of the bed and turned back to look in his hooded black eyes. "There's everything to talk about. There's how you feel about what happened. How you're…holding up. And there's the question of why you won't let a good plastic surgeon have a look at that scar."

His eyes flashed dark fire. "I feel like bloody hell about what happened, thank you. I'm in one piece, in good health and I'm now the earl of Hartmore, so I would say that I'm holding up just fine. As to my face, it may not be pretty, but I really don't give a damn. If you don't want to look at me, then simply look away."

"Oh, Rafe, that's not fair. You can't just—"

He cut her off by reaching for her, yanking her close and smashing his lips down on hers in a hard, angry kiss.

She shoved at his shoulders until he let her go. "What is the matter with you?"

"Leave. It. Alone." Each word came out as hard and cold as a stone.

Her lips still tingled from the force of his kiss. She pressed her fingertips to them, soothing them. "This isn't like you."

"I mean it, Gen. Edward is dead. There's nothing more to say on the subject."

"Of course there is. There's *everything* to say. I know you loved him, as he loved you. I know it has to be killing you, that he's gone, that—"

"Enough." He threw back the covers and got up. "Good night." And then he left her, just like that.

She watched him stride through the door that led to the other bedroom, pausing only to close it behind him so carefully, hardly making a sound.

She longed to jump up and go after him.

But no.

She'd tried. It hadn't gone well. She needed to let it be, at least for now. She settled back against the pillows, sliding her hand under the blankets, resting her palm on her belly where their baby slept.

It will get better.

They would somehow work through all the awfulness. Somehow they would find each other, as friends. As lovers. As husband and wife.

She absolutely refused to admit that she might have made a terrible mistake, that she'd married a man she no longer even knew.

* * *

It was after three in the morning when she finally fell into a fitful sleep.

She woke at a little past nine, feeling exhausted, as though she hadn't slept at all. But she couldn't stay in bed forever. So she rose and showered and dressed and resisted the temptation to check the other bedroom.

Finally, at the very last minute, before she went down to breakfast, she went to the door of the other bedroom and gave it a tap.

Nothing.

She knocked again. When he still didn't answer, she went ahead and pushed it open. He'd already gone. No one had made the bed yet; the sheets were in tangles. She couldn't help taking selfish satisfaction from the evidence that he hadn't slept all that well, either.

Out in the hallway, her bodyguard, Caesar, was waiting. He followed her to the Morning Room, positioning himself just outside the door, ready in case she might need protecting.

Which she did not. But after her brother Alex's kidnapping and four-year captivity in Afghanistan, everyone in the family had security whenever they traveled outside the principality.

Her marriage to Rafe changed that. Now she was part of Rafe's family and as such allowed to choose whether she still wanted security or not. She chose not. Caesar would be going home with her parents. Nothing against him. He was quiet and unobtrusive and easy to have around. But she looked forward to getting along without a soldier following her everywhere.

In the Morning Room, the staff kept a buffet breakfast on the sideboard until eleven. The room was empty, the table set, the silver chafing dishes lined up and waiting.

Her stomach felt a bit queasy. Pregnancy and a wedding-night argument were not a good combination. She took toast and apple juice and sat at the table.

Rory came in as she debated whether or not to try the raspberry jam. "Any news?"

Genny glanced up from the jam pot. "News about what?"

Rory got some coffee and took the seat next to Genny. "No one told you?"

"Apparently not. What are you talking about?"

Rory set down her china cup without taking a sip. "Geoffrey's disappeared. Brooke went to his room at eight to get him ready for the drive up to London. He wasn't there. He'd left a note on his pillow saying he hated school and was running away and never coming back."

Chapter Four

Genny's stomach lurched. "Geoffrey...ran away?"

Rory nodded. "Rafe, Eloise, two of the gardeners and a stable hand are out beating the bushes looking for him. I offered to help, but Eloise turned me down. She said maybe later, if they don't find him in any of his favorite places."

"What about Brooke? And Mother and Father?"

"Brooke's in her rooms having her nineteenth nervous breakdown. Mother and Father are out on the terrace, waiting for Rafe or one of the others to come back—hopefully, with Geoffrey in tow."

Genny pushed back her chair. "Where did they go to look for him?"

"They mentioned the lake trail and the boat jetty, the walled garden...a couple of other places, I think."

"What about the castle?" Built in the thirteenth century, Hartmore Castle was now a roofless ruin. She and Geoffrey had spent an afternoon exploring there last summer.

"No," said Rory. "I don't think the castle made the list—and where are you going?"

Genny was halfway to the door. "To check the castle."

"I'll come!"

"No, stay here. I'll be fine...."

Rory grumbled that she hated getting stuck at the house, but Genny hardly heard her. Caesar left Rory's bodyguard by the door and fell in behind her as she ran to her room to change into a pair of jeans and some trainers. She left the house from a side door and took off on foot across open parkland in the quickest, most direct route to the castle. Caesar followed close behind.

She felt terrible about Geoffrey. She'd promised herself she'd make time for him yesterday. But in the last rush to get ready for the wedding, she'd never quite managed it. If she found him at the castle, they'd have a few minutes together. She could apologize for yesterday. And she could try to make him see that running away solved nothing. With a little coaxing, she hoped she could get him to return to school voluntarily.

On foot, at a steady clip, it was a good half hour to the ruins, past Saint Ann's, through the old cemetery, onto a public footpath that once was a turnpike road. The path cut through the former pleasure grounds of the estate, from back before the construction of Hartmore House, when the DeValerys lived at Hartmore Hall, long since demolished. From the path, she crossed the deer park, and from there she took a heavily wooded trail that wound in upon itself, with the ruined castle at the center.

Before she rounded that last curve in the circular track, she turned to her bodyguard. "I'm hoping Geoffrey is at the castle and I want to speak with him alone. Will you stay out of sight unless I call for you?"

"Of course, ma'am." The bodyguard stepped off the

path and into the trees, vanishing almost instantly from her sight.

She turned again for the castle, emerging a few minutes later into the open space where the crenellated ruin loomed against the sky. The stone hall and courtyard fortress were beautiful in their stark, gray, weather-beaten way. The tower still stood, though the lower wing had been plundered over the centuries to get stone for other buildings. The empty rectangular windows and door arches gaped like dark unseeing eyes.

Genny opened her mouth to call for Geoffrey, and then shut it without a sound. Even on a sunny, almost-June morning, the place had a haunted, otherworldly feel about it. She didn't want to scare him off.

And surely he wouldn't go inside. He'd been warned, and sternly, that it wasn't safe in there. More stones could topple at any time.

The castle was built into the side of a hill. She circled the structure, climbing the steep east slope, crossing around behind it on the tower side, keeping her eye out for Geoffrey along the way.

She found him as she started down the west slope. He was huddled against the outer wall of the castle, his legs drawn up, thin arms wrapped around his knees. He looked unhappy, but unharmed.

Relief, like cool water on a sweltering day, poured through her. "Hello, Geoffrey."

He had a streak of dirt on his cheek and he glared at her mutinously. "*Now* you have time for me."

She went over and dropped to the damp, patchy grass at his side. "Yesterday, it was just one thing after another. I kept meaning to…" She stopped herself. He deserved better than a bunch of lame excuses. "Geoffrey, I messed up. I didn't make time for you. And I'm so sorry. Sometimes... Well, sometimes even a true friend will mess up."

He pressed his lips together and looked away. "I'm not going back. I'm running away forever and I'm *never* going back."

"I wish you wouldn't run away. We would all miss you way too much."

"Oh, no, you won't. You won't miss me in the least. You don't even care about me. Nobody does. My father has new children. He's forgotten all about me. He lives all the way over there in America and if he never sees me again, it won't matter in the least to him."

She wanted to demand in outrage, *Who told you that?* But she had a very strong feeling that Brooke might have done it. Brooke too often forgot that she was supposed to be a grown-up. "Your father loves you," she said, for lack of anything better. Geoffrey's reply was a scoffing sound. She asked, "Do you want to go and live with your father?"

Geoffrey gasped. "No! I want to live here, at Hartmore, with you and Uncle Rafe and Great-Granny Eloise."

"And you do live at Hartmore. But you go away to school."

"Because nobody wants me here."

She braced her arms on her knees and rested her cheek on them. "That's not true. We want you here and we love you, Geoffrey. *I* love you. I know I let you down yesterday, but if you think back to all our times together, you'll remember that I do care about you, that you're very important to me. And if you left, if you ran away, well, I just couldn't bear it."

He looked at her then, narrowing his eyes, as though trying to see inside her head and determine whether she really meant what she said. Finally, with a heavy sigh, he leaned her way, sagging against her.

She dared to hook an arm loosely around him, and he rested his head on her shoulder. He smelled of dirt and clean sweat and she ached to grab him hard and close and never let him go.

"I hate boarding school. I'm only almost nine. Most of the boys my age there are day boys. I have to live in a house where everyone is older and they treat me like a baby. Why can't I stay at Hartmore with you and Rafe and Great-Granny? Why can't I go to the village school and have my tutor back until I'm at least thirteen like Uncle Rafe was when he went away? Or even go to St Anselm's in Bakewell, like the Terrible Twins?" He meant Dennis and Dexter, Fiona Bryce-Pemberton's ten-year-old sons. "Why can't I just wait to go away until I'm old enough to attend St Paul's?"

"Because you are very smart, that's why. And it's important for you to get the best education possible."

"St Anselm's is one of the top prep schools in the country. It's not fair. Mum just wants to get rid of me."

Even Genny, who was no fan of Brooke's, didn't believe that. Brooke was self-absorbed and a hopeless drama queen, but she loved her son. She just didn't know how to deal with him. "No, your mother does not want to get rid of you. Your mother wants the very best for you and your new school *is* the very best."

"I hate it."

"Well, then, you will have to find ways to learn to like it."

"I will never be able to do that."

"Yes, you will. Also, I know it must seem that you'll never get home, but doesn't the summer term end soon?"

"No. It's forever. It's practically a whole month."

"Well, a month may seem like forever now, but it *will*

pass. You'll be home for all of July and August, here, with us. I'll be looking forward to that."

"All the boys are awful. I don't have any friends."

"Well, then, you will find a way to make some."

"Making friends takes effort," said a deep voice from the ridge above them. "But you can do it."

"Uncle Rafe!" Geoffrey jumped up, so happy to see Rafe that he forgot to be angry.

Looking much too big and manly for Genny's peace of mind, Rafe hobbled his Belgian Black gelding and came down the slope to them. His gaze found hers—and then they both looked away, to Geoffrey, who stared at Rafe with mingled guilt and adoration. Rafe knew what to do. He held out his arms.

With a cry, Geoffrey flung himself forward. Rafe scooped him up, hugged him and then put him down again. They both dropped to the ground, Geoffrey on Genny's left, Rafe on Geoffrey's other side.

Rafe took out a cell phone and called the house. "Yes, hullo, Frances." Frances Tuttington served as housekeeper for the East Wing. She took care of the family. "Will you tell my sister we've found him?…Gen did, yes." He gave her a quick nod and she felt absurdly gratified. He spoke into the phone again. "He's fine. He's well. We're at the castle.…Yes. We'll be heading back there soon." He put the phone away.

Geoffrey was looking sulky again. "I mean it. I don't want to go back."

"We can see that," Rafe answered gently. "But you will, won't you? For me? For Gen? For yourself, most of all."

Geoffrey groaned and looked away.

Rafe said, "You know, I hated school myself when they first sent me away."

"But you were older."

"I was, yes, a little. But still, I hated it. Until I started realizing that I could learn things there I couldn't learn at Hartmore."

"I like science class," Geoffrey grudgingly admitted. "I don't much care for cricket. But aikido is interesting."

"Ah," said Rafe. "And you wouldn't be studying aikido at the village school, now, would you?"

Geoffrey picked up a twig and poked at the mossy ground with it. "Did you...make friends at St Paul's?"

"Not at first. I was sure they all hated me and I was determined to hate them right back."

"Yes," Geoffrey muttered. "Exactly."

"But then I found out that some of them missed home as much as I did. I found out that they were a lot like me." He chuckled low. "Or at least, more like me than I had thought at first. It worked itself out. By second term, I got on well enough. I even made a lifelong friend or two during my years at school...."

Genny watched the two of them—the blond, delicate-featured eight-year-old boy and the scarred, dark giant. Rafe didn't hurry things, didn't rush them back to the house. He took his time. Watching him being so good to Geoffrey, saying just the right things to ease a confused eight-year-old's loneliness and fear, Genny couldn't help but be reminded of all she so admired about him.

Surely they could overcome this strangeness and distance between them and forge a union of mutual love and respect.

"All right," said Geoffrey at last. "I guess they'll all be waiting, wondering. Mum will be crying. We should get back."

"Excellent," said Rafe.

They stood up and brushed the bits of grass from their clothes.

They all three walked back together, the gelding trailing on a lead behind Rafe, Caesar taking up the rear. As they approached the East Wing, a groom appeared and took charge of the horse.

Brooke was waiting in the East Entrance Hall, still in her dressing gown, crumpled on a delicate white-and-gold side chair, sobbing into her hands, her long hair falling forward. At the sound of their footsteps on the inlaid floor, she yanked her shoulders up and raked all that hair back off her forehead. "Geoffrey. My God. You have scared me out of my wits!" She leapt up and ran to him. Dropping to a crouch in front of him, the long, filmy skirts of her robe fanning on the floor like the petals of some giant flower, she grabbed him in a hug and sobbed on his small shoulder. "How could you?"

Genny and Rafe shared a glance. She knew he wanted to intervene as much as she did, to try to get Brooke to ease off. But intervening would most likely only make things worse.

So they said nothing as Brooke cried, "You horrid, cruel little beast!"

Geoffrey turned his head away and mumbled in obvious misery, "Sorry, Mum...."

"Sorry? Sorry!" She grabbed him by the shoulders and glared at him furiously. "Don't you ever, ever—"

"Brooke." Rafe did cut in then. "He's back. He knows he did wrong. Could you dial it down a notch?"

Brooke gasped, released Geoffrey and surged to her feet. She shot her brother a venomous look—a look that seemed to bounce off his huge shoulder and end up aimed straight at Genny. "You…" She let out a hard, ragged breath full of pure venom. Her blue eyes shone with righteous fury. "Rory told us you took off for the castle without telling a soul."

"Well, but you just said it yourself, Brooke. I did tell Rory," Genny reminded her hopefully.

Brooke sniffed, all wounded nobility now. "The point is you should have told *me*. I'm his mother after all. I'm the one who has the right to know every bit of new information first in a terrifying situation such as this. But you didn't tell me, did you, Your Highness? You didn't say a word to me. You just ran off to save him, to have all the glory for yourself."

Rafe said warningly, "Brooke…"

Genny silenced him with a touch of her hand on his big, hard arm. "I apologize. I'm sorry you weren't informed." She spoke gently, hoping to diffuse the coming tirade before it really got going.

But that only brought another outraged gasp from Brooke. "Oh, please. You're not the least sorry and we both know that." Right then, Eloise and the housekeeper came in from the hallway behind Brooke. Brooke never turned, never even paused for breath. "I know you, Genevra, so sweet and *sincere*. So very *kind* to everyone."

Geoffrey tugged on her robe. "Mum, don't…"

She ignored him and went right on while everyone watched, struck speechless, like witnesses to a horrible accident. "They all adore you, don't they? You are just the sweetest thing. And yet somehow you never fail to find a way to make yourself the center of attention."

"Enough!" Rafe roared.

And Geoffrey fisted his small hands hard at his sides and shouted, "Stop it, Mum, you stop it! You leave Aunt

Genny alone!" And then he whirled on his heel and fled up the stairs.

Brooke let out a cry. "Geoffrey! Oh, darling..." The waterworks started in again as she lifted the long hem of her robe and took off after him.

That left the rest of them standing in the entrance hall staring at each other. Genny felt awful, as though she'd been somehow at fault for Brooke's tantrum. Worse than that, she worried for Geoffrey. What a nightmare.

Rafe reached out and drew her into his side. She went willingly, their troubles of the night before forgotten in that moment. He was so huge and warm and strong and just his touch made her feel better about everything.

Eloise shook her head. "So much drama, and it's not even noon yet." She went straight to Genny. "My dearest girl. Are you all right?" Genny pressed her lips together and gave a quick nod, to which Eloise whispered, "But of course you are."

The others—Genny's mother and father and Rory, too—appeared from the hallway then. They all three looked a little bewildered. No doubt they'd heard the shouting.

Eloise said. "Frances, do make sure that everyone has eaten." She turned for the stairs. "I'll just go and assure myself that things have settled down...."

They all went to the Morning Room. Genny and Rafe had breakfast. The others poured fresh cups of coffee. They visited, chatting about everyday things, everyone determined to put a better face on the day.

Eloise joined them. She said that Brooke would ride along with Geoffrey back to London. "And how about we all go out to the lake later?" Everyone agreed that the weather was beautiful and a day at the lake would be lovely. "We'll have a picnic."

"I'll get a few more candid shots," said Rory.

Adrienne nodded. "It's an excellent idea."

Brooke and Geoffrey appeared a few minutes later. Brooke was fully dressed, her makeup perfect, her manner subdued. Geoffrey's hair was wet and slicked down. He wore his school uniform.

Eloise said, "Come along, you two. Eat before you go."

So they filled plates from the buffet and joined the group. It wasn't too bad. They all did their best to pretend that nothing out of the ordinary had happened. It worked, more or less.

Brooke ate hardly anything. When she slipped her napkin in beside her plate, she turned a somber face to Genny. "Genevra, I wonder if I might have a word with you."

Rafe started to say something, but Genny beat him to it. "Of course." She pushed her chair back and followed Rafe's sister out to the terrace garden.

They found a bench by one of the fountains. Brooke sat on one end, Genny on the other, with plenty of space between them.

There was a long, bleak silence.

Finally, Brooke said, "I'm sorry, all right? I'm a hopeless bitch. Everyone knows it. I've embarrassed myself and my family in front of Princess Adrienne and your father. I don't know what gets into me."

Genny tried to decide how to respond. Best to patch things up.

But anger, like a burning pulse, beat beneath her skin— for Geoffrey, for all that the woman at the other end of the bench insisted on putting him through. She tried to remind herself that Geoffrey was doing fine overall, that Brooke did love her son, she just didn't really know *how* to love. Brooke inevitably managed to make everything that happened all about her.

Genny understood that Brooke felt left out of her own family. Edward had been the old earl's favorite. Their mother had adored Rafe. Brooke had never been anyone's special darling.

And then Genny had come along. From the age of five, Genny had been the princess of Hartmore. The earl had pampered her. Brooke's mother had lavished affection on her and Eloise had welcomed her with open arms. Brooke remained nobody's favorite—only from then on, she had Genny to blame.

Plus, there was the Geoffrey situation. Genny would have been wiser not to pay so much attention to him, not to love him so completely. But how could she help it? He was sweet and smart and funny. Genny's heart had been his from the first time she saw him, the summer he was three, when Brooke had divorced her American husband and brought Geoffrey home to Hartmore.

"Nothing to say to me?" Brooke muttered, growing surly again.

Genny turned and faced the other woman squarely. "I accept your apology."

Brooke stared back at her, defiant. She made a scoffing sound. "As if I believe you."

Genny had a very powerful urge to scream. "What do you want from me, Brooke?"

"Oh, I don't know. Everything you took from me?"

A sudden wave of nausea rolled through her. The baby didn't like all this tension. She stood. "I know you resent me. I even understand why. But in reality, I didn't take your place, and we both know it. That you feel somehow...left out, well, Brooke, that's *your* feeling. You would be dealing with the same emotional issues whether I was here or not."

Brooke sighed. For once, it wasn't a dramatic sigh. She let her shoulders slump. "I promised Granny I would make things up with you. And I promised Geoffrey, too. Somehow, we have to learn to get on together."

Genny put her hand against her belly and took a slow breath. "Fair enough. Let's call a truce. Put some real effort into getting along with me. I'll do the same. We'll muddle through somehow."

Brooke regarded her, narrow eyed, her head tipped to the side, her dark hair tumbling along her arm like a waterfall of silk. "You're pregnant, aren't you?"

Genny longed to deny it. She didn't want to give Brooke the satisfaction of knowing for certain why Rafe had married her. But please. Brooke would know soon enough anyway. "Yes, I am."

"Suddenly it all makes sense."

Genny refused to rise to that bait. "Rafe and I are thrilled. So is Eloise."

Brooke produced a slow, mean smile. "Allow me to congratulate you."

"Thank you."

"Granny's asked me to go away, did you know? For a week. I'll stay with Fiona." Brooke's lifelong friend had a house in Chelsea. "It's partly a reprimand for my behavior this morning. But it's mostly for you, of course. To give you time settle in as countess of Hartmore without having to deal with me."

"Do you want me to tell Eloise to let you stay, is that it?"

"Oh, no. I wouldn't dream of that." Brooke stared up at her, defiant.

"Brooke, I'm not going to beg you to stay." And who was she kidding? It would be a relief to have the woman gone.

"It's fine." Brooke gave a lazy shrug. "Time away from here with someone who loves me is just what I need about now."

Genny wanted to grab her and shake her. "Why does it have to be my fault that you feel unloved at Hartmore?"

"Did I say I felt unloved?"

"You didn't have to."

Brooke made a humphing sound. "Well, you can take what I said however you want to."

Genny asked with excruciating civility, "Was there anything else you needed to discuss with me?"

"Not a thing."

"Then, let's go back in."

Brooke swept to her feet and they turned together for the house.

The remainder of the day passed uneventfully. Brooke and Geoffrey left for London.

In the afternoon, the rest of them walked down to the lake, where they threw sticks for the dogs to fetch. Rory took more pictures and they shared a picnic. And that night, they all enjoyed a lovely dinner in honor of the bride and groom and the visiting Bravo-Calabrettis.

After the meal, Genny's father and Rafe disappeared into Rafe's study. Eloise pleaded exhaustion and went to bed. Genny, her sister and her mother went out to sit at an iron table under the stars in the terrace garden. It was good to have a little time together, just the three of them.

At a quarter past eleven, her father and Rafe came out. Genny glanced up and Rafe met her eyes....

Her heart gave a lurch, and a prickly, hot shiver raced down the backs of her knees. Would he leave her to sleep alone again?

She really had no idea what he would do. And she used to think she knew him better than anyone. Those days were over. Now she hardly knew him at all.

Her mother and sister got up. Everyone said good-night.

Rafe and Genny were left alone. He held out his hand to her.

So. He was coming upstairs with her, then? Her skin felt overly sensitized suddenly. And her breath came short.

She rose and went to him.

"What happened with Brooke this morning when you went outside?" he asked.

They'd taken turns in the bathroom, though there were two sinks and plenty of room in there. Now they lay, propped on piles of pillows, side by side in the bed. He wore his boxers and she'd put on a short summer night-gown much less revealing than the one she'd worn the night before. It tied with pink bows high on her shoulders.

The lamps on either side of the bed cast a soft glow across the bedcovers—and over the powerful planes and angles of her husband's broad chest. He had the body of a laborer—everything hard and big and honed. And every time she looked at him, her stomach hollowed out with longing. The crescent scar looked more pronounced than ever in the slanting lamplight.

He was watching her now, eyes black as pitch beneath the strong shelf of his brow. His inky hair curled on his wide forehead. His skin was brown all over, rich and dark against the white pillowcase. "About Brooke?" he asked again, one black brow lifting.

She shook herself from her trance of hopeless yearning and answered him. "We called a truce and agreed to get along with each other. And I told her about the baby—or rather, she guessed."

He stared at her intently, as though seeking a point of entry. Or maybe testing her expression for lies. "Did she make you want to strangle her?"

"Only a little bit."

He made a low sound—of frustration, or annoyance. "I can't believe Geoffrey's not a holy terror, the way she carries on."

She bumped him with her elbow, a tap of reassurance. "Well, he's not a terror and shows no signs of becoming one."

"Gen. He ran away this morning."

"Yes. But almost every child runs away at one time or another."

"Did you?"

She thought back. "No. But I considered it. Everyone in the family was so much more adventurous and exciting than I ever was."

Humor lit those black eyes. "You considered running away to make yourself more exciting?"

"I did, yes. And I happen to know you spent most of your first thirteen years running wild all over Hartmore. You didn't *have* to run away to be exciting."

He actually leaned a fraction closer. He smelled of toothpaste and very faintly of cigar smoke. She'd never much cared for the smell of cigars. But on him, it worked.

On him, since those four days in March, everything worked.

And what were they talking about?

She remembered. "And about Geoffrey…"

"Yes?" Low and rough and so, so lovely.

"He has you and Eloise. And Brooke may be a mess, but she does love him. I think he knows that."

"*And* he has you." He said it softly.

"Yes. Yes, he does—and what exactly went on with you and my father in the study for all that time tonight?"

"Cigars. Brandy. A little fatherly advice."

"Was it awful?"

"Not at all. I've always liked your father. He's wise. And he's kind."

"What advice did he give you?"

"Sorry." He touched her chin, a breath of a touch that sent darts of sensation zipping all through her. "I can't tell you."

"Oh. So what happens in the study stays in the study?"

"Something like that." His index finger went roving along the ridge of her jaw, up under her hair. "You always smell of roses. And vanilla, too."

Yearning made her chest ache. Heat pooled low down. "It's my perfume," she heard herself whisper, a lame response if there ever was one.

He gave a slow, lazy shake of his head. "No. Forever. Since you were a child. Do you know that any time I smell roses, I think of you?"

She stared into those wonderful, dangerous eyes of his. "What a beautiful thing to say."

He traced the shape of her ear, tugged gently on a lock of her hair. All the breath seemed to have fled her body. She was absolutely still, waiting.

Hoping.

If she didn't do anything to chase him off, would he make love with her tonight, kiss her and hold her and touch her all over?

He clasped her bare shoulder, his thumb flicking the pink satin bow that held up her nightgown. And then he leaned even closer. His rough cheek brushed her smooth one. She heard him draw breath through his nose, scenting her. "A little musky now. And creamy, too, beneath the roses and vanilla. That's the grown-up Gen. The woman. *My* woman now."

She drew a shaky breath. "Oh, Rafe…" She wanted—everything. His big body pressed against her, naked. Him inside her, moving, blowing the world away to nothing, shattering all the barriers.

They were frightening to her, the barriers. And they all began with Edward and the things Rafe wouldn't tell her about the night of the accident, about the secrets of his heart.

But then, well, he *had* married her, and brought here to the one place she'd always wanted to be, brought her to Hartmore to live with him and Eloise—and Geoffrey, whenever he came home. And their baby.

Their baby would grow up here. It was her lifelong dream come true. He'd given her everything. Her heart's desire.

She could wait—she *would* wait—until he was ready to tell her the dark things he was keeping from her. Until he was willing to forgive himself for whatever had happened the night Edward died.

He turned his head and his lips touched her ear, sending sparks across her scalp, down the side of her throat. "That first time I kissed you—really kissed you—at the villa?"

"What about it?" It was in the foyer. She'd pounded on the front door until he'd finally let her in. And then he'd asked her, please, to leave him. To go away and not come back. And she'd started shouting at him for shutting her out, for refusing to see her when he needed her most. For four whole months, he'd avoided her. When she'd gone to Hartmore for the funeral, he was still in the hospital recovering from his injuries. But he was conscious. He'd had visitors. Yet when Genny went to see him, he'd made the nurses turn her away.

For four months, he never let her near. She'd sent emails, messages, even letters—actual, physical letters on fine linen stationery. No reply. She'd called several times and not once had he called back.

Finally, when he'd come to Montedoro to see to the refurbishing of the villa, she had cornered him there. It had broken her heart all over again to see him—the angry, red scar, the deadness in his eyes, the slight limp when he walked. And then, when he'd ordered her to go, she'd snapped.

She'd started shouting, telling him that no, she wasn't leaving. She was never leaving. Not until he talked to her, not until he told her what was going on with him, what she'd done to him to make him treat her so shabbily. How could he do this, cut her out in the cold, when they had lost Edward, when she needed him—and *he* needed *her?*

"I remember you kept saying my name, 'Gen, Gen,' over and over, trying to stop my tirade, trying to get me to go."

"But you wouldn't go."

"And finally you just grabbed me. And you kissed me. That did shut me up, I'll give you that."

"The taste of you." The low, rough sound of his voice sent ripples of excitement through her. "I kissed you and I never wanted to stop."

She accused, "But you did stop."

"At first, yes…"

"And we stood there, both of us breathing too hard, glaring at each other…"

"Until I couldn't stand it anymore. I kissed you again."

"Oh, yes, you did. And that time, you didn't stop." She heard the triumph in her own voice. "You scooped me up and carried me to the nearest bedroom."

"Limping all the way."

"I was glad. So glad—although I did worry that you would reinjure your leg." She couldn't help smiling. "We found that box of condoms in the back of the bedside drawer, remember?"

"How could I ever forget?"

"I was so happy we did, because I knew that if we had to go out and buy some, you would have time to come up with some reason why we couldn't go through with it."

"But we did go through with it."

She touched his cheek—the unscarred one this time. "It was glorious."

"You don't...regret what happened?"

"No, I do not. You?" *Please, please. Tell me you don't regret it.*

But he couldn't. "I took advantage of you."

"Oh, stop. You did not. I'm not a child anymore, Rafe. I did what I wanted to do. I wanted you and I...took you."

"Oh, did you?" Was he pleased? Oh, she hoped so. So often nowadays, it was hard to tell what he felt.

"Yes, I did," she said staunchly. "And I have no regrets that I did—though I will admit that we really should have checked the date on the condom box."

"The miracle of hindsight." He pressed his forehead to hers, his big hands clasping her shoulders. And then his fingers were moving—so light, his touch, for such a huge, hard man. He caught the tails of the ribbons on her shoulders.

And he pulled.

Chapter Five

The bows came undone.

Very slowly, he began to lower them, pulling them away from her body and down. Her innocuous pink nightgown went with them.

"Rafe?" she asked on a sharp, indrawn breath.

"You have objections?" He stopped lowering the ribbons.

She looked down. Her nightgown didn't seem quite so wholesome now that the tops of her breasts were showing. "I…"

"Do you want me to stop?"

"No. I do not want you to stop."

"You're certain?"

"Don't torment me. It's cruel."

He slanted her a dark look, still holding the ribbons. Her nightgown covered her nipples, but barely. "What would you know of cruelty?"

She sucked in another sharp breath. Her whole body ached. For his touch, his kiss, to be joined with him. She gritted her teeth at him. "Do not stop. If you do, I'll start shouting. Just like I did at the villa. I'll shout the house down. My father will come running. You don't want to get into trouble with my father. He seems like a nice man. But he's a Bravo, born and bred in the American West. Bravos can be dangerous when provoked."

"Now you've got me terrified. Say *please.*"

"I could easily become really angry with you."

"Say *please.*"

Under the covers, she pressed her thighs together, trying to ease the ache of wanting just a little. It only made her more aroused. She gave in. "Please."

And he only sat there, watching her, holding those two sweet pink ribbons. "Honestly, Gen, you are the hottest thing. I think you might burn me."

"Please."

"Just sear me to a cinder, right here in this bed. They'll find me in the morning, nothing but a pile of ash."

"Take it down," she commanded. "Do it now, Rafe."

"Sweet little Genevra. Who could've known?"

She gave up. On the pleas. On commanding him. She just sat there and glared at him, eye to eye.

Until, at last, way too slowly, he began pulling on the ribbons once more. Slowly, so slowly, her curves were revealed. Until she felt the cool air of the room across her naked breasts, felt her nipples drawing tighter from excitement.

From the burning heat in his gaze.

He swore low. And then he threw back the blankets that covered them. "Sit up. Away from the pillows."

Her breathing coming ragged, her heart battering the walls of her chest, she obeyed.

The hem of the nightgown, which she'd been very careful to smooth into place when she'd climbed into bed with him, came to the tops of her knees. He reached for it, began to gather it in his big fists, his skin brushing hers as he took it up her thighs. She stifled a moan of equal parts agony and pleasure.

He said, "Lift up."

She did. He got the fabric out from under her and clear of her hips. Now she had the whole thing in a wad at her waist. She was bare above and below it. She never wore panties to bed.

"Beautiful," he whispered. And he bent close and pressed a kiss on the dark gold curls at the juncture of her thighs.

Oh, it felt so good. Just the brush of his soft lips so near where she burned for him. She put her hand, very lightly, on his head, her fingers sifting in the thick, curling black strands.

But then he sat up again. "Raise your arms."

"Rafe..."

"Do it. Now. Raise them high.... Yes, that's the way. Don't move."

She said a very naughty word. But she didn't move.

He tipped his head to the side, studying her with her dress around her waist and her arms up in the air. He took his slow, sweet, infuriating time about it. And then, even more slowly, he licked those soft lips of his. "Beautiful."

"I'm going to kill you," she informed him quietly.

"You shall do as you wish with me, I've no doubt on that score. Keep your arms up. Sit still."

She did as instructed. But nobody said she couldn't look.

And she did look. At his fine, corrugated belly, at his huge, thick horseman's thighs, at the deep scar that furrowed his right leg, from midcalf to several inches above the knee.

And at the front of his boxers. Tented high.

Good. If he had to play this game, at least he should be suffering right along with her.

A memory, sharp and sweet and full of meanings she hadn't understood at the time, washed over her.

She was...what? Fourteen? That would have made him twenty-two. A time when they were completely forbidden to each other in any sexual way, when it never would have occurred to her that someday she would find him at Villa Santorno and spend four days naked all over the house with him.

Yes. She was fourteen that summer. And she'd come to Hartmore for a three-week visit. That had been a more innocent time, a time when her family had seen no need for bodyguards. It had just been just her and her Aunt Genevra. Genevra was older and wanted to rest from the trip. She'd retired to her room.

Edward had been there, she remembered. And he'd greeted her with a kiss on the cheek. He'd smiled and flirted with her in a harmless way. She'd felt feminine and all grown-up, and she had loved it. Edward always made her feel sophisticated and brilliant. In his presence, she saw herself as someone clever and charming and fun.

But then, some of Edward's friends drove up. He got in the car and went off with them. And she was anxious to see Rafe, to tell him...what, exactly? She couldn't remember now. Something that had seemed terribly important at the time. Whatever it was, she went looking for him.

And she found him at the lake, on the boat jetty. With a pretty dark-haired woman who looked about his age. When she saw them, she gasped and ducked out of sight behind a mound of flowering yellow gorse. They sat with their shoes off, their cuffs rolled, their feet in the water. They were talking so softly. The woman laughed. And then he bent close to her and kissed her.

Genny had to slap her hand over her mouth to keep from crying out. And then there was fury. Deep, burning fury that she didn't understand.

Whatever happened next between Rafe and the young woman, she had no idea.

She only knew that they mustn't know she had seen them. She had to get away. Staying low at first, she'd turned and raced for the house. By the time she got there, she was running upright and full-out, calling herself an idiot, wondering what in the world was wrong with her to be spying on Rafe like that, to get so upset. She decided to forget all about it, about the woman with Rafe, about that kiss on the jetty.

When she saw him later at dinner, he was alone. She never saw the woman again. And though, at the time, she always told Rafe everything—anything that happened to her, every single thought that flitted through her mind— she'd never told him she'd seen him kiss a strange woman on the jetty.

He was watching her face way too closely—as he always did. "Gen, love. Where *are* you right now?"

She did wonder who that woman had been, and she considered sharing the old, secret memory at last. But what if that ruined the mood somehow? She would spontaneously combust if he stopped now. "I'm right here. Wearing only a wad of cloth around my waist, aching for you, Rafe. Oh, and my arms are starting to get tired...."

"Aching for me, did you say?"

"Let me put my arms down. I'll show you how much."

"In a minute."

"Seriously. You're a dead man."

But then he leaned close again. She smelled toothpaste and heat. Electric now, the scent of him. Electric and burning. His beard-rough cheek brushed her shoulder, and his warm breath ghosted across her upper chest. He whispered something. She couldn't quite make out the word.

But then it didn't matter. Nothing mattered but the caress of his breath, the brush of his black, silky hair on her skin.

And then…oh, then…

He stuck out his tongue and flicked her right nipple with it. And then he blew on it, bringing a shiver that coursed through every inch of her body.

That did it. She moaned.

And then he leaned even closer. He took that nipple in his mouth.

It was too much.

She lowered her arms and speared her fingers in his hair and held him close to her while he did truly wonderful things, first to that right breast and then to the other one.

And then he pulled back. She growled low in her throat and tried to reach for him.

"Wait," he commanded.

"Fine." She sat still, glaring at him, as he took her wrinkled clump of nightgown and started easing it up. With a small moan of impatience, she lifted her arms again and, at last, the thing was off and out of her way.

She went for his boxers, to get rid of them, too.

But he beat her to it, whipping them down and off and tossing them between the bed curtains toward a chair.

With a low cry, she reached for him.

And he didn't refuse her that time. He wrapped his steely arms around her and he took her down to the pillows, surrounding her in his heat and his hardness. The sheer size of him thrilled her. It was like being swallowed by manliness, just to have him hold her close in his arms. And she did glory in it.

He touched her, those big hands wandering. She lifted her body toward him, offering him everything, yearning only for him to take it—take all of her. Right now.

But of course, what he took was his time.

His hot mouth opened on her skin. She felt the quick, wet swipe of his tongue. And then the sharp nip of his teeth.

She made noises, pleading noises.

But he wouldn't hurry. He touched her all over. And where his hands went, his hot mouth followed.

She lost herself in pure sensation and she really didn't care if she ever got found. For the longest, sweetest time, he lay with his head between her open thighs, kissing her endlessly, using his clever tongue and hungry mouth to drive her mad.

Beautifully, happily, completely mad.

She clutched the sheet in her fists and lifted herself higher, tighter against that thrilling, relentless kiss. Heat curled up her spine, exploded across her chest, and then raced back down to her core, where it opened her up, hollowed her out, sent currents of pleasure pulsing along every burning nerve.

And he went on kissing her.

When she came, crying out his name, he only kept on using his rough tongue, soft lips and sharp teeth to make her come again.

And then, after the third time, when she was limp and drowsing, and hardly able to move, he swept up her body and covered her, bracing on his forearms to keep from crushing her.

Rafe. All over her, pressing her down in the most delicious way. His erection nestled, hard and so ready, right where she wanted him. Right where she needed him.

She groaned, aroused all over again. A moment before, she'd been limp. Finished.

That hadn't lasted long.

She groaned again, sliding her arms around him, down low at his waist. And then lower. She clutched his rock-hard buttocks in either hand—so good, the feel of his tight skin and hard muscles under her palms, the slick of sweat between their bodies, the press of him, there, where she was so ready for him.

"Rafe…"

"Shh…"

"Please…" She rocked her hips, lifting her legs to wrap them around him, trying to lure him in.

It worked, to a degree. The tip slid in. And she was so wet and open. Her body called to his.

Why wouldn't he answer?

"Wait," he whispered. So softly. So patiently.

She growled low in her throat. "I mean it." She opened her eyes and looked into his midnight black ones. "I will kill you…."

The scar pulled at the corner of his lip, a mockery of a smile. "Don't worry. You have. You are."

And suddenly, she not only desperately needed him inside her, she wanted to cry. "I was afraid we would never have this again."

"Shh…" He lifted his torso away from her, bracing up on those bulging arms, the hard, thick length of him nudging deliciously deeper within her.

Twin tears escaped. They ran down her temples into her hair. "You wouldn't take my calls. I tried so hard to reach you. If not for the baby…"

"Shh. I didn't know, didn't understand. I thought it would be better for you if we didn't see each other again."

"Liar."

"I swear it, Gen. It's true." He bent his head, kissed her on either cheek and then at her temples, his wonderful, pliant lips brushing the tracks of her tears. "And we *do* have this." And then he took her mouth in a kiss so sweet and gentle—at first. Until it went deeper, became a tangle of tongues, a nipping of teeth.

"Now," she whispered against his lips. "Now, please…"

And at last, he gave her what she craved, sinking into her slowly, all the way.

She stared into his eyes as they began to move together. He didn't look away. He held her gaze endlessly, as the pleasure washed over them.

It lasted the longest time. She reveled in every stroke, every sigh, every aching, perfect moan.

Because he was so right.

No matter, all the questions. All the secrets, the pain, the terrible loss and even the lies.

They did have this. And it was glorious. Raw and simple and marvelous.

Together in this, at least, they both were set free.

Chapter Six

"I was wondering…" He held her close. They had turned off the lights.

"Mmm?" She floated on a gentle sea of satisfaction.

"Would you like some kind of wedding trip?" He kissed the top of her head.

She pressed her lips to the hard curve of his shoulder. "Maybe, sometime…"

He stroked her hair. "That's not very specific."

"Honestly, for now, I would just like to stay here, at Hartmore, to settle in, work with Eloise in the gardens, spend time with my new husband…"

He guided her hair behind her ear. "Fair enough. But remember, if all this domesticity starts driving you out of your mind—"

"It won't."

"Fine, but if it does, let me know and we'll plan a holiday somewhere."

She put her hand against his cheek—on the safe side, the unscarred side. "I've been thinking about the West Wing roof."

"How romantic."

She kissed his square jaw. "Listen."

"Do I have a choice?"

"None. I remember you told me a couple of years ago that you'd pushed Edward into commissioning a structural survey of the West Wing…"

"I did, yes."

"Last year, you said the survey uncovered exactly what we'd expected. There's extensive roof damage, right?"

"That's right."

"So, then. I think we need to move on that and have the roof replaced. I'm more than willing to see it paid for out of my inheritance."

He made a sound that might have been a chuckle. "So you think you'll make the West Wing roof your wedding gift to Hartmore?"

"That's a perfect way to look at it, yes."

"Very generous, but that won't be necessary."

"But Rafe, if we need the roof…"

"We do. And the repairs will begin in November, when we close the house to the public for the winter. The work is projected to take the whole winter. As it turns out, the survey revealed that the entire roof needs replacing—both wings and the central block. So we'll be doing just that, with extensive structural and interior repairs required in the West Wing."

"You've already arranged to replace the roof…the *entire* roof?"

"Yes."

"Well, Rafe, I'm…"

"Speechless?" He was definitely teasing her. "That's a first." For that, she bit his shoulder. "Ouch!"

She kissed the spot she'd bitten. "I know how to be quiet when I should."

"Of course you do." He said it way too fast to be sincere and she was tempted to bite him again.

But she decided to be nice and let it go. "I admit I'm used to thinking of Hartmore as barely struggling along." So few of the best country houses were privately owned anymore. They simply cost too much to run and keep in good condition. Most had been put under a trust or in the care of one historical society or another. And there were rules for historic buildings in England. Hartmore House was a Grade I listed building, a building of highest architectural and historic interest. That meant the new roof would be required to match the style and materials of the original as closely as possible, as would repairs inside. It all added up to enormous outlays of cash.

"We're doing all right now," he said.

"Yes, we are." She stretched up to brush a kiss across his lips. "You will let me pitch in, though? The damage must be extensive."

"It is, and we are dealing with it."

She pushed up on her elbow and peered down at him through the shadows. "All the rooms with water damage are going to need attention. And we need to do something about the castle, too, before it all falls in on itself."

"One thing at a time. But yes, you will be allowed to spend your money liberally."

"And to be *involved,* to be included in the decision-making…"

"Yes." He stroked her hair again. "Of course."

Satisfied for the moment, she settled into his arms again. "It's so strange. I knew you'd done well for yourself. And I promise I *was* paying attention in all those meetings with the lawyers last week…." She tried to think how to finish.

But then she didn't need to finish, because he understood. "You always pictured yourself coming to Hartmore's rescue, didn't you?"

"That's it. I would ride in on a white horse, brandishing a giant checkbook."

"That was when you were going to marry Edward." He said it evenly, without heat, it seemed to her. But she couldn't see his expression in the dark.

She dared to take it further. "Not that he ever came close to asking me."

"He would have asked you." The words were flat, bleak. The conversation had veered very close to forbidden territory.

Still, she pushed for more. "How do you know that?"

"Gen. Please. We all knew it. Just as we all knew you couldn't wait to say yes to him."

Because I wanted Hartmore, she thought, but didn't quite have the courage—or the integrity—to say out loud. Dear God. No wonder Brooke hated her.

She was a princess by birth. An heiress with money to burn. She had it all, but she'd wanted more. She wanted to be countess of Hartmore, to be a DeValery in fact as well as in her heart. She would have married Edward simply to get what she wanted. Deep down, she'd always known that.

But until recently, she'd been able to tell herself pretty lies about it—that she loved Edward, that he was the man for her and she was only waiting for him to see that and take action.

The pretty lies weren't working anymore.

Not since two months ago.

Not since the first time Rafe had kissed her in the foyer at Villa Santorno.

"Sleep now," Rafe whispered.

Sleep. Yes. A good idea—much better than trying to talk about the difficult things.

Much better than facing too much painful truth.

The next day, Monday, the Bravo-Calabrettis departed. Genny's mother and father went home to Montedoro. Rory was on her way to Colorado. Genny, Rafe and Eloise saw them off after breakfast.

Genny spent half the day in the West Wing, looking over the rooms with water damage, trying to get something of an idea of what would have to be done. Many of the damaged areas were former servants' quarters. The servants' quarters and hallways were plain, the walls of stone or sometimes wood. The repairs would be simpler in those rooms, but no less critical.

Later, Rafe took her to his study and showed her the plans for the new roof. It was a truly impressive undertaking.

First off, extensive scaffolding and a temporary roof would be built above the existing one, so that the repairs could go on regardless of winter weather. Included in the project was a complete redesign of the West Wing roof structure, necessary because of design errors in alterations made back in 1838. The new roof would have a hundred-year design life upon completion and would require fifty metric tons of new sandstone to match the old, degraded stone, and eighty metric tons of continuously cast lead roof coverings to replace large sections of defective slate slabs.

"It's so exciting," she said.

They stood over his desk. He snaked out an arm and hauled her in close. Desire, like a pulse, coursed through her as he pressed his lips to her hair. "Only you would find roof repair exciting."

She thought of the things they'd done the night before. Of what they would do in the nights to come. Of how good his big body always felt when he was pressing it against her....

And then she made herself concentrate on the business at hand. "Hartmore will get what it needs, and I do find that exciting—and I'm going to want to go through all the furniture that's been moved into storage. I want to hire the best people to put the rooms back together. It all has to be done right, you know."

"Your eyes are shining." He touched the side of her face.

She realized she was as happy as she'd ever been. And that turned everything around again. The joy and excitement vanished. She wanted to cry.

Rafe eased his hand around her neck, his warm fingers tender, insistent. "Whatever you're thinking, stop." He tucked her head beneath his chin.

She sucked in the wonderful, arousing scent of his skin. "It's only hormones," she lied.

"Shh."

She lifted her head and looked up into his unforgettable ruined face. "Lately, you're shushing me a lot."

"Only because you need it." He kissed the end of her nose.

"You don't understand."

"Maybe you should explain it to me."

"Oh, Rafe. My sisters are all so brilliant and accomplished. They each make it a point to do good things in the world. Rory's a successful photographer. Arabella is a nurse who travels the world raising money so that poverty-stricken children can get the medical care they so desperately need. Rhia oversees acquisitions and restorations at

Montedoro's National Museum. She finds great art and she *saves* great art. Alice is a genius breeder and trainer of the world's finest horses. And I? I have no calling. I have no real *work*. Except this, what we're doing now. To be...in your family."

"It's *your* family now."

"I have a liberal-arts education. I studied a little bit of everything. English literature, botany. Landscape design, architecture, interior design—it was all for Hartmore, so I would know how to take charge when the time finally came."

"Gen." So patient, so kind. "I know all of this."

"It's everything, all I ever wanted. To take care of Hartmore, to provide Hartmore with an heir."

"And look how quickly you've managed that."

"Rafe. It's not funny."

He chided, "Don't sulk."

"I'm not—or at least, not exactly."

"I can see I have no choice but to distract you." He tipped up her chin with a finger. And then he lowered his mouth to hers.

It worked. For a lovely string of thrilling moments, she thought of nothing but the pleasure of being held by him, the heat and beauty in his kiss. When he finally lifted his head, he said, "All right. You were born for this. And now you are living the life you were born for. What's wrong with that?"

She let out a small, bewildered laugh. "Well, nothing. When you put it that way."

"What other way is there to put it? It's the simple truth."

"But not *all* the truth."

His expression darkened. "Don't borrow trouble, Gen."

She knew he was right. And her mouth still tingled from the press of his lips. "I love it when you kiss me."

"Good." He traced a lazy finger down the side of her throat. Her eager flesh seemed to rise to meet his touch.

She'd had two lovers before him, because Edward had never got around to proposing and she had started to feel that no man would ever want her.

Two lovers before Rafe. Nice men, both of whom she remembered with a sort of vague fondness. They simply did not compare.

She went on, "When you kiss me, I...well, I just didn't know, before you, what a kiss could be. What sex could do, that it could hollow me out and fill me up, both at the same time. That it could carry me away to a place where nothing else matters but to have you putting your hands on me, kissing me, doing all those things to me that you do so very well." She stared up at him, a little embarrassed, certain she'd just given him way more information than he needed.

But he didn't look uncomfortable with what she'd just said. On the contrary, his eyes had changed, gone darker, deeper. "Keep talking. We'll be trying out my desk."

Her breath got all tangled somewhere in the bottom of her throat. "Now, why does that sound like a really good idea?"

He turned for the door.

"Rafe, wait. What did I say? Where are you going?" He shut the door and turned the lock. "Oh!" she squeaked, finally putting it together. She watched him come back to her, all muscle and man, so tall, so broad. He hollowed her out, all right. And now he was going to fill her right up. "Ahem. Well. The desk it is, then."

He closed the program with the roof plans and put his laptop on a guest chair, the mouse on top. Then, with one broad sweep of his arm, he cleared the wide, inlaid desk of everything else. Pens, a paperweight, the desk pad, a stack of books, they all went flying.

"Oh, my…" she whispered, wide-eyed.

And then he grabbed her hand and yanked her close. "You shouldn't talk like that unless you're looking for action."

She licked her lips. Like a tiger scoping out the slowest gazelle, he watched her do it. "I, well, yes. I think that I actually am, er, looking for action."

He smiled then. Or something close to it. And then he dipped his head and claimed her lips.

Not two minutes later, she was naked on the desk. He'd peeled all her clothes off in record time. Most of his were still on. She kept thinking she wanted them off him.

But then he unzipped his trousers and positioned her just so at the edge of the desk. She stared up into his black, black eyes.

And everything flew away but the wonder of him touching her, caressing her, filling her in one long, slow, deep glide. She lifted her legs and wrapped them around him and let him sweep her away to that place where there was nothing but the two of them and the sweet, mindless pulse of pleasure beating between them.

In the week that followed, the scandal sheets and royal-watching bloggers got hold of their story. Their pictures were all over the internet. The headlines were silly, as always: The Earl's Princess Bride, Princess Genevra Takes an Earl, Princess Genny's Hasty Wedding.

Rafe grumbled about the invasion of their privacy.

Genny told him to be grateful she was so far down the tabloid food chain. Her older brothers couldn't go anywhere without some paparazzo popping up, snapping pictures frantically and shouting rude personal questions.

"That's just so wrong in so many ways," he said.

And she replied, "Maybe so. But it's a fact of life if you're a prince of Montedoro."

During that week, they moved forward with their plans to repair the West Wing interiors. Rafe commissioned structural surveys of Hartmore Castle and the stables, as well. Genny toured the gardens with Eloise. They discussed enlarging the range of income-generating events at Hartmore. Within the next few years, they wanted to add a Medieval Faire in the late spring and an annual Christmas at Hartmore celebration.

Over the generations, earls of Hartmore had taken wealthy wives and sold off income-generating land to keep the house and grounds intact. The goal in this generation, Rafe, Genny and Eloise agreed, was to make it so that Hartmore could provide for itself.

From Colorado, Rory sent a wedding book full of beautiful pictures, not only of the ceremony and the reception, but of all of them out by the lake. There were pictures of the dogs and Eloise, of Geoffrey with a tiny kitten cradled in his arms. There were beautiful shots of Brooke. And of Hartmore in all its glory. And so many of Genny and Rafe. They looked happy in the pictures. They looked like two people in love. Seeing them filled Genny with hope for the future.

She called her sister. "The pictures are beautiful. Rory, I can't thank you enough."

"I'm so glad you like them. I sent you a link to all the pictures in an album online, too."

"I got it, yes. Rory, I love them."

"Be happy."

"I will," she promised, because she fully intended to be just that. She told Rory about the baby.

Rory congratulated her. And then she said, "Walker's

here." Walker McKellan was a friend of the Justice Creek Bravo family, a rancher, fireman and search-and-rescue leader. According to Rory, he could do anything: communicate with mountain lions and speak the language of ravens, build a cabin with a pocketknife and some willow bark. "I have to go."

"Tell the mountain man your sister says hello."

"Will do. Later, then…"

The next morning, Genny went to see the DeValery family doctor in nearby Bakewell. He said that both she and the baby were doing well, gave her a prescription for prenatal vitamins and a due date of December 20.

The days were full. And the nights were magic.

No, she and Rafe had not spoken again of what had happened the night Edward died. Genny told herself she was all right with that. For now anyway. In time, she hoped her new husband would open up to her about the most difficult things.

But the here and now wasn't bad at all. She knew a certain fragile joy, a sense of something very like fulfillment. She was finally living the life she'd always yearned for. Yes, all right. It was a life she was supposed to have led with Edward. But she was going to try to be like Eloise, to roll with the punches, as they said in America. Life had given her Rafe.

And it was working out just fine.

On the second Monday in June, Rafe left for a series of business meetings in London. Genny stayed at Hartmore. She watched him drive away at nine in the morning and missed him already—which was silly. He would only be gone for two days.

Brooke arrived home early that evening. Fiona Bryce-Pemberton came with her. The two had traveled down from London together. Fiona had green eyes, a turned-up nose and long, gorgeous red hair. She lived half the time with her banker husband in Chelsea and half the time at her country house, Tillworth, right there in Derbyshire. Her husband, Gerald, came to Tillworth on weekends and holidays when he could manage it. Her twin sons went to school in nearby Bakewell and lived at Tillworth, where there was always the staff to look after them while their parents were in London.

The weather was lovely that day, so they had dinner outside on the terrace, with the dogs lazing at their feet. It was just the four of them: Eloise, Brooke, Fiona and Genny.

Fiona had decided to stay the night. "Truly, I can't deal with the boys just yet. I'll see them tomorrow. It's soon enough." She took a big gulp of wine and flicked Genny a quick, disdainful glance as she set the glass down.

Genny always felt edgy around Fiona. She had the definite sense that Fiona didn't like her, which wasn't especially surprising. Fiona and Brooke were BFFs after all. No doubt Fiona disliked Genny as a matter of course, out of loyalty to her longtime friend.

Out past the terrace, a nightingale cried.

Brooke shivered. "It always seems so quiet at Hartmore, after London." She aimed a forced smile at Genny. "Too bad Rafe's run off. Married barely a week and he's left you all alone." Eloise sent a warning look in Brooke's direction. Brooke waved a hand. "What? It's just conversation, Granny."

Genny spoke up. "He's off on business." She was proud of how casual and relaxed she sounded. "Just until Wednesday. He wanted me to go with him, of course." Well, he *had* asked her if she'd like to go. "But I decided to stick it out here with Eloise. It's so beautiful this time of year. The buttercups are in bloom now. The daisies and wild roses, too."

Fiona hid a yawn. "Right. The country. Don't we just love it?"

"Yes, we do," replied Eloise strongly. She launched into an enthusiastic description of the success of the weekly market in Hartmore Village, of the upcoming County Show to be held in Elvaston Parish. It promised to be bigger than ever this year.

Fiona hid more yawns and Brooke got a glazed look in her eye.

When Eloise finished, Brooke started in about the new clothes she'd bought in London. "At Fresh," she announced. "It's a shop. A wonderful shop. Granny, you remember Melinda Cartside?"

"Of course. From the village. Nice girl. Melvin and Dora's only daughter." Eloise explained to Genny, "The Cartsides run the post office and village store." She turned to Brooke again. "Melinda went off to Paris, didn't she?"

"She did, yes. But now she's in Chelsea and she is the genius behind Fresh."

"Well, I'm so pleased to hear she's doing well. Dora was brokenhearted when she went away."

"Well, she needed to make a life that worked for her," said Brooke, more than a little defensively.

"I know, I know," Eloise replied mildly. "Children have to go out and make their own way."

Fiona drank more wine and said that everything Brooke had bought was fabulous. And then Brooke told them that she'd invited Melinda for a visit. "Just a short one. Overnight."

Eloise agreed that it would be lovely to see her and Genny tried not to wonder what Brooke was up to now—which was pretty small-minded of her, and she knew it. Why shouldn't Brooke have her friends come to visit?

The meal wore on. Somehow, they got through it without Brooke or Fiona saying anything too awful. After the dessert of fresh berries and cream, Brooke decided to open another bottle of wine.

Eloise shook her head. "You'll have a headache in the morning."

"Oh, for God's sake, Granny. It's just a little wine."

"No, dear. You've *had* a little wine. When you finish another bottle, you'll have had a *lot* of wine."

Brooke only laughed. "And then I will most likely feel happier about everything."

Fiona snickered. "After which, we'll need *more* wine— to celebrate so much happiness."

"And I will not be here for that," said Eloise mildly. "I believe I shall call it a night."

"Good night, Granny," Brooke said much too sweetly.

"Yes," agreed Fiona. "Good night. Lovely dinner."

"So pleased you enjoyed it." Eloise got up. The dogs jumped up, too, eager to follow wherever Eloise might lead them.

Genny started to stand. "I'll come up with you."

"Oh, no," said Brooke, much too eagerly. "Genny, don't go." *Genny.* Brooke never called her Genny. Was it a good sign? Genny couldn't help but doubt that.

"Yes," agreed Fiona, flashing her pretty white teeth. "You must stay with us. Have a glass of wine. We'll talk about old times…"

Brooke, Fiona and too much wine. Not a good combination. Genny knew if she stayed things could easily get ugly.

But her pride pricked at her. It seemed so cowardly just to run away from them. They resented her. To them, she had it all by a mere accident of birth. They were the same, of course. Born into good families, both had married wealthy men. But Genny's luck beat theirs. She was higher born *and* had an enormous inheritance. Plus, as it turned out, Rafe's fortune was nothing to sneeze at. So she'd married well, too.

Rafe.

She wished he were there. With him at the table, Brooke and Fiona wouldn't dare go too far.

And then she felt like a spineless nothing, a total wimp, longing for her husband at her side to protect her.

Eloise laid a gentle hand on her shoulder. Genny glanced up into those wise blue eyes. "Thanks," she said to Brooke and Fiona. "But I'm a little tired tonight." She pushed back her chair and stood.

"Fine." Brooke put on her sulky face. "Be that way."

Genny went on smiling. "Good night. Brooke, good to have you home. So nice to see you, Fiona."

The two nodded and smirked—and Brooke poured them more wine.

Genny had a long bath, put on her most comfortable nightgown and a comfy dressing gown over it and then watched television in the sitting room of the suite for a while.

By eleven, she still felt edgy and wide-awake. She missed Rafe, missed him terribly. Which was pretty absurd. He'd been gone just fourteen hours.

She had tonight and Tuesday night to get through without him. Her body ached for him. It was the strangest thing. It had been the same after their four-day fling or affair or whatever it could be called, in March.

Like withdrawing from some addictive drug, to be without him. Without his big hands caressing her, his broad, hard body curved around her when she fell asleep...

She let her head fall to the sofa back and stared up at the intricate plaster moldings in the ceiling. Yes, the bed would feel lonely without him. But at some point, she would to have to crawl between the covers and try to get some sleep.

Might as well get going on that now. She dragged herself to her feet.

And someone tapped on the outer door.

A prickle of alarm sent a shiver down her back. What possible good could come of someone knocking on her door at this hour?

The tap came again.

Rafe? Her heart grew lighter in her chest.

But no. He wouldn't knock on the door to his own rooms.

Genny gave up trying to guess who it might be and went to find out.

"Well," said Fiona on a blast of wincy breath. "All ready for beddy-bye, I see." Brooke's friend had her right arm braced on the door frame and a woozy look on her pretty face. She wore the same yellow sleeveless dress she'd worn at dinner, and her peep-toe Manolo Blahniks dangled from the fingers of her left hand. Clearly, a lot more wine had been consumed since Genny and Eloise had left the table. "May I come in?"

Whatever for? Genny couldn't remember ever having had a private conversation with Brooke's friend. "You know, Fiona, it's late and I was just—"

"A little chat, that's all, just you an' me." Fiona peeled herself off the door frame. "I won't stay long, promise. Only a minute or two…"

It was either shove her backward and slam the door in her face—or go along. For now. Genny waved her in.

"Super." Fiona dodged around her and headed for the sofa, plunking down on it with a huffing sound and dropping her yellow shoes to the rug. She lifted both arms and spread them wide along the sofa back. "I understand congratulations are in order." There was definite smirking. "A baby. How nice."

"Thank you." Genny took one of the wing chairs. She wasn't the least surprised that Fiona knew. No way Brooke could have resisted the temptation to tell her—especially not after the two of them had poured down large amounts of wine. "Rafe and I are very excited."

"Oh, well, I'm sure you are." Fiona listed to the left a bit, but then righted herself once more. "When are you due—if you don't mind my asking?"

"Not at all," Genny sweetly lied. "December 20."

"Ah. A Christmas baby."

"Yes."

"Aren't those good luck?"

"Christmas babies, you mean?"

"Yes." Fiona blinked several times in rapid succession, apparently trying to focus. "I'm sure I heard once that... um..." The sentence wandered off unfinished.

This was getting a little scary. "Fiona, let me help you to your room." Genny started to stand.

"In a minute, Yer Highness." Fiona stared at her through narrowed eyes—because her vision was blurry or as a drunken attempt at a glare, Genny couldn't tell which. "I have...things which I need to say to you."

Genny slowly lowered herself back into the chair. Fiona looked pretty bad. Was she going to pass out? She needed to be in her own room before that happened. "Fiona, I think it's time you let me help you to your—"

"A minute. Just a minute. I only, well, I wanted to tell you. How ver' sorry I am. For Rafe. For...how difficult it must be for him..."

Genny really, really did not like where this was going. She braced for the big insult.

"So terrible," Fiona barreled on, "knowing he's not a

DeValery by blood, but only the, um, bastard son of some nobody, some gardener."

Genny gulped. Alrighty, then. Completely different insult than she'd been expecting. "That's enough, Fiona. You're talking nonsense."

The awful woman wouldn't stop. She only sniffed loudly—and kept on. "I mean, Rafe has a good heart. He means well. He tries. I know that. We all know that. And he must feel terribly guilty about the accident. It's so obvious. I mean, that hideous scar he's done nothing about. He's leavin' himself scarred as a penance for the accident, isn't he?"

"Of course not. Fiona—"

"I know, I know." She waved a hand. "He wasn't driving. They have all those forensic things they do now. They proved, somehow, that he wasn't at the wheel. But will we ever really know? Will we ever—?"

"Fiona. Hello!" Genny tried again to shut her up. "You don't know what you're talking about."

"Oh, don't I, then? You'd be surprised what I know, what I've been through. How I've suffered." The green eyes filled with tears. "What I have had that you will *never* get. Ver' surprised. Oh, yes, you would." The tears overflowed and ran down her cheeks.

"Fiona, it's time for you to—"

"Who can tell, is all I'm saying? Who can know? Except that Edward is gone," she sobbed. "And that leaves Rafe to ape his betters and pretend to be the lord and heir that he can never, ever be...." Her shoulders shook. She swiped at her streaming eyes. "It's only that I can't bear it, you see? Sometimes I wish I could die. Sometimes I just want to curl into a li'l ball of misery and die."

But Fiona didn't die. She only covered her face with

both hands, fell over sideways on the sofa and dissolved completely into an ugly fit of soggy snorts and heavy sobs.

Genny did nothing for several seconds. She sat there and watched Fiona cry and longed to get up, march over there, grab Brooke's BFF by her long red hair and slap her good and hard across her snot-soaked, splotchy little face.

Chapter Seven

Genny gave herself a count of ten to let her violent urges fade down to a slow-burning rage. And then she said, slowly and clearly, "I'll say it again. I don't know what you're talking about. I'm as sorry as anyone that Edward is gone. But Rufo is doing Hartmore proud and he is every inch the earl in every way. And if you know what's good for you, you'll stop spreading vicious lies."

Fiona only went on sobbing. "I can't bear it. I never s'pected he would… That it would end. It *can't* end. That's not how it was supposed to be.…"

Clearly, there was no point in talking to her.

Genny got up, went to the door to the hallway and opened it wide. Then she marched into the bedroom and took the box of tissues from the dressing table. She carried it back to the sitting room and stood above the sobbing, shoeless woman in the yellow dress. "Fiona."

"What?" Fiona dragged herself to a sitting position. Her

dark eyeliner had dribbled down her cheeks. She blinked at the tissues. "Ugh. Thanks." She whipped out a handful and dabbed at the mess on her face. "I'm…" She let out an enormous belch. "Oh. S'cuse me. So sorry…"

"Take it." Genny shoved the box at her.

Fiona caught it, fumbling, and blinked up at her. She was catching on at last. "Oh, my. I do b'lieve you're bloody cheesed off…."

"Yes, I am." She grabbed Fiona's shoes in one hand. With the other, she took Fiona's arm and hauled her upright. "And you are going to your room."

"I don't think that's such a good idea…walking and all that. I'm a li'l woozy…"

Genny ignored her. She jerked the arm she held, guiding it up and across her shoulders.

"Ow! You're *hurting* me…."

"You're going now." Genny started moving, taking Fiona with her, to the door and through it.

Half walking, half dragging the other woman, Genny somehow managed to keep them upright and moving down to the end of that hallway and on to the next.

Halfway down that second hallway, Fiona dropped the box of tissues. "Stop," she whined. "The tissues…"

Genny only snapped, "Never mind that," and kept them lurching along toward the room Fiona always used when she came to Hartmore.

It took forever. With each step, Genny feared Fiona would pass out completely. Or chuck up all that wine she'd drunk.

But they made it to Fiona's room at last. Genny dropped Fiona's shoes on the threshold and shoved open the door.

Inside, Genny dragged the other woman past the small sitting area and over to the neatly turned-back bed. She backed them both to the mattress and sat Fiona down on it, then eased out from under the limp weight of her arm. Fiona swayed in place for a moment—and then collapsed back across the bed, her shoeless feet dangling over the side.

Genny stared down at her, thoroughly disgusted. She tried to think of one final thing to say to her, the right words that would shut her evil little mouth about Rafe once and for all.

But then Fiona started snoring.

Genny went to the door, scooped up the yellow shoes and tossed them into the room. Then, quietly, she shut the door and returned to the East Bedroom, only pausing to get the fallen box of tissues on the way.

She turned off the lights and crawled into bed and lay awake for hours, missing Rafe, thinking that in the morning, Fiona probably wouldn't even remember what she'd done and said while she was so thoroughly plowed.

As for the old story about Rafe being some gardener's son? It was one of those big secrets that a lot of people seemed to be in on. Genny had heard the whispers about Rafe's "real" father long ago—from an English girl she'd met at school who knew the DeValerys, and also from a village boy one summer when she'd come to Hartmore for a long visit. It seemed to her that she'd always known.

Fiona getting sauced and deciding to throw the old rumor in Genny's face didn't really amount to all that much—beyond providing yet more proof that Brooke's BFF was a raving bitch. Genny had never cared in the least that Rafe might be the product of a forbidden liaison between his mother and one of the staff.

What really mattered was her own unwillingness to raise the subject with him. Even back in the old days, when she and Rafe could talk so easily about so much, they never discussed the ugly rumors concerning his "real" father.

It was another one of those things they didn't speak of. Like the pretty woman on the jetty the summer she was fourteen; like the night Edward died. Like the shameful truth that she would have married Edward just to get Hartmore.

She believed Rafe did know what people whispered behind his back. And she assumed it must be hurtful to him. She was reasonably certain that most of his difficulties with his father, Edward II, went back to those rumors. The old earl had too much pride to disown him, but had never treated him as a true son.

Genny wished they *could* talk about it. But she feared if she brought it up, things would go the way they had on their wedding night. She would only upset him and push him away.

The next day, Fiona failed to appear in the Morning Room for breakfast.

Brooke, nursing what looked like one hell of a hangover, seemed unconcerned. She waved a dismissive hand. "Fiona left. Said she had a lot to attend to at Tillworth."

Genny felt only relief not to have to deal with her.

That day, she went out with Eloise to the walled garden, which supplied fruits and vegetables for Hartmore. The garden, on the far side of the lake, was large and well tended, with modern glasshouses for protecting more delicate plants and a beautiful old pavilion-type structure that served as a giant storage shed.

The walled garden had always provided much more than the DeValerys could eat themselves. The extra they carted to the village market for sale. That day the garden staff was digging new potatoes, picking runner beans and tomatoes, as well as raspberries and strawberries for pies and desserts.

In the afternoon, before walking back to the house, Genny and Eloise sat together on a stone bench under an elm tree and made more plans for the future. Eloise said she'd always dreamed that someday they might open a restaurant by renovating the stables and the cobbled courtyard outside them. The DeValerys still kept horses, but only a few now. They could build smaller, modern stables farther from the house and use the old, rambling stone stables for the restaurant. They could sell Hartmore produce there, too. And maybe, eventually, they should have a gift shop. It would fit in the stable area, as well.

Genny agreed. The more income they produced, the better.

"It's so satisfying," Eloise said, "to feel we're really going somewhere now, that we're doing all we can to keep the house in good repair, to plan ahead and build on what we have. It's no small thing, to keep an old pile like Hartmore standing—let alone in the family."

Genny thought of the rotten things Fiona had said the night before. "Rafe's doing a wonderful job, I think."

Eloise patted her hand. "Oh, yes. God knows, we all loved Edward, rest his soul. But he was never a planner, was he? Not one to look ahead and decide what will need doing, not one to apply himself to the basic questions of survival. He was a beautiful charmer, that one…."

"Yes."

"We'll miss him. But we must count our blessings. And Rafael is very much among them."

Genny longed to confide in Eloise, to tell her about Fiona's drunken ramblings last night, to ask if Eloise thought the old story about Rafe's parentage was true.

But she hardly knew how to start such a difficult conversation. Surely Eloise had heard the rumors, too. Still, what if she hadn't? It wasn't the kind of thing the old woman even needed to know about. Whatever the truth of his birth, Rafe *was* the earl of Hartmore now. Digging around in the secrets of the past wouldn't change that.

Better to let it go.

Or, if she just *had* to discuss it with someone, it really ought to be with the man himself. Maybe. Someday…

Eloise asked, "Shall we go, then?"

They got up and left the garden, taking the lake path back to the house.

That evening at dinner, Brooke was downright pleasant. She mentioned Geoffrey's birthday, which was about a month away, on the first Saturday in July. He would be home from school by then. She'd decided to throw a birthday party for him.

Eloise reminded Brooke that Geoffrey didn't like a lot of fuss. "But if we keep it small and simple…"

"Of course," Brooke said brightly. "That's exactly my plan."

Genny agreed that a party would be nice. And she decided to take Brooke's new attitude for a good sign that Rafe's sister really was trying to get along, that things would be better between them from now on.

Rafe was due back on Wednesday in the afternoon. Genny woke early that morning thinking, *Today, he comes home.*

All morning, she had that edgy, excited feeling, like a child who'd been promised some special treat. She kept busy, spending most of the morning in the center of the house, helping out wherever she was needed. They had a steady stream of visitors that day.

By one, she felt downright anxious. She couldn't wait to see him. It was almost embarrassing—the sense of longing, the way her heart seemed to have got stuck up high in her chest at the base of her throat. It was pounding away in there, yearning and burning. And her cheeks felt much too warm.

Ridiculous. Really.

She decided she needed exercise. She would work off some of the tension caused by all this crazy anticipation. It was a clear, bright day. Perfect for a run. She changed into shorts and a pair of trainers and put her hair in a ponytail. Then she took Moe and Mable and headed to the lake.

She ran half the way, the dogs bounding on ahead, circling back and taking off again. When she couldn't run another step, she found sticks and threw them for the collies to fetch. Now and then, she passed a visitor or one of the gardeners or someone from the village. They all smiled and waved as she raced by, the dogs at her heels. No doubt she'd get a bad reputation: that wild, young princess who married the earl.

By the time she was on her way back to the house, she dripped sweat and her hair was falling down. She had mud spattered all over her trainers, halfway to her knees. She needed a hot shower and clean clothes.

But she did feel more settled within herself, not so achy and hormone crazed. Funny, how it was all turning out. Even with the things that lay unspoken between her and Rafe, even with the guilt she felt over getting pregnant during their four-day fling, even given the sadness and regret over Edward's tragic death, she was glad, so glad that she'd married him.

And not because of Hartmore, either.

Really, who did she think she was kidding? The truth was so simple. She not only loved him, as she always had, as her dearest friend in the world. No. It was more than friendship for her now. She was falling *in* love with him.

How could she not? He was so smart and true and good at heart. She loved how he looked out for Geoffrey, how he treated his grandmother, with respect and real affection, how he was patient and forgiving with Brooke, who, let's face it, was the kind of woman who could try the patience of a saint. He was also thoughtful and kind to the staff and the local people. Not to mention way better in bed than any man had a right to be.

She wanted to tell him, to just say it right out: *Rafe, I'm falling in love with you. I'm falling deeper and deeper every day.*

But then she had no idea how he would react to such news. And she felt like such a complete fraud, after all those years of waiting for Edward, telling herself she was in love with *him*. Wasn't it way too convenient that she'd suddenly decided she loved Rafe now?

She probably shouldn't rush it. Better to give it time, think it over. Surely a woman shouldn't just spring something like that on an unsuspecting man.

Even if he was her husband.

She dropped the dogs off with Eloise, who was busy in the rose garden, and let herself in at the East Entrance the family used, pausing just inside the door to check the soles of her trainers. Unlike the tops, the soles were clean, wiped off by all that running across the damp grass. She wouldn't be tracking mud up and down the fine old floors and carpets. She took off for the stairs to the first floor.

And then she heard the voices. They were coming from the Blue Drawing Room not far from the stairs: a woman's voice. And Rafe's. Her heart did that leaping thing and got lodged in her throat again.

"Never change," he said, his tone warm and easy.

And the woman laughed in a husky, intimate way. "No danger of that."

Genny veered from the stairs and over to the wide-open doors to the drawing room. Rafe and a slim, dark-haired woman stood over by the Palladian window that looked out on the wide swathes of open parkland rolling away from the north front of the house.

Rafe spotted her. "Gen—there you are."

The woman turned to smile at her.

It was the woman he'd kissed on the boat jetty eleven years before.

Genny's mind went blank—and then started spinning. What was going on here? She didn't like it—no, worse.

She *hated* it.

She hated *herself* for hating it.

He held out his big hand. "Come here, love. I want you to meet Melinda Cartside."

Melinda. So that was her name—a name Genny had heard recently. Hadn't she? Melinda…

Right. The shop owner in Chelsea that Brooke had gone on about. The woman who'd grown up right here, in the village.

Rafe had spoken so fondly to her. Too fondly. And the way she had laughed, so husky and teasing…

Did he still have a thing going on with her, after all these years? He'd just come from London. Had he been with this woman there?

Genny wanted to scratch the woman's wide brown eyes out. Not only was she much too good-looking to be laughing intimately with someone else's husband, she had a really fabulous sense of style. She wore an ankle-length full skirt, of all things. The skirt was a swirling pattern of red and fuchsia-pink. Into the skirt, she'd tucked a crisp white oxford shirt. And she had sky-high, very ladylike black pumps on her delicate feet.

Genny poked at her sweaty, falling-down ponytail. The elastic came loose and she stuck it in her pocket, then swiftly raked the tangled mess behind her ears. She wanted a shower and to put on something really pretty.

And then to kill Melinda Cartside.

All these overwhelming emotions. Was this what falling in love did to you? It wasn't fun in the least, and she was growing so tired of it.

"Gen?" Twin lines drew down between Rafe's black brows: worry. He looked worried.

And he *should* be worried if he was fooling around with this Melinda person. They might have gotten married because of the baby. He might not love her the way she'd begun to love him. But still. They *were* married. She needed to have a little talk with him about what marriage meant to her.

And what it had better mean to him.

He was still watching her, still looking worried.

Genny put on her friendly face and entered the Blue Drawing Room. "Hello." She aimed a thousand-watt smile at the other woman. Rafe put out a hand to pull her close to his side. She jerked away. "I've been out running, throwing sticks for the dogs. You'll be covered in mud."

"I don't mind." He pulled her close anyway, up nice and snug against his beautifully cut jacket and gray silk trousers. It felt so good—his warmth and size, the smell of his aftershave that was fresh and green, a little bit musky. And so, so manly. "Gen. Melinda."

The woman gushed, "Your Highness. I'm so pleased." She actually managed to sound sincere.

"You must call me Genny," she said, and thought she sounded friendly and gracious and not the least bit murderous after all.

"Melinda grew up in the village," Rafe said. "But she lives in London now."

"I own a shop," Melinda provided. "Women's fashion."

Right. The shop. Brooke had mentioned the shop and all the clothes that she'd bought there....

"I hear you've made a big success," Rafe said.

"It's going rather well, I must admit."

Genny needed more information. "And what brings you to Hartmore?"

"I invited her," said Brooke from the doorway—which meant that Rafe hadn't.

Good. And Genny should have remembered that. Brooke had said that the woman was coming for a visit.

Dear God, this was awful. Love had addled her mind and stolen her memory. She could hardly recall the things she'd been told night before last.

"Brooke, hello!" exclaimed Melinda.

Brooke took a step into the room and pirouetted on her heel. She wore a bubblegum-pink blazer over a wonderful featherlight blush-colored dress. "All Fresh."

"I'm flattered," said Melinda. She explained to Genny, "Fresh is the name of my shop."

"That's right." Genny hoped her smile didn't look like a grimace. "Brooke has told us all about it."

Brooke was still preening. "I love everything I bought."

"I'm so pleased." Melinda glowed and gave a little wave of her left hand. She wasn't wearing a wedding ring.

Brooke asked, "Genevra, did you fall in the lake?"

Genny laughed. It sounded easy and natural and she was glad about that. "No, but the dogs and I did have a good run around it." She eased out from under Rafe's arm. "Excuse me, everyone. I do need to wash the mud off." She aimed herself at the foyer and she kept going until she was through it, up the stairs, down the hallway and safely in the East Bedroom.

* * *

Genny didn't hear the shower door open.

She was too busy rinsing the sweat and mud away—
and trying not to wonder what Melinda Cartside and Rafe
were doing downstairs. Then a hard arm hooked around
her waist. She knew it was Rafe, but a shriek of surprise
still got away from her as she found herself reeled in tight
against his big bare chest.

"Rafe!" She bopped him one, using the heel of her hand
against the giant bulge of his shoulder. "You'll give me a
heart attack."

He gazed down at her, looking all lazy and pleased with
himself. Water plastered his hair to his head, ran down his
cheeks and off the end of his nose. It also splashed over his
broad chest, catching in the dark trail of hair there, making little sparkling rivulets that joined into bigger rivulets
and trickled lower. And lower… "I'm happy to be home."
He was definitely glad to see her. It was in his eyes as he
looked at her—and there was also that lovely hardness rising against her belly.

Apparently, he would rather be with her than Melinda.
That was gratifying. She stared up at him and thought
about kissing him, about climbing all over him right then
and there, with the shower raining down on them.

But then she thought about all the things they never
seemed to talk about. And she decided they really needed
to start somewhere.

Why not Melinda?

Oh, please. She knew very well why not Melinda.

What if he really was having an affair with her?

She didn't want to know.

But then again, she *needed* to know.

Was this where married people went wrong? They
avoided the difficult things and before they knew it, ev-

erything was difficult and there was nothing true left between them.

"You're looking at me strangely." He dipped his head and pressed his cheek to hers. The water streamed between them, tickling a little. "What?" he whispered into her ear.

She pushed on his shoulders until she could meet his eyes. "I need to tell you something."

He tried to keep teasing her. "This is sounding much too serious."

She just gazed at him somberly through the veil of running water. "Well, yes, Rafe. It is rather serious, as a matter of fact."

He stepped back clear of the shower spray then. His expression was not the least encouraging. The scar pulled harder than ever at the corner of his mouth—but it didn't come close to making him look as if he might smile. "What is it?" he asked again, this time in a thoroughly discouraging tone.

She backed from under the shower head, too, putting even more distance between them. "Don't look so worried. It's not about Edward or the night that he died."

He leaned near again, but only in order to reach around her and shut off the water. Then he pushed open the shower door and grabbed a fluffy bath sheet from the heated rack on the nearest wall.

She stood silent, watching his unreadable face as he blotted water from her hair and then wrapped the toasty towel around her. "Thank you," she whispered finally, tucking it, sarong-style, above her breasts.

He said nothing, just grabbed another towel, rubbed himself down quickly and hooked it around his waist. They got out of the shower, went into the bedroom and sat, side by side, between the curtains, on the edge of the bed. She tried to think how to start.

When the silence stretched too long, he said, "All right, then. Whatever it is, tell me. I'm waiting."

Her insecurities tried to take control. They urged her to get on his case, to take the offensive. She longed to demand hotly, *Are you, or have you ever been, Melinda Cartside's lover?*

But that was hardly fair. And what would she accomplish by jumping all over him? What would that do but push him away?

No. She wanted him to talk with her, to be frank with her. And she really needed him to understand what was bothering her. He should know upfront why she had suspicions about him and the Cartside woman.

And that meant she had to share the little secret she'd been keeping since she was fourteen years old.

She gulped and got after it. "Eleven years ago, when I came for a summer visit, I went looking for you. You know how I was then, always with a thousand things I needed to tell you immediately or sooner." She tried a laugh. It came out all strangled sounding. He didn't laugh with her. He only waited, watching her guardedly. So she said the rest. "I ran down to the lake and I saw you sitting out on the jetty with a woman I'd never seen before."

He knew then. "Melinda."

She nodded. "You were laughing together. And you kissed her. I ran away, back to the house, before you could see me. I never saw her again until today."

"You never said a word…"

She fiddled with the towel, tucking it a little tighter. "I felt…embarrassed. Confused. Angry, too, though I knew I had no right to be."

He touched her then, easing a soggy curl away from her cheek with a slow caress of his index finger. Something hard and painful inside her softened, melted. "You were angry?"

"Yes. Well, actually, I was furious. Do not ask me to explain that. I don't think I can."

"What else?"

"Today, before I came into the Blue Room, I heard you two talking. You sounded…affectionate toward her. You told her never to change and she laughed. I didn't know at that moment that she was the woman from the jetty. But it was a husky, too-friendly laugh, I thought." She straightened her shoulders. "And it bothered me. A lot."

"There's nothing between Melinda and me." His voice was calm. Level. "Not anymore."

"But there *was* something eleven years ago?"

"Gen…"

"I want to know, Rafe. You were lovers then, is that what you're saying?"

"For that summer, yes."

"But how? I never saw her again, though I followed you everywhere during that visit. When did you have time to be her lover?"

He made a low sound. It might have been a chuckle. "I got away on my own now and then, believe it or not."

"Hmph. Eloise never mentioned her. Neither did Brooke or Edward, or your mother. Were you keeping things secret, the two of you?"

"We were, yes."

"But why?"

He frowned a little. "We always we knew it wasn't going to last forever. She wanted to keep what we had just between us, didn't want her parents or anyone getting ideas about some kind of future between her and me—or worse, having people deciding that I was somehow taking advantage of a nice village girl. Melinda always planned to get out, to see the world. And that fall, she did. She went to France. We drifted apart. It's nothing mysterious."

"And since then?"

"That first year after she left the village, I went to Paris to see her a couple of times. And then, well, she got on with her life. I had mine. I ran into her once after Paris, a chance meeting in the village about five years ago. She was home on holiday. We said hello, wished each other well. And that was it until today, when I found her waiting in the Blue Room. I was surprised to see her. When you came in, she was telling me about her shop, about how much she loves living in London."

"All very innocent, then?"

"Gen…" His voice teased her. So did the light in his eyes. He wrapped an arm around her. She allowed him to ease her back across the bed. He braced on an elbow and gazed down at her. "Did you think I was having a little something on the side with Melinda, is that it?"

She started to deny it, just out of pride. But truth was the point here and pride only got in the way of the truth. "Well, yes. I did wonder."

"I'm not." He leaned closer. "You're the only one I'm having a little something with." He breathed the words against the still-damp skin of her throat. "Scratch that. With you, it's a whole lot of something." She did like the sound of that.

She liked it a lot. "Really?"

"Really."

She knew she was blushing. "It's only that we got married so fast…"

"We've known each other since you were five. Twenty years, Gen. For at least the first fifteen of those twenty, you told me all your secrets."

She pulled a face. "Whether you wanted to hear them or not."

"Except now I learn that you saw me kissing Melinda

Cartside and never told me until today. How many other secrets are you keeping from me?"

How many are you keeping from me? she thought, but couldn't quite make herself ask.

Yet.

And that had brought her back around to the ugly things Fiona had said Monday night. Should she go there now, try to get him to talk about the cruel old stories concerning who his real father might be?

Maybe not. They'd covered enough dangerous emotional territory for one day.

He added, "A wife should tell her husband everything."

"Of course you would say that. You're the husband."

He caught the edge of her towel. She tried to hold on, but he wouldn't stop tugging on it. With a low, nervous laugh, she let go. He peeled it back. Then he took the other side and peeled it back, too. When she tried to wrap her arms across her bare breasts, he shook his head. "Don't."

"You're very bossy." She put her arms down.

"I like to look at you. It was bad in London."

"Bad? Why?"

"You weren't there."

Gratifying. Definitely. "So you missed me?"

He nodded. "I find I've grown accustomed to having you in my bed. I don't like it when you're not there…to look at. To touch." He put his big hand, fingers spread, on her belly. "A little fuller, I think."

She blew out her cheeks with a breath. "Yes. I'll be fat as an old cow in no time."

"You're not the least old."

"Oh, you…" Her hand was wedged between them. All it took was a twist of her wrist and she was tugging on his towel. It came undone.

"Careful." He bent over her and pressed those wonderful lips to her stomach, right where his hand had been.

She sighed. It ended on a tiny moan. "We never talked…"

"About?"

"Being true…"

"Do you want us to be true?" He kissed the words onto her skin right over where their baby slept.

"Yes. I want only the two of us in this marriage—you and me. Nobody on the side."

He opened his mouth, brushed her belly with his tongue, nibbled on her belly button. Pleasure shimmered through her veins, flashed across her skin.

She murmured, "I know we started all wrong…"

"There are worse ways to start." He laid a sweet string of nipping kisses up over her ribs to her left breast.

She moaned again as he sucked her nipple into his mouth. "I want a *real* marriage, Rafe. I'm a Bravo-Calabretti after all. We marry for…" *Love,* she thought, but didn't let herself say. She let a moan of pleasure suffice.

He sucked more strongly and did something amazing with his tongue. She closed her eyes. A thread of pleasure seemed to connect her breast to her core. Fire licked along that thread.

And then he stopped.

She moaned in protest and blinked up at him.

He gazed down at her, eyes low and lazy, soft mouth a little swollen, red from kissing her. "Just you and me, then," he whispered. "No one else."

"Good." She lifted the hand that wasn't tucked in between them and finger combed his thick, inky hair.

It hadn't been so awful—not awful at all, really. To reveal an old secret. To find out what she needed to know. To come to a workable agreement between the two of them.

They should do that more often—and she intended to see that they did.

"Gen."

"Um?"

He bent close and bit her chin. Lightly. "Did *you* miss *me?*"

"Terribly."

"That's what I like to hear. I think next time I go up to London, you'll have to come with me. That way I won't have to go to bed without you."

"I *might* go with you."

He rubbed his nose against hers. "You will."

"Bossy, bossy, bossy. Just because I want us to be true to each other doesn't mean we shouldn't have time apart now and then. It's healthy for a couple to have some separate interests."

"You're becoming very opinionated."

She laughed. "You're bossy. I'm opinionated. It's good we found each other. Who else would have us?"

"It doesn't matter. We've got each other. And a workable agreement between us. *And* you missed me." He kissed her. "Say it."

"What?"

"You know what. Say you missed me."

"I said it already."

"Say it again."

"I...I missed you, Rafe." She breathed the words, a little bit raggedly, against his lips.

He eased his arm down with hers, between them. And he caught her hand and guided her fingers to the silky, hard length of him. "Now I want you to show me, Gen. Show me how much...."

She did what he wanted. With enthusiasm. Because it was what she wanted, too.

Chapter Eight

They stayed in the bedroom for the rest of the afternoon. Rafe insisted that no one would fault them.

After all, they were newlyweds.

They made love; they shared a long bath. And then they made love again.

He told her he'd been to see Geoffrey.

She asked, "How's he managing?"

"Better, I think. He says he's on a team in Geography. They work together to do the assignments. There's one other boy on the team he thinks he might be friends with. And he's counting the days until the summer term is over and he can come home."

"Brooke says she's giving him a birthday party."

Rafe was lying on his back, his hair crow-wing black against the white pillow. He put his arm across his eyes. "A small one, I hope."

"Eloise suggested the same thing. Brooke seemed to agree."

"You know how she is. You can tell her a hundred times that less is more. Not to Brooke."

"So true. To Brooke, more is more."

"Worse." He put his arm down and arched a dark brow at her. "To Brooke, more is never enough."

There were five of them at dinner: Rafe, Genny, Eloise, Brooke and Melinda. They ate in the family dining room.

"We have exciting plans." Brooke beamed at Melinda. "We're doing a fashion shoot. For Fresh. With Hartmore as the setting."

Melinda said, "I think we could get some beautiful shots. I couldn't pay a lot, but the pictures should get good exposure—in magazines and online. Fresh has a website, of course. We sell the clothes on the site as well as at the shop. I've been thinking of possibly doing a redesign of the website home page...."

"A home page featuring Hartmore as a backdrop for all those fabulous clothes," Brooke finished for her. Then Brooke fluttered her long lashes in Rafe's direction. "But of course, we'll need to get permission from Lord Hartmore."

He turned to Eloise. "What do you think?"

"It sounds lovely. Good for Hartmore—and for your shop, I would think, Melinda." She told Brooke, "You would need to work with the house team." The house team managed the public, income-producing face of Hartmore. They juggled tours, wedding parties and other events. And they handled the day-to-day running and upkeep of the State Rooms.

"No worries," said Brooke. "We'll clear everything with them."

"We'll be sure to stay out of the way," Melinda promised. "There are so many good locations—the deer park, the castle, the gardens, as well as the house, the terrace, the lake… The possibilities go on and on. We can easily work around whatever's already scheduled."

Rafe turned to Genny then. "How do you feel about this?"

Melinda looked at her hopefully.

Brooke's eyes narrowed—probably at the reminder that Genny now had a say in decisions regarding Hartmore. But then she forced a bright smile. "Genevra. Come on, now. You know it will be fabulous."

Genny understood that the photo shoot would essentially be a favor to Melinda, who'd been careful to say that she could only pay a limited fee. That was no problem. Doing favors created goodwill. And after getting the facts from Rafe about his relationship with Melinda, she didn't feel threatened by the other woman anymore.

As usual, Brooke wanted her answer and she wanted it now. "Well?"

Rafe said, "Don't rush her. She's thinking it over."

Brooke made a sour face and gulped down some wine. "Honestly. How difficult a decision can it be?"

Genny almost stalled a little longer, just to give Brooke a taste of her own medicine. But Rafe and Eloise were looking at her expectantly. So she said, "I think it's a terrific idea," and it was decided.

Melinda beamed and Brooke started in about which locations on the property were the ones they absolutely must include.

"Do you really think Melinda's photo shoot is a terrific idea?" Rafe asked much later, when they were alone in bed, after they'd made slow, tender love.

She turned toward him and wrapped her leg across his

and felt very comfortable and wonderfully intimate with him. "I think it's a nice favor to do for her, yes."

He admitted, "I always get nervous when Brooke gets a plan."

"I get nervous whenever she looks in my direction."

He made a sound low in his throat. It might have been a chuckle. "I know sometimes you want to pop her one."

"It's true. So far, though, I've restrained myself."

"You're a saint."

"No. I just try to remember that she's your sister and you love her."

He shifted, rolling to his back and pulling her over to rest her head against his shoulder. "I keep thinking that she'll work it out, find something to do that makes her happy. I'd hoped, when she married Derrick, that she'd be happy with him, in America. But she hated Atlanta." Derrick Landers was from an old Georgia family. "The marriage lasted...what?"

"Four years?" Derrick was in property development. He'd done well for himself and he'd been generous, in terms of money anyway, when he and Brooke had divorced.

"Four years," Rafe repeated, his deep voice echoing beneath her ear. "She came back to us angry. And she's been angry ever since."

"I don't know, Rafe. It seems to me she's always been angry, as far back as I can remember."

"Maybe so."

"Definitely so."

He made a low noise that she took for agreement. "I'm continually amazed that Geoffrey's so well-adjusted, to tell you the bald truth."

"I do worry for him. But then I try to remember that Brooke loves him absolutely. She may not be very good at showing it, and she never met a situation she couldn't make into a crisis. But I think he knows that she loves him, even if he's often frustrated with her. It gives him a certain balance, a basic feeling of security—which is something Brooke herself doesn't have."

He touched her jaw, her cheek. She sighed in pleasure at the sweet caresses and he whispered, "You always see the best in people."

She snorted out a laugh at that. "Your sister might disagree."

He kissed the crown of her head. She felt his lips against her hair and knew complete happiness in that moment. Then his fingers strayed beneath the covers. He found her hand and guided it lower. "I have something to show you...."

She tipped her head up enough to press her lips to his throat. "I think I've already seen it."

He lifted her chin higher with a finger and kissed her, his tongue meeting and tangling with hers, making her breath catch and her heart beat hard and deep. "Bored with me already, eh?"

Down beneath the blankets, she closed her fingers around him, stroking. "Not bored," she whispered against his lips. "Not in the least."

He groaned.

And she ducked her head under the covers, moving down.

He lifted the covers and peered under them at her. "Where *are* you going?"

"I'm going to have another look after all...."

His deep chuckle ended on another groan.

Genny woke up in the morning smiling.

Rafe was already gone. But he'd left her a note on her

night table: "Off for an early meeting with the house team. Tonight, I have something to show you. You might remember it from last night."

Laughing, she snatched up the note and pressed it to her chest. Her husband might not be *in* love with her, but he certainly cared for her. They had so much in common, shared a life they both wanted. And he wanted *her*. He'd proved that more than once last night.

Things were good between them—better every day.

She showered and dressed and went down to the Morning Room, where Brooke and Melinda had their heads together about the photo shoot. Genny dished herself up some oatmeal, adding blueberries and cream. Then she poured a tall glass of milk and sat down with them.

Melinda flashed her a warm smile. "Good morning."

"Morning," she replied.

Then Brooke went on talking.

Genny left them to their plans and concentrated on her food. She was starving for some reason. Could be the baby. Or maybe all the exercise she'd had last night. She giggled to herself at the thought.

The other two women stopped chattering and swung questioning glances her way. Melinda seemed to be waiting politely for her to say something. Brooke wore her usual impatient glare.

"Oops," she said. "Sorry. Just a happy thought, that's all." A very happy thought, as a matter of fact. She put on her most innocent expression and spooned up another heaping bite of oatmeal and berries.

The other two went back to their plans. The photo shoot was tentatively scheduled for the end of the next week. Melinda would call the photographer and the modeling agency right away and be sure that everyone she needed would be available. They were going to keep it simple, so

Melinda could try to keep costs down. Brooke seemed happy, animated. Maybe it was having a project that interested her. Or maybe it was having a friend to laugh and make plans with....

Genny ate the oatmeal and then returned to the sideboard for sausages and a scone slathered in clotted cream and jam made from Hartmore strawberries. She'd polished off the scone and was finishing up the last sausage when the other two women fell silent.

She looked up to find Rafe, in old jeans and a worn polo, standing in the doorway to the hall, watching her. He had a streak of soot on his unscarred cheek, and in his eyes she could see all the lovely things they'd done the night before. She swallowed that last big bite of sausage and reached for her napkin.

"Rafe, good morning," said Melinda, her voice a little too bright. Genny slid her a glance. What she saw startled her. A look of...what? Yearning? Hurt?

Whatever it was, it only lasted a split second. The strange expression vanished, replaced with a sweet, agreeable smile.

"Melinda," Rafe replied with a nod and turned back to Genny. "Almost done?" he asked her. She was still kind of stuck back there with that look on Melinda's face. He prompted, "Gen?"

She tucked her napkin in at the side of her plate. "Finished, yes. Have you eaten?"

"Later. Right now, there's something you need to see."

Deep in the center of the house, below the State Rooms, they stared at the ancient oil heater that provided warmth to the rooms above.

He said, "I'll have the man in from the village to look

at it. I think he can keep it going until the end of the season, at least."

"How old is it, exactly?" she asked.

"Twenty-three years."

"That's old, isn't it—for a heater, I mean?"

He nodded. "It's guzzling sixty thousand pounds a year now just for the oil, with another forty thousand for the electricity to run it."

"We'll have to replace it, won't we?"

He hooked an arm around her, pulled her close and pressed his lips to her hair. "I think we might, yes."

"This winter, then, while they're doing the roof and refurbishing the West Wing?"

He made a low, thoughtful sound of agreement as he rubbed his hand up and down her arm lightly, with a casual sort of intimacy that stole her breath—and made her feel she belonged to him, that they belonged together. "Visitors pour in and out of here every day," he said. "They see rooms full of art, Chinese wallpaper and Chippendale furniture. It all looks so well maintained."

She knew exactly where he was going. "But the trouble is behind the scenes, where people *don't* see—and you know what?"

He gave her shoulder a squeeze. "You have an idea."

"Maybe. Did you read about the new heating system they put in at Castle Howard? It was a few years ago."

"That's right. I'd completely forgotten. Ground-source heat, wasn't it called? A system of coils filled with heat-absorbing glycol under the lake. The heated glycol is then pumped up into the house and through the radiators, same as oil."

"From what I read, the savings are enormous for them. And they got government aid, because God knows the British government loves anything green." She turned into his arms and tipped her head up to grin at him. "Heating oil is not going to get any cheaper, you know."

He guided a curling lock of hair behind her ear. There was such warmth in his eyes. "We should look into it."

"Definitely." She reached up and rubbed that streak of soot off his cheek.

He gazed at her so...fondly. As though she were the only other person in the world. "Only you would have been reading casually about ground-source heating."

"You know about it, too, which means you did the same—and yes. It's what you said the day you showed me the plans for the new roof."

He remembered. "You were born for this." He bent his head to kiss her—a light, brushing, so-sweet little kiss. "We'll whip this old pile into shape in no time."

"Just stay away from Melinda." She hardly knew she was going to say it until the words were out of her mouth.

He stiffened and his eyes grew wary. "What do you mean?"

She stared up at him, wordless at that moment. She'd shocked herself when she blurted it out like that.

Now he was looking offended. "I told you everything, Gen. There's nothing between Melinda and me. Not for years."

She drew a slow breath—and set about making amends. "I believe you."

"Then, what's this about? Why demand I stay away from her?"

"Rafe, I mean it. I honestly don't believe you've done anything wrong." She put a hesitant hand against his hard chest—and breathed a little easier when he wrapped his fingers around it.

"I'll ask again," he said low. "What's this about?"

She tried to think how to explain it. "You're going to say I'm imagining things...."

A hint of his former good humor returned. "Let me decide for myself what I think."

"It was...the way she looked at you."

He seemed bewildered. "Looked at me when?"

"In the Morning Room, just now."

He shook his head. Slowly. "You're basing your suspicions on a look?"

"Yes. Yes, I am. It was a hurt, hungry sort of look. A very intense look."

"I have to say, I missed it completely."

"It was very fast. There and then gone. Just like that. And you weren't looking at her when it happened."

"Let me guess. I was looking at you. That should tell you something, don't you think?"

"This isn't about me and you. It's about Melinda."

"From where I'm standing, I would say it's very much about you and me. About whether you trust me—or not."

"I do trust you." For that, she got a grunt of disbelief. And she could easily grunt right back at him. He did have secrets, things he wouldn't—or couldn't—share with her.

But she didn't believe that Melinda was one of them. He'd been frank and open with her about his former girlfriend.

It was Melinda she was worried about. "I think she's still in love with you."

He groaned. "That's insane. With an extra helping of crazy sauce."

"Oh, well. Thank you very much."

"She was never in love with me. I told you how it was."

"You told me how it was for *you*. You told me about the agreement you had with her. You really can't have any idea what was going on inside her head and heart—and stop looking at me like that."

"Like what?"

"Like I'm a few mallets short of a full croquet set."

"I do not think you've lost your mind."

"Oh, excuse me. Wasn't it you just talking about crazy sauce?"

"I was exaggerating for the sake of affect."

"Gee, Rafe. Good to know."

"And Gen, I have to say, I do think you're very… possessive."

"Of course I'm possessive. You're my husband. I've made it very clear I don't want you fooling around."

"Then we can stop this conversation right here. I'm not fooling around."

"You're also not understanding what I'm trying to tell you."

"No kidding."

Men were so dense. "Rafe, I'm not only possessive, I'm feeling insecure."

"Why?"

"Oh, please. You married me because I'm having your baby."

He blinked. Bright hope rose within her, that he might take issue with the point, say he'd married her because he *wanted* to marry her.

Didn't happen. "So?"

So I'm in love with you, you idiot. She opened her mouth to say it. "So, I'm…" And then she just couldn't. She took the coward's way. "I have…worries, doubts about whether we'll make it together in the long run."

"We'll make it." He said it grimly, with determination. As though their marriage was some long, hard slog he'd set himself on, a goal he would reach no matter the cost.

She held on to her patience and spoke with admirable calm, she thought. "Rafe, I'm only saying that a baby coming is probably not the best reason to marry someone."

"It's a fine reason. A damn good enough reason."

"Yes, well. All right. It's reason enough for us."

"What in hell are you getting at?"

Oh, this was not going well at all. "I'm, er... We have an agreement, that's what. Last night, you agreed to be true to me."

He threw up both hands. "I don't know what you're worried about. How much clearer can I make myself? I haven't for years and am never again, under any circumstances, having it off with Melinda Cartside. I don't want anyone but you. If I've yet to convince you of that, let me see what I can do."

And with that, he grabbed her by the arms, hauled her close and slammed his mouth down on hers in an angry, punishing kiss.

She twisted her mouth away. "Rafe. Please..." His dark eyes burned down at her. She fully expected to see smoke coming out of his ears. "Rafe..." She flattened both hands on his chest that time, to put at least a few inches between his body and hers. His big heart was pounding away in there, like a giant hammer against a thick stone wall. He looked down at her hands. But he didn't take them in his this time. Then again, he didn't jerk away, either. "Rafe, I'm... I don't want anyone but you, either." *Because I'm in love with you. Totally, completely, achingly in love with you.*

"Then what is the problem? Why don't you trust me?"

"But I told you. It's Melinda I don't trust. You can't trust a woman—or a man—who's all eaten up with unrequited love."

"Eaten up? Gen, listen to yourself. What you're saying is absurd."

"No, I don't think it is."

"Think again. What real proof do you have? You can't just assume that Melinda's carrying some decade-long torch for me. Not from just one look. You hardly know her."

"Well, all right. When you put that way, I..."

"See? You don't know. You can't be sure."

She couldn't. And she had to admit that. "All right. I take your point. Maybe, just possibly, I have it all wrong."

"Of course you do."

She pushed at his chest. "Don't make me smack you one."

He caught her hands before she could escape. "You're a violent little thing." He dipped his head again.

And again, she turned away. "Listen. I mean it."

"Say it, then," he growled in her ear.

"I only... Well, just for the sake of argument, say I was right."

"But, Gen, you're *not* right."

"It doesn't matter."

"Of course it matters."

"Rafe. Please. Just for the sake of argument, let's say that I'm right. Let's say that Melinda is and always has been in love with you. And let's say she did make a pass at you. What would you do?"

"This is ridiculous."

"But what would you *do?*"

"Well, I would say no. That I'm not interested."

"And then, not only would she be suffering from unrequited love, she would have to live with your outright rejection."

He blew out a hard breath. "If a woman is going to make

a move on a married man, she deserves what she gets—in fact, I'll go further."

"Oh, well. Please do."

"We all risk rejection any time we go after something we want—or some*one* we want. If Melinda was so in love with me, why didn't she say a word about it all those years ago, when both of us were free?"

She looked at him, loving him, shaking her head, longing to demand, *If she had, would you have said you loved her, too?*

But no. If he answered yes, she'd only die a little inside. And it wasn't a fair question anyway. Better to stay in the here and now.

And then she found herself thinking about those two months after their four days at Villa Santorno. She had waited every day, every hour, every beat of her heart, for him to contact her, for him to tell her he wasn't ready yet for it to be over. Thinking about that time had her understanding Melinda better.

"Oh, Rafe. Don't you see? Eleven years ago, she was only waiting for a sign from you, a signal that maybe, just maybe, you felt what she felt."

He stared down at her with a thoughtful expression. For a moment, she thought he understood. But then, just like a man, he argued, "And maybe you have no idea what you're talking about."

She was so tempted to start yelling at him then. But no. She'd done the best she could with this. They needed to move on. "Just in case, will you please be careful around her? Be observant, watch your step?"

He snorted out a hard laugh. "You are the most stubborn woman I've ever known."

"Not half as stubborn as you. *Will* you?"

He looked thoroughly put-upon. "I suppose, for the sake

of peace between the two of us, I'll have to, won't I?" And then he dipped his head a third time.

She leaned back, so his lips couldn't quite touch hers. "Was that a yes?"

He caught her by the shoulders. "Kiss first."

She sucked in a shivery, yearning breath. "Will you?"

And he lifted one hand and cradled the back of her neck. His warm, knowing fingers slid into her hair. He held her there with very little effort as his mouth came down and plundered hers.

She didn't fight it. It felt too good. She parted her lips for him, inviting his clever, hot tongue inside.

For a long, lovely string of moments, everything faded away. There was only his burning kiss and the pleasure zipping along her every nerve.

And then, when he finally released her mouth, he pressed his forehead to hers. "Gen…"

She asked, one more time, "Will you?"

He teased, "What were we talking about?"

"Answer the question."

And finally, he gave in. "Yes, all right. I'll watch my step around Melinda."

Chapter Nine

Rafe had to go up to London again the next week. Genny went with him. They stayed at his house in Kensington. They ate out at good restaurants and attended the theater.

And they spent long, lazy hours in bed. They laughed a lot and discussed their plans for Hartmore. Genny felt relaxed and content with her life and her new husband. In her third month of pregnancy now, she was in excellent health and definitely eating for two.

Twice, they picked up Geoffrey after his school day was through. The first time, when he saw her, he let out a whoop and ran to her arms. "I'm so glad you've come, Aunt Genny. And you can come often, can't you? Now that you live at Hartmore with us."

She hugged him tight and agreed that yes, she certainly could and she definitely would.

They went to a film, the three of them. And they visited the Science Museum and ate at the Rainforest Café. He was cheerful and chatty. He said school wasn't so bad after all. And he couldn't wait to come home for two whole months.

Genny and Rafe returned to Hartmore late Friday afternoon. Melinda's photo shoot was just wrapping up. The sky had clouded over with a promise of coming rain and a car waited to take the models back to London—or the train station, Genny wasn't sure which.

The photographer and his assistant had already left, Eloise told them when they found her in the Blue Drawing Room.

"It's all been so very exciting," she said, and then lowered her voice to a stage whisper. "Best of all, it's almost over."

The three of them—Rafe, Eloise and Genny—stood at the Palladian window and watched the five tall, willowy models get into the waiting car and drive away.

Eloise explained, "Melinda will be staying the night and driving her van with all the clothes back tomorrow. She and Brooke have really hit it off. Melinda has been here every day since you two left for London. She goes back and forth between us and the village. Evidently, there's some tension between Melinda and her family. They never wanted her to leave the village all those years ago, from what I've gathered. They hoped she would stay home and marry some local man. So now they're making it up between them, Melinda and her mum and dad. I must say, I'm happy for that. Melvin and Dora are getting on in years. It's a time of life when you want to have peace with your children."

Rafe put his arm around Genny. She glanced up at him. He gathered her closer to his side.

Eloise shrugged and added, "Well, at least that's the sense that I have of the situation. I can't say for sure, though. I'm just an old woman and no one's been terribly forthcoming with me."

Rafe teased, "Granny, are you feeling sorry for yourself?"

"Of course not. I have my gardens and my family. Genevra belongs to us now." The pale blue eyes twinkled. "And in December I shall have another great-grandchild to spoil. Life is just as it should be—oh, and did I mention, Fiona's here, too? She invited herself for the photo shoot and will also be staying the night."

Fiona.

Genny knew she'd been unrealistic to hope she'd never have to see the woman again. But where Brooke went, Fiona eventually followed. Genny sometimes wondered about Fiona's marriage. The banker husband seemed to have a completely separate life from his horrible wife. And what about her children? Fiona seemed to have no time for the twins.

The rain was coming down, a dreary drizzle, by dinnertime. They ate in the family dining room. Brooke, Melinda and Fiona chattered away, sipping too much wine.

Genny tried not to look at Fiona. She feared if she did, her dislike would show on her face.

Melinda, on the other hand, seemed friendly in an easy, unpretentious way. She offered Genny smiles, asking her questions about her childhood in Montedoro, about how she was settling in at Hartmore. And she really did seem interested in Genny's answers. Not once did Genny catch her looking longingly at Rafe.

Had Rafe been right, then? Had Genny made a big deal about Melinda when there'd been no need? Genny really did begin to wonder if she'd completely mistaken that glance in the Morning Room a week before.

Apparently, Genny's pregnancy was now general knowledge. Which was fine. Good, even. It wasn't a secret anyone could keep for all that long—and somehow, in the past few weeks, she'd moved beyond wanting it to be a secret anyway. Melinda said how happy she was for her and Rafe.

And Fiona suggested, "Enjoy yourselves while you can. Once they're born, they're always in your hair."

Genny longed to reply that Fiona's sons didn't seem to be cramping her style one bit. But she didn't. She only gave Fiona a nod and quickly looked away.

Then Brooke started in about the party she was giving for Geoffrey's birthday. She'd decided to invite several children from the village. And Fiona's twins would be attending, as well. There was talk of paintball—a child's version, Brooke assured them, with smaller paint guns and softer ammunition, perfectly safe, totally painless—a petting zoo, a balloon act and a magician. The menu went on forever. The cake would be shaped like the main characters from Geoffrey's favorite video game. And there would be loot bags. Big ones.

Rafe reminded his sister, "I thought you were going to keep it low-key."

Brooke dismissed him with a wave of her wineglass. "He's only nine once, Rafe. I want it to be a party he'll remember."

Rafe let it go at that. Genny understood why. Once Brooke had decided to do something, it caused nothing but misery to argue with her plan.

Before dessert, Genny excused herself for a quick trip to the loo. She used the half bath not all that far from the East Dining Room. It was down a rather dim corridor. She took care of business, washed her hands and primped her hair.

When she pulled open the door, she almost ran into Fiona. "Oh!" It came out like a shriek of fright. And in a way, it was. "Fiona, you surprised me." She wanted out of there, and fast. "All yours, then." She dodged around the redhead.

But Fiona caught her arm. "Just a minute. Please, Genevra." Her voice was frantic, the light in her eyes nothing short of desperate.

Genny's stomach rolled, the baby making it clear yet again that he or she didn't appreciate intense emotions. She longed to jerk away and race toward the light at the end of the hallway.

But she didn't. She pulled it together, gently disengaged her arm and said, "All right. What is it?"

Fiona put her hands together—and started wringing them. "About that night last week…" Her mouth twisted, her misery obvious even in the darkness of the hallway. She tried a laugh. It came out a frenzied little screech. "I'd had a lot to drink and I have no idea what I might have said or done. It's all a complete blur to me. And I do hope you won't take whatever I said that night seriously. I…I could have said anything. Made up things, you know?"

Genny ought to let it go. There was nothing antagonistic in Fiona's attitude now. On the contrary, she seemed to want to reassure Genny that the things she'd said last Tuesday night would never cross her lips again. But then, who could tell with Fiona? "Which things, exactly, are you talking about?"

More hand wringing. "Well, I…I told you, I don't really know—because I can't remember, you see? I only wanted to apologize for barging in on you like that. It was so rude and disgusting of me."

"Then you do remember coming to my room?"

"I… Yes. I do. I remember you let me in. And after that, it's all a blur. All of it. Everything. I woke up in the morning in my room with a blazing hangover and I had no idea how I—"

"Gen?" Rafe stood down at the far end of the hallway, his broad form silhouetted against the light. "Everything all right?"

"Oh!" Fiona cried. "Rafe, hello there. Everything is fine, fine…" She flashed Genny a huge, ghastly smile. "Well, wonderful, then. Wonderful." She whirled, darted into the powder room behind her and quickly shut the door.

Genny went to Rafe.

He looked her over as though checking her for injuries. "After you left the table, she jumped up and said she'd be right back. I didn't like the look in her eyes."

"So you came to rescue me?" She went on tiptoe and brushed a kiss against his jaw.

He was still frowning. "What was that about?"

Scary question. Genny considered blowing the whole thing off, reassuring him, the same as Fiona had, that it was nothing. But he was no fool. He would know she was lying. And they'd been doing so well together. Truth mattered. They needed, slowly, to work their way through all the sad secrets of the past.

"Gen?" he prompted.

Right now, however, was not the time. "Long story. How about if we talk about it later?"

He hesitated. "You're sure you're all right?"

"I am, absolutely."

He offered his arm and they returned to the dining room.

All evening Genny stewed over what she would tell him when they were alone.

Everything, demanded her conscience.

Nothing, said the coward within who only wanted this fragile happiness they shared to continue forever, no matter the cost.

After dessert, Brooke, Fiona and Melinda went off to watch a film on the big-screen television in the Back Sitting Room. Eloise seemed to want to visit for a while. Rafe suggested Scrabble, as he knew his grandmother enjoyed trouncing everyone at a good word game. They played for three hours. Eloise won. She always did.

By midnight, Genny and Rafe were alone in the East Bedroom. She waited for him to ask about Fiona, but he only undressed her slowly and took her to bed.

Maybe he'd forgotten.

Or maybe he really just didn't want to go there.

Fine with her. The coward inside her was perfectly content to forget all about it. He worked his usual magic on her willing body and she let herself get lost in the beauty of every sensation.

Afterward, he turned off the lights and she lay tucked against him, drifting toward sleep, when he said, "Have you changed your mind about telling me what happened tonight with Fiona?"

She stifled a groan and lay very still in his arms, knowing they needed to talk about it, yet still longing to forget it and pretend she was already fast asleep.

"Gen?"

She tipped her head back and looked at him through the darkness.

His black eyes were waiting. "Well?"

"You're not going to like it."

He touched the side of her face, a tender caress that did her heart good. "Given that it concerns Fiona, you're probably right."

"Great. Go to sleep."

"Fat chance." He reached through the curtains and turned on the light.

No getting out of it now. She plumped the pillows and

sat up beside him. "Last week, while you were in London, Brooke and Fiona came back together. Fiona stayed the night. There was a lot of wine at dinner. Both Fiona and Brooke got pretty drunk. Eloise and I came up to bed early, essentially to get away from them. Much later, there was a knock on the sitting room door...."

Rafe sat silent at her side as she told him everything, all she could remember, of what Fiona had said to her that night.

When she'd finished, he asked gently, "Is that all?" His calm, his seeming unconcern, surprised her. She had thought he would be angry. But he took it all with a hint of a smile—or maybe that was just the crescent scar making it seem that he was smiling.

Mixed in with her relief that he hadn't shut her out, she found she was angry *for* him. "It's more than enough, don't you think? I swear, Fiona is such an evil cow."

"She has her agendas," he said wryly.

"What agendas?"

He shook his head. "What was that in the hallway tonight?"

She considered pressing her point, asking again exactly what agendas he meant. But she let it go. "Fiona seemed frantic to convince me that she couldn't recall a thing she'd said that night last week, that none of it was true anyway—which is funny, considering she said she didn't know what 'it' was. I think she meant to have me believe she'd had some kind of blackout during which she babbled nonsense, and I should simply forget it ever happened."

He framed her face in his wonderful, huge hands. "My poor love, it must have been gruesome."

"It was. I wanted to slap her until her ears rang and tear out her hair. Instead, I gave her tissues to mop up her tears and then I dragged her back to her room."

He brushed her cheeks with his thumbs. "And you were never going to tell me?"

"I was, yes. Eventually. When…I thought the time was right."

Those obsidian eyes gleamed at her. And then he kissed her, slow and tender. "Would you hate it so much to know you were married to a gardener's bastard and not a true DeValery after all?"

That one was easy to answer. "I wouldn't, no, not at all. I've always known anyway."

"Known what? That I'm a bastard?"

"No. That some people *think* you are."

"What people?"

She was in all the way now. She confessed, "Some English girl I went to school with, a boy in the village years and years ago…"

"People love to carry tales."

"Yes, they do."

He made a chiding sound with his tongue against his teeth. "And you never once brought it up to me."

"I told you, I didn't care. And I was afraid that it would hurt you. I didn't want that. You are the finest man I know and I…" She couldn't do it. Couldn't quite say the most dangerous word. "I'm so very, very fond of you."

He studied her face for a long, uncomfortable moment. And then he said, "As I am of you."

She was thinking that she should try again, make herself say it. *I've fallen completely in love with you, Rafe.* But before she could work up the nerve, he shoved the covers back and jumped from the bed.

"Rafe, what in the world?"

"I want you to come with me. I'll get you a dressing gown." He turned for the dressing room.

She stared at his magnificent backside as he walked away from her. "Come with you where, exactly?"

He disappeared in the other room for a minute. When he returned, he wore track pants, a T-shirt and house shoes. He carried her favorite kimono in one hand and her slippers in the other. "Here you go."

"But it's the middle of the night. Where are we going?"

"You'll see. Come on."

So she put on the kimono and slippers. Then he grabbed her hand and led her out into the sitting room, where he got a flashlight from a side-table drawer. He went to the outer door, pulled it open and waved her out.

She gave in and simply went out ahead of him.

He shut the door and took the lead. One hallway led to another. In the soft light from the wall sconces, they worked their way toward the glorious State Rooms at the heart of the house and then on from there, along a central hallway to the damaged West Wing.

In the West Wing, he turned on the flashlight. No one lived or worked in the West Wing. At night, the dim hallway wall sconces were left off.

It was sad, really, even by flashlight, even when they were sticking only to the hallways, to see the water stains on the ceilings and walls, the emptiness where marble-topped hall tables had stood and beautiful art used to hang. Yes, much of the West Wing had once been servants' quarters, but the central hallways used to be as finely put together as the rest of the house. There was the faint smell of moisture there now. For the sake of the West Wing, winter and the new roof couldn't come soon enough.

Rafe led her up the stairs and along another hallway until finally they came to the West Wing Gallery, a long red room on the top floor with all its furnishings intact. The gallery and the rooms below it were protected by a small section of undamaged roof replaced forty years before.

The West Wing Gallery was not among the finest rooms at Hartmore. All the most treasured paintings and portraits hung in the State Rooms or in the East Wing where the family lived and could enjoy them. The West Wing Gallery was for all the pictures no one really cared all that much about, for portraits of forgotten ancestors painted by unimportant artists. For undistinguished landscapes by painters no one remembered anymore.

Rafe turned on the lights.

Genny stood in the middle of the room and stared up at the beautiful painted ceiling. The El Grecos, the Titians and Turners were in other rooms. Still, there were gorgeous gilt mirrors here and serpentine columns flanked the arched windows.

Rafe came up behind her and clasped her shoulders. She leaned back into the solid heat of his body—but only for a moment. Because he ran his palm down her arm and caught her hand again. "Here. Let me show you...."

He led her to a shadowed corner, to a grouping of mediocre portraits in unremarkable frames. "This one." He shone the flashlight on a portrait of a young, powerfully built dark-eyed man with thick black hair and sideburns. The fellow wore a fitted, single-breasted tailcoat. There was a spill of snowy-white—what they used to call a cravat—at his throat. His doeskin breeches tucked into shiny black Hessian boots and he held a silk top hat to his breast. He stared into the middle distance with an expression of great seriousness.

It wasn't a very good painting. The eyes weren't quite right and the proportions were odd. But the likeness was still striking—eerie, even.

Genny's heart was suddenly racing and her mouth had

gone dry. She said in a whisper, "Rafe, he looks just like you."

"He does, doesn't he? This was painted in 1819."

"But…who is he?"

"Richard DeValery, a second son. Like me, he was never expected to inherit. But then his older brother, James, died in a hunting accident. And that left Richard to become the fifth earl of Hartmore."

Chapter Ten

Genny stared in amazement at the portrait of Richard DeValery. "How long have you known about this?"

"I was ten when I first saw it."

"But...how did you know to look here?"

"Granny brought me here."

"Eloise." That made perfect sense. "Of course. Had someone said something to you then, about the old rumors?"

"My father had called me an ugly, hulking bastard. He'd muttered under his breath that I wasn't any son of his."

"Oh, Rafe..."

"And he'd beaten me again for no reason that I could understand. I had been trying to behave in a civilized manner. To pay attention at school. But it didn't help. I couldn't catch a break with him. That day, I can't remember having done anything to make him furious with me—other than just being there, in his sight. Afterward, Granny found me crying like a baby in the stables. She wanted to know if I was injured. I told her no. And I wasn't. The beatings hurt, but he never broke a bone or made me bleed. It was the way he looked at me, and the verbal abuse, that killed me. He was a master at that. Anyway, when Granny found me in the stables, I told her to go away, to leave me alone, that I wasn't a true DeValery and everyone knew the truth about me."

"But she wouldn't go."

"You know Granny...."

Genny did know. "She would have had a little lecture ready, I'm guessing."

"Yes, she did. She said my father was a cruel and narrow-minded man and sometimes she was ashamed to call him her son. But that *his* father had been a cruel man, too. 'And the best revenge,' she said, 'against a cruel husband or father is to live a productive, rich life anyway, and to hell with them.'"

"What did you say then?"

"I just told her again to leave me alone."

"But she wouldn't."

"Not Granny. She held down her hand to me and said she had something I needed to see. I tried to ignore her. But she only waited, her hand outstretched. Finally, I took it and she brought me here, to the West Wing Gallery. She showed me this portrait and she said, 'You are just as much a DeValery as your father or your brother or your little sister and you must never, ever forget that you are.'"

Genny swallowed down the lump that had formed in her throat. "I do adore Eloise."

He nodded toward the portrait. "Lord Richard was rumored to be the child of one of the gardeners."

"And two hundred years later, they're saying the same thing about you. It does make you wonder..."

"What?"

"Well, who's to say Richard wasn't legitimate, too? Who's to say he didn't just take after some other long-ago, long-forgotten ancestor way back in the DeValery line?"

He put on a severe expression. "Because a true De-Valery isn't built like a common laborer. He doesn't have a broad nose, dusky skin and coarse black hair."

"Rafe, that's just so much crap."

"It's good you never let my father hear you talk like that."

"It's strange. He was so awful to you. And yet, I was never afraid of him. Toward me, he was always kind and gentlemanly."

"Because you're someone who matters, a princess of Montedoro—even if your father is a damned upstart American."

She sighed. "He was not only cruel, your father. He was a terrible snob, wasn't he?"

"Yes, he was." He gathered her close to him. "My father was a very proud man. And every time he looked at me, he was reminded that we all all of us proud DeValerys might have a common gardener's blood running in our veins."

The next morning, Saturday, Rafe woke her with kisses.

She sighed in pleasure and twined her arms around his neck.

He kissed her again—and then shoved back the covers.

"Rafe!" she protested.

He only laughed and jumped from the bed. "Come on. The sun's out. Get up. No laying about. Get dressed. Wear riding gear. We'll go after breakfast, a nice ride around the lake, to the deer park, maybe to the castle—and we'll take it slow, in consideration of your delicate condition."

She leaned out between the curtains on her side of the bed, grabbed up one of her slippers and threw it at him as he strode for the dressing room. He dodged before it hit him in the shoulder. "Missed me," he said smugly, without bothering even to turn around. He put the dressing room door between them before she could find something else to throw.

They went down to breakfast together. Brooke, Fiona and Melinda all came down a few minutes later.

Fiona behaved as though the incident by the powder room the night before had never taken place. She had coffee and a brioche and talked about the County Show at the show grounds near Elvaston the next day. She and her husband would be taking their boys.

"Besides all the horse competitions and the livestock show, there will be the usual tractor show and vintage car exposition." Fiona hid a yawn. "Gerald loves old cars. And then there's the carnival. The boys are like wild animals over candy floss, toffee apples and the giant blow-up slide."

Brooke said, piling on the sarcasm, "Don't forget the hedge laying and dry stone walling exhibitions."

And Genny couldn't resist throwing in somberly, "Hedge laying matters, Brooke. Hedgerows are important habitats for wildlife. They make natural fences between fields and properties. They serve as a windbreak for cattle."

Brooke sent her a quelling look and said, "I know Granny will want to go. Rafe?"

He looked at Genny, one dark brow lifted.

Brooke groaned. "You two. It's becoming embarrassing. Are you joined at the hip now?"

After last night, Genny felt closer than ever to Rafe. Even Brooke's scorn couldn't get to her that morning. "We're newlyweds. Being joined at the hip is what newlyweds do—and yes, I think we should all go together."

"Good idea," said Rafe.

"I never said *I* was going," Brooke shot back.

"We're *all* going," said Eloise from the doorway. "Together. So that's the end of that."

Nobody argued. Eloise rarely laid down the law, but on the rare occasions when she did, they all went along. She crossed to the sideboard and began filling a plate.

Fiona ate the last bite of her brioche. "I've got to get back to Tillworth. Gerald will be home from London by eleven. And it's Saturday, which means the boys are there." She added sourly, "They'll all be expecting me for a little family togetherness." She left them to grab her things.

Melinda said wistfully, "I wish I could stay for the County Show. It's been years and I'm feeling so... sentimental about old times lately."

Brooke's eyes lit up. "Why don't you? You can come with us."

"But I need to get back."

"So go. Come back in the morning. Isn't Fresh closed on Sundays?"

"But it's a long drive, hours each way."

"Take the train."

"On Sunday? It's not practical." Melinda sipped her coffee. "It's so strange. As the years go by, I find I miss home—and Hartmore Village *is* home to me—though when I was growing up, I couldn't wait to get away."

Eloise set down her full plate and pulled out the chair on Genny's left. "Why not just stay? Have a nice, relaxed visit with your parents in the village. Go back on Monday— or tomorrow evening, if you must. You won't make it to London before noon today anyway."

"Granny's right," insisted Brooke. "You'll have more time with your mum and dad. They'll appreciate that. And then you'll stay with us here at Hartmore, of course."

About then, Genny was starting to feel like a jealous cow. She ought to behave like a proper hostess, to chime in and urge Melinda to stay, as the woman so obviously longed to do. But both she and Rafe had sat silent through the whole discussion about whether or not Melinda ought to go. Genny, because she suspected Melinda was after her husband. Rafe, because he knew what Genny suspected.

And truly, Genny now doubted herself on the issue. There had only been that one glance the other morning. Was she really so certain she'd seen it at all?

Melinda murmured hesitantly, "I *could* call my store manager, see if she's getting on all right without me…."

And Genny couldn't take it anymore. "Yes, why don't you? Stay the weekend. We'd all love to have you."

"Not one word," Genny muttered out of the side of her mouth as she and Rafe walked beneath the oaks on their way to the stables.

He grabbed her arm, pulled her off the path and backed her up against one of the enormous old tree trunks, bracing his hands to either side of her, boxing her in. "It's your fault she's staying, you know." He looked infuriatingly pleased with himself.

She made a face at him. "Oh, don't rub it in. It just seemed rude, the two of us sitting there not saying anything…"

He leaned closer, whispered, "Admit it. She's a nice woman with no interest in me whatsoever, beyond a pleasant sort of friendliness. You had it all wrong about her."

"But I could have sworn…"

He bent even closer. Now his wonderful mouth was just inches from hers. "Admit it."

Genny gave it up. "Fine. Maybe I misunderstood that look she gave you."

He brushed his lips against hers. She tried not to sigh in delight and leaned into him. He pulled back. "Only maybe?"

She turned her head away. "I don't want to kiss you anyway."

"Liar." And he caught her chin in his hand and turned it back.

And then, at last, he kissed her. A lovely, lingering sort of kiss. A kiss just deep enough to make her knees go to jelly and turn the butterflies loose in her stomach.

When he finally lifted his head she stared up at him dreamily. "Melinda? Who's Melinda?"

He laughed.

She studied his wonderful wreck of a face. "You seem... happier lately."

He rubbed the back of his index finger along the side of her throat, bringing a sweet little shiver to skitter beneath the surface of her skin. His eyes gleamed as black as polished agates. "Marriage must agree with me."

Her heart lifted and the words were right there, at the base of her throat, pushing to get free. *I've fallen in love with you, Rafe. I'm so happy that I married you.* She longed to say it. It should be so easy. How could she go wrong to tell him she loved him?

No matter if he didn't feel the same, he would never be cruel about it. He would let her down gently, at least....

But gentle or not, it would hurt if he didn't feel the same. It would hurt no matter how kind and understanding he was about it.

And that was ridiculous. Because he seemed happy. And she *was* happy.

And maybe rather than bringing the big, fat *L* word into the equation, she ought to exercise a little good sense and leave wonderful enough alone.

His eyes had grown guarded. "What's the matter?"

And she said, "Nothing. Nothing at all." And really, there wasn't. Just her silly heart aching to know if he loved her as she loved him. She slid her hand down his arm and clasped his fingers. "Come on. Let's have that ride."

They rode around the lake and the village, and then they circled back toward the house, going on past it and the chapel, too, to the deer park and the castle. Later, he went to his study to catch up on some paperwork and she helped the house team with the tours and a late-afternoon wedding.

Rory called just after the wedding party had moved to the terrace for the reception. Genny excused herself and left the team and the caterers to manage the party.

There was always a deserted room somewhere at Hartmore. She found a bedroom overlooking the terrace with a nice window seat and a view of the wedding party, and she and Rory talked for over an hour.

It was nice to talk to someone from home. She and Rory had always gotten along well, though they'd never been all that close. Not like Rhia and Alice, who'd been best friends practically from birth.

Rory's big news was that their eldest brother, Maximilian, was engaged to be married again. Max had lost his first wife, Sophie, several years ago and had made it clear to everyone that he would never remarry. So his engagement was something of a shocker to Genny. That he was marrying the former nanny, Lani Vasquez, was kind of rich, too.

But everyone loved Lani. And Rory said Max was happy again, at last, after all those years of dragging around looking like someone had cut out his heart.

It was to be a Christmas wedding.

"So mark your calendar," Rory instructed. "You and Rafe will be coming. I hope Eloise can make it, too."

And Genny said regretfully, "I doubt if we'll make it."

"Why not?" Rory demanded. "It's going to be beautiful. And it's Christmas. Everyone will be expecting you."

"The thing is…"

"Oh, my God. Are you all right? What…?"

"I'm pregnant, Rory. The baby is due December 20."

Rory gasped. "Why, you little…"

"I'm sorry. I should have told you sooner."

"Mother and Father…?"

"Yes. They know."

"Wow."

Genny groaned. "Really. We were careful. But I think the condoms were expired."

Rory confessed, "Well, I did kind of wonder. I always thought that you and Edward…"

"Yes. I was wrong about that. Way wrong."

"So you *are* in love with Rafe?"

"Absolutely. I…just haven't drummed up the courage to tell him yet."

"This all sounds beyond delicious, I have to say."

"I *am* going to tell him," Genny insisted, and knew she sounded defensive.

The always bubbly Rory was silent. But only for a moment. "Are you happy?"

That was easy. "Yes. I am. Very happy."

"Well, then, that's what matters. Everything else will work itself out."

That night, Genny and Rafe went to dinner at a nice hotel in the Peak District, not all that far from Hartmore. It was just the two of them. After the meal, they strolled the gardens around the old inn, holding hands, whispering together, laughing often.

The next day was the County Show. Genny had a great time. She especially enjoyed the horticulture exhibits and the beekeeping exhibition, and the displays of rural crafts always impressed her. She and Eloise made a point to attend both the hedge laying and the dry stone walling demonstrations.

And Melinda went back up to London that evening. All weekend, Rafe's old girlfriend had been sweet and agreeable. And if she'd been giving Rafe more yearning glances, neither he nor Genny had spotted a single one. That night Genny admitted she'd been completely off base about Rafe's old flame.

Rafe only said "I told you so" once.

They spent that week at Hartmore, together.

And on Friday, Geoffrey came home from school. They were all waiting for him outside the family entrance when his car arrived. He jumped out and ran to them, hugging first Brooke, then Eloise, then Rafe and finally Genny, laughing the whole time.

"There now," he said, smiling broadly as they turned to go in. "You all know how happy I am to be home."

To celebrate, they had his favorite, pork chops and chips, for dinner.

Brooke was all over him, her beautiful blue eyes constantly threatening to overflow with tears, insisting she'd been missing him terribly, promising him she was giving him a birthday party he would never forget.

His face fell.

Brooke cried, "What is that? A long face? What in the world are you upset about now?"

Carefully, he told her, "Mum, I wish you wouldn't."

"Wouldn't *what,* for God's sake?"

"The party, Mum. I don't need that. I would rather just have a little cake and the family."

Brooke made a disgusted sound. "Don't be silly. You're like an old man, my darling, I swear you are. Not even nine years old. And ancient already. It makes me much too sad."

"I have a list of video games I want," he suggested hopefully. "And a chart with minerals I'd like to have."

"Minerals?" Brooke made the word sound like it tasted bad in her mouth. "What kind of minerals?"

"Rare rocks is what they are, Mum. I'd like specimens of quartz crystals and iron pyrites. And malachite. A fire agate. Oh, and I'd love a few geodes..."

"Rocks. You want rocks."

"Yes, and the video games. That's really all I'm needing. Please."

She waved her hands. Both of them. "Of course you'll have your video games. And the rocks, too, as many as you want. But there *will* be a party and it will be spectacular. We'll have a magician, a waterslide, paintball out on the old archery field. We'll have all your friends from the village. And Dennis and Dexter..."

Now Geoffrey was looking as though *he* might cry. "Not the Terrible Twins. Please, Mum."

"Don't call them that. That's just rude. And of course they're coming. Fiona says they can't wait to see you."

"Mum. They hate me. When no one is looking, they trip me and poke me and push me down."

"Stop, stop." Brooke put her hands over her ears like the spoiled child she was. "I don't want to hear it. La, la, la. You know it's not true."

It was like watching a train wreck. Genny, Rafe and Eloise never knew how to stop it before the collision became inevitable.

That night, Eloise was the one who tried. "Brooke, dear, I thought the plan was to keep it small and—"

Brooke didn't even let her finish. "Stay out of it, Granny."

And Geoffrey cried out, "Yes! What Great-Granny said. I don't want a lot of people. I go to *school* with a lot of people. When I come home to Hartmore and have my birthday, I want it to be just us."

"Well, it's *not* going to be just us and you'd better get used to it. I'm giving you a fabulous, unforgettable birthday party and that's the end of it."

"But I don't want one!" Geoffrey shouted.

At which Brooke jumped up and waved her hands about frantically. "That's it. That just cuts it. You've shouted at me. I mean it, Geoffrey. You're giving me fits. It's all for you and you don't even want it—and I... Oh, well, I just can't take it anymore." And with that, she burst into tears and ran from the room.

Geoffrey watched her go with a look of abject misery on his face.

After a minute, Eloise stood and said what she always said whenever Brooke ran off in tears. "I'll just go and have a word with her."

But then Geoffrey delivered the shocker. "No, Great-Granny. Please sit down."

His calmly uttered request was such a surprise to Eloise, she sank back to her chair without a word.

And he said so seriously, "I've been thinking a lot, about me and Mum and the way it always goes with us. I don't want it to be like that anymore and I mean to do better, I really do. But she just..." He stopped himself, swallowed hard. "No. What I want to say is that I *will* do better." He pushed back his chair. "So *I* will go and talk to her and make her stop crying. And we'll have the party, and everything will be..." He seemed not to know how to go on from there.

Rafe said gingerly, "Geoffrey, if you don't want the party—"

Geoffrey put up his little hand. "No. Uncle Rafe, I mean it. She surprised me is all. And the party will be fine. I will enjoy it very much, I'm sure." And with that, he pushed in his chair in and went to talk to his mother.

Genny stared after him, aching for him. No almost nine-year-old boy should have to be that wise.

A few minutes later, mother and son came down together.

Brooke apologized for running off like that. And then she beamed them all a dewy smile. "Geoffrey has told me he wants his party after all. So we all have something lovely to look forward to."

In the week between Geoffrey's arrival from school and his birthday party, things went along pretty well, Genny thought. Brooke was all wrapped up in making the final arrangements for the big celebration.

Geoffrey was sweet and open, as always. And he seemed so happy to be home. He went riding with Rafe and he spent time in the gardens with Genny and Eloise.

By the end of the day Thursday, the giant waterslide had been set up not far from the lake and the archery field was ready for paintball. The magician would put on his show on the family side of the terrace. There was a candy-floss machine and one for popcorn, too. The East Terrace was done up in a carnival theme. The children would bring clean clothes for the magic show and the food and cake. Before that, they could get wonderfully wet and messy on the waterslide, in the aboveground pool Brooke had had created nearby, and in the archery field playing paintball.

Thursday at dinner, Brooke told them that Melinda was coming. She would be arriving tomorrow afternoon. "She offered to come," Brooke explained. "She'll stay the weekend. With all the stress of the party, I need my friends round me."

Melinda came by car. When she drove up to the family entrance at five Friday afternoon, Brooke ran out to meet her, crying glad greetings. The two hugged as if they hadn't seen each other in years.

Genny watched them from the doorway, annoyed with both of them. It was Geoffrey's birthday tomorrow, but as usual he would be lost in the shuffle of Brooke's plans and Brooke's friends. She only hoped they could make it through the party without Brooke staging one of her big, emotional scenes.

Fiona arrived a half an hour later—minus the twins and the banker husband. At dinner, she announced that her driver would bring the boys for the party tomorrow.

Dinner was at eight that night. Geoffrey didn't join them. He'd eaten earlier.

"And besides," Brooke said, "it's nice now and then to have just the grown-ups, to take our time, enjoy our wine…" Melinda and Fiona both made eager noises of agreement.

Later, when Genny and Rafe were alone, she couldn't resist remarking snidely, "I've been meaning to ask. Is the party for Geoffrey—or Brooke?"

"Do you really *need* to ask?" He smoothed her hair to the side.

She let out a slow sigh. "But Geoffrey does seem to be holding up all right, don't you think?"

"So far, so good." He brushed a trail of kisses out from her nape, along her bare shoulder.

She turned in his arms and settled herself against the

pillows, sliding a hand up to finger comb his unruly hair. "Once I had to admit that Melinda wasn't out to seduce you, I started to like her...."

"Why do I hear a 'but' in there somewhere?"

"I don't know. Tonight, she seemed as bad a Fiona, seconding everything Brooke said. Laughing too much about things that aren't even funny."

"I think they'd all three had too much wine."

"I think they all three *always* have too much wine— and I sound like a bitter old witch, don't I?"

"You're not the least—"

"Don't you dare say it. And I just had a horrible thought. Do you think the twins will be staying over tomorrow night? I hope not. Geoffrey will be scarred for life."

He frowned in thought. "It's entirely possible. But then again, Fiona will probably send them home after the party. If they stay, she'll have to look after them. She doesn't ever seem up for that."

Genny laughed. "Now *you* sound like the spiteful one. Good. At least I'm not alone. And you know, I haven't seen much of the boys yet this year—just a quick hello at the County Show. Are they still as awful as Geoffrey says?"

He kissed the tip of her chin. "Worse, I'm afraid."

"Dennis and Dexter. Seriously? Remember *Dennis the Menace?* And Dexter, the serial killer. Who names their sons after a menace and a serial killer?"

"Fiona, apparently." He buried his face against her throat and chuckled. "And have you *met* the twins?"

"Ha-ha."

"And wait a minute. I don't think the *Dexter* series started until after the twins were born."

"Well, that's reassuring—although not a whole lot."

"Stop thinking about the twins."

"I can't. They're too scary."

He started kissing his way down her body, slowly. "I have something to show you...."

She put on her bored voice. "Is it the same thing as last night?"

He lifted his head from kissing her breast. She gasped at the wonderful gleam in his eyes. "I'm afraid so."

She fisted her hands in his hair and pulled him closer again. "Show me, then. Show me...everything. And do it for a long, long time...."

He made a rough noise of agreement. And then he got busy giving her just what she'd asked for.

Much later, as he slept in her arms, she thought about how much she loved him. She really did need to tell him so.

Life went by and anything could happen. She could live to regret not having said what was in her heart.

Even if he didn't say it back to her, she wanted him to know.

Maybe after the weekend, when things had settled down a little. Yes. After the party.

That would be soon enough....

He stirred in her arms.

She kissed his cheek. *I love you.* She said it in her head. With all her heart.

But she failed to say it out loud.

Because she still couldn't stand to think he might not feel as strongly as she did, that she loved him more and that put her at a disadvantage somehow. As long as she didn't say the words, she could always imagine he felt the same....

"Rafe?" She knew he was gone from the bed before she opened her eyes. She stretched out her hand to the other side, his side.

Empty.

And then she sat up and switched on the lamp.

"Rafe?" She pushed back the covers and got out of the bed.

He wasn't in the bathroom or the dressing room or the smaller bedroom beyond. The sitting room was empty, too.

She returned to perch on the edge of the bed and told herself to get back under the covers and go to sleep. He'd probably just gone down to the family's kitchen for a snack. He did that now and then.

But she found herself feeling a little needy, a little lonely. She put her hand on her rounded belly and whispered to her baby, "I want your papa now."

So, then. She would go and get him. If he was snacking, she would sit with him until he finished and they could come back up together.

She put on her kimono and slippers and left the suite. Tiptoeing along the first-floor hall, she turned down another hall to the back stairs, which were narrow, lit by low-wattage bulbs in the ceiling at each landing and descended at a sharp angle to the lower floor.

At the ground floor she stopped on the landing. Four more stairs led down into the family's kitchen, which was smaller than the original main kitchen beneath the center of the house. The family kitchen had been created from a back sitting room forty years before and updated now and then as the decades went by.

But the back stairs didn't look modern at all. The back stairs was a catacomb of narrow passageways all through Hartmore. They remained pretty much as they'd been over two hundred years ago, when Hartmore was built.

She hesitated there on the old, narrow landing, before turning and going the rest of the way down. The low light directly overhead cast odd shadows on the whitewashed wall. The kitchen wasn't visible, not from there, not until she went down those last few stairs and emerged from the narrow back hall, which connected to the stairway there.

But she could hear something—movement?—in the kitchen. A dish clattered against a counter.

And a man said something.

Rafe. She couldn't make out the words, but she knew the sound of his voice, knew it instantly, knew it to her bones, to the deepest core of herself.

A woman spoke in a passionate whisper.

Genny's stomach went hollow and her heart was suddenly pounding out a sick, hard rhythm under her breast.

She didn't want to go down.

But she *had* to go down.

Her feet in the little red slippers felt as though they weren't even connected to the rest of her. She looked down and they were moving, one step, and another.

She descended the last step and emerged from the short hallway. And saw Rafe in track pants and an old T-shirt. He stood by the big Wolf cooker, his back to her. On the counter, there was toast on a plate, something hot in a cup, a curl of steam rising up.

Melinda stood with him—right there next to him, oblivious to anything but him. The woman stared up at him in the same haunted, hungry way she'd done that morning three weeks before.

He lifted one powerful arm and raked his hand back over the top of his head.

And then Melinda was reaching for him, wrapping her arms around his shoulders, spearing her fingers up into his hair—and going on tiptoe to press her open mouth to his.

Chapter Eleven

Genny didn't remember making a noise.

But she must have—a cry of shock and hurt. A gasp of outrage, maybe.

There must have been something.

Because Rafe not only swiftly grabbed Melinda's hands from around his neck and pushed her away, he also whirled to find Genny standing there. "Gen." He looked…hurt. Brokenhearted.

Or maybe just sorry.

Yes. Sorry that she'd caught him.

Melinda grabbed him by the shoulders. "Oh, Rafe…"

He shrugged Melinda off. His black eyes were only for her. "Damn it, Gen. Don't."

She almost wished he hadn't seen her. That she could turn and sneak away.

Now there was nothing left but to draw the shreds of her dignity around her, to stand tall and ask in a voice that only shook a little bit, "What, exactly, is going on here?"

Rafe said, "It's simple. You were right." He never let his gaze stray from her face. "I should have listened. But I swear, I didn't know. I'm an idiot, yes. But I'm no cheater. I didn't know."

"Rafe, please, darling." Melinda tried to clutch at him again. "I only—"

"Hands off." He jerked his shoulder free of her grip. "Wait," he said to Genny. "Right there. I'm going to turn away and get rid of her. Do not go."

Fine. She could do that. If it killed her, she could do it. "All right."

So she waited.

And he turned to Melinda and said, "You shouldn't have done that."

The tears came then. "Oh, but, Rafe, really. Why not? I love you. Always. All those years ago, I kept waiting. For you to say you wanted more. You never did. And I only wanted a chance, that's all. I only wanted—"

"Stop." He said it coldly. "I don't want to hear it. Neither does my wife. Whatever there was between you and me has been over for ten years."

"No. No, don't say that. You cared. You *used* to care. And I know you only married *her* because of the—"

"Do. Not. Say. It. Don't even think it. You're wrong." He said it strongly, firmly. Genny felt marginally better—even if it wasn't true. He *had* married her for the baby's sake after all.

Melinda let out another sad little cry. "Oh, but I…I only thought if I kissed you, you would remember how it was between us, you would—"

He silenced her with a hard chop of his hand through the space between them. And then he said, very gently, "I want you to go and get your things together. I want you to leave this house. And I want you never to come back."

"But how can I do that? Brooke won't understand. She knows nothing about—"

"Brooke will understand completely. I will explain it to her."

"Oh, my God…" Melinda covered her face and sobbed into her hands.

It was awful. Genny wanted to scratch the woman's eyes out and then cut off her head. At the same time, she couldn't help feeling just a little bit sorry for her.

The disorienting swirl of mixed emotions made her stomach churn. She swallowed bile. Fisting her hands, pressing her fingernails into her palms as hard as she could, she used the pain to distract her from the urge to be sick right there in front of her husband and the woman who had just grabbed him and kissed him.

Melinda cried harder, great, gulping sobs.

Rafe tried again. "Melinda. Get control of yourself. You have to—"

Genny couldn't take it anymore. "Rafe." He turned to her. He looked furious—and in way over his head. She said, "You'd better let me help her."

He swore then. A very bad word. "Don't be absurd. This is not your problem."

It wouldn't be if only you'd listened to me. "What are you going to do, pick her up bodily and carry her to her car? No. Let me help. Please."

He drew in a slow breath—and then he stepped aside.

Genny went to the other woman and took her by the shoulders. Softly, she coaxed, "Melinda. Come on, now. You know that it's time to go."

With a cry of pure heartbreak, Melinda surged up and fell against Genny. It was not a fun moment and reminded Genny sharply of Fiona on that awful night weeks ago.

Genny gritted her teeth and wrapped her arms around

the other woman. "All right. Come on, now. Let's get you upstairs...."

Rafe followed after her as she led Melinda, sobbing all the way, up the back stairs to her room.

Genny pushed the door open and coaxed her in and over to the bed. "Come on. It's all right. Sit down...."

With a moan, Melinda dropped to the bed. Genny found the tissues and handed them over. Melinda dabbed at her streaming eyes, blew her nose—and went on crying.

"What now?" Rafe asked from the doorway.

"Oh, Rafe. Look at her. We can't kick her out tonight. It's just too cruel."

He looked like he wanted to put his fist through a wall, but he held it together. "What do you suggest?"

Genny sat next to Melinda and put her arm across her shoulders. Melinda sagged against her. "Listen," Genny said softly. "Melinda, are you listening?"

"Mmm-hmm?" A sad little squeak of acknowledgment.

"You're not going anywhere tonight. Go to bed. Try to sleep. In the morning, after breakfast, you'll make your excuses to Brooke and you'll go."

"Oh, God..."

"It's up to you what you tell her. I would suggest honesty."

A horrified cry. "No!"

"It's your call. Whatever you say to Brooke, please don't come back to this house, or we'll have to tell Rafe's sister and grandmother why, exactly, it is that Rafe and I don't want you here."

"I'm just going to tell you exactly what happened tonight," Rafe said when they were alone in their sitting room.

She didn't really want to hear it, didn't *have* to hear it.

"I believe you, Rafe. I know you didn't encourage her." She knew he'd done nothing wrong—well, beyond being a thickheaded, know-it-all *man*. "I'm not blaming you."

"I just want to say it. I need for you to know everything."

So she gave in and sat on the sofa. "All right."

He sat beside her carefully, as though unsure if she'd let him stay there. "I woke up. You were sound asleep—and I wanted a snack."

She realized she'd been staring straight ahead. If he *had* to give her the details, she should at least look at him while he did it. She faced him. And her love for him welled up, so powerful it hurt. "You're saying you had no agreement to meet with her secretly in the kitchen. Is that what you're getting at?"

"That's right. It never occurred to me that she would be down there. And she wasn't, not at first. I made toast. And hot chocolate. She came down just as I was about to carry my plate and cup to the table. She said she couldn't sleep. I suggested hot milk. And then, out of nowhere, she gave me this intense look. I knew then that there was trouble, that you'd been right when you said she…" He hesitated, his expression pained. "That she still had feelings for me. I tried to decide how to get out gracefully—and you don't have to give me that look."

"But I'm not—"

"Yes, you are. Listen, I get it, all right? It was my mistake not to take you seriously earlier. And tonight, it was my mistake again even to hesitate. Once she gave me that look, I should have gotten the hell out fast. She said my name. Just my name, and then she grabbed me. I was pushing her off when I heard you behind me." He fell silent.

What to say now? "Is that it?"

"That's everything, yes."

"Then can we go to bed now?"

He only looked at her. Deeply. "You do blame me."

"No." And she didn't, not really. "But I didn't like seeing that woman all over you. I didn't like it at all."

Something blazed in his eyes. "I didn't like *having* her all over me. I swear it. I meant what I said. I am, and always will be, true to you."

"Good." But she still felt put out with him for being so damn dense. And she kept thinking of Fiona, for some strange reason—of the odd parallels between Fiona's drunken behavior weeks ago and what Melinda had done an hour before. The similarities seemed to be about more than just two women behaving badly in the middle of two different nights.

"There's something you're not telling me. What is it?" he demanded.

It would have been so simple to say it was nothing, to soothe him—soothe them both—and take him to bed.

But she knew there were truths about the night Edward died that he refused to share with her. She knew that he lied to her by omission. And now, because he hadn't taken her warning seriously, she would have to live the rest of her life with the image of Melinda spread all over the front of him, her hands in his hair as she sucked on his face. It all got her back up just enough that she went ahead and gave him exactly what he asked for.

"The night she got drunk and came here to our rooms, Fiona said a few very strange things."

His big body went absolutely still. "Fiona? Why are we suddenly talking about Fiona?"

"I thought you wanted to know what I *wasn't* telling you."

"Gen." He spoke so gently. "Maybe we should—"

She stopped him with an upraised hand. "That night,

when she came here to find me, Fiona talked about the accident."

"What does what she said matter? You said she was drunk half out of her mind."

"She talked about how she'd suffered, about how she'd 'had' what *I* would never get. How she'd never expected 'it' to end, that 'it' couldn't end. That 'it' wasn't supposed to end…"

"What, for God's sake, is 'it'?"

"Well, I don't know, Rafe. I thought maybe *you* would know."

"I…?" He seemed to gather calm about himself. "What are you getting at, Gen? You'd better just say it."

"All right. Have you ever had…?" Dear Lord, this was gruesome. "I mean, you and Fiona, have you ever been in love with her—or have you ever, you know, had sex with her?"

He gaped at her. "Fiona? Seriously?"

"Don't mock me, Rafe."

"I'm not. It's only… You really don't think that, do you? Fiona and *me*?"

"Answer the question, please."

"All right." He sounded hopelessly weary. "Then, no. Never. She's so completely *not* the woman for me, not in any way. And after what happened tonight, I can't blame you if you question my judgment—but I would swear on the graves of all my proud DeValery ancestors that Fiona has no more interest in being my lover than I have in being hers."

Genny stared at him for several endless seconds, right into his black, black eyes.

"What?" he demanded. And then he whispered, "Please don't say you don't believe me."

"I do believe you," she said at last. And she did. "Absolutely."

He reached up and rubbed the back of his neck. "Well. Thank God for that."

She chewed her lower lip. "I just don't understand what Fiona meant that night."

"She was drunk, remember? Drunks say incoherent things."

"Yes. I suppose so...."

He stood and held down his hand. "Enough for now. We're both tired. Come to bed."

She looked up at him. And there was that welling feeling within her, a sensation both painful and pleasurable at once. A rising feeling, a sense of something overflowing.

Love.

Oh, she did love him. So very much. She ached with it—and yet never quite managed to tell him about it. The moment was never right.

And tonight...?

No way. Not tonight. She wasn't saying *I love you, Rafe,* with the image of him and Melinda so fresh in her mind.

"Take my hand, Gen."

That, she could manage. She put her fingers in his.

He pulled her up and led her into the bedroom. They undressed and got into bed. He switched off the light.

She turned on her side and scooted away from him, but he only reached out, pulled her close and spooned himself around her. It felt good.

Really good. With a sigh, she let sleep carry her away.

Genny woke to find the morning sun streaming in the front window. Rafe stood staring out, his broad back to the bed. He was fully dressed in tan trousers and a knit shirt.

Genny dragged herself to a sitting position against

the pillows and pulled up the blankets to cover her bare breasts. "Rafe?" He turned to her. "Have you already been down to breakfast?"

He looked strangely determined. "No. I waited for you."

She blinked sleep from her eyes and looked at the clock. "It's almost ten." She thought about that snack he'd never gotten to eat last night. "You must be starving."

"No way was I leaving this room without you. Not with Melinda in the house."

"Oh, please. I said I believe you about last night. And I meant it. I think you're being a little extreme."

He squared his huge shoulders. "You're angry with me."

"No, not angry. Just…"

"Disappointed, then."

"All right, yes. A little disappointed." *Admit the rest,* her conscience chided. So she muttered, "And jealous, too."

His expression softened. "You have no reason to be."

She stared at him steadily. "I'll get over it. Go on down and eat."

"Get up and come with me."

"It'll take me a few minutes…."

He dropped into the slipper chair by the window. "I'll wait."

Brooke and Fiona were alone in the breakfast room sipping coffee and whispering heatedly together when Genny and Rafe got there. They served themselves and sat across from the two women.

Rafe asked, "Where's everyone?"

Brooke said, "Geoffrey's gone off with Granny and the dogs. They've promised to be back by noon at the latest to get cleaned up for the party."

Genny doggedly poked a bite of sausage into her mouth and waited for him to ask the important question.

Finally, he did. "And Melinda?"

Fiona groaned.

Brooke said, "She's gone, just like that. She left practically at the crack of dawn, Frances told me. She gave Frances a note for me."

"Ah," said Rafe. Genny could hear the relief in his voice.

But Brooke was not pleased. "The note was three lines. She had to go. She was sorry. There was an emergency in London. She gave no details. None. I have no idea what happened, but it makes no sense to me."

Fiona sniffed. "Rather rude of her, I must say."

Brooke shrugged. "Well, I don't know what to think. I hope she's all right...."

Fiona made a humphing sound.

Rafe said nothing. Genny didn't, either. What was there to say?

The children from the village began arriving with their parents at a few minutes before two. There were twenty of them total, twelve boys and eight girls, ranging in age from eight to ten. A few of the parents stayed on for the party, but most dropped off the youngsters and promised to return at six to collect them.

At two-fifteen, Fiona's chauffeur arrived with the twins. He dropped them off and left.

It was a warm, sunny day and Brooke had planned on two hours on the waterslide and in the pool first. She'd set up a pair of changing tents—one for the boys, one for the girls—out by the jetty. The children handed their gifts to Frances, who took them to the terrace. Then Brooke and Fiona herded them toward the tents.

Rafe, Genny, Eloise and the few parents who'd stayed pitched in to keep the excited guests corralled. With twenty-three of them running about, you never knew who might fall in the lake or run off into the parkland, never to be seen again.

The water sports went well enough. The twins dominated, as always. They shouted the loudest and pushed the other children aside so they could go down the waterslide first.

Fiona kept telling them to behave themselves and they kept pretending not to hear her. She finally gave them a five-minute time-out. They lasted about ninety seconds. When they got up and ran away from her, Fiona just let them go.

Geoffrey seemed to be holding up pretty well. He avoided Dennis and Dexter. And he got along well with the children from the village. Genny saw him laughing, his head tipped back, the space where his baby teeth were missing showing, as he went down the slide.

They played Marco Polo in the pool and batted various water toys around. Frances and a couple of the women who came in twice a week to clean served cold drinks to anyone who wanted them. That meant there were several trips to the toilets and back. It was hectic, but it seemed to be going nicely, all things considered.

At a little past four, they moved on to paintball on the archery field. It started out well enough, with the children hiding behind boulders and hay bales and jumping out to splatter each other with paint from child-size plastic guns. They were all laughing at first. But the twins quickly became overly aggressive, leaping out and shooting the village girls in the face mask—and some of the boys, as well.

Geoffrey started looking grim during the paintball. There was screaming and some crying. Genny and Eloise took charge of comforting the crying girls, leading them away, getting them out of their vests and headgear, hosing off the paint and then herding them to the girls' tent to put their on their dry clothes.

As the paintballing progressed, Brooke's temper started to fray. Apparently, she hadn't figured out that inviting the Terrible Twins and then handing them guns filled with balls of bright paint probably wasn't the best brainstorm she'd ever had. She started shouting, "No, now!" and "Careful, now!" and "Dennis, you stop that this instant!"

She and Fiona traded angry words when Brooke demanded that Fiona control the twins and Fiona insisted it wasn't their fault. "They've had nothing but sugared drinks since noon. What do you expect? They need nourishing food."

Finally, Eloise whipped out her Acme Thunderer Titanic Commemorative Whistle and blew a halt to paintball. They hosed off the children who remained on the field, got them all dry and dressed and moved on to the east side of the terrace, where there were banners and streamers strung about and the sandstone walls of the house had been decorated up to look like an old-time carnival caravan. Frances and her helpers handed out SpongeBob lunch boxes to everyone, adults included.

The food was surprisingly healthy, Genny thought, and gratefully dug in. They had sandwiches and fruit, each with a bag of crisps and a bottle of water. Of course, there were also the candy floss and popcorn machines. Frosted treats and other goodies sat in bowls and on platters, available for the taking.

While they ate, the magician appeared. He pulled things out of a top hat and made animals with balloons. Genny found him a bit lackluster and the children, simultaneously overstimulated and worn-out, quickly lost interest. The twins started throwing things.

By then it was half past five. They'd yet to do the cake

and presents. The magician took his final bow. Brooke had blue paint on her white skinny jeans and her Jimmy Choo ballerina flats were splattered with yellow. And she was shouting a lot.

"Frances, the cake!" she called, grabbing a very somber-looking Geoffrey by the arm and pushing him down into the chair of honor, which had been done up to look like some kind of circus clown's throne. "Settle down now, everyone. It's time to sing Happy Birthday to Geoffrey!"

The children quieted. But only for about a half a minute. They were laughing and whispering together again when Frances finally emerged with a tower of a cake consisting of three figures from the Skylanders: Giants video game, each figure with three flaming birthday candles sprouting from the top of its head.

Dexter shouted something and one of the girls let out a yelp. Eloise hustled over to settle them down. Fiona, Brooke and the other adults started singing Happy Birthday, a few of the children catching on and joining in.

Frances set the cake in front of Geoffrey. Genny didn't think he'd ever looked so miserable in his life.

"Make a wish, darling!" Brooke shouted. "Make a wish and blow out your candles!"

Geoffrey shut his eyes. Genny could almost *feel* the poor sweetheart counting to ten.

"Geoffrey, come on now!"

He sucked in a big breath.

And someone threw an apple. Apparently, it was Dexter, because Fiona shouted, "Dex, no!"

Too late. The apple flew straight at the throne of honor. It didn't hit Geoffrey, but it did plow through the cake, mowing down the candles and decapitating the three Skylanders action figures.

* * *

They'd yet to get to the huge pile of presents and were serving the half exploded cake when the parents started arriving to pick up their children.

Brooke ended up just handing out the loot bags and letting them all go. Fiona went home with her sons. Brooke hardly bothered to wave her goodbye.

Nobody realized that Geoffrey had gone off somewhere until all the guests and their parents had left. About then, Brooke decided the family could watch while he opened his gifts.

She shouted for him, "Geoffrey, where are you? Time to open your gifts!" He failed to appear. "Where's he gone now?" she muttered crossly. "Geoffrey, come here this instant! Geoffrey!"

Eloise said, "He's probably up in his room…." She went to get him. But when she came back down, she was shaking her head. "He's not there."

Brooke started pacing. Never a good sign. "Dear sweet God, what a balls-up. Geoffrey, Geoffrey!" She fled toward the lake, frantically yelling his name.

Rafe said resignedly, "We'd better find him."

Eloise assigned each of them a different area to search. Genny got the stables and stable yard.

She found him in the second stall, which was empty except for him and the gray kitten he cradled in his thin arms. He was crying softly to himself.

He looked up and saw her peeking over the stall door. "I'm not going back out there." He sniffed and swiped the tears from his flushed cheeks with the back of his hand.

She opened the door, went in and dropped down beside him onto the bed of hay scattered across the floor. He stared straight ahead and petted the kitten, which purred out its contentment with every stroke of Geoffrey's paint-spotted hand.

"May I pet him, too?"

"I don't care."

Genny scratched the sweet little creature behind its overly large ear. "It's not such a bad thing, that your mum would put in a lot of time and effort to give a big party for you."

"I never wanted it." He stuck out his lower lip. "It was awfuler even than I thought it would be. The slide and the pool weren't so bad. But the rest of it was crap. And Dennis and Dexter…" He gave a little shudder of disgust. "Some boys are just bad."

"Let's hope they grow out of it," she said. Geoffrey made a doubtful sound. "And look at it this way. Some of it was fun, you said so yourself."

He seemed to think about that for a bit. And then he asked, "Aunt Genny?"

"Hmm?"

"I'm glad you're my aunt now. You're really in our family. I like that very much."

Suddenly *she* felt like crying. It wasn't an easy family she'd married into. But they were hers now—all of them: Geoffrey and Eloise, Rafe most of all. And yes, even her impossible, beautiful bitch of a sister-in-law.

She wrapped her arm around Geoffrey's narrow shoulders. "I'm glad to *be* your aunt."

He put the kitten down in the hay. It meowed cheerfully and then bounded off through the stall's open door. "All right, Aunt Genny. Let's go back now."

Genny and Geoffrey returned to the terrace. Eloise and the dogs joined them shortly after and then Rafe came, too.

Frances and her helpers were picking up trash and cleaning off the tables.

Brooke appeared last, striding swiftly across the wide swath of lawn leading up to the terrace. At the sight of all them waiting there, Geoffrey among them, she walked even faster.

A hot flush stained her cheeks and her mouth was a thin line. She marched right up to Geoffrey. "What is the matter with you? You'll be the death of me. Where have you been?"

"Mum, I...went to the stables, that's all. For a minute."

"The stables!" She threw up her arms. "Oh, you are the most ungrateful little... Oh, I just..." She glanced hotly up from her son—and locked gazes with Genny, who had made a big mistake and stood directly behind him. She braced her fists on her hips. "And I'll just bet that *you* were the one who found him."

Genny stood tall. "Well, yes. Yes, I was."

"What did I tell you last time he ran off? If you know where he is, you're to come and tell *me*."

Rafe said, "She didn't know. We each took an area. Gen got the stables. It's hardly a plot against you, Brooke."

Brooke's face flamed hotter. "Oh, what is the matter with you? You're always defending her. And she's just... well, you know what she is."

"Brooke," Genny said carefully, levelly. "Don't do this. Dial it down."

Brooke fisted her hands at her sides, tipped her head back and let out a screech of pure fury. "I will not dial it down. Not when you're trying to steal my son from me."

"Brooke, dear..." Eloise tried to catch her hand.

Brooke jerked away and went right on. "You were born with so much. You had it all. But you just weren't satisfied.

You had to have more. Do you think you're fooling anyone? Well, guess again. You're not. We all know what you did."

Rafe said, "Brooke. Stop."

Brooke did no such thing. "All your scheming to get Edward to marry you went nowhere. So with him barely cold in the ground, you fell into bed with Rafe and got yourself pregnant to guarantee you'd get Hartmore after all."

"Brooke!" Eloise gasped.

"That's enough, Brooke!" Rafe shouted.

Brooke whirled and opened her mouth to shout right back at him.

But Geoffrey shouted first. "Mum, you leave Aunt Genny alone! She's a good person and she loves us all very much and I only wish that *she* was my mum!"

"Oh, dear God…" Genny didn't know she would say it aloud until the anguished words fell from her lips. She clapped her hand over her mouth.

And Brooke? She let out a loud, wounded cry. And then she did what she always did when one of her tantrums spiraled out of her control. She burst into tears and ran for the house.

Eloise turned and went after her, the dogs at her heels.

Frances and her crew went on staunchly cleaning up, trying their hardest to pretend that none of this was happening.

Geoffrey stood still for a moment, his small body vibrating with fury. And then he took off running, back toward the stairs that led down to the parkland.

Genny would have followed him.

But Rafe caught her arm. "Are you all right?"

She wasn't, not really. But she nodded anyway. And then she looked down at his hand on her arm. "Let me go. I need to see that Geoffrey's—"

"Gen." He caught her chin and tipped it up so she met his eyes.

"Don't," she cried. "Let me go…"

"Gen. Listen."

She shut her eyes, sucked in a slow breath. "Yes. What?"

Quietly, he told her, "I'll go. I'll talk to him. It's better if I go."

She wanted to jerk away, to demand again that he release her, to insist that she would do it, go to Geoffrey. That she *needed* to do it, that Geoffrey needed *her* now.

But she didn't jerk away. Because she knew he was right. The fight drained out of her, leaving her shoulders drooping, her arm limp in his grip.

She loved Geoffrey with a deep, unconditional, very motherly sort of love.

But she *wasn't* his mother.

And in this delicate moment, for her to take his mother's place and go to him when Rafe could do it just as well as she could…

That would be wrong.

She said in a flat voice of reluctant surrender, "I think he'll just go to the stables again." She wanted to burst into tears and run off wailing. Did that make her as bad as Brooke?

Probably.

He took her by the shoulders. "Are you sure you're all right?"

And she made herself nod. "Yes. I'm all right. Go talk to him. He needs you now."

"Gen, I…"

If he kept looking at her like that, she really would start crying. "You're wasting time. Go. Go now."

At last, he released her. She stood numbly watching as

he went the way the way that Geoffrey had gone, to the stairs and down to the rolling expanse of lawn.

Frances stepped up and asked if the crew should take the gifts inside.

Off in the distance, clouds gathered. But there was no imminent danger of rain. "Leave them for now. Ask Eloise when she comes back down. Or Brooke…" *If she comes back down.* "And, Frances, I think I'll go for a walk." She needed to do something, get away, clear her head, soothe her aching heart. "Around the lake, I think. Maybe out to the castle, too." She had on her sturdy trainers, so suitable for chasing after party-mad children. "I have my phone if anyone needs to reach me. And I'll be back by dark."

"Good enough, then." The housekeeper gave her a nod.

Genny dug an elastic from a pocket. She swiftly smoothed her hair up into a ponytail, out of the way. Then she left the terrace and headed for the lake, setting herself the goal of briskly walking the perimeter. That would take a good hour, minimum.

Time enough to have a nice cry and get herself under control.

The tears welled up and spilled over. She let them come, now and then lifting a hand to swipe them away. She hurried on, past the tents, the aboveground pool and the jetty. Several members of the house team were there, cleaning up. She gave them a wave and went on down that long stretch that led eventually to the graveled road around the walled garden.

Her unspoken love for Rafe seemed to be eating her up from inside. She ached to say the words, to have them out. He was a good man with a true heart.

And yet she feared to give him that kind of power over her. It was a mostly groundless fear. She knew that Rafe would not betray her. He'd given her his word to be true, and he lived by his word.

Still, she kept flashing on that moment last night when Melinda had flung herself into his arms and slammed her open mouth to his.

To banish that image, she broke into a run—until she had to stop and catch her breath. She paced in circles, pausing to bend at the waist, sucking in great gulps of air, finally stretching her calves a little with the help of a sturdy oak tree to lean against.

Out on the lake, a couple drifted in a rowboat. They waved to her and she waved back. She put her hand on the slight swell of her belly.

All was right with the baby. He—or she—was safe and cozy in there. But Genny promised herself she would slow down a little, not push so hard. She only needed to keep going for a while, needed solitude and steady movement to think everything through.

She walked on at a brisk pace, Brooke's furious accusations echoing in her head. It wasn't that anything Brooke had said was news. It was only to have to hear it right out loud like that, in front of everyone. Because she *had* wanted Hartmore, more than anything. And no romantic illusions about Edward were left to her now. She would have married Rafe's brother simply to get Hartmore, just as Brooke had said.

And she *had* managed to get herself pregnant, causing Rafe to insist on marrying her—and resulting in her getting what she'd always wanted: to be a DeValery and mistress of Hartmore.

She veered off the lake path and walked fast beside a crumbling stone wall. By then, she was hardly aware of her location, let alone of the direction her swiftly moving feet were taking her. The stretched-out elastic slid down her ponytail and fell off. She ignored it, shoving her hair behind her ears and letting it hang free.

Eventually, she did pause. She looked around and tried to figure out exactly where she'd come to. How long had she been moving blindly along this unknown path? She hadn't seen a single soul since she'd waved to that couple boating on the lake.

And when had she left the lake trail? Definitely before she reached the road to the walled garden.

Had she come to the garden road along this path? She seemed to remember running across it, the crunch of gravel beneath her shoes.

Ahead, just off the path, she saw a stone wall and a heavy wooden gate. Ivy climbed the wall, growing thick, digging into the stone. She approached and pushed on the gate. It opened reluctantly with a creak of rusty hinges.

Inside, she found an overgrown garden and a small stone house with the thatch roof half caved in. She didn't know the place. Perhaps a gardener's cottage fallen into disuse, or maybe a tenant farmer's house, abandoned with the changing times.

Fascinated by the magical feel of the place, she picked her way through all the undergrowth toward the house.

What time was it?

She took her phone from her back pocket and shook her head. Late. Almost eight. She needed to start thinking about getting back. A rotting plank creaked underfoot, but she didn't really stop to think what that might mean to her.

Still walking, she auto-dialed the house and put the phone to her ear. Before she heard a ring, the plank gave way beneath her. With a cry of surprise, she plummeted into darkness.

Chapter Twelve

Rafe

As Gen had predicted, Rafe found his nephew in the stables looking broody and sullen, petting one of those rangy, big-eared kittens born to the mistakenly named Samson at the end of May. Rafe sat down with him. They played with the kitten for a long time until Geoffrey was ready to talk.

Rafe let him get his frustrations off his chest. Geoffrey whispered that he hated his mum sometimes—or he said that at first. As he kept talking, he admitted that maybe he didn't really hate Brooke. But he hated things she did.

"Like how she never listens to me, Uncle Rafe. And like how she's mean to Aunt Genny, who only wants to love us and have us all be happy together." He also hated that his mum was always getting mad and yelling and then running off crying. "I hate that a lot, Uncle Rafe."

Rafe said that he didn't like it, either. And he thought

about Gen, about the numb misery in her big brown eyes when he'd left her on the terrace.

He thought about what a damn coward he was. All the years of loving her. You'd think he could say it. Such a simple thing. *I love you, Gen. You are the only woman for me.*

But he'd been a cheat and a liar—and not with Melinda. No. He'd cheated and lied in ways he didn't know how to explain to her. The truth had a lot of ugliness in it. And he felt so bloody guilty about the way it had all turned out.

And once he told her how much he loved her, the ugly truth of what had really happened the night Edward died was sure to follow. That wouldn't be fair. Wouldn't be right. She shouldn't have to know any of it. It was all in the past and best left alone.

He took Geoffrey back to the house, where Frances reported that Gen had gone for a walk around the lake and possibly to the castle. She'd promised to return before dark.

The lake *and* the castle? Before dark? What the hell?

He shouldn't have left her on the terrace like that after the rotten things Brooke had said to her. But there had been Geoffrey to deal with....

It was all such a mess.

And maybe getting off to herself for a while would be good for her. Frances said she had her phone. So if she needed someone to give her a ride back from wherever she'd gone off to, she could simply call.

He and Geoffrey went on up to Brooke's room. Granny was still with her.

Brooke seemed subdued. At the sight of her son, her face crumpled again.

Granny said, "Brooke, dear. Please."

Brooke pulled it together and asked with surprising calm and real concern, "Geoffrey, are you all right?"

Geoffrey stood very straight. "Mum, I'm sorry for what

I said. I love Aunt Genny very much, but I don't wish she was my mum. *You're* my mum and I'm happy that you are." He pressed his lips together and then added bleakly, "Most of the time."

Brooke drew a slow, careful breath. "I was awful," she said, and seemed sincere. "I don't blame you for what you said. I am going to find a way to be…better than I have been. I promise you. And I owe Aunt Genevra an apology, I know that. As for you, I only hope you can forgive me for the terrible things I said, and for pushing you into a party you didn't want, for…yelling at you and crying and calling you ungrateful when I should have been trying to understand what was bothering you."

Geoffrey looked down at his shoes and seemed not to know what to say to that.

Eloise caught Rafe's eye. He nodded. She said, "Shall we leave you two alone, then?"

Brooke had eyes only for her son. "Geoffrey? Do you mind if Granny and Uncle Rafe go?"

He was still looking at his shoes. But finally, he answered, "All right."

As soon as they were out the door and Eloise had shut it behind them, she asked, "Where is Genevra? How is she?"

He repeated what Frances had told him.

Granny frowned at that. "What time is it?"

"A little past eight."

"Call her."

So he took out his phone and dialed. It went directly to voice mail, without a ring. He left a message. "Gen. Please call me as soon as you get this." He disconnected.

"She's not answering?"

"No, and it didn't ring. I think she may have turned it off."

"That's not like her, to take her phone so that we can reach her—and then to turn it off."

"Maybe she just wants some time to herself. That was damned gruesome, what Brooke did." And it had come right on the heels of that god-awful encounter with Melinda last night. Had it all become more than Gen was willing to put up with?

Had she left him?

No. She wouldn't do that. She wasn't a leaver. No matter how bad things got, Gen stuck it out and worked it through. It was one of the million and two things he loved about her.

Plus, if she was going, she would pack a bag and tell him to his face that she was done with him. No way would she promise to be home before dark and then just wander off on foot with only the clothes on her back.

But what if she'd finally had enough—of him and his sister, of Fiona and Melinda?

If she had, no matter what it took, he would find a way to change her mind.

"Rafe, are you listening?"

"Er, of course I am, Granny."

She peered up at him doubtfully. "I *said,* Brooke's behavior is completely unacceptable. She's agreed to take steps to deal with her temper. She's finally volunteered to see a therapist."

He would believe that when he saw it. "It's a start."

"Even *she's* finally seeing that she went too far and it has to stop—but right now it's Genny I'm concerned for. She should be here, with us, where we can tell her how very much we love her and ask her to forgive us for all the ways we failed to protect her from the jealous spite of her own sister-in-law."

"Are you lecturing me, Granny?"

"Oh, well, not exactly. I'm certainly as guilty as you are

of not stepping in decisively before Brooke said all those unconscionable things to her."

Did she want reassurance? He could use some himself. "I'm sure she's all right. She told Frances she'd be back by dark."

Eloise made a low, unhappy noise. "I just don't like it. She wouldn't turn off her phone. I think we should do something."

He agreed. "Frances said she took the lake trail first. And she said she might go to the castle. I'll saddle a horse and start with the lake trail."

"Take your phone with you. And do not turn it off."

It was full dark by nine. He'd been around the lake and hadn't found her.

He tried her phone for the fourth time. Straight to voice mail, as each time before.

So he called Eloise. Gen wasn't back yet.

Clouds had gathered overhead. He returned to the stables, got a torch and rode for the castle.

No sign of her on the way. And the old ruin was deserted except for an owl hooting somewhere up in the battlements. He returned to the house and turned his gelding over to one of Frances's helpers who sometimes worked with the horses.

They were all waiting in the family's foyer at the East Entrance—Granny, Brooke, Geoffrey and Frances—huddled together, looking worried. He had no idea what to say to them. He only wanted Gen back.

She'd said she would be home by dark. But night had fallen an hour ago. She wasn't home and she hadn't called. Every minute that ticked by now made it more likely that something had happened to keep her from doing what she'd told Frances she would do.

He didn't want to think about all the things that might have happened to her.

At the same time, those things were *all* he could think about.

He called the number for the local policing team to report Gen missing. The sergeant was patient and sympathetic. He said it was more than likely she would return soon and that Rafe should call anyone who might know of her whereabouts. And then he told Rafe he would be at Hartmore in twenty minutes.

Rafe called Rory in Montedoro. Rory agreed that if Gen wasn't where she'd said she would be, something wasn't right. She said she would go and speak with her mother and Prince Evan and get back to him right away.

After Rory, he remembered the names of a couple of Gen's school friends and managed to dig up their numbers. He left a message for one and the other answered on the third ring. She said that no, Gen hadn't been in touch.

The sergeant arrived. He had a short list of questions, which Rafe answered. And he wanted a recent photo of Gen. Rafe gave him one of the pictures from their wedding album. The sergeant said he wouldn't put the information in the system until tomorrow.

"One other question, Your Lordship. Does your wife have any health problems?"

The baby. He'd been purposely *not* thinking about the baby. "Not a problem, exactly. But she's pregnant. Almost four months along."

"Any difficulties with the pregnancy…?"

"None. She's perfectly healthy. She's been to Dr. Eldon, in the village, and he says she's doing fine."

"Good, then." The sergeant nodded, as though in approval. "I'm sure you'll be hearing from her tonight." The man was clearly trying to be encouraging. Rafe wanted to

grab him and shake him and demand some action, *now.*
"But it's good to have the basic information ready," the
sergeant went on briskly, "just in case."

Gen's father called a few minutes after Rafe waved
the sergeant out the door. Rafe took the call in his study.

He told the prince consort the basic facts. That Gen
had gone for a walk and not returned when she'd said she
would, that her cell was dumping calls directly to voice
mail. "She hasn't been seen since around seven."

"And it's after eleven there now. I don't like it. She
wouldn't turn off her cell phone like that."

"I know."

"Something's kept her from returning when she said
she would."

"Yes. I think so, too."

"We should have made her keep Caesar with her, at least
for a while…" Rafe's gut twisted. Evan was right. Dear
God in heaven, were they going to be getting a ransom
call, then? But then Evan asked, "Was anything bothering
her when she went for that walk?"

And Rafe hesitated too long before answering.

"You had better tell me," said Evan, his tone surprisingly patient.

"All right. Brooke's always been jealous of Gen. Today,
Brooke threw a party for Geoffrey's birthday…" He told
the rest of it straightforwardly, making no attempt to pretty
it up.

"Anything else?" Evan asked.

Rafe had always trusted and respected Evan. And besides, at this point, with Gen's safety in question, her father
had a right to know. As simply as he could, he explained
his epic fail involving Melinda the night before.

"I take it you've yet to tell my daughter that you love
her." It was gently said, but an accusation nonetheless.

Evan knew way too much—because Rafe had told him. On that Sunday night, the day after the wedding, when the two of them had spent hours drinking brandy and smoking excellent cigars, Rafe had told the prince the truth: that he was in love with his bride, but he'd yet to tell Gen. "And never mind," added Evan. "Your silence is your answer. The good news is that if she's upset, it's possible she did turn off her phone, that she decided she needs more time to sort things out."

"God, I do hope so."

"We'll wait until morning," Evan said. "If she hasn't contacted you by then, her mother and I will be on our way to Hartmore."

After ringing off with Evan, Rafe hardly knew what to do with himself. He was tempted to put on his walking shoes, grab another lantern and scour the pitch-dark countryside shouting her name all night long until he found her at last. It was raining by then. He stood at the window looking out on the darkness, watching the raindrops slide down the panes. He prayed that, wherever she was, she was safe and dry, with food in her belly.

There was a tap at the door.

Gen? He spun around at the sound.

But it was only Brooke. "I need a minute. Please."

He went to the desk, dropped into his chair and demanded flatly, "What?"

She shut the door and came over and stood facing him with the desk between them. She looked awful, hollow-eyed. Troubled.

He had no sympathy for her. She *should* be troubled.

"I just got a call from Melinda."

He swore. An ugly word. "I don't want to hear about Melinda."

Brooke didn't crumble. She wrapped her arms around

herself and kept her spine straight. "Melinda told me what she did last night. I had no idea. I swear it, Rafe. Just now, she said you two had been together, years ago, before she left for Paris."

He stared at the paperweight in the corner of the desk. It would be so satisfying to grab it and hurl it at the far wall. To resist that temptation, he fisted his hands on his thighs. "Let me make myself clear. I don't give a good damn about Melinda. And what is the point of this, I'd like to know? Gen is missing. Nothing else matters right now."

"I just… I didn't *know,* all right? I had no idea that Melinda was after you. It's not like with Fiona. I mean, Fiona was my friend first, *before* anything happened with—" He surged upright again, so fast that she gasped. "Rafe! What?"

"Have you lost your mind completely, to come in here tonight and talk to me about *Fiona?*"

Brooke put up both hands. "All right. I'm sorry. Forget about Fiona."

"Go to bed."

"I will, yes. In a minute. It's just, well, I mean it when I say I had no idea that Melinda had a secret agenda. I actually believed that she only wanted to be my friend."

"Surprise," he said, more cruelly than he should have.

Brooke didn't even flinch. For once in her life, she just stood there and took it. "Melinda apologized for her behavior. She won't be back."

"Damn right she won't."

She hesitated. Then, "Please, Rafe. Can you tell me, is there any word about Genevra?"

"None. If we aren't in touch with her by morning, her parents are coming and an organized search will begin."

She swallowed, hard. "Oh, God. I'm a terrible person, aren't I?"

Wearily, he waved her off. "Go to bed, Brooke." He waited for her to start crying and carrying on. As soon as she did, he planned to march around the desk, grab her by the arm, put her out the door and lock it behind her.

But she surprised him. There were no tears. She only pleaded softly, "Tell me that she's all right."

He sank back to the chair again. "I don't know what will happen, Brooke. Go on now, go to bed. You'll need your rest. I have a feeling tomorrow will be a hellish day."

She nodded and turned for the door.

But she stopped when she got there and faced him once more. "I always... She's so strong. She looks so sweet and delicate, but we all know she's not. She's as tough as they come. I can't imagine her broken. Even beyond the fact that if something happened to her, it would be my fault, I don't *want* anything to happen to her. I know you won't believe this, but in my own sad, twisted way, I love her. She is a sister to me. Not all sisters get along, you know? Sisters have...rivalries. Jealousies. That's me. The jealous sister. But if...*when* she comes home, I'm going to find a way to make it different between us, to make it what it should have been all along." She opened the door.

And he relented, just a little. "Brooke?"

"Yes?"

"It's not *all* your fault, you know. There's plenty of blame to go around."

By morning, the rain had stopped and the sky was clear. Gen had neither called nor come home.

No one—not anyone at Hartmore, not her parents or her siblings or her old school chums—had heard a word from her since she left the terrace the day before.

Rafe called Evan and Princess Adrienne and they told

him they would be there by afternoon. Next, he called the police sergeant.

The sergeant said he would put the information Rafe had given him last night into the system. Then he came back out to Hartmore. He said he would need to interview everyone—family members and staff. He asked for the names of everyone who'd come to Geoffrey's party. And he wanted to have a look around the East Bedroom.

He spoke of what would happen within the next twenty-four hours. Search teams with rescue dogs would be mobilized, a missing-persons flyer put into circulation.

Rafe thanked him, turned him over to Eloise and went out to the stables to saddle his horse. He got the black gelding ready and led him out of the stable.

Geoffrey and Brooke were waiting for him in the cobbled courtyard.

"We want to search with you, Uncle Rafe," Geoffrey said. "Mum and me."

Both had dressed for riding. Brooke carried a rucksack. They stood side by side and looked up at him so seriously, with such complete determination. He thought that they'd never looked more alike than they did at that moment.

He said, "The police sergeant will want to speak with both of you."

Brooke shrugged. "Later. Geoffrey and I want to help. Now. Plus, we're going mad with the waiting."

What could it hurt? Brooke was an excellent horsewoman and Geoffrey was competent enough. He asked Brooke, "Do you have your phone?"

"I do."

"Saddle up, then. I'm going to the castle first to have another look. Last night I didn't get there until after dark. After the castle, I'll ride over the north parkland and the chapel area. You two take the lake trail. I rode around it while it was still light out yesterday. Nothing. But today, pay attention to trails leading off the main one. She might have taken a detour at some point. We'll need to try those. Call me every half hour to check in."

"Will do," said Brooke.

Geoffrey grabbed her hand. "Come on, Mum. Let's hurry."

A half hour later, Rafe was at Hartmore Castle, and finding no more sign of Gen than he had the evening before. Brooke called. She and Geoffrey were on the lake trail, almost to the jetty. They'd seen nothing worth reporting.

An hour after that, on their third check-in, Rafe was combing the north parkland. Brooke and Geoffrey had been around the lake once. They'd found no sign of Gen.

"We're going to circle the lake again," Brooke said. "We'll take the branching trails as we come to them."

Rafe thought they needed to put a limit on how far to wander along each trail.

Brooke agreed. "We'll follow each trail for twenty minutes, looking for signs of something, anything, that would hint that Genevra might have been down it." If there was nothing, they'd backtrack to the lake and try the next trail.

When Rafe put his phone away that time, he stopped in the shadow of an oak and considered the hopelessness of this entire exercise. They'd have the trained rescue people and the dogs out by tomorrow, people who knew the way to set up an effective search, who knew what signs to look for.

He and Brooke and Geoffrey were likely only to make the real search more difficult by mucking up the ground with their horses, destroying the scent trail and any possible footprints Gen might have left. They would make it all the tougher for dogs—or trained rescuers—to find where she'd been.

Rafe got out his phone again to tell Brooke to call it off.

But then he couldn't do it, couldn't go back to the house and sit around waiting for someone else to do something. He'd done that all night long. He couldn't bear to give in and do it again.

And he knew that his sister and his nephew couldn't, either.

They went on with it.

Two hours and fifteen minutes later, as he was about to call the whole thing off all over again, his phone rang. It wasn't check-in time.

"Brooke?"

"We found a hair elastic," she said. "Blue and orange, striped."

"A what?"

"You know, a rubber band thing for a ponytail. Genevra uses them to keep her hair out of the way when she works up a sweat."

"A hair elastic." His hopes sank. "A lot of women use those, don't they?"

"Well, yes…"

"Then what makes you think it might be hers?"

"Rafe. *Geoffrey* thinks it's hers."

"I do, Uncle Rafe!" Geoffrey's excited voice came through the phone. "I just know it has to be!"

"Did you hear that?" Brooke asked.

He got the message. Geoffrey believed they were on to something. Brooke refused to dash his hopes. "Yes," he said resignedly. "I heard."

"We're almost twenty minutes on this trail, but we're going to continue."

He asked which trail it was and she described it, the

second path after the boat jetty, the one that crossed the road to the walled garden. "I know the one," he said. "It continues on past a couple of abandoned farmers' cottages, in and out of stands of elm and ash trees. Eventually, it curves back and comes out at the lake again."

"Then we'll just go on, follow it all the way around and back to the lake."

"And we'll call right away when we find her!" Geoffrey shouted.

Rafe smiled in spite of everything then, and felt the scar on his cheek pulling, reminding him again of all the things he hadn't said, all the truths too dangerous to share. "All right, then. Keep me in the loop."

Brooke made a low sound in her throat. "Geoffrey will make absolutely certain that I do."

Again, Rafe put his phone away and rode on, moving back toward the house and circling around to the south front, heading for the lake. He was going to join forces with Brooke and Geoffrey. Why not? He'd been searching since half past nine and he'd gotten exactly nowhere. They might as well all be together and fail to find her as to wander around separately praying for a clue.

Plus, he had to admit that Geoffrey's enthusiasm was inspiring. He decided not to think about what would happen when Geoffrey finally became discouraged, too.

Rafe's phone rang as he reached the lake trail, at a point just beyond the old woodland garden, which Gen and Eloise were planning to start whipping into shape next year. His heart slamming into overdrive, he pulled the phone from his pocket.

But it was only Eloise. "The sergeant is asking for you. Princess Adrienne and Prince Evan have landed at East Midlands. They should arrive here within the hour. And I called Brooke. She told me to call you."

"Put the sergeant off. I know you. You can handle him."

"Do you really think you're going to find her?"

"Geoffrey does. And we're not giving up as long as he's hard on the case."

Eloise gave in. She promised she would take care of the sergeant for him.

Rafe shoved the phone in his back pocket and rode on toward the boat jetty. He was past it and almost to the trail Brooke and Geoffrey had taken when his phone rang again.

That time it was Brooke.

His hand was shaking as he put it to his ear.

"Rafe!" Brooke's voice shook as hard as his hand. "Rafe, are you there?"

"Yes. What—?"

And then he heard Geoffrey shout, "Uncle Rafe, we found her! We found Aunt Genny and she's stuck in the well!"

Chapter Thirteen

Genny stared up through the darkness, toward the light beyond the broken boards, and at Geoffrey's dear, perfect little face. "Is he coming? Tell me he's coming."

"Don't worry, Aunt Genny. Mum told him to get a ladder first, but he said to call Great-Granny and tell her we found you and Great-Granny would get the ladder to us."

Brooke's face appeared opposite Geoffrey's. "Rafe's coming. Turns out he'd decided to join up with us, so he was already on his way."

Genny's heart filled with pure love for her—for Brooke, of all people. Tears of relief and happiness were rolling down her face. And then one of the boards up there creaked. "You two, be careful! Get away from the edge! You'll end up down here with me."

Both dear faces disappeared. Genny clapped her hand over her mouth to keep from calling them back. Just the sight of them meant so much. It made her injured ankle stop aching, made her forget the stinging scrapes on her hands, her arms and her knees.

It made the absolute loneliness of being down in the darkness for hour upon hour fade almost to nothing. It made the fear that had chewed on her soul, fraying it to a bloody scrap, vanish as if it had never been. She'd even forgotten for a moment how thirsty she was. Fear that it might somehow be contaminated had kept her from drinking the water she stood in. So far anyway…

And then both beloved faces appeared again.

Genny sniffed and swiped the tears away. "I said, get back!"

"It's safe," argued Brooke. "We're on solid ground."

"Are you sure?"

Brooke laughed. "I would tell you to trust me, but how likely is that?"

"If either of you falls in here, I will strangle you, Brooke."

"Hah." Brooke's arm appeared. In her hand, she held a miracle: a bottle of water. "Are you thirsty?"

"Are you kidding?"

"Can you catch it?"

"Drop it straight down."

"Count of three. One, two…"

Genny caught it. "Oh, thank you, God." She screwed off the cap and took a slow, heavenly sip. "Wonderful." She sipped again. "Oh, I cannot tell you…"

Brooke asked, "What happened to your phone?"

Genny indulged in another glorious sip. "I dropped it. It's down here somewhere. There's muddy water to just below my calves." During the rain last night, it had risen to her knees. That hadn't been fun. She'd been freezing and sure she was going to drown. "I felt around for it for hours, it seemed like. Haven't found it yet."

"Are you cold?" Brooke asked. "We have a blanket."

"Mum thought of it as we were leaving the stables," Geoffrey proudly announced.

Suddenly, she was shivering again. She capped the water and stuck it under her arm. "Pass it down here, please."

Brooke got the blanket and carefully dropped it down. Genny caught it neatly and managed to wrap it around herself without letting any of the edges trail in the muck. It was heavy and scratchy, the most fabulous thing she'd ever felt in her life.

Well, next to Rafe's kiss, his rough whisper in the middle of the night, the feel of his big, hot body curled around her as she slept. Next to the knowledge that she and their baby had somehow survived way too many hours alone in the dark wondering how anyone was ever going to find them....

Brooke asked, "Are you hungry? We have sandwiches and fruit and muesli bars."

Genny's stomach rumbled. She smiled through her tears. "I've got the blanket and the water." She shifted, getting the water bottle out from under her arm, trying to hold the blanket and keep her weight off her bad ankle at the same time. "I'm bound to drop something if I have to catch anything else. I'll be okay until you get me out of here." She got the cap off the bottle and took a longer drink that time.

Brooke said, "Rafe should be here any minute..."

And he was. Not five minutes later, she heard the pounding of horse's hooves echoing through the muddy walls that surrounded her.

"It's Uncle Rafe!" Geoffrey shouted. "He's here."

She heard him pull the horse to a stop. And then he

was there, much too far above her, his beloved face staring down at her, black eyes finding hers.

"Gen."

Her heart felt too big for the cage of her chest. "I'm all right. *We're* all right, me and the baby, too. I lost my phone. I…hurt my ankle and couldn't see any way to get out of here. I didn't know what to do…." Her voice caught on a sob.

"Just hold on, love. We'll get you out."

Brooke said, "I called Granny. They should be here with the ladder and ropes and…whatever else they need soon."

Rafe broke eye contact with her to talk to his sister. "Soon isn't good enough. I can barely see her face, but I can tell that she's shivering. She's freezing down there. It's an old well, hand dug, not more than twenty feet deep, probably less. A ladder seven or eight feet would do it. She can climb to the top and I'll reach down and pull her the rest of the way up. Even a sturdy rope might be workable. Let's check in the cottage and around back. I think there's a storage shed. We'll see what we can find."

Wait. He was leaving? Genny cried out, "No! Just stay there. Just…I need to see you."

"Gen." He held her yearning gaze so steadily. She needed his arms around her. Needed them desperately. "I'm just going to have a look around the cottage. I won't be long."

And Geoffrey said, "I'll stay here, Aunt Genny. You can look up and see me."

Of course, she knew she was being ridiculous. But that didn't make the terror of losing sight of Rafe now any less. All those endless hours and hours, where she hadn't known if she would ever see his face again.

She swallowed her tears—and her fear. "Yes. That would be all right. Of course it would."

"You're sure?" Rafe asked gruffly.

And Geoffrey said, "She's sure. See if there's a ladder. Mum, you help him. I will stay here where Aunt Genny can look at me."

So Rafe and Brooke disappeared from her sight. Genny stared hard up at Geoffrey and clutched the blanket tighter around her shaking shoulders.

They really didn't take that long. It only seemed like half a lifetime.

And then Rafe was there again, looking down, finding her, giving her his crooked wreck of smile. "We found one."

"A ladder?"

"Yes—you said something about your ankle?"

"I sprained it. It hurts, but I can get up a ladder." By God, she would do it no matter the pain. Her ankle would hold her. She'd drag herself up by her arms alone if she had to.

"We could wait," he suggested.

Brooke said, "I can call and find out how long they're going to be."

"No! Get me out of here, Rafe."

Brooke caught Rafe's eye again. "When she gets that tone, you should do what she wants."

"Listen to your sister," Genny warned. "She knows how I am. And I want out of here. Now," she added, just to be perfectly clear on the issue.

"All right, love." He disappeared from her view for an instant. And then he was hoisting the ladder into the well. It was of weathered wood, an old harvest ladder, wider at the base than at the top. "Get up against that side there, underneath where Brooke is. I'll ease it down to you...."

"Wait." She drank the rest of the water and let go of the bottle. Then she tied the corners of the blanket around her neck. "All right." She limped back against the slimy wall. "I'm ready."

He lowered the ladder into the well, dropping to his belly in order to ease it as far as he could with his long arms. "Can you reach it?"

She stepped forward to catch it—and let out a moan when she put too much weight on her bad ankle.

"Gen. If you can't do it—"

"Do not tell me what I can't do. I *will* do it." She got under the ladder, keeping most of her weight on her good leg, and she reached up and wrapped her hands around the side rails, about a foot from the base. "It's long enough. If I can get to the top, you can pull me the rest of the way."

"All right." He sounded doubtful—probably about her ability to climb with only one good leg—but he didn't try to tell her again that they should wait. "Have you got it?"

She stepped back again, taking care not to let the groan of pain escape her lips. "You're just going to have to let it go. I'll try to guide it down."

"Good, then."

"Now," she said.

He let go. She bent with it as it dropped. Slivers speared her already injured palms and pain sang up her leg. She gritted her teeth and did what she had to do, bending to follow the ladder down. Muddy water splashed up into her face.

"Are you all right?" Rafe called to her.

She armed the water out of her eyes. "Fine. Yes. I've got it."

"Ease it up as close to the wall as you can. And then lift it, and drop it hard. You need to be sure it's planted firmly at the base."

Her ankle ached every time she moved it, but she managed to lift the ladder and shove it hard into the muck.

Once that was done, she grabbed a rung and gave it a tug. It seemed stable. She looked up at Rafe's face above her—and thought of that night at Villa Santorno, when she'd told him about the baby.

There had been a ladder involved then, too. As well as a twisted ankle.

He frowned down at her. "It's all right to wait...."

Not a chance. "I'm coming up. Ignore the groaning. I am not stopping. Are we clear?"

"Nine steps," Brooke called down. "You can do it."

"And I'm right here to pull you out." Rafe held down his big hand.

Genny started climbing. Every other step was an agony. But it was funny about pain. The closer she got to Rafe's reaching hand, the less the hurting mattered.

By the time she reached the top with her hands, she was putting her full weight on her bad foot. She kept going, stepping up one rung and then the next, until her upper body was beyond the ladder and she had to press her torso against the slimy wall of the well, trying to distribute her weight so that the ladder wouldn't topple away beneath her.

And then there were no more steps. She eased her hand upward on the muddy wall, reaching for Rafe's fingers.

"Careful, careful..." He whispered the words. She saw only his face, his reaching hand, heard only that "Careful," so tenderly whispered as he lured her upward.

He reached. She reached. She had both legs on the top rung. Inches to go before he clasped her hand and brought her up out of there.

And then the ladder jolted, one of the legs giving way—or maybe sinking. She couldn't tell.

Alarm rattled through her. Pain seared her hurt foot. She let out a shriek and knew she was lost as the ladder dipped to the side and she started to fall.

Except she didn't fall.

Because Rafe somehow reached deeper. He reached and he caught her, his hand grasping her wrist at the last possible second. She grabbed on, too.

And then she was rising, moving up and up and into the light.

Geoffrey was shouting. "You got her, you caught her!"

And then she was blinking at the brightness of the afternoon sun. Tears streamed down her face as Rafe's big, hard arms gathered her close.

Rafe carried her back on the front of his horse.

They met the others on the lake trail. Rafe gave orders that they should put warning signs around the well and secure the cottage gate. Then he took her the rest of the way home to Hartmore, with Brooke and Geoffrey following behind.

He carried her up to the East Bedroom in his arms, calling for Eloise to send Dr. Eldon.

When he closed the door to the hallway and they were alone, she told him, "I'm filthy."

He carried her to the bathroom, drew her a bath and took off her torn, muddy clothes. The left shoe was the hardest. Her foot was swollen, her ankle black-and-blue. With such tender care, he lowered her into the warm, lovely water and he washed her, careful of her cuts and scrapes and bruises, so gentle with her swollen foot.

"You should stay off ladders, I think," he teased as he used tweezers to get the slivers from her palms.

They shared a look. She said, "Are you remembering that night at the villa, too?"

"Yes, I am."

She smiled at him. "I'm also going to try to avoid falling down wells."

"A fine plan."

He got her a soft, old nightgown from the dressing room and helped her put it on. Then he carried her back to the bedroom and tucked her into bed.

She was starving, so Frances brought up a tray of eggs, juice and toast.

Eloise came in a moment later and reported that her parents had arrived.

Rafe said, "Tell them she's all right and so is the baby. Let her eat and see the doctor before they come in."

"One thing more. The sergeant has returned to the village. He said he'll want a concluding interview. It's a formality. He asked if you would call him tomorrow." She kissed Genny on the forehead. "I'm so glad you're home, dearest girl."

"Oh, Eloise. So am I."

Eloise left them alone again. Genny filled her empty stomach, and then Dr. Eldon appeared. He examined her, declared her ankle badly sprained and started giving her instructions for its care.

By then, her eyes just wouldn't stay open. "I can't... stay awake...."

Dr. Eldon nodded. "Sleep, then. Rest is the best healer. I'll tell His Lordship what to do for that ankle."

With a contented sigh, she closed her eyes. Her ankle throbbed. But not enough to keep sleep from settling over her.

When she woke, it was ten in the evening. Her injured ankle was outside the covers, in a soft brace. It ached, but not as bad as it had before.

Her mother was there, at her bedside. Her father and Rory sat in the two slipper chairs near the dark window.

They told her they loved her, that they were so glad she

and the baby were safe and well. She explained how Rafe and Brooke and Geoffrey had saved her.

Her father said, "So, then. You're happy, here at Hartmore, with the DeValerys?"

She laughed. "I *am* a DeValery now, Papa. And there is no place I would rather be than here at Hartmore with them."

"But are you happy?"

She answered, "Yes, I am," without even having to stop and think about it. All right, there were…issues. Things she and Rafe did need to talk about. But being lost at the bottom of a well overnight had put it all in perspective for her somehow.

She and Rafe would work it out. There would be truth and it might be difficult. But she'd chosen her life with him and she would fight tooth and nail to keep it.

"Do you love him?" her father asked. "Are you *in* love with him?" Somehow, he always knew how to hit to the heart of the matter.

"I do and I am."

He laid his warm hand on her brow. "Then I think you'll manage."

"Papa," she said fondly. "You know that I will."

They talked a little more. She learned that her brother Damien and his fiancée, Lucy Cordell, were getting married in Las Vegas at the end of the week. Lucy was studying fashion in New York. They had planned originally to wait until she graduated.

"But they don't want to wait any longer," said her mother.

And Genny laughed softly. "I can understand that."

Later, after her parents had left so that she could rest, Rafe came back.

He stood by the bed in dark trousers and a white shirt,

so broad and solid. He was all she'd ever wanted. Too bad it had taken her so much longer than it should have to figure it all out. He asked if she wanted a mild painkiller. "Dr. Eldon said acetaminophen should be all right, for the baby."

She shook her head. "It's not bothering me that much. And there are things we need to talk about."

"Later," he said in a rough whisper. "When you're stronger."

She shook her head. "We've waited far too long already."

He stood there, just looking at her, for a full count of ten. "All right. If you're certain."

"I am."

He dropped into the chair her mother had sat in earlier. "There are a few things that happened while you were missing."

"Tell me."

"Melinda called Brooke, came clean about everything and promised never to darken our doorstep again."

"I'm glad that she told Brooke the truth."

"And speaking of Brooke, I actually think she's had a change of heart."

Genny nodded. "She seemed…different this afternoon. In a good way."

"She told me she considers you her sister. That she loves you."

Genny gave a low chuckle and felt the slight burn of tears at the back of her throat. "Believe it or not, I always knew that. I love her, too."

"Love…" He repeated the word so softly. She couldn't tell whether he meant it as a musing remark, or his pet name for her.

She drew in a slow breath. "I…had a lot of time to think. That can happen when you're trapped down a well."

He sat forward slightly. "And?"

"I started…I don't know, reliving, remembering moments, events from the past. It helped to distract me from the pain in my ankle and the darkness and the rain coming down, from the water that kept rising, from my terror that I would die in there and so would our baby."

"God, Gen…" There was real pain in his face—pain for *her,* for what she'd lived through in the long night before.

"I'm here." She reached out her hand. He caught it, clasped it. When he let go, she pressed her palm to the slight swell of her belly. "Both of us are safe and well—and I'm not trying to upset you. It's only that there are things that I really do need to tell you."

He sat back purposefully. "Go ahead."

"I thought of you, Rafe. I thought of all the years we've known each other. I thought of our four hot, wild days and nights in March, and the beautiful days and nights since then. And I…I thought of Edward, too."

Rafe shut his eyes. She feared he would turn from her. But then he opened them again and he looked at her steadily.

She continued, "I remembered that day again—that summer day when I was fourteen and saw you kissing Melinda on the boat jetty. Before I came to the lake looking for you, I saw Edward, did I tell you that?"

"I don't think so."

"He flirted with me the way he always did, charming me, making me feel important and feminine and all grown-up. And then some friends of his drove up. He went out to get in the car with them. He ducked into the backseat—and this is the important part. Because I had forgotten what happened next. I think I forgot because I really didn't want to remember...."

"What?" He said it warily, watching her so closely.

"Fiona was in the car, waiting in the backseat. She would only have been nineteen at the time. It couldn't have been more than a few months before she married Gerald. I...saw her face, just a glimpse. She smiled at Edward and reached out a hand to pull him close to her. There was something in the way she looked at him...a look I didn't really understand then. A look of heat and anticipation. Of powerful desire. And last night, in the well? That was when it finally hit me. Fiona was in love with Edward. She was talking about Edward that night last month when she got so drunk. They were lovers, she and Edward. And from what she said that night a month ago, it didn't end when she married Gerald."

Rafe closed his eyes again. He let his head drop back against the chair.

Genny waited—for as long as she could bear it. And then, finally, she pleaded, "Please, Rafe. I need to know. I need the truth. I need to understand."

And in the end, he didn't disappoint her. He lifted his head and he gazed at her, unwavering. "Yes. They were lovers. I think it started when she was very young, fifteen or sixteen. And it kept on. They hid it from Granny and the parents, but not from us—not from Brooke and me. They were...crazy with it, the two of them. Fiona wanted him to marry her. But he wouldn't. So she found her banker and married him, mostly to get even with Edward for not making her his countess."

"But the affair didn't end when she married Gerald."

"No. It went on."

"Dennis and Dexter—they're the banker's, right?" she

asked. At his nod, she added, "I thought so. They look just like Gerald."

"She would have dumped Gerald in an instant if she could have had Edward's baby. And Edward didn't want that, because he never planned to marry her." He slanted her a weary look. "Are you sure you want the rest of it?"

"I do. Yes. All of it, please. I want to know what happened the night of that party at Tillworth, the night of the accident."

He sat forward again. "You won't like it."

"I don't need to like it. I just need the truth."

He braced his elbows on his knees and rested his chin on his fists. "That night, the night of the party, I caught Edward and Fiona in a clinch in the upstairs hall."

"Oh, my God. That's bad. Right there in Gerald's house?"

"Yes. It made me furious. He'd told me the day before that he was going to propose to you, that he was flying to Montedoro at the end of the next week to 'sweep you off your feet.'"

"He actually said that—and then the next night you caught him and Fiona going at it in her husband's house?"

"I'm ashamed to say, my response to the problem was to get very drunk."

"Oh, Rafe. I'm so sorry…"

"You have nothing—*nothing*—to be sorry for." He gathered calm about him and sank back into the chair again. "And then later, because I was thoroughly bagged, Edward insisted he would drive me home."

"Oh, dear Lord…"

"On the way, I got into it with him for planning to drag you into the dog's dinner he'd made of his life. Edward was unrepentant. He said that he loved Fiona, but he'd never thought she would make him a suitable wife. She would bring him no status, not the way that you would. Plus, there was your fortune. He said, 'You know how it is, Rafe. Hartmore requires the earl to take a bride with money.' He said that he was fond of you and you loved Hartmore, so it was perfect. You and he would marry— and he and Fiona could go on as always."

Genny said nothing. Her mouth was hanging open. She remembered to shut it.

And Rafe continued, "So I offered to give him money. I told him I would see that he had whatever funds he needed—and he could leave you out of it. He became offended. Because the earl of Hartmore can marry his money, but he certainly can't stoop to living off the largesse of his younger brother. He insisted again that he was going to marry you. And that's when I pulled out all the stops. I told him that I wouldn't allow it. I said, 'I'm going to go to Gen. And I'm telling her what you just told me.'"

Her heart ached with love for him. "What did he say then?"

"He couldn't believe that I would dare. I think he forgot he was driving. He turned and snarled at me that of course I would never tell you any of it. He said that he knew very well that I was in love with you and you would only hate me if I did such a thing."

Genny's heart soared. "You...were in love with me?"

He didn't answer that. He just went on, "The next turn in the road came up fast. He didn't see it coming. I said, 'Look out!' But he kept on, straight ahead. He was still telling me off when he hit the oak tree."

"Oh, my darling," Genny whispered. "How completely awful."

He stood up, went to the dark window and stared at his own shadowed reflection for a time.

"Rafe. Come here, please. Here to me...."

And he turned and came back to her and stood above her by the side of the bed. "It's all so ugly and shabby and sad. I didn't want you to have to know it."

She reached out, clasped his hand and brought it to her cheek. "Having the truth is never as bad as not knowing, not understanding. And honestly, I only feel sorry. Edward was just a mess, loving one woman and planning to marry another. And I was no prize, was I? Brooke said it. I would have married your brother to be mistress of Hartmore."

He rubbed his thumb so carefully across her bruised cheek. "You love Hartmore. In spite of all of Brooke's carrying on yesterday, nobody here faults you for that."

She gulped. "But they should. I had it all wrong. I wanted Hartmore, so I told myself I loved Edward. It was lies all round."

Keeping hold of her hand, he sat on the bed beside her. "I meant what I said to him. I would have told you the truth before you ever made it to altar. You were never going to marry him. No matter how much you hated me for telling you the truth, I wasn't about to let you ruin your life."

"Oh, Rafe..."

"I regret that I threw it in his face, though. He wouldn't be dead now if I'd only kept my mouth shut that night."

"We can never know what might have happened. You didn't do anything wrong. It really was just an accident. A terrible accident. You've been blaming yourself, and that needs to stop."

He brought her hand to his lips and brushed a kiss across her fingers. "You really are a very domineering woman."

"Yes, I am. And I have deep flaws. But I'm working to improve myself. It's true I've been much too obsessed with Hartmore."

He looked at her unflinching, with such complete acceptance. "It's all right. I understand. Hartmore is and always has been your greatest love."

"Oh, Rafe. That's not true. Not anymore. But I have to confess that I did marry you partly to get Hartmore."

He smiled then. And it was a real smile, more than just the crescent-moon scar. "Only partly?"

"Well, there was the baby and the great sex. And *you*. I mean, we had been such dear friends. I hoped we might find our friendship again."

"And we did, didn't we?"

"Oh, yes. And now, I… Well, for weeks now I've been trying to find a way to tell you…"

He turned her hand over, brought her palm up and pressed his warm lips to it. She shivered in pleasure at that little kiss. And then he asked, "What?"

"You, um, mentioned that Edward said you were in love with me…."

He watched her face for the longest time. At last, he spoke. "I've always loved you, as a friend, as a true comrade, since that summer when you were five and I was thirteen and you talked to me as if I mattered, as though I was more than just my father's oversize, wild-haired whipping boy."

"Oh, my darling…"

"But then you came to us that summer you were seventeen and you had suddenly grown up. And it hit me like a bullet to the chest. I knew that summer that you were the only woman for me. And I also knew that all you'd ever wanted was to marry my brother."

"Dear Lord…since I was seventeen? I can't…"

"Love, you're sputtering."

"Of course I'm sputtering. You just told me that for eight years, you've been in love with me."

"I did. I have."

"But you never said a word to me. I can't believe…"
She thought again. And she found that she *could* believe.
She drew a slow breath. "Sometimes it's so hard to say the
words that matter most."

"It is, yes. You were seventeen and I realized I was in
love with you—and you had been telling me for years that
you were going to marry Edward."

"God, what a twit I was."

He chuckled. "You were very determined. And I had
a lot of pride. I told myself that if you wanted Edward,
well, you could have him. I tried to forget you. And then I
watched all the goings-on with him and Fiona. I realized
that it was going to be a disaster for you if you married
him. When I saw him with Fiona at Tillworth that last
night, I made up my mind, finally, to tell you about the
two of them, no matter if you hated me for it. No matter
if you never spoke to me again. And then Edward died."

"And you blamed yourself."

"I did, yes."

"Truly, Rafe, it wasn't your fault."

"Yes, it was, at least partly. So I tried to stay away
from you."

"But I wouldn't allow that. I tracked you down at Villa
Santorno."

"And then—" he put his hand on the soft swell of her
belly, so gently "—there was the baby. I convinced you
to marry me—and got exactly what I'd always wanted
all along."

"I mean it, Rafe. It's not your fault that Edward died.
And it's not wrong that we are happy together. It's…what
Eloise said to you that day she took you to the West Wing
Gallery and showed you the portrait of Richard DeValery,
that what we all need to do is to live a productive, rich life
anyway, in spite of everything."

He gazed at her so tenderly. "We both know that's not exactly what she said."

"Close enough—and where were we? Ah. You and me, married, and you still hadn't told me how you really felt."

"I couldn't get the words out. I knew that when I finally did say it, when I told you how much I love you, I would have to tell you all of it, about Edward and Fiona and the night Edward died. I knew that the whole story was going to come out."

"Just like it has, at last, tonight."

"Exactly."

"And you weren't ready to do that yet."

"No."

"But tonight...?"

"I knew I had to tell you."

"Because...?"

"Because you didn't come home last night. Because I was afraid I had lost you, lost you without ever telling you what you mean to me. I knew last night that if— *when*— we brought you back to us, there would be no more putting it off."

The tears came then. She swiped them away. "Come here. Right now." She grabbed him against her, jostling her injured ankle in the process. "Ow!"

He tried to pull away. "Your ankle..."

She pulled him close again. "It's fine."

"But—"

"Wrap your arms around me, Rafe. Do it now."

He kicked off his shoes, swung his long legs up on the bed and gathered her into his embrace. "Satisfied?"

She kissed his throat, his chin, his mouth. She traced the crescent scar and he didn't object or try to stop her. And then she said, "I'm in love with you, too. Maybe I've always been in love with you, from the very first, when I was only five. However long it's been that I've been yours in my heart, I couldn't let myself admit that you were the one I loved. I thought it was Hartmore that I longed for. I was such a fool."

"No."

"Yes. I was. A fool. I couldn't see my love for you until after you married me and we had a life together and I realized that somehow, in spite of my own idiocy and pigheadedness, I had gotten exactly what I wanted, what I needed, whom I loved. I used to be blind. But I'm not blind now. I love you with all my heart, Rafe. And I only want to be exactly where I am—and I'm not talking about Hartmore. I would be your wife if we both woke up tomorrow without Hartmore, without a penny to our names. I would still count myself a lucky woman, as long as I could be at your side in the daytime, and in your big arms at night."

He pulled her closer. "It won't be a problem. I'm going nowhere. You're stuck with me."

"Good. That's exactly my plan."

"Forever, Gen."

"Yes, Rafe. Forever and always. We are together in all the ways that matter. We have the truth, together. We have love and commitment and family—and a little one on the way. And nothing and no one can ever tear us apart."

Epilogue

December 18

Genny told Rory goodbye and hung up the phone. Outside, night was falling. A light snow drifted down.

Brooke, over at the window, looked up from the baby she held in her arms. "Thomas Richard DeValery. I like it. And I swear. Two days old and he already looks just like Rafe."

Genny chuckled. "Oh, he's a handsome one, all right."

Brooke came back to the bed and gently put Tommy into his bassinet. She gazed down at him adoringly. "I think I'm going to love being an auntie."

Genny sighed and settled back against the pillows. "It's wonderful, believe me. Aunties get all the glory and they rarely have to say the word *no*."

"Yes." Brooke slanted her a grin. "Being an auntie is definitely for me—and how are you feeling?"

"As though I've been run down by a lorry. But it's better every day. I had to walk up and down hospital hallways more than once before they'd let us out of there."

"Take it easy."

"Well, Brooke. You know that's not my style."

Brooke made a face at her. "You've always been disgustingly resilient. I had postpartum with Geoffrey. It was grim. But I know you'll be up and singing Christmas carols by tomorrow morning, checking on the roof project, telling everyone what to do."

"And you'd better do what I tell you to," Genny advised. "Or you'll be sorry."

Brooke said, "You're such a bitch."

And Genny said, "It's good that we have so much in common." And they both started laughing—until Genny put her hand to her stomach and groaned. "Don't make me laugh. Not for a day or two yet anyway."

The door out in the sitting room opened and shut. Rafe appeared. Genny's heart lifted just at the sight of him. "Geoffrey's looking for you," he said to his sister. "He wants your help wrapping presents. The Sellotape is not cooperating. Granny said she'd help, but he claims you wrap the prettiest packages and he wants his to look as good as yours."

"I'm on it. Genevra, are you hungry? I can have something sent up...."

"Thanks. Not right now."

Rafe said, "I'll see that she eats something later." Brooke left them. Rafe took her place by the bassinet. "Look at him. Sleeping so peacefully. Not a care in the world..."

She held out her hand. Rafe came around and sat beside her on the bed.

He said in a bemused tone, "My sister is happy." Brooke

had been getting counseling and it had really paid off for her.

"Yes, she is."

"Will wonders never cease?"

"It's good to see her doing so well."

"That she wants to be a therapist is a little surprising." He looked vaguely concerned—for Brooke or her future patients, Genny couldn't be sure.

Genny shrugged. "She wants to help others now she's finding out what it's like to clear out all the old emotional baggage. I think she'll be a good therapist—and come closer."

He leaned toward her just a little.

"Closer," she whispered. He bent near enough that their lips could touch. She kissed him, just a light brush of her mouth across his. Her heart felt so full of love. It filled her up, spilling over, bringing light and goodness and complete happiness. She reached up and stroked his scarred cheek. The scar was no more than a thin red line now. In time, it would almost disappear. Or so the plastic surgeon had promised.

He asked, "What did Rory have to say?"

"She told me all about her adventures up in the Rocky Mountains with Walker."

"Walker?" Rafe frowned.

"Yes, Walker, the rancher and trail guide and search-and-rescue expert. It all sounded very exciting—but she's back in Justice Creek now. The wedding's on Saturday." Their Bravo cousin, Clara, was marrying Walker's younger brother, Ryan. "And then she'll fly straight back to Montedoro for Max and Lani's wedding."

He asked, "Are you sad to have to miss your brother's wedding?" Max was getting married two days before Christmas.

"A little. But I knew all along that, with Tommy coming, I wouldn't be able to make it. And besides, I'll have Christmas with you at Hartmore." She gestured toward the window. "And it looks as though there will even be snow."

"Beautiful," he whispered. He wasn't looking out the window.

"Merry Christmas, my darling."

Dark eyes held hers. "Merry Christmas, love. For this year, and all of our years to come."

* * * * *

Watch for Rory and Walker's story,
A BRAVO CHRISTMAS WEDDING,
coming in December 2014.

"Sorry, I didn't mean to take advantage of you like that," he told her, still cupping her cheek with the palm of his hand.

Her voice felt as if it was going to crack at any second as she told him, "You didn't. And there's nothing to be sorry about, except…"

"Except?" he prodded.

Lily shook her head, not wanting to continue. She was only going to embarrass herself—and him—if she said anything further. "I've said too much."

"No," he contradicted, "you've said too little. "'Except' what?" he coaxed.

Lily wavered. Maybe he did deserve to know. So she told him.

"Except maybe it didn't last long enough," she said, her voice hardly above a whisper, her cheeks burning and threatening to turn a deep pink.

"Maybe it didn't," he agreed. "Let's see if I get it right this time," he murmured just before his mouth came down on hers for a second time.

* * *

Matchmaking Mamas:
Playing Cupid. Arranging dates.
What are mothers for?

DIAMOND IN THE RUFF

BY
MARIE FERRARELLA

Published in Great Britain 2014
by Mills & Boon, an imprint of Harlequin (UK) Limited,
Eton House, 18-24 Paradise Road, Richmond, Surrey, TW9 1SR

© 2014 Marie Rydzynski-Ferrarella

ISBN: 978-0-263-91324-8

23-1014

Harlequin (UK) Limited's policy is to use papers that are natural, renewable and recyclable products and made from wood grown in sustainable forests. The logging and manufacturing processes conform to the legal environmental regulations of the country of origin.

Printed and bound in Spain
by Blackprint CPI, Barcelona

A *USA TODAY* bestselling and RITA® Award-winning author, **Marie Ferrarella** has written more than two hundred books for Mills & Boon, some under the name Marie Nicole. Her romances are beloved by fans worldwide. Visit her website, www.marieferrarella.com.

To
Rocky and Audrey
who made my life so much richer
in their own unique way.

Prologue

"You don't remember me, do you?"

Maizie Connors, youthful grandmother, successful Realtor and matchmaker par excellence, looked at the tall, handsome, blond-haired young man standing in the doorway of her real estate office. Mentally, she whizzed through the many faces she had encountered in the past handful of years, both professionally and privately. Try as she might to recall the young man, Maizie came up empty. His smile was familiar, but the rest of him was not.

Ever truthful, Maizie made no attempt to bluff her way through this encounter until she either remembered him or, more to the point, the young man said something that would set off flares in her somewhat overtaxed brain, reminding her who he was.

Instead, Maizie shook her head and admitted, "I'm afraid I don't."

"I was a lot younger back then and I guess I looked more like a blond swizzle stick than anything else," he told her.

She didn't remember the face, but the smile and now the voice nudged at something distant within her mind. Recognition was still frustratingly out of reach. The young man's voice was lower, but the cadence was very familiar. She'd heard it before.

"Your voice is familiar and that smile, I know I've seen it before, but…" Maizie's voice trailed off as she continued to study his face. "I know I didn't sell you a house," she told him with certainty. She would have remembered that.

She remembered *all* of her clients as well as all the couples she, Theresa and Cecilia had brought together over the past few years. As far as Maizie was concerned, she and her lifelong best friends had all found their true calling in life a few years ago when desperation to see their single children married and on their way to creating their own families had the women using their connections in the three separate businesses they owned to find suitable matches for their offspring.

Enormously successful in their undertaking, they found they couldn't stop just because they had run out of their own children to work with. So friends and clients were taken on.

They did their best work covertly, not allowing the two principals in the undertaking know that they were being paired up. The payment the three exacted was not monetary. It was the deep satisfaction that came from knowing they had successfully brought two soul mates together.

But the young man before her was neither a professional client nor a private one. Yet he *was* familiar.

Shrugging her shoulders in a gesture of complete surrender, Maizie said, "I'm afraid you're going to have to take pity on me and tell me why your smile and your voice are so familiar but the rest of you isn't." Even as she said the words aloud, a partial answer suddenly occurred to her. "You're someone's son, aren't you?"

But whose? she wondered. She hadn't been at either of her "careers"—neither the one involving real estate nor the one aimed at finding soul mates—long enough for this young man to have been the result of her work.

So who are you?

"I was," he told her, his blue eyes on hers.

Was.

The moment he said that, it suddenly came to her. "You're Frances Whitman's boy, aren't you?"

He grinned. "Mom always said you were exceedingly sharp. Yes, I'm Frances's son." He said the words with pride.

The name instantly conjured up an image in Maizie's mind, the image of a woman with laughing blue eyes and an easy smile on her lips—always, no matter what adversity she was valiantly facing.

The same smile she was looking at right now.

"Christopher?" Maizie asked haltingly. "Christopher Whitman!" It was no longer a question but an assertion. Maizie threw her arms around him, giving him a warm, fond embrace, which only reached as far up as his chest. "How *are* you?" she asked with enthusiasm.

"I'm doing well, thanks." And then he told her why he'd popped in after all this time. "And it looks like we're going to be neighbors."

"Neighbors?" Maizie repeated, somewhat confused.

There'd been no For Sale signs up on her block. Infinitely aware of every house that went up for sale not just in her neighborhood, but in her city as well, Maizie knew her friend's son was either mistaken or had something confused.

"Yes, I just rented out the empty office two doors down from you," he told her, referring to the strip mall where her real estate office was located.

"Rented it out?" she repeated, waiting for him to tell her just what line of work he was in without having to specifically ask him.

Christopher nodded. "Yes, I thought this was a perfect location for my practice."

She raised her eyebrows in minor surprise and admiration.

"You're a doctor?" It was the first thing she thought of since her own daughter was a pediatrician.

Christopher nodded. "Of furry creatures, large and small," he annotated.

"You're a vet," she concluded.

"—erinarian," he amended. "I find if I just say I'm a vet, I have people thanking me for my service to this country. I don't want to mislead anyone," he explained with a smile she now found dazzling.

"Either way, you'll have people thanking you," Maizie assured him. She took a step back to get a better, fuller view of the young man. He had certainly filled out since she had seen him last. "Christopher Whitman," she repeated in amazement. "You look a great deal like your mother."

"I'll take that as a compliment," he said with a warm smile. "I was always grateful that you and the

other ladies were there for Mom while she was getting her treatments. She didn't tell me she was sick
until it was close to the end," he explained. It was a
sore point for him, but under the circumstances, he'd
had to forgive his mother. There hadn't been any time
left for wounded feelings. "You know how she was.
Very proud."

"Of you," Maizie emphasized. "I remember her
telling me that she didn't want to interfere with your
schooling. She knew you'd drop out if you thought she
needed you."

"I would have," he answered without hesitation.

She heard the note of sadness in his voice that time
still hadn't managed to erase. Maizie quickly changed
the subject. Frances wouldn't have wanted her son to
beat himself up over a decision she had made for him.

"A veterinarian, huh? So what else is new since I
last saw you?" Maizie asked.

Broad shoulders rose and fell in a careless shrug.
"Nothing much."

Habit had Maizie glancing down at his left hand.
It was bare, but that didn't necessarily mean the man
wasn't married. "No Mrs. Veterinarian?"

Christopher laughed softly and shook his head.
"Haven't had the time to find the right woman," he
confessed. It wasn't the truth, but he had no desire
to revisit that painful area yet. "I know Mom would
have hated to hear that excuse, but that's just the way
things are. Well, when I saw your name on the door, I
just wanted to drop by to say hi," he told her, adding,
"Stop by the office sometime when you get a chance
and we'll talk some more about Mom," he promised.

"Yes, indeed," Maizie replied.

As well as other things, she added silently as she watched Christopher walk away, anticipation welling in her chest. *Wait until the girls hear about this.*

Chapter One

Okay, how did it get to be so late?

The exasperated, albeit rhetorical, question echoed almost tauntingly in her brain as Lily Langtry hurried through her house, checking to make sure she hadn't left any of her ground-floor windows open or her back door unlocked. There hadn't been any break-ins in her neighborhood, but she lived alone and felt that you could never be too careful.

The minutes felt as if they were racing by.

There was a time when she was not only on time but early for everything from formal appointments to the everyday events that took place in her life. But that was before her mother had passed away, before she was all alone and the only one who was in charge of the details of her life.

It seemed to her that even when she was taking care

of her mother and holding down the two jobs that paying off her mother's medical bills necessitated, she had usually been far more organized and punctual than she was these days. Now that there was only one of her, in essence only one person to be responsible for, her ability to be on top of things seemed to have gone right out the window. If she intended to be ready by eight, in her mind she had to shoot for seven-thirty—and even that didn't always pan out the way she hoped it would.

This morning she'd told herself she would be out the door by seven. It was now eight-ten and she was just stepping into her high heels.

"Finally," she mumbled as she grabbed her bag and launched herself out the front door while simultaneously searching for her keys. The latter were currently eluding detection somewhere within the nether regions of her oversize purse.

Preoccupied, engaged in the frantic hunt that was making her even later than she already was, Lily wasn't looking where she was going.

Which was why she almost stepped on him.

Looking back, in her defense, she hadn't been expecting anything to be on her doorstep, much less a moving black ball of fur that yipped pathetically when her foot came down on his paw.

Jumping backward, Lily's hand went protectively over her chest to contain the heart that felt as if it was about to leap out of it. Lily dropped her purse at the same time.

Containing more things in it than the average overstuffed suitcase, the purse came down with a thud, further frightening the already frightened black ball of fur—which she now saw was a Labrador puppy.

But instead of running, as per the puppy manual, the large-dog-in-training began to lick her shoe.

Since the high heels Lily had selected to wear this morning were open-toe sandals, the upshot was that the puppy was also licking her toes. The end result of that was that the fast-moving little pink tongue was tickling her toes at the same time.

Surprised, stunned, as well as instantly smitten, Lily crouched down to the puppy's level, her demanding schedule temporarily put on hold.

"Are you lost?" she asked the puppy.

Since she was now down to his level, the black Labrador puppy abandoned her shoes and began to lick her face instead. Had there been a hard part to Lily's heart, it would have turned to utter mush as she completely capitulated, surrendering any semblance of control to her unexpected invader.

When she finally rose back up to her feet, Lily looked in both directions along the residential through street where she lived to see if anyone was running up or down the block, frantically searching for a lost pet.

It was apparent that no one was since all she saw was Mr. Baker across the street getting into his midlife-crisis vehicle—a sky-blue Corvette—which he drove to work every morning.

Since it wasn't moving, Lily took no note of the beige sedan parked farther down the block and across the street. Nor did she notice the older woman who was slouched down in the driver's seat.

The puppy appeared to be all alone.

She looked back at the puppy, who was back to licking her shoes. Pulling first one foot back, then the other, she only succeeded in drawing the dog into her house because the Labrador's attention was completely focused on her shoes.

"Looks like your family hasn't realized that you're missing yet," she told the puppy.

The Lab glanced up, cocking his head as if he was hanging on her every word. Lily couldn't help wondering if the animal understood her. She knew people who maintained that dogs only understood commands that had been drilled into their heads, but she had her doubts about that. This one was actually making eye contact and she was *certain* that he was taking in every word.

"I have to go to work," she told her fuzzy, uninvited guest.

The Labrador continued watching her as if she was the only person in the whole world. Lily knew when she'd lost a battle.

She sighed and stepped back even farther into her foyer, allowing the puppy access to her house.

"Oh, all right, you can come in and stay until I get back," she told the puppy, surrendering to the warm brown eyes that were staring up at her so intently.

If she was letting the animal stay here, she had to leave it something to eat and drink, she realized. Turning on her heel, Lily hurried back the kitchen to leave the puppy a few last-minute survival items.

She filled a soup bowl full of water and extracted a few slices of roast beef she'd picked up from the supermarket deli on her way home last night.

Lily placed the latter on a napkin and put both bowl and napkin on the floor.

"This should hold you until I get back," she informed the puppy. Looking down, she saw that the puppy, who she'd just assumed would follow her to a food source, was otherwise occupied. He was busy gnawing on one of the legs of her kitchen chair. "Hey!" she cried. "Stop that!"

The puppy went right on gnawing until she physically separated him from the chair. He looked up at her, clearly confused.

In her house for less than five minutes and the Labrador puppy had already presented her with a dilemma, Lily thought.

"Oh, God, you're teething, aren't you? If I leave you here, by the time I get back it'll look like a swarm of locusts had come through, won't it?" She knew the answer to that one. Lily sighed. It was true what they said, no good deed went unpunished. "Well, you can't stay here, then." Lily looked around the kitchen and the small family room just beyond. Almost all the furniture, except for the TV monitor, was older than she was. "I don't have any money for new furniture."

As if he understood that he was about to be put out again, the puppy looked up at her and then began to whine.

Pathetically.

Softhearted to begin with, Lily found that she was no match for the sad little four-footed fur ball. Closing the door on him would be akin to abandoning the puppy in a snowdrift.

"All right, all right, all right, you can come with me," she cried, giving in. "Maybe someone at work will have a suggestion as to what I can do with you."

Lily stood for a minute, studying the puppy warily. Would it bite her if she attempted to pick it up? Her experience with dogs was limited to the canines she saw on television. After what she'd just witnessed, she knew that she definitely couldn't leave the puppy alone in her house. At the same time, she did have the uneasy feeling that the Labrador wasn't exactly trained to be obedient yet.

Still, trained or not, she felt as if she should at least *try* to get the puppy to follow her instructions. So she walked back over to the front door. The puppy was watching her every move intently, but remained exactly where he was. Lily tried patting her leg three times in short, quick succession. The puppy cocked its head, as if to say, *Now what?*

"C'mon, boy, come here," Lily called to him, patting her leg again, this time a little more urgently. To her relief—as well as surprise—this time the puppy came up to her without any hesitation.

Opening the front door, Lily patted her leg again—and was rewarded with the same response. The puppy came up to her side—the side she'd just patted—his eager expression all but shouting, *Okay, I'm here. Now what?*

Lily currently had no answer for that, but she hoped to within the hour.

"Hey, I don't remember anyone declaring that this was 'bring your pet to work' day," Alfredo Delgado, one of the chefs that Theresa Manetti employed at her catering company, quipped when Lily walked into the storefront office. She was holding a makeshift leash, fashioned out of rope. The black Lab was on the other end of the leash, ready to give the office a thorough investigation the moment the other end of the leash was dropped.

Theresa walked out of her small inner office and regarded the animal, her expression completely unfathomable.

"I'm sorry I'm late," Lily apologized to the woman who wrote out her checks. "I ran into a snag."

"From here it looks like the snag is following you," Theresa observed.

She glanced expectantly at the young woman she'd taken under her wing a little more than a year ago. That was when she'd hired Lily as her pastry chef after discovering that Lily could create delicacies so delicious, they could make the average person weep. But, softhearted woman that she was, Theresa hadn't taken her on because of her skills so much as because Lily's mother had recently passed away, leaving her daughter all alone in the world. Theresa, like her friends Maizie and Cecilia, had a great capacity for sympathy.

Lily flushed slightly now, her cheeks growing a soft shade of pink.

"I'm sorry, he was just there on my doorstep this morning when I opened the door. I couldn't just leave him there to roam the streets. If I came home tonight and found out that someone had run him over, I wouldn't be able to live with myself."

"Why didn't you just leave him at your place?" Alfredo asked, curious. "That's what I would have done." He volunteered this course of action while bending down, scratching the puppy behind its ears.

"I normally would have done that, too," Lily answered. "But there was one thing wrong with that—he apparently sees the world as one giant chew toy."

"So you brought him here," Theresa concluded. It was neither a question nor an accusation, just a statement of the obvious. A bemused smile played on the older woman's lips as she regarded the animal. "Just make sure he stays out of the kitchen."

Lily gestured around the area, hoping Theresa would see things her way. This was all temporary. "Everything here's made out of metal. His little teeth can't do any damage," she pointed out, then looked back at Theresa hopefully. "Can he stay—just for today?" Lily emphasized.

Theresa pretended to think the matter over—as if she hadn't had a hand in the puppy's sudden magical appearance on her pastry chef's doorstep. After Maizie had mentioned that their late friend's son was opening up his animal hospital two doors down from her real estate office and went on to present him as a possible new candidate for their very unique service, Theresa had suggested getting Christopher together with Lily. She'd felt that the young woman could use something positive happening to her and had been of that opinion for a while now.

The search for a way to bring the two together in a so-called "natural" fashion was quick and fruitful when, as a sidebar, Cecilia had casually asked if either she or Maizie knew of anyone looking to adopt a puppy. Her dog, Princess, had given birth to eight puppies six weeks ago, and the puppies needed to be placed before "they start eating me out of house and home," Cecilia had told her friends.

It was as if lightning had struck. Everything had fallen into place after that.

Theresa was aware of Lily's approximate time of departure and had informed Cecilia. The latter proceeded to leave the puppy—deliberately choosing the runt of the litter—on Lily's doorstep. Cecilia left the rambunctious puppy there not once but actually several times before she hit upon the idea of bribing the little dog with a large treat, which she proceeded to embed in the open weave of the welcome mat.

Even so, Cecilia had just barely made it back to her sedan before Lily had swung open her front door.

Once inside the catering shop, the puppy proceeded to make himself at home while he sniffed and investigated every inch of the place.

Lily watched him like a hawk, afraid of what he might do next. In her opinion, Theresa was a wonderful person, but everyone had their breaking point and she didn't want the puppy to find Theresa's.

"Um, Theresa," Lily began as she shooed the puppy away from a corner where a number of boxes were piled up, "how old are your grandchildren now?"

Theresa slanted a deliberately wary look at the younger woman. "Why?"

Lily smiled a little too broadly as she made her sales pitch. "Wouldn't they love to have a puppy? You could surprise them with Jonathan."

Theresa raised an eyebrow quizzically. "Jonathan?" she repeated.

Lily gestured at the Labrador. "The puppy. I had to call him something," she explained.

"You named him. That means you're already attached to him," Alfredo concluded with a laugh, as if it was a done deal.

There was something akin to a panicky look on Lily's face. She didn't want to get attached to anything. She was still trying to get her life on track after losing her mother. Taking on something new—even a pet—was out of the question.

"No, it doesn't," Lily protested. "I just couldn't keep referring to the puppy as 'it.'"

"Sure you could," Alfredo contradicted with a knowing attitude. "That you didn't want to means that you've already bonded with the little ball of flying fur."

"No, no bonding," Lily denied firmly, then made her final argument on the matter. "I don't even know *how* to bond with an animal. The only pet I ever had was a goldfish and Seymour only lived for two days." Which firmly convinced her that she had absolutely no business trying to care for a pet of any kind.

Alfredo obviously didn't see things in the same light that she did. "Then it's high time you got back into the saddle, Lily. You can't accept defeat that easily," he told her.

Finding no support in that quarter, Lily appealed to her boss. "Theresa—"

Theresa placed a hand supportively on the younger woman's shoulder. "I'm with Alfredo on this," she told Lily. "Besides," she pointed out, "you can't give the dog away right now."

"Why not?" Lily asked.

Theresa was the soul of innocence as she explained, "Because his owner might be out looking for him even as we speak."

Lily blew out a breath. She'd forgotten about that. "Good point," she admitted, chagrinned by her over-sight. "I'll make flyers and put them up."

"In the meantime," Theresa continued as she thoughtfully regarded the black ball of fur and paws, "I suggest you make sure the little guy's healthy."

"How do I go about doing that?" Lily asked, completely clueless when it came to the care of anything other than humans. She freely admitted to having a brown thumb. Anything that was green and thriving would begin to whither and die under her care—which was why she didn't attempt to maintain a garden anymore. The thought of caring for a pet brought a chill to her spine.

"Well, for starters," Theresa told her, "if I were you I would bring him to a veterinarian."

"A vet?" she looked at the puppy that now appeared to be utterly enamored with Alfredo. The chef was scratching Jonathan behind the ears and along his nose, sending the Labrador to seventh heaven. "He doesn't look sick. Is that really necessary?"

"Absolutely," Theresa answered without a drop of hesitation. "Just think, if someone is looking for him, how would it look if you handed over a sick dog? If they wanted to, they could turn around and sue you for negligence."

Lily felt hemmed in. The last thing she wanted was to have to take care of something, to get involved with a living, breathing entity.

Eyeing the puppy uncertainly, Lily sighed. "I should have never opened the door this morning."

"Oh, how can you say that? Look at this adorable little face," Theresa urged, cupping the puppy's chin and turning his head toward Lily.

"I'm trying not to," Lily answered honestly. But Theresa was right. She didn't want to chance something happening to the puppy while it was temporarily in her care. Emphasis on the word *temporarily,* she thought. "Okay, how do I go about finding an animal doctor who's good, but not expensive? I wouldn't know where to start," she admitted, looking to Theresa for guidance since the woman had been the one to bring up the matter of a vet to begin with.

Theresa's smile bordered on being beatific. "Well, as luck would have it, I happen to know of one who just opened up a new practice a few doors down from one of my best friends. She took her dog to him and told me that he performed nothing short of a miracle on Lazarus." The fact that Maizie didn't have a dog named Lazarus, or a dog named anything else for that matter, was an unimportant, minor detail in the grand scheme of things. As a rule, Theresa didn't lie, but there were times—such as now—when rules were meant to be bent if not altogether broken. "Why don't I call her to get his phone number for you?" she suggested, looking at Lily.

That sounded like as good a plan as any, she supposed. "Sure, why not?" Lily replied with a vague shrug, resigned to this course of action. "What do I have to lose? It's only money, right?"

Theresa knew that times were tight for the younger woman. She saw what she was about to propose as an investment in Lily's future happiness.

"I tell you what. We've had a great month. I'll pay for 'Jonathan's' visit," she offered, petting the eager puppy on the head. The dog stopped roaming around long enough to absorb the head pat and then went back to sniffing the entire area for a second time. "Consider it my gift to you."

"How about me?" Alfredo said, pretending to feel left out. "Got any gifts for me, boss?"

"I'll pay for your visit to the vet, too, if you decide

you need to go," Theresa quipped as she retreated into her office.

Once inside, Theresa carefully closed the door and crossed to her desk. She didn't care for cell phones. The connection was never as clear as a landline in her opinion. Picking up the receiver, she quickly dialed the number she wanted to reach.

Maizie picked up on the second ring. "Connors' Realty."

"Houston, we have liftoff," Theresa announced in what sounded like a stage whisper to her own ear.

"Theresa?" Maizie asked uncertainly. "Is that you?"

"Of course it's me. Who else would call you and say that?"

"I haven't the vaguest idea. Theresa, I mean this in the kindest way, but you've definitely been watching too many movies, woman. Now, what is it that you're trying to say?"

Impatience wove through every word. "That Lily is bringing the puppy to Frances's son."

"Then why didn't you just say so?"

"Because it sounds so ordinary that way," Theresa complained.

"Sometimes, Theresa, ordinary is just fine. Is she bringing the puppy in today?"

"That's what I urged her to do."

"Perfect," Maizie said with heartfelt enthusiasm. "Nothing like being two doors down from young love about to unfold."

"I don't see how that's any different from Houston, we have liftoff," Theresa protested.

"Maybe it's not, Theresa," Maizie conceded, not because she thought she was wrong, but because she knew Theresa liked to be right. "Maybe it's not."

Chapter Two

The first thing that struck Christopher when he walked into Exam Room 3 was that the woman was standing rather than sitting. She was clearly uneasy in her present situation. The puppy with her appeared to have the upper hand.

Smiling at her, he made a quick assessment before he spoke. "This isn't your dog, is it?"

Lily looked at the veterinarian, stunned. "How can you tell?" she asked.

All she had given the receptionist out front was her name. The dark-haired woman had immediately nodded and told her that "Mrs. Manetti called to say you'd be coming in." The young woman at the desk, Erika, had then proceeded to call over one of the veterinary aides, who promptly ushered her and Jonathan into an exam room. As far as she knew, no details about her nonrelationship to the animal she'd brought in had been given.

Maybe she was wrong, Lily realized belatedly.

"Did Theresa tell you that?" she asked.

"Theresa?" Christopher repeated, confused.

Okay, wrong guess, Lily decided. She shook her head. "Never mind," she told him, then repeated her initial question. "How can you tell he's not mine?" Was there some sort of look that pet owners had? Some sort of inherent sign that the civilian non–pet owners obviously seemed to lack?

Christopher nodded toward the antsy puppy who looked as if he was ready to race around all four of the exam room's corners almost simultaneously. "He has a rope around his neck," Christopher pointed out.

He probably equated that with cruelty to animals, Lily thought. "Necessity is the mother of invention," she told him, then explained her thinking. "I made a loop and tied a rope to it because I didn't have any other way to make sure that he would follow me."

There was a stirring vulnerability about the young woman with the long, chestnut hair. It pulled him in. Christopher looked at her thoughtfully, taking care not to allow his amusement at her action to show. Some people were thin-skinned and would construe that as being laughed at. Nothing could have been further from the truth.

"No leash," he concluded.

"No leash," Lily confirmed. Then, because she thought that he needed more information to go on— and she had no idea what was and wasn't important when it came to assessing the health of a puppy—she went on to tell the good-looking vet, "I found him on my doorstep—I tripped over him, actually."

The way she said it led Christopher to his next conclusion. "And I take it that you don't know who he belongs to?"

"No, I don't. If I did," Lily added quickly, "I would have brought him back to his owner. But I've never seen him before this morning."

"Then how do you know the dog's name is Jonathan?" As far as he could see, the puppy had no dog tags.

She shrugged almost as if she was dismissing the question. "I don't."

Christopher looked at her a little more closely. Okay, he thought, something was definitely off here. "When you brought him in, you told my receptionist that his name was Jonathan."

"That's what I call him," she responded quickly, then explained, "I didn't want to just refer to him as 'puppy' or 'hey, you' so I gave him a name." The young woman shrugged and the simple gesture struck him as being somewhat hapless. "He seems to like it. At least he looks up at me when I call him by that name."

Christopher didn't want her being under the wrong impression, even if there was no real harm in thinking that way.

"The right intonation does that," he told Lily. "I'll let you in on a secret," Christopher went on, lowering his voice as if this was a guarded confession he was about to impart. "He'd respond to 'Refrigerator' if you said it the same way."

To prove his point, Christopher moved around the exam table until he was directly behind the puppy.

Once there, he called, "Refrigerator!" and Jonathan turned his head around to look at him, taking a few follow-up steps in order to better see who was calling him.

His point proven, Christopher glanced at the woman. "See?"

She nodded, but in Christopher's opinion the woman appeared more overwhelmed than convinced. He had been born loving animals, and as far back as he could remember, his world had been filled with critters large and small. He had an affinity for them, something that his mother had passed on to him.

He was of the mind that everyone should have a pet and that pets improved their owners' quality of life— as well as vice versa.

"Just how long have you and Jonathan been together?" he asked. His guess was that it couldn't have been too long because she and the puppy hadn't found their proper rhythm yet.

Lily glanced at her watch before she answered the vet. "In ten minutes it'll be three hours—or so," she replied.

"Three hours," he repeated.

"Or so," she added in a small voice. Christopher paused for a moment. Studying the petite, attractive young woman before him, his eyes crinkled with the smile that was taking over his face.

"You've never had a dog before, have you?" The question was rhetorical. He should have seen this from the very start. The woman definitely did not seem at ease around the puppy.

"It shows?" She didn't know which she felt more, surprised or embarrassed by the question.

"You look like you're afraid of Jonathan," he told her.

"I'm not," she protested with a bit too much feeling. Then, when the vet made no comment but continued looking at her, she dialed her defensiveness back a little. "Well, not entirely." And then, after another beat, she amended that by saying, "He's cute and everything, but he has these teeth…"

Christopher suppressed a laugh. "Most dogs do. At least," he corrected himself, thinking of a neglected dog he'd treated at the city's animal shelter just the other day, "the healthy ones do."

She wasn't expressing herself correctly, Lily realized. But then, communication was sometimes hard for her. Her skill lay in the pastries she created, not in getting her thoughts across to people she didn't know.

Lily tried again. "But Jonathan's always biting,"

"There's a reason for that. He's teething," Christopher told her. "When I was a kid, I had a cousin like that," he confided. "Chewed on everything and everyone until all his baby teeth came in."

As if to illustrate what he was saying, she saw the puppy attempt to sink his teeth into the vet's hand. Instead of yelping, Christopher laughed, rubbed the Labrador's head affectionately. Before Jonathan could try to bite him a second time, the vet pulled a rubber squeaky toy out of his lab coat pocket. Distracted, Jonathan went after the toy—a lime-green octopus with wiggly limbs.

High-pitched squeaks filled the air in direct proportion to the energy the puppy was expending chewing on his new toy.

Just for a second, there was a touch of envy in her eyes when she raised them to his face, Christopher thought. Her cheeks were also turning a very light shade of pink.

"You probably think I'm an idiot," Lily told him.

The last thing he wanted was for her to think he was judging her—harshly or otherwise. But he could admit he was attracted to her.

"What I think," he corrected, "is that you might need a little help and guidance here."

Oh, God, yes, she almost exclaimed out loud, managing to bite the gush of words back at the last moment. Instead, she asked hopefully, "You have a book for me to read?"

Christopher inclined his head. He had something a little more personal and immediate in mind. "If you'd like to read one, I have several I could recommend," he conceded. "But personally, I've always found it easier when I had something visual to go on."

"Like a DVD?" she asked, not altogether sure what he meant by his statement.

Christopher grinned. "More like a *P-E-R-S-O-N.*"

For just a second, Lily found herself getting caught up in the vet's grin. Something akin to a knot—or was that a butterfly?—twisted around in her stomach. Rousing herself, Lily blinked, certain that she'd somehow misunderstood the veterinarian.

From his handsome, dimpled face, to his dirty-blond hair, to his broad shoulders, the man was a symphony of absolute charm and she was rather accustomed to being almost invisible around people who came across so dynamically. The more vibrant they were, the more understated she became, as if she was shrinking in the sunlight of their effervescence.

Given that, it seemed almost implausible to her that

Christopher was saying what it sounded as if he was saying. But in the interest of clarity, she had to ask, "Are you volunteering to help me with the dog?"

To her surprise, rather than appearing annoyed or waving away the question entirely, he laughed. "If you have to ask, I must be doing it wrong, but yes, I'm volunteering." Then he backtracked slightly as if another thought had occurred to him. "Unless, of course, your husband or boyfriend or significant other has some objections to my mentoring you through the hallowed halls of puppy ownership."

Her self-image—that of being a single person—was so ingrained in her that Lily just assumed she came across that way. That the vet made such a stipulation seemed almost foreign to her.

"There's no husband or boyfriend or significant other to object to anything," she informed the man.

She was instantly rewarded with the flash of another dimpled grin. "Oh, well then, unless you have any objections, I can accompany you to the local dog park this weekend for some pointers."

She hadn't even been aware that there was a dog park anywhere, much less one here in Bedford, but she kept that lack of knowledge to herself.

"Although," the vet was saying, "I do have one thing to correct already."

Lily braced herself for criticism as she asked, "What am I doing wrong?"

Christopher shook his head. "Not you, me," he told her affably. "I just said puppy ownership."

She was still in the dark as to where this was going. "Yes, I know, I heard you."

"Well, that's actually wrong," he told her. "That

phrase would indicate that you owned the puppy when in reality—"

"The puppy owns me?" she guessed. Where else could he be headed with this? She could very easily see the puppy taking over.

But Christopher shook his head. "You own each other, and sometimes even those lines get a little blurred," he admitted, then went on to tell her, "You do it right and your pet becomes part of your family and you become part of his family."

For a moment, Lily forgot to resist experiencing the exact feelings that the vet was talking about. Instead, just for that one sliver of time, she allowed herself to believe that she was part of something larger than just herself, and it promised to ease the loneliness she was so acutely aware of whenever she wasn't at work.

Whenever she left the people she worked with and returned to her house and her solitary existence.

The next moment, she forced herself to lock down and pull back, retreating into the Spartan world she'd resided in ever since she'd lost her mother.

"That sounds like something I once read in a children's book," she told him politely.

"Probably was," Christopher willingly conceded. "Children see the world far more honestly than we do. They don't usually have to make up excuses or search for ways to explain away what they feel—they just *feel*," he said with emphasis as well as no small amount of admiration.

And then he got back to the business at hand. "Since you can count the length of your relationship with Jonathan in hours, I take it that means you have no information regarding his rather short history."

She shook her head. "None whatsoever, I'm afraid," she confessed.

Christopher took it all in stride. He turned his attention to his four-footed patient. "Well, I'm making a guess as to his age—"

Curious about the sort of procedures that involved, she asked, "How can you do that?"

"His teeth," Christopher pointed out. "The same teeth he's been trying out on you," he added with an indulgent smile that seemed incredibly sexy to her. "He's got his baby teeth. He appears to be a purebred Labrador, so there aren't any stray factors to take into account regarding his size and growth pattern. Given his teeth and the size of his paws in comparison to the rest of him, I'd say he's no more than five or six weeks old. And I think I can also safely predict that he's going to be a *very* large dog, given the size of the paws he's going to grow into," the vet concluded.

She looked down at the puppy. Jonathan seemed to be falling all over himself in an attempt to engage the vet's attention. No matter which way she sliced it, the puppy *was* cute—as long as he wasn't actively biting her.

"Well, I guess that's something I'm not going to find out," she murmured, more to herself than to the man on the other side of the exam table.

Christopher watched her with deep curiosity in his eyes. "Do you mind if I ask why not?"

"No."

"No?" he repeated, not really certain what the answer pertained to.

Her mind was *really* working in slow motion today,

Lily thought, upbraiding herself. "I mean no, I don't mind you asking."

When there was no further information following that up, he coaxed, "And the answer to my question is—?"

"Oh."

More blushing accompanied the single-syllable word. She really was behaving like the proverbial village idiot. Lily upbraided herself. What in heaven's name had come over her? It was like her brain had been dipped in molasses and couldn't rinse itself off in order to return to its normal speed—or even the bare semblance of going half-speed.

"Because as soon as I leave here with Jonathan, I'm going to make some flyers and post them around town," she told the vet. She was rather a fair sketch artist when she put her mind to it and planned to create a likeness of this puppy to use on the poster. "Somebody's got to be out looking for him."

"If you're not planning on keeping him, why did you bring him in to be examined?"

She would have thought that he, as a vet, would have thought the reason was self-explanatory. She told him anyway.

"Well, I didn't want to take a chance that there might be something wrong with him. I wouldn't want to neglect taking care of something just because I wasn't keeping it," she answered.

"So you're like a drive-by Good Samaritan?"

She shrugged off what might have been construed as a compliment. From her point of view, there was really nothing to compliment. She was only doing what

anyone else in her place would do—if they had any
kind of a conscience, Lily silently qualified.

Out loud, she merely replied, "Yes, something like
that."

"I guess 'Jonathan' here was lucky it was your front
step he picked to camp out on." He crouched down to
the dog's level. "Aren't you, boy?" he asked with affection, stroking the puppy's head again.

As before, the dog reacted with enthusiasm, driving the top of his head into the vet's hand as well as
leaning in to rub his head against Christopher's side.

Watching the puppy, Lily thought that the Labrador
was trying to meld with the vet.

"Tell you what," Christopher proposed after giving the puppy a quick examination and rising back up
again, "since he seems healthy enough, why don't we
hold off until after this weekend before continuing with
this exam? Then, if no one responds to your 'found'
flyers, you bring Jonathan here back and I'll start him
out on his series of immunizations."

"Immunizations?" Lily questioned.

By the sound of her voice, it seemed to Christopher
that the shapely young woman hadn't given that idea
any thought at all. But then she'd admitted that she'd
never had a pet before, so her lack of knowledge wasn't
really that unusual.

"Dogs need to be immunized, just like kids," he
told her.

Somewhere in the back of her mind, a stray fact
fell into place. She recalled having heard that once or
twice. "Right," she murmured.

Christopher smiled in response to her tacit agreement. "And," he continued, "if you don't get a call from

a frantic owner by this weekend, why don't we make a date to meet at the park on Sunday, say about eleven o'clock?" he further suggested.

"A date," she echoed.

Given the way her eyes had widened, the word *date* was not the one he should have used, Christopher realized. It had been carelessly thrown out there on his part.

Very smoothly, Christopher extricated himself from what could potentially be a very sticky situation. "Yes, but I have a feeling that Jonathan might not be comfortable with my advertising the situation, so for simplicity's sake—and possibly to save Jonathan's reputation," he amended with a wink that had her stomach doing an unexpected jackknife dive off the high board—again, "why don't we just call the meeting a training session?"

Training session.

That phrase conjured up an image that involved a great deal of work. "You'd do that?" she asked incredulously.

"Call it a training session? Sure."

"No, I mean actually volunteer to show me how to train Jonathan—provided I still have him," she qualified.

"I thought that part was clear," Christopher said with a smile.

But Lily had already moved on to another question. "Why?"

"Why did I think that was clear?" he guessed. "Because I couldn't say it any more straightforwardly than that."

She really *did* need to learn how to express herself

better. "No, I mean why would you volunteer to show me how to train the dog?"

"Because, from personal experience, I know that living with an untrained dog can be hell—for both the dog and the person. Training the dog is just another name for mutual survival," he told her.

"But aren't you busy?" she asked him, feeling guilty about taking the vet away from whatever he had planned for the weekend. Grateful though she was, she wondered if she came across that needy or inept to him.

Christopher thought of the unopened boxes that were throughout his house—and had been for the past three months—waiting to be emptied and their contents put away. He'd moved back into his old home, never having gotten around to selling it after his mother had passed away. Now it only seemed like the natural place to return to. But the boxes were taunting him. Helping this woman find her footing with the overactive puppy gave him a good excuse to procrastinate a little longer.

"No more than the average human being," he told her.

"If the dog is still with me by the weekend," she prefaced, "I still can't pay you for the training session. At least, not all at once. But we could arrange for some sort of a payment schedule," she suggested, not wanting to seem ungrateful.

"I don't remember asking to be paid," Christopher pointed out.

"Then why would you go out of your way like that to help me?" she asked, bewildered.

"Call it earning a long-overdue merit badge."

She opened her mouth to protest that she wasn't a

charity case, but just then one of his assistants knocked on the door.

"Doctor, your patients are piling up," she said through the door.

"I'll be right there," he told the assistant, then turned to Lily. "I'll see you at the dog park on Sunday at eleven," he said. "Oh, and if you have any questions, don't hesitate to call. I can be reached here during the day and on my cell after hours."

"You take calls after hours?" Lily asked him, surprised.

"I've found that pets, like kids, don't always conveniently get sick between the hours of eight and six," he told her, opening the door.

"Wait, how much do I owe you for today?" she asked, forgetting that there was a receptionist at the front desk who would most likely be the one taking care of any and all charges for today's visit.

Christopher started to head out. He could hear his next patient barking impatiently from all the way down the hall. Without breaking stride, he told Lily, "I don't charge for conversations."

He was gone before she could protest and remind him that he *had* given Jonathan a cursory examination.

Chapter Three

Lily was certain she hadn't heard the man correctly. Granted, Jonathan hadn't received any shots or had any specimens taken for a lab workup, but the veterinarian *had* spent at least twenty minutes talking to her about the puppy and he *had* looked the Labrador over. In her book, that sort of thing had to constitute an "office visit."

Didn't it?

While she was more than willing to do favors for people, Lily had never liked being on the receiving end of a favor because it put her in the position of owing someone something. She was grateful to the vet for taking an interest in the puppy that was temporarily in her care and she was happy that he'd offered to instruct her on how to maintain a peaceful coexistence with the ball of fur while the puppy *was* in her care, but she wasn't about to accept any of that for free.

It wouldn't be right.

Taking a breath, Lily extracted her checkbook from her jumbled purse and then braced herself for her next confrontation with the puppy.

Doing her best to sound stern, or at least authoritative, she looked down at Jonathan and said, "We're going out now, Jonathan. Try not to yank me all over this time, all right?"

If the puppy understood what she was asking, then he chose to ignore it because the minute she opened the door, he all but flew out. Since the rope she had tethered to the Labrador was currently also wrapped around her hand, the puppy, perforce, came to an abrupt, almost comical halt two seconds later. He'd run out of slack.

The puppy gave her what seemed to Lily to be a reproving look—if puppies could look at someone reprovingly.

Maybe she was reading too much into it, Lily told herself.

Still, she felt compelled to tell the puppy, "I asked you not to run."

Making her way out to the front of the clinic, Lily saw the receptionist, Erika, looking at her. She flushed a little in response. "You probably think I'm crazy, talking to the dog."

Erika's dark eyes sparkled. "On the contrary, most pet owners would think you're crazy if you didn't. They understand us," she explained with easy confidence, nodding toward Jonathan. "They just sometimes choose not to listen. In that way, they're really no different than kids," Erika added. "Except that pets are probably more loyal in the long run."

"I'm not planning for a 'long run,'" Lily told the receptionist. "I'm just minding this puppy until his owner turns up to claim him," she explained. Placing her checkbook on her side of the counter, she opened it to the next blank check, then took out her pen. All the while, Jonathan was tugging on the rope, trying to separate himself from her. "Okay, how much do I make the check out for?" She flashed a somewhat shy smile at the receptionist. "I warn you, it might be slightly illegible."

Jonathan was tugging on his makeshift leash, desperately wanting to escape from the clinic—and in all likelihood, from her, as well. Legible writing under those circumstances went out the window.

Erika glanced at the paperwork that had just been sent to her computer monitor a moment ago. She looked up at the woman on the other side of her desk. "Nothing," she answered.

That couldn't be right. Could the vet really have been serious about not charging her? "For the visit," Lily prompted.

"Nothing," Erika repeated.

"But Dr. Whitman saw the dog," Lily protested.

Erika looked at the screen again.

"Well, he's not charging you for seeing the dog," Erika told her. "But now that I look, I see that he does have one thing written down here," the receptionist informed her, reading the column marked "special instructions."

Lily could feel her arm being elongated by the second. For a little guy, the Labrador was uncommonly strong in her opinion. She tugged him back. "What?" she asked the receptionist.

Instead of answering her immediately, Erika said, "Just a minute," and opened the large side drawer. She started rummaging through it. It took her a minute to locate what she was searching for.

"Dr. Whitman wants me to give you this."

"This" turned out to be not one thing but two things. One item was a small, bright blue braided collar made to fit the neck of a dog just about the puppy's size and the other was a matching bright blue braided leash.

Erika placed both on the counter in front of Jonathan's keeper.

"It's a collar and leash," Erika prompted when the woman with Jonathan continued just to look at the two items. "Dr. Whitman has a 'thing' against ropes. He's afraid that a pet might wind up choking itself," she confided.

Given the Labrador's propensity for dashing practically in two directions at the same time, getting a sturdy leash that wouldn't bite into his tender throat did make sense to her, Lily thought. She certainly wasn't about to refuse to accept the collar and leash.

"Okay, so what do I owe you for the collar and leash?" she asked.

The answer turned out to be the same. "Nothing," Erika replied.

She'd heard of nonprofit, but this was ridiculous. "They have to cost *something,*" Lily insisted.

All of her life, she'd had to pay, and sometimes pay dearly, for everything she had ever needed or used. Taking something, whether it involved a service that was rendered or an item that was given to her, without the benefit of payment just didn't seem right to Lily. It also offended her sense of independence.

"Just pennies," Erika told her. When she looked at the young woman skeptically, the receptionist explained, "Dr. Whitman orders them practically by the crate full. He likes to give them out. Just think of it as a gesture of goodwill," Erika advised.

What she thought of it as was a gesture of charity placing her in debt, however minor the act seemed to the vet.

Lily tried one last time. "You're sure I can't pay you, make a contribution to your needy-dog fund, *something?*"

"I'm sure," Erika replied. She pointed to her monitor as if to drive the point home. "It says right here, 'no charge.'" The woman hit two keys and the printer on the stand behind her came to life, spitting out a hard copy of what was on her monitor. She handed what amounted to a nonreceipt to the puppy's keeper. "See?" Erika asked with a smile.

Lily took the single sheet of paper. Unable to pay for either the office visit or the two items now in her possession, all she could do was say thank you—which she did.

"No problem," Erika replied. She got up from her desk and came around to the other side, where the Labrador stood fiercely yanking against the rope.

"Why don't I put the collar on him while you try to hold him in place?" Erika suggested. "This way, he won't make a break for it."

"You're a godsend," Lily said with a relieved sigh. She'd been wondering just how to manage to exchange the rope for the collar and leash she'd just been given without having the puppy make a mad dash for freedom.

"No, just an animal clinic receptionist who's been at it for a while," Erika corrected modestly.

She had the collar on the puppy and the leash connected to it within a couple of minutes. Only at that point did she undo the rope. The next moment, the rope hung limp and useless in Lily's hand.

Lily was quick to leave it on the desk.

Standing up, Erika told her, "You're ready to go." The words were no sooner out of her mouth than Jonathan made an urgent, insistent beeline for the front door. "I think Jonathan agrees," Erika said with a laugh. "Here, I'll hold the door open for you," she offered, striding quickly over to it.

The instant the door was opened and no longer presented an obstacle, the dog made a break for the outside world and freedom. Lily was nearly thrown off balance as he took her with him.

"Bye!" she called out, tossing the words over her shoulder as she trotted quickly in the dog's wake, trying hard to keep up and even harder to keep from falling. Jonathan seemed oblivious to any and all attempts to rein him in.

Erika shook her head as she closed the door and went back to her desk. "I give them two weeks. A month, tops," she murmured to herself.

The second she and her energetic, furry companion returned to Theresa's catering shop, Lily found herself surrounded by everyone she worked with. They were all firing questions at her regarding Jonathan's visit to the new animal hospital. He was the center of attention and appeared to be enjoying himself, barking and licking the hands that were reaching out to pet him.

To her amazement, Lily discovered that of the small band of people who worked for Theresa's catering company, she was the only one who had never had a pet—if she discounted the two-day period, twenty years ago, during which time she had a live goldfish.

Consequently, while keeping Jonathan out of the kitchen area for practical reasons that in no small way involved the Board of Health's regulations, the puppy was allowed to roam freely about the rest of the storefront office. As a result, Jonathan was petted, played with, cooed over and fed unsparingly by everyone, including Theresa. He became the company's mascot in a matter of minutes.

Because their next catering event wasn't until the next evening, the atmosphere within the shop wasn't as hectic and tense as it could sometimes get. Alfredo and his crew were still in the planning and preparation stages for the next day's main menu. Zack Collins, Theresa's resident bartender, was out purchasing the wines and alcoholic beverages that were to be served at the celebration, and Lily was in the semifinal preparation stage, planning just what desserts to create for the occasion.

Checking on everyone's progress, Theresa observed that Lily was doing more than just planning. She was also baking a tray of what appeared to be lighter-than-air crème-filled pastries.

"Did you decide to do a dry run?" Theresa asked, coming up to the young woman.

"In a manner of speaking," Lily replied. Then, because Theresa was more like a mother to her than a boss, Lily paused for a moment and told the woman what was on her mind. "You know that vet you had me bring Jonathan to?"

Theresa's expression gave nothing away, even as her mind raced around, bracing for a problem or some sort of a hiccup in Maizie's plan.

"Yes?"

"He wouldn't let me pay him for the visit," Lily concluded with a perturbed frown.

"Really?" Theresa did her best to infuse the single word with surprise and wonder—rather than the triumphant pleasure, laced with hope, she was experiencing.

"Really," Lily repeated. "I don't like owing people," she continued.

"Honey, sometimes you just have to graciously accept things from other people," Theresa began. But Lily interrupted her.

"I know. That's why I'm doing this," she told Theresa, gesturing at the tray she'd just taken out of the oven. "I thought that since he was nice enough to 'gift' me with his knowledge by checking out Jonathan, I should return the favor and 'gift' him with what I do best."

By now, Theresa was all but beaming. Maizie had gotten it right again, she couldn't help thinking.

"Sounds perfectly reasonable to me," Theresa agreed. She glanced at her watch. It was getting to be close to four o'clock. Maizie had mentioned that Christopher closed the doors to the animal clinic at six. She didn't want Lily to miss encountering the vet. "Since we're not actively catering anything today, why don't you take a run back to the animal clinic and bring that vet your pastries while they're still warm from the oven?" Theresa suggested.

Lily flashed her boss a grateful smile since she was perfectly willing to do just that. But first she had to take care of a more-than-minor detail.

Lily looked around. "Where's Jonathan?"

"Meghan's keeping him occupied," Theresa assured her, referring to one of the servers she had in her permanent employ. In a pinch, the young, resourceful blonde also substituted as a bartender when Zack was otherwise occupied or unavailable. "Why?" She smiled broadly. "Are you worried about him?"

"I just didn't want to leave the puppy here on his own while I make a run to the vet's office." She didn't want to even *begin* to tally the amount of damage the little puppy could do in a very short amount of time.

"He's not on his own," Theresa contradicted. "There are approximately eight sets of eyes on that dog at all times. If anything, he might become paranoid. Go, bring your thank-you pastries to the vet. Sounds as if he might just have earned them," the older woman speculated.

At the last moment, Lily looked at her hesitantly. "If you don't mind," Lily qualified.

"I wouldn't be pushing you out the door if I minded," Theresa pointed out. "Now shoo!" she ordered, gesturing the pastry chef out the door.

She was gone before Theresa could finish saying the last word.

When the bell announced the arrival of yet another patient, Christopher had to consciously refrain from releasing a loud sigh. It wasn't that he minded seeing patients, because he didn't. He enjoyed it, even when he was being challenged or confounded by a pet's condition. Plus, his new practice took all his time, which he didn't mind. It was paperwork that he hated. Paperwork of any kind was tedious, even though he readily admitted that it needed to be done.

Which was why he had two different receptionists, one in the morning, one in the afternoon, to do the inputting and to keep track of things.

However, on occasion, when one or the other was away for longer than ten minutes, he took over and manned the desk, so to speak.

That was what he was currently doing because Erika had taken a quick run to the local take-out place in order to buy and bring back dinner for the office. He looked up from the keyboard to see just who had entered.

"You're back," Christopher said with surprise when he saw Lily coming in. The moment she stepped inside, she filled the waiting area with her unconscious, natural sexiness. Before he knew it, he found himself under her spell. "Is something wrong with Jonathan?" It was the first thing that occurred to him.

And then he noticed that she was carrying a rectangular pink cardboard box. Another animal to examine? No, that couldn't be it. There were no air holes punched into the box, which would mean, under normal circumstances, that it wasn't some stray white mouse or rat she was bringing to him.

"You brought me another patient?" he asked a little warily.

"What?" She saw that he was eyeing the box in her hand and realized belatedly what he had to be thinking. "Oh, this isn't anything to examine," she told him. "At least, not the way you mean."

He had no idea what that meant.

By now, the savory aroma wafting out of the box had reached him and he could feel his taste buds coming to attention.

"What *is* that?" he asked her, leaving the shelter of the reception desk and coming closer. He thought he detected the scent of cinnamon, among other things. "That aroma is nothing short of fantastic."

Lily smiled broadly. "Thank you."

He looked at her in confused surprise. "Is that you?" he asked, slightly bemused.

Was that some sort of new cologne, meant to arouse a man's appetites, the noncarnal variety? He could almost *feel* his mouth watering.

"Only in a manner of speaking," Lily replied with a laugh. When Christopher looked even further confused, she took pity on him and thrust the rectangular box at him. "These are for you— and your staff," she added in case he thought she was singling him out and trying to flirt with him—although she was certain he probably had to endure the latter on a regular basis. Men as good-looking as Christopher Whitman *never* went unnoticed. From his thick, straight dirty-blond hair, to his tall, lean body, to his magnetic blue eyes that seemed to look right *into* her, the man stood out in any crowd.

"It's just my small way of saying thank you," she added.

"You bought these for us?" Christopher asked, taking the box from her.

"No," Lily corrected, "I *made* these for you. I'm a

pastry chef," she explained quickly, in case he thought she was just someone who had slapped together the first dessert recipe she came across on the internet. She wasn't altogether sure what prompted her, but she wanted him to know that in her own way she was a professional, too. "I work for a catering company," she added, then thought that she was probably blurting out more details than the man wanted to hear. "Anyway, since you wouldn't let me pay you, I wanted to do something nice for you. It's all-natural," she told him. "No artificial additives, no gluten, no nuts," she added, in case he was allergic to them the way her childhood best friend had been. "It's all perfectly safe," she assured him.

"Well, it smells absolutely terrific." He opened the box and the aroma seemed to literally swirl all around him. "If I didn't know any better, I would have thought I'd died and gone to heaven," he told her.

"I'm told it tastes even better than it smells," she said rather shyly.

"Let's see if they're right." Christopher took out a pastry and slowly bit into it, as if afraid to disturb its delicate composition. His eyes widened and filled with pleasure. "Heaven has been confirmed," he told her before giving in and taking a second bite.

And then a third.

Chapter Four

Despite the fact that she really was enjoying watching the veterinarian consume the pastry she'd made, Lily did feel a little awkward just standing there. Any second now, someone would either come in with a pet that needed attention, or one of the doctor's assistants would emerge and the moment she was experiencing, watching him, would vanish.

It would be better all around if she left right now.

"Well, I just wanted to drop those off with you," Lily said, waving a hand toward the contents of the opened pink box. With that, she began to walk out of the clinic.

Christopher's mouth was presently occupied, involved in a love affair with the last bite of the pastry that he'd selected. Not wanting to rush the process, he also didn't want Lily to leave just yet. He held up his hand, mutely indicating that he wanted her to stay a moment longer.

"Wait." He managed to voice the urgent request just before he swallowed the last bite he'd taken.

Lily stopped just short of the front door. She shifted slightly as she waited for the vet to be able to speak, all the while wondering just why he would ask her to remain. Was he going to tell her that he'd changed his mind about charging her for today? Or had the man had second thoughts about his offer to meet her in the dog park on Sunday?

And why was she suddenly experiencing this feeling of dread if it was the latter?

"You really made these?" Christopher asked once he'd regained the use of his mouth.

"Yes," she answered slowly, her eyes on his as she tried to fathom why he would think that she would make something like that up.

Unable to resist, Christopher popped the last piece into his mouth. It was gone in the blink of an eye. Gone, but definitely not forgotten.

"They're fantastic," he told her with feeling. Executing magnificent restraint, he forced himself to close the rectangular box. "Do you do this professionally?" he asked. "Like at a restaurant? Do you work for a restaurant?" he rephrased, realizing that his momentary bout of sheer ecstasy had temporarily robbed him of the ability to form coherent questions.

"I work for a caterer," Lily corrected. "But someday, I'd like to open up a bakery of my own," she added before she could think better of it. The man was only making conversation. He didn't want her to launch into a long monologue, citing her future plans.

Christopher nodded and smiled warmly as he lifted the lid on the box just a crack again. There was a little dab of cream on one side. He scraped it off with his fingertip which in turn disappeared between his lips as he savored this last tiny bit.

He looked like a man who had reached Nirvana, Lily couldn't help thinking. A warm, pleased feeling began to spread all through her. Lily forgot to be nervous or uncomfortable.

"You'd have standing room only," Christopher assured her. "What do you call these?" he asked, indicating the pastries that were still in the box.

She hadn't given the matter all that much thought. She recalled what Theresa had called them the first time she'd sampled one. "Bits of Heaven."

Christopher's smile deepened as he nodded his approval. He turned to face her completely as he said, "Good name."

That was when she saw it. The tiny dot of white cream just on the inside corner of his lips. Obviously not all of the dessert had made it *into* his mouth. She thought of ignoring it, certain that the more he spoke, the more likely that the cream would eventually disappear one way or another.

But she didn't want him to be embarrassed by having one of his patients' owners point out that his appearance was less than perfect.

"Um, Dr. Whitman," she began, completely at a loss as to how to proceed. She'd always felt out of sync pointing out someone else's flaws or shortcomings. But this was because she'd brought in the pastries so technically the remnants of cream on his face was her fault.

"Your pastry just made love to my mouth, I think you can call me Chris," Christopher told her, hoping to dismantle some of the barriers that this woman seemed to have constructed around herself.

"Chris," Lily repeated as she tried to begin again.

He liked the sound of his name on Lily's tongue. His smile reflected it. "Yes?"

"You have a little cream on your lip. Well, just below your lip," she amended. Rather than point to the exact location on his face, she pointed to it on hers. "No, the other side," she coached when he'd reversed sides to start with. When Christopher managed to find the spot on his second try, she nodded, relieved. "You got it."

Amused, Christopher was about to say something to her, but he was stopped by the bell over the door. It rang, announcing the arrival of his next patient: a Himalayan cat who looked none too happy about being in a carrier, or about her forced visit to the animal hospital for that matter.

The cat's mistress, a rather matronly-looking brunette with a sunny smile, sighed with relief as she set the carrier down on the floor next to the front desk. "Cedrick is *not* a happy camper today," she said, stating the obvious. Then, before Christopher could turn to the cat's file, the woman prompted, "Cedrick's here for his shots."

That was definitely her cue to leave, Lily thought. She'd stayed too long as it was. Theresa's people were watching Jonathan, but she had a feeling that she was on borrowed time as far as that was concerned.

"Well, bye," she called out to Christopher as she opened the door for herself.

She was surprised to hear his voice following her out of the office as he called, "Don't forget Sunday."

The butterflies she'd just become aware of turned into full-size Rodans in a blink of an eye.

Lily darted out of the office and hurried to her vehicle.

"You look like someone's chasing you," Theresa observed when she all but burst through the front door of the catering shop. "Is everything all right?" the older woman asked.

"Fine. It's fine," Lily answered a little too quickly.

Theresa opted to leave her answer unchallenged, asking instead, "How did he like your pastries?" When Lily looked at her blankly, her expression not unlike that of a deer caught in the headlights, Theresa prompted helpfully, "The vet, how did he like the pastries that you made for him?"

"Oh, that. He liked them," Lily answered. "Sorry, I'm a little preoccupied," she apologized. "I'm thinking about the desserts for tomorrow night's event," she explained. Because she always wanted everything to be perfect—her way of showing Theresa how grateful she was to the woman for taking such an interest in her—she was constantly reviewing what she planned on creating for any given event.

This time it was Theresa who waved a hand, waving away Lily's apology. She was far more interested in the topic she had raised.

"Well, what did he say?" she asked. "Honestly, child, sometimes getting information out of you is just like pulling teeth." Drawing her over to the side, she repeated her request. "Tell me what he said."

She could feel her eyes crinkling as she smiled, recalling the exact words. "That he thought he'd died and gone to heaven."

Theresa nodded in approval. "At least he has taste," she said more to herself than to Lily. Maizie had come up with a good candidate, she couldn't help thinking. "It's an omen," she decided, giving Lily's hand a squeeze. "We'll go with Bits of Heaven for the celebration tomorrow night." And then, because Lily didn't seem to be inclined to say anything further about Christopher for now, she changed topics. "By the way, if you're wondering where Jonathan is, Meghan took him out for a walk. Until he gets housebroken, one of us is going to have to take him out every hour until he finally goes," Theresa advised.

Utterly unaccustomed to anything that had to do with having a pet, Lily looked at her, momentarily confused. "Goes? Goes where? You mean with his owner?" she guessed.

Theresa suppressed a laugh. "No, I meant as in him relieving himself. Unless made to understand otherwise, that puppy is going to think the whole world is his bathroom."

Lily looked at her in complete horror. "Oh, God, I didn't think of that."

"Don't beat yourself up, Lily," Theresa told her kindly, putting her arm around her protégé's shoulders. "You've never had a pet before." Then, to further ease the young woman's discomfort, Theresa told her, "There were always dogs around when I was growing up. This is all like second nature to me."

If she felt that way, maybe there was a chance that she could convince her boss to take the puppy if no one came forward to claim him. Lily gave it one more try. "Are you sure that you don't want to—"

Immediately aware where this was going, Theresa deftly headed it off. "Not a chance. My Siamese would take one look at Jonathan and scratch his eyes out, then go on strike and not eat her food for a week just to make me suffer. As long as that prima donna resides with me, I can't have any other four-footed creatures coming within a yard of the house." Theresa gave her a sympathetic smile. "I'm afraid that until you find his owner, you and Jonathan are going to be roomies."

Lily nodded, resigned—for the moment. "Then I'd better get started trying to find his owner," she told Theresa.

With that, Lily retreated into the glass-enclosed cubbyhole where she came up with her recipes. It was a tiny office at best, with just enough space to fit an undersize desk and chair. She couldn't complain. It suited her needs. There was enough space on the desk for her laptop, which was all she required. That and the wireless portable printer she had set up on a folding table.

Lily got to work the second she sat down.

Deciding that an actual picture would do a better job than a drawing, she'd taken a picture of Jonathan earlier with the camera on her cell phone. After attaching her phone to the laptop, she proceeded to upload the photograph—adorable in her opinion—onto her laptop.

"Why would anyone not realize you were missing?" she murmured to the photograph. "Okay, enough of that, back to work," she ordered herself.

Centering the photograph and cropping it to focus on his face, she wrote in a few pertinent words about

the puppy—where and when he was found—then put
down her phone number.

Reviewing everything on the screen, Lily went
ahead and printed one copy as a test run. Except for
the fact that she needed to tweak the color a little to get
it just right, the results looked fine to her. She adjusted
the color and changed a couple of the words she'd initially used, then saved this copy over the first one. She
printed a copy of this version.

She reviewed the poster one final time, decided she
was satisfied with both the message and Jonathan's
photograph and saved *this* version for posterity. Then
she ran off an initial twenty-five posters. She intended
to put them up on trees and poles throughout her entire
residential development.

Hopefully, that would do it. If she received no response to the flyers, she'd be forced to widen her circle and take in the adjacent development, but for the
moment, she was hoping that it wouldn't have to come
to that.

If Jonathan *had* been her puppy, she'd be frantically
searching for him by now. It only seemed right to her
that his real owner would feel the same.

Once she and Jonathan left the catering shop for the
day, Lily put her plan in motion. With the rear window cracked just far enough to let him have air, but
not enough to allow the puppy to make an escape, she
would drive from location to location within her development. She'd then get out—leaving the Labrador
sitting in the backseat of her car—and put the flyers
up on two to three trees.

Because she was trying to blanket the entire development, it took Lily more than an extra hour to get home. Jonathan barked louder and louder each time she got out, registering his growing displeasure at this game that seemed to be excluding him.

"You'll thank me when your owner turns up," Lily told the dog, getting in behind the wheel again. She had just tacked up the last of the posters.

Weary, she pulled up to her driveway. Jonathan began to bark again, as if anticipating that she was going to leave him behind.

"I'm coming," Lily assured him.

She rounded the hood of her vehicle to get to the rear passenger side. When she opened the rear door, she did her best to grab the leash the vet had given her but Jonathan was just too fast for her. He eluded her attempts and dove right between her legs as he made his break for freedom.

With a sigh, Lily gave up and let him go. She wasn't about to chase the animal down. With her luck, she'd fall flat on her face. Instead, she went to her trunk and unlocked it.

Theresa had insisted on making her a home-cooked meal—if home was a catering company—so that she'd have something substantial to eat for dinner.

"I know how you get all caught up in things and forget to eat, especially if you have to prepare something. Well, this time, you have no excuse," Theresa had told her as she thrust the large paper bag at her. The bottom had been warm to the touch.

It still was, Lily thought as she took the carefully packed, large paper bag out of the trunk.

Armed with her dinner, she walked up the drive-

way to the front door and then came perilously close
to dropping the bag.

Jonathan was sitting on her front step. By all appearances, the puppy looked as if he was waiting for her.

"What are you doing here?" she cried, stunned. "I
thought you'd be long gone by now."

Jonathan's expression was mournful as he glanced
up at her. His tongue was hanging out and he was
drooling onto her front step. The moment she inserted
her key into the lock, the Labrador shot to his feet. His
tail was thudding rhythmically on the step.

"I suppose you're going to want to come in," she
said. As if he understood her—or perhaps he just
wanted to be annoying, she speculated—Jonathan responded by barking at her. Barking even more loudly
than he had before. The sound made her absolutely
cringe as it echoed in her head. "House rule," she told
the puppy as she pushed the door open with her shoulder. Jonathan was inside the house like a shot. She had
to be careful not to trip on him—this was getting to be
a habit. The puppy seemed to be everywhere at once.
"Use your inside voice," she said firmly.

He chose to ignore her.

Jonathan barked again, just as loudly as before. Temporarily surrendering, Lily sighed as she closed the
door and then made her way into the kitchen.

"Maybe you don't have an inside voice. I'm beginning to think that you didn't run off, someone *dropped*
you off. Someone who didn't want to spend the rest of
their life living on headache medication."

Jonathan ran around her in a circle then, suddenly
and inexplicably, he apparently opted to become her

shadow. He started to follow her every move, staying within a couple of steps from her at all times.

"It's just going to be a matter of time before you make me fall, isn't it?" she predicted, putting down both the bag Theresa had prepared for her and the one Alfredo had given her earlier in the day. The chef had sent his assistant out to the pet store to buy some cans of dog food for Jonathan.

She might not have adopted the Labrador yet, but it seemed as if everyone else had, Lily thought as she unpacked the cans and set them on the counter. There were ten cans in all, each one for a different kind of meal.

"Boy, dogs eat better than most people, don't they?" she marveled. Jonathan was now running back and forth, eagerly anticipating being fed. "Can you smell this through the can?" she asked incredulously. Jonathan just continued pacing.

She took a moment to choose a can for her houseguest, decided that she couldn't make up her mind and finally made her selection by closing her eyes and plucking a can out of the group. One was as good as another, she reasoned. She had a feeling the puppy would have made short work of cardboard had she decided to serve him that.

The can conveniently had a pop-top. "At least I won't have to look for the can opener."

Lily pulled the top off and emptied the contents of the can into a soup bowl. Placing the bowl gingerly before the Labrador, she managed to take a couple of steps back, out of his way. That took a total of three seconds, possibly less.

Jonathan was finished eating in six.

Lily stared at the empty bowl. "Don't you even *chew?*" she asked in amazement. The puppy followed her when she picked up the bowl to wash it out. As before he seemed to be watching her every move intently. "If you think I'm going to give you any more food, you're going to be sadly disappointed. Your kitchen is closed for the night, mister. Water is all you're going to be getting until tomorrow."

Drying the bowl, she then filled it with cold water and placed it back on the floor where it had stood before. The dog taken care of, she turned to her own dinner. Lily opened up the containers of food that Theresa had sent home with her.

The woman had made her favorite, she realized. Beef stroganoff. One whiff of the aroma had her appetite waking up, reminding her that she hadn't eaten very much today.

"God bless Theresa," she murmured.

Putting together a serving, Lily sat down at the table. Jonathan placed himself directly by her feet. The Labrador watched every forkful of food she placed between her lips, seemingly mesmerized.

Lily did her very best to ignore the puppy and the soft brown eyes that were watching her so very closely. She held out against feeding Jonathan for as long as she could—nearly seven minutes—then finally capitulated with a heartfelt sigh.

"Here, finish it," she declared as she put her plate down on the floor.

She barely had enough time to pull her hand away. Even so, her thumb was almost a casualty. Jonathan's sharp little teeth just grazed the skin on her thumb as he proceeded to make the last of the stroganoff disappear from her plate.

"You know," she told the animal, "if we're going to get along for the duration of the time that you're here, we're going to need some boundaries. Boundaries that you're going to have to abide by or it's 'hit the street' for you, buddy. Am I making myself clear?" she asked the puppy.

Getting up from the table, she deposited the nearly immaculate plate in the sink and made her way to the family room. Her shadow followed. Jonathan's tongue was hanging out and he had started to drool again. This time he left an erratic, wet trail that led from the kitchen to the family room.

Turning around, Lily saw the newly forged trail. With a sigh, she took her sponge mop out of the closet and quickly went over the drool marks, cleaning them up. Finished, she left the mop leaning against the kitchen wall—confident she would need it again soon—and looked down at the puppy.

Now what? "Hey, Jonathan, are you up for a hot game of bridge?"

The puppy looked up at her and then began to bark. This time, the sound also rattled her teeth, not just her head.

"Didn't think so. Maybe I'll teach you the game someday." Her words played back to her. "Hey, what am I saying? You're not going to be here 'someday.' By the time 'someday' comes, you, my fine furry friend, will be long gone, eating someone else out of house and home and turning their home into a pile of rubble. Am I right?"

In response, Jonathan began to lick her toes.

She sank down on the sofa and began petting Jonathan's head. "You don't fight fair, Jonathan."

The puppy barked at her, as if to tell her that he already knew that.

Lily had a feeling it was going to be a very long night.

Chapter Five

Christopher glanced at his watch and frowned. It was five minutes later—four and a half, actually—since he'd last looked at it.

He was standing in the dog park, where he'd been standing for the past fifty minutes. From his vantage point, he had a clear view of the park's entrance. No one could enter—or leave—without his seeing it. It was another "typical day in paradise" as someone had once referred to the weather here in Bedford, the Southern California city where he'd grown up, but he wasn't thinking about the weather.

The frown had emerged, albeit slowly, because Lily and her Labrador puppy were now almost an hour late.

She didn't strike him as someone who would just not show up without at least calling, but then, he wasn't exactly the world's greatest judge of character, he reminded himself. Look how wrong he'd turned out to be about Irene.

He laughed shortly as the memory insisted on replaying itself in his mind. He would have bet money—and despite his outgoing nature, he didn't believe in gambling—that he and Irene were going to be together forever.

Idiot, he upbraided himself.

They'd met the first week at college. Helping each other acclimate to living away from home, they discovered that they had the same interests, the same goals—or so he'd thought. But while he went on to attend Cornell University to become a veterinarian, Irene's career path had her turning to the same New York University they'd gone to as undergraduates to get an advanced degree in investment banking.

The latter, he came to learn, was the career of choice in her family. She had her sights set on Wall Street. That was when their very serious first major conflict occurred. She wanted to remain in New York while he had always planned on eventually returning back "home" to set up his practice.

When he discovered that his mother was not only ill, but dying, he felt it was a sign that he really *needed* to return to Bedford. It was then that things between him and Irene began to unravel and he found that he really didn't know the woman the way he thought he did. Irene had made a halfhearted attempt to be understanding. She even said she was willing to take a short hiatus—she was already working at her father's firm—to accompany him to Bedford for one last visit to his mother.

The tension between them grew and he wound up

going back home to see his mother without her. Irene required "maintenance" and while that didn't bother him too often, he knew it would interfere with the time he wanted to sped with his mother.

As it was, that time turned out to be shorter than he'd anticipated. One month to the day after he had arrived back in Bedford, his mother lost her fight to stay alive. He was heartsick that she hadn't told him about her illness sooner, but grateful that at least he'd had those precious few weeks to spend with her.

When he returned to New York and Irene, things went from bad to worse. Their relationship continued to come apart. The night that he saw things clearly for the first time, Irene had told him that she wanted him to seriously consider turning his attention to doing something a little more "prestigious" than dealing with sickly animals.

She went on to say that in her opinion, as well as the opinions of her father and uncles, being a veterinarian didn't fit in with the upwardly mobile image that she was going for.

Irene had stunned him by handing him a list of "alternative careers" he could look into. "I kept hoping you'd come to this conclusion on your own, but if I have to prod you, I will. After all, what's a future wife for if not to get her man on the right path where he belongs?"

She'd actually meant that.

He knew then that "forever" had a very limited life expectancy in their particular case. He broke off the engagement as civilly as he could, being honest with Irene and telling her that much as he wanted to be with her, this wasn't the way he envisioned them spending their lives together: rubbing elbows with people more interested in profit than in doing some good.

Enraged, Irene had thrown her engagement ring at him. He left it where it fell, telling her she could keep it, that he didn't want it. Two days later, it showed up in his mailbox. He decided that he could always hock the diamond ring if he needed money for a piece of medical equipment.

He left New York for good the day after that.

In an incredibly short spate of time, he had lost his mother and the woman he had thought he loved.

It had taken him a while to get back into the swing of things. A while to stop thinking of himself as one half of a couple and to face life as a single person again. But then, he would remind himself when times were particularly tough emotionally, his mother had done it practically all of his life. His father, a policeman, had been off duty picking up a carton of milk at the local 7-Eleven when a desperate-looking gunman had rushed into the convenience store, waving his weapon around and demanding money. His father, according to the convenience store owner, tried to talk the gunman down.

The latter, jittery and, it turned out, high on drugs, shot him in the chest at point-blank range. The gunman got off three rounds before fleeing. He was caught less than a block away by the responding policemen. But they had arrived too late to save his father.

His mother had been devastated, but because he was only two years old at the time and they had no other family, she forced herself to rally, to give him as good a life as she could.

When he was about to go off to Cornell, he'd felt

guilty about leaving her alone. He remembered asking her why she'd never even dated anyone while he was growing up. She'd told him that she'd had one really great love in her life and she felt that it would have been greedy of her to try to get lightning to strike again.

"Your dad," she'd told him, "was a one-of-a-kind man and I was very lucky to have had him in my life, even for a little while. I don't want to spoil that by looking for someone to fill his shoes when I already know it can't be done."

However, he thought now with a smile, his mother would have told him that just because Irene hadn't turned out to be "the woman of his dreams," that didn't mean that there wasn't someone he was meant to be with out there, waiting for him to find her.

And then again, maybe not, he concluded with a sigh.

It wasn't that he was looking for a relationship. It was still too soon to be contemplating something like that. But nonetheless, he did find himself wanting to spend time with Lily.

Christopher looked at his watch again. Five more minutes had gone by.

Okay, he'd been at this long enough, he decided with a vague shrug. For whatever reason, Lily and her overenergetic puppy weren't coming and the woman hadn't seen fit to call him and let him know.

The possibility that the Lab's owner had turned up and claimed "Jonathan" did occur to him, but even in that event, Lily would have called to cancel, wouldn't she?

Unless, maybe, she'd lost his card.

You can stand here all day and come up with a

*dozen excuses for her, but the fact is that she's not here
and you are. It's time to go home, buddy,* he silently
ordered himself.

With that, Christopher straightened up away from
the lamppost he'd been leaning against and began to
head for where he had parked his car, a late-model,
light gray four-door Toyota.

That was when he heard it.

A loud, high-pitched whistle literally seemed
to *pierce* the air. It was an irritating sound, but he
dismissed it—until he heard it again. His curiosity
aroused, he looked around to see where the sound was
coming from.

Before he could zero in on the source, a puppy was
excitedly running circles around him.

The puppy.

There was a leash flying behind him like a light
green streamer. For the moment, the puppy was a free
canine.

With a laugh, Christopher stooped down to the puppy's level, petting him and ruffling the fur on his head.
The animal responded like a long-lost friend who had
finally made a connection with him against all odds.

"Hi, boy. Where's your mistress? Did you make a
break for it?"

Christopher looked over his shoulder and this time
he saw her. Lily. Her chestnut hair flying behind her,
she was running toward him. Lily was wearing a striking green T-shirt that was molding itself to her upper
torso and faded denim shorts, frayed at the cuff, which
only seemed to accentuate her long legs.

Lily was covering a lot of ground, trying to catch

up to the dog that had obviously managed to get away from her.

Seeing that Jonathan had found the man they were both coming to meet, Lily slowed down just a tad, allowing herself time to catch her breath so that she could speak without gasping.

"Hi," Christopher greeted her warmly, the fifty-five-plus minutes he'd been waiting conveniently vanishing into an abyss. "I was beginning to think you weren't coming."

"I'm sorry about that," she apologized. "I'm usually very punctual." Since Christopher was still crouching next to the puppy, she dropped down to the ground beside him. It seemed easier to talk that way. "Jonathan decided he wanted to give me attitude instead of cooperation." She wasn't trying to get sympathy from the vet, she just wanted the man to know what had kept her from being here on time. "I had a terrible time getting him into the car. It was like he was just all paws, spread out in all directions. And then, when I finally got to the park and opened the rear door, he raced out of the car before I could get hold of his leash. I tried to grab it, but Jonathan was just too fast for me." She shook her head. "He obviously has a mind all his own."

It was hard to believe that the whirlwind of stubbornness she was describing was the same dog that now appeared to be all obliging sweetness and light. Not only that, but the Labrador had just flipped onto his back, paws resting in the begging position because he wanted to have his belly rubbed.

Christopher obliged. The puppy looked as if he was in heaven. "Was that you I heard, whistling just now?" Christopher asked her incredulously.

He was wording his question politely, she noted. Embarrassed, Lily nodded.

"I know the whistle was kind of loud." The truth of it was that she didn't know *how* to whistle quietly. "But I was desperate to get him to at least stop running away even if he wasn't coming back to me."

Christopher found it rather amusing that someone as petite and graceful as Lily whistled like a sailor on shore leave gathering his buddies together. But he decided that was an observation best kept to himself, at least for now. He had a feeling that if he mentioned his impression to her, Lily would take it as criticism and it would undoubtedly cause her to feel self-conscious around him. That was the *last* thing he wanted to do. If nothing else, it would get in the way of her being able to adequately relate to the puppy she was so obviously meant to bond with.

So instead, Christopher aimed his attention—as well as his words—at the black furry creature that all but had his head squarely in his lap, still silently begging for attention and to be petted.

This, Christopher decided, was a dog that thrived on positive reinforcement. That should ultimately make it easier for Lily.

"Have you been giving your mistress a hard time, Jonny-boy?" Christopher laughed, continuing to stroke the puppy. "Well, that's going to stop as of right now, do I make myself clear?" he asked in a pseudostern voice.

Eager-to-please brown eyes stared up at him, and then Jonathan's pink tongue darted out to quickly lick his hand. The same hand that had just been petting the animal.

Christopher pulled his hand out of the dog's reach.

"No more of that for a while. You're not fooling anyone. We're here to work," he told the dog as he got up off the ground. The next moment, the leash in one hand, he offered his other hand to Lily. "C'mon, it's time to start both your training lessons."

Taking his hand, Lily had the momentary sensation of being enveloped and taken care of. The man had strong hands. He also wasn't as quick to let her hand go as she would have thought. It was just an extra second or so, but it registered.

Feeling herself start to flush, Lily quickly changed the subject. "You made it sound as if you're going to be training me, as well," she said with a nervous laugh.

The laugh dissipated in her throat when he looked at her with a wide smile and replied good-naturedly, "That's because I am."

Lily was so stunned by his answer that for a couple of minutes, she had no reply to render, snappy or otherwise. And then her brain finally kicked in.

"I'm happy to say that I'm housebroken," she told Christopher.

She watched, nearly mesmerized, as the corners of his mouth slowly curved. She found herself being drawn into his smile. The line "resistance is futile" flashed through her brain.

"Good to know," Christopher told her, "but that isn't exactly what I have in mind for you."

"Oh?"

She looked at him warily, unaccountably relieved that they were out in the open, in a fairly crowded area. For the life of her, she wouldn't have been able to explain why the thought of being alone with the man made her fingertips tingle and the rest of her feel nervous. She did her best not to let him see the effect he was having on her.

"And what is it that you have in mind for me?" she asked, brazening it out. It was a loaded question and had they been friends for some length of time, or at least at a stage where they knew one another a little better, the answer that flashed through her brain might have been obvious.

"I intend to train you on how to train Jonny here," he told Lily. "There's a right way and a wrong way to do just about everything. With a dog, the wrong way won't get you the results you want and it could get you in trouble. Remember, it's important to maintain positive reinforcement. I don't care if it's a treat—a small one," he emphasized, warning, "or you'll wind up with a severely overweight dog—or lavish praise, as long as it's positive. Remember, kindness works far better than fear," he told her as they began to walk to the heart of the park.

"Fear?" she repeated uncertainly. The word conjured up vivid memories of her own reaction to Jonathan and his nipping teeth.

Christopher nodded. "I've seen people scream at their pets, hit them with a rolled-up newspaper or anything else that happened to be handy. The pet was always the worse for it. You don't want your pet to be obedient out of fear but out of love. I can't stress that enough," he told her. And then he curtailed the rest of his lecture, as if not wanting to get carried away. "Although I have to admit that you don't look like the type who would take a stick to a dog."

Lily shivered at the very thought of someone actually beating their pet. Why would anyone get a pet if they had no patience? Every relationship, whether strictly involving humans, or extending to pets, required a large dose of patience unless it happened to be unfolding on the big screen in the guise of a popular studio's full-length cartoon feature.

"Also," he continued as they made their way to a more open section of the park, "regarding housebreaking—there will be occasional setbacks," he warned her. "I don't recommend dragging Jonny back and sticking his nose into what just came out his other end while sternly denouncing him, saying, 'No, no!' Best-case scenario," Christopher explained patiently, "all that teaches him is to do it somewhere a little more out of the way so he won't get reprimanded for it."

"And worst-case scenario?" she asked, curious what he thought that was since what he'd just described *was* worst-case scenario as far as she was concerned.

Christopher laughed softly. "Your puppy just might find he has a taste for it. I've heard of more than one dog who believed in recycling his or her own waste products." He stopped walking, taking a closer look at Lily's face. "You look a little pale," he noted. "Are you all right?"

She put her hand over her stomach, as if that would keep her hastily consumed breakfast from rising up in her throat and purging itself from her stomach. Opening her door to this puppy had consequently left her open to more things than she'd ever dreamed of, no pun intended she added silently.

"I just didn't realize all the things that were involved in taking in a stray—even temporarily. The only dogs I ever knew were up on a movie screen," she confessed. Admittedly it had been a very antiseptic way of ob-

taining her knowledge. "They didn't smell, didn't go
to the bathroom and had an IQ just a tad lower than
Einstein's." She smiled ruefully as she elaborated a
little more, realizing while she was at it that she was
underscoring her naïveté. "The kind that when their
owner said, 'I need a screw driver' would wait until
he specified whether it was a flathead or Phillips head
that he wanted."

Christopher grinned. He liked that she could laugh
at herself. The fact that Lily had a sense of humor was
a very good sign, as far as he was concerned.

"In the real world, if you don't bathe them, dogs
smell, and they don't do long division in their heads."
And then he went on to list just a few of the positive
reasons to own a dog. "But they *do* respond to the
sound of your voice, are highly trainable and will come
to an understanding with you, given the time and the
training—coupled with a lot of patience. Always remember, anything worth doing is worth doing well.
You let a dog into your life, remember to show him
that while you love him, you're the one in charge, and
you will never regret it."

Christopher paused for a moment. He caught himself looking into her eyes and thinking how easily he
could get lost in them if he wasn't careful.

Taking a breath, he told himself that he needed to
get down to business before she got the wrong idea
about him and why he was here.

"Now then, are you ready to get started?" he asked
Lily.

"Ready," she answered with a smart nod, eager to
begin.

"All right," he said, stooping down to the dog's level

again to remove the leash he'd given her. He replaced it with a long line, a leash that was three times as long as the initial one. Getting back up to his feet, Christopher told her, "The first thing we want to teach Jonny here is to come when you call."

She watched as he slowly backed up, away from Jonathan. "Um, how about housebreaking?" she asked hesitantly.

She would have thought that would be the very first thing the dog would be taught. She'd had to clean up several rather untidy messes already and couldn't see herself doing that indefinitely. To be honest, she'd rather hoped that the vet had some sort of magic solution regarding housebreaking that he was willing to pass on to her.

The sympathetic expression on his handsome, chiseled face told her that she'd thought wrong.

"That's going to take a little longer for him to learn, I'm afraid. I can—and will—show you the basics and what to say, but for the most part, that's going to require dedication and patience on your part. A *lot* of dedication and patience," he emphasized. "Because you're going to have to take Jonny here out every hour on the hour until he goes—as well as watch for signs that he's about to go."

This was completely new territory for her and something she had never given any attention to before now. "How will I know what signs to look for?"

"That," he replied with a smile that would have curled her toes had she allowed it, "is a very good question." Leaning in to her as if to confide a secret, he lowered his voice and said, "This would be the part where *you* get trained."

Drawing his head back again, he gave her a wink that seemed to flutter through layers of skin tissue and embed itself smack in the middle of her stomach.

"Okay, back to getting him to come when you call," he said, taking a firm hold on the long line. With that, he proceeded to go through the basics for her slowly and clearly before he went on to demonstrate what he'd just said, allowing her to see it in action.

Chapter Six

"Okay, now you try," Christopher said after successfully getting Jonathan to come to him when he called the puppy. The vet held out the long line to her.

Instead of taking it from him, Lily looked at the elongated leash uncomfortably. "Me?"

If there was one thing she really hated, it was appearing inept in front of people, even someone who seemed as nice as this man. Doing so only seemed to underscore her feelings of insecurity, not to mention that it reinforced the shyness that she grappled with every day.

Christopher instinctively knew when a situation required an extra dose of patience. Usually, it involved the animals he treated, but occasionally, he could sense the need to tap into his almost endless supply when dealing with a person. He could see that Lily's reluctance had nothing to do with being stubborn or reticent. From her stance, she was far from confident.

That had to change. If he could sense it, the dog definitely could. While he had a soft spot in his heart for all things canine, he also knew that dominance had to be established. If it wasn't, this cute little black ball of fur and paws was going to walk all over the woman beside him and most likely make her life a living hell— or at least turn her home into a shambles.

"Well, yes," Christopher told her. "Unless you intend to have me come home with you and take over raising Jonny here, you're going to have to learn how to make him obey you. Emphasis on the word *obey*," he said, still holding the end of the long line before her.

Lily pressed her lips together. The only thing she hated more than looking like a fool was looking like a coward. She took a deep breath and wrapped her fingers around the end of the long line.

Glaring at the puppy, she said as authoritatively as she could, "Come!" When Jonathan remained where he was, she repeated the command even more forcefully. "Come!" At which point Jonathan cocked his head and stared at her, but made no attempt to comply.

Taking pity on her, Christopher bent close to her ear and said in a low voice, "Remember to preface each command with his name and give the long line a little tug the way I did. He'll get the hang of it eventually."

Christopher's breath along the side of her face and neck would have caused an involuntary shiver to shimmy down her spine had she not steeled herself at the last moment.

Lily felt her cheeks growing pink. Use the puppy's

name. How could she have forgotten something so simple so quickly?

"Right. Jonathan, come!" she ordered, simultaneously giving the elongated leash a little tug.

Despite its length, the impact of the play on the line telegraphed itself to the Labrador. Then, to her surprised relief, Jonathan trotted toward her, coming to a halt almost on top of her feet.

"He did it," she cried excitedly, stunned and thrilled at the same time. "He came!"

Christopher wasn't sure which was more heartening to him, seeing the animal respond to Lily's command or seeing Lily's joy *because* the animal had responded to her command.

"Yes, he did," Christopher acknowledged with a pleased smile. "Now give him that scrap of doggie sausage as a reward and play out the long line so you can do it again."

Jonathan appeared to be in sheer ecstasy as he swallowed his "reward" without so much as pausing a second to chew it.

It was a toss-up as to which appeared to be more eager for a repeat of what had just happened, Christopher mused: Jonathan or his mistress.

The brief exercise played out more smoothly this time.

"Again," Christopher instructed her after Lily tossed the treat to the eager puppy.

Lily and Jonathan repeated the training exercise a total of five times before Christopher decided it was time to move on to the next command.

"This is the exact opposite of what you've just taught him," Christopher told her. He noticed that instead of the reluctance she had initially exhibited, Lily seemed to be almost as eager as the puppy to undertake the next "lesson." "You're going to train him to stay where he is. Now, not moving might seem like it's an easy thing to get across, but for an antsy puppy that's approximately six to seven weeks old, staying put is not part of their normal behavior—unless they're asleep," he told her. "Okay, instead of tugging on the long line, you're going to use a hand gesture—holding your hand out to him as if you were a cop stopping traffic—plus a calm voice and patience. Lots of patience," Christopher emphasized.

"Okay," she said, nodding her head.

In a way, he couldn't help thinking that she reminded him of the puppy—all eagerness and enthusiasm. Without fully realizing it, she'd gone a step up in his estimation of her.

"You tell him to stay and then slowly back away from him," Christopher instructed, standing directly behind her and ready to match her step for step as she backed up. "Until he responds for the first time and stays in place for as long as you've designated, you don't take your eyes off him. *Make* him obey you. Your goal ultimately is to get Jonny to obey the sound of your voice *without* being bribed to do it or being watched intently. And that," he told her firmly, "is going to take doing the same thing over and over again until he gets it, until he associates what he does with the key words you use."

"I was never very good at being authoritative," Lily admitted ruefully. But even so, her enthusiasm was still high.

"Then you're going to have to keep that little secret

to yourself. As far as Jonny here is concerned, you are the lord and master of his world—or mistress of it if you prefer," he amended.

She didn't seem like the type to take offense over words where none was intended, Christopher thought, but since they were still in the getting-to-know-each-other stage, he wasn't about to take anything for granted.

Lily smiled at him. There was something about the way she looked at him that made him feel connected to her. It was as if, without his exactly knowing why, they were in sync to one another. "Either way is fine with me," she told him.

In all honesty, she'd never thought of herself in those sort of lofty terms. She was neither a mistress *nor* a master. Or at least she hadn't been until now, she thought with a smile.

"Okay." Christopher nodded toward their subject. "Let's see you make him stay."

"You're not going to do it first?" she asked Christopher.

"You mean warm him up for you?" he asked, amused. "He's your dog," he told her, wanting to subtly build up her confidence. "You should be the main authority figure he listens to."

"But he's not my dog," she protested. "I have these flyers out in my development. His owner might still come looking for him." Although, she had to admit, she was now just a tad less eager for that to happen than she had been just a little while ago.

He looked at Lily for a long moment, seeing through the veneer she'd put up. "Then tell me again why you're going to all this trouble for an animal you might not get to keep?"

There was a struggle going on inside of her, a struggle between logic and emotions. At any given moment, she wasn't quite sure just which way she was leaning.

But for the sake of appearances and the role she was trying to maintain, Lily replied, "I'm trying to train Jonathan so that I can survive with him until his owner *does* turn up." She did her best to sound cool and removed as she added, "I don't want to get attached to him and then have to give him up."

"I hate to break this to you, Lily, but watching the two of you, in my opinion, you already *are* attached to him—and it looks to me as if he's attached to you as well, as much as an overenergized puppy can be attached to one person," he qualified with a laugh. "Don't get me wrong," he was quick to explain. "Dogs are extremely loyal creatures, but puppies tend to sell their souls for a belly rub and have been known to walk off with almost anyone—unless they've been given a better reason to stay where they are."

Christopher searched her eyes. He could readily see that Lily was grappling with the problem of wanting to keep the dog at an arm's length emotionally—while wanting to throw caution to the wind and enjoy the unconditional love that the puppy offered.

"And if I could add two more cents." Christopher paused, waiting for her to nod her head.

Surprised, she told him, "Go ahead."

"Personally, I don't think anyone is going to come looking for Jonny here," he told her. "The way I see it, his mom probably had a litter recently and this one made a break for it when he was old enough to explore the world and no one was watching him. Most likely, his mom's owner was busy trying to find a good home for him and his brothers and sisters. When Jonny took off, the owner probably took it to be a blessing—one less puppy for him to place.

"*Or* he might have been so overwhelmed that he didn't even notice Jonny was missing—especially if his dog had had an unusually large litter." A fond smile curved his lips as he gazed down at the Labrador that had taken to momentarily sunning himself and was stretched out in the grass. "These little guys move around so fast, it's hard to get a proper head count."

She couldn't quite explain the happy feeling growing inside of her, especially since she was trying so hard to maintain her barriers, so hard to not get attached and thereby leave herself open to another onslaught of pain.

Attempting to sound removed—and not quite succeeding—she said, "So what you're telling me is that I'd better get used to the idea of vacuuming up fur several times a week."

For the sake of her charade, Christopher inclined his head—even though he saw right through her performance. "That's another way of putting it."

She was on shaky ground and she had a feeling that she wasn't fooling him—or herself. "What if I don't like the idea of having to vacuum that often?" she posed.

Rather than tell her that he would take the dog—which he actually would do if he believed she was serious—Christopher decided to play on her sympathies and create a heart-tugging scenario.

"Well, in that case, you could always bring Jonny

to the animal shelter and leave him there. Bedford out-
lawed euthanizing animals after a certain period of
time the way they do in some other cities, so there's no
chance of his being put to sleep. Of course, he might
not get all the love and attention he needs, getting lost
in the shuffle because there are a large number of animals at the shelter. The city had to cut back on employ-
ees even though the animals all need care and attention.

"Not to mention the fact that lately the number of
volunteers who come by to walk, feed and play with
the animals has dropped off, too, but at least the little
guy would still be alive—just not as happy as he would
be here with you."

Beneath the steel exterior she was trying to maintain was a heart made of marshmallow. But even if
there wasn't, Lily would have seen what the veterinarian was trying to do.

Shaking her head, she told him, "You left out the
violins."

The comment, seemingly coming out of the blue,
caught him by surprise. "What?"

"Violins," she repeated, then elaborated. "As background music. You left them out. They should have
been playing while you painted that scene for me. They
could have swelled to a crescendo right toward the end.
But other than that, you just created a scenario that's
bordering on being a tearjerker."

"Just wanted you to know what these little critters
are up against," he told her with a very straight face.
"Now, let's see if you can get Jonny to stay. In place,"
he added with emphasis in case she thought he was
still referring to the dog staying with her. And then
he winked at her.

Again.

Her reaction was exactly the same as it had been the first time he'd winked at her. Her breath caught in her throat and butterflies fluttered in her stomach. The only difference was that it seemed to her that there were even more now than there had been the first time he'd winked at her.

How could something that could technically be described as a twitch create such pure havoc inside of her? Was she really *that* starved for attention that any hint of it had her practically melting into tiny little puddles and reminding herself to breathe?

Lily had no idea how to begin to make any sense of that.

For the moment, she blocked it all out and turned her attention to what Christopher had just said, not how she'd reacted to how he'd looked as he said it.

"Okay, let's see if I can get him to listen."

"Oh, he'll listen," Christopher assured her. "That's not the issue. Whether he'll obey is a totally other story."

This particular story turned out to have a good ending some ninety minutes later.

With Christopher urging her on, she had managed to get the Labrador puppy to stay in place for a total of ten seconds as she backed away from him. This happened several times, building up her confidence both in herself and in her relationship with the eager Labrador. She'd still had to maintain eye contact with Jonathan, but Christopher promised her that that would change and the next time they got together, they'd work on her just turning her back on the Labrador and *still* getting the animal to remain in place.

"Next time?" Lily repeated. It wasn't exactly a question so much as she wanted to make sure that she'd heard him correctly.

"Yes, next weekend," Christopher answered.

He slanted a glance at her, wondering if he'd pushed a little too hard too fast. Normally, he wouldn't have given it a second thought, but this woman needed a little more delicate care in his estimation. He also felt certain she was worth it. Something about her aroused both his protective nature as well as an inherent response from him as a man. Though a little soured on the idea of relationships, he still genuinely *liked* this woman.

"I thought since you were having such success at this, you might want to push on, get a few more commands under your belt, so to speak. Unless you don't want to," Christopher said, giving her a way out if she really wanted one.

"Oh, I want to." She'd said that a little too eagerly, Lily realized and dialed back her enthusiasm a notch as she continued. "But what I'm really interested in is getting him housebroken," she confessed, wondering if she was putting the veterinarian out too much, taking advantage of his generosity.

"For that to get underway, we can't be out here," he told her. "We'd have to work with him at your home. Jonny can't be taught to observe his boundaries if one of those boundaries is missing," he pointed out.

"Can't argue with that," she agreed. And then she glanced at her watch.

Christopher saw something that resembled an apologetic expression on her face. Had he missed something? "What's the matter?"

"I feel guilty that you're spending all this time helping me train Jonathan when you could be doing something else with your time. I wouldn't feel so bad if you were letting me pay you for your time, but you're not."

"I'm not about to charge you for something I volunteered to do." He could see that wasn't going to assuage her guilt. He thought of the other day—and went with that. "However, if you feel compelled to make some more pastries anytime soon, well, I couldn't very well refuse those, now could I?"

"How about dinner?" She was as surprised as he was to hear her make the suggestion. It seemed to have come out all on its own. For a second, she lapsed into stunned silence.

The sentence was just hanging there between them, so he took a guess at what she was saying. "You mean like going out to dinner first?"

You put it out there, now follow up on it before the man thinks he's spending time with a crazy woman.

"No, I mean how about if I make you dinner before the dessert? Like a package deal," she concluded with a bright, albeit somewhat nervous smile.

For just a heartbeat, he found himself mesmerized by her smile. Some people had smiles that seemed to radiate sunshine and make a person feel the better for being in its presence. Lily had such a smile.

"I wouldn't want you to go to all that trouble," he finally said when he recovered his ability to make coherent sentences. But he uttered it without very much conviction.

"Not that it's any actual trouble," she countered,

"but why not? It seems to me like you're going through a lot of trouble helping me train Jonathan."

There were two people running around the perimeter of the park with their whippets. Moving out of their way, Christopher waited until they were out of earshot before continuing their verbal dueling match.

"I don't consider working with a dog as any sort of 'trouble.' To be honest, I can't remember a time when I didn't want to be a veterinarian," he told her. "My dad died when I was very young and my mother thought that having a dog—or two—around the house would somehow help fill the void in my life that his death left. Without knowing it, she inadvertently set me on a career path that shaped the rest of my life. I really appreciated what she tried to do, but to be honest, you can't miss what you don't remember ever having, can you?"

"Actually, you *could* miss it if you find yourself imagining what it would have been like to have a father and then realize that no matter what you do, it was never going to be that way."

There was a sadness in her voice that caught his attention. "You sound like someone who's had firsthand experience with that."

Ordinarily, she would have just glossed over his observation, shrugging it off and simply saying no, she didn't. But lying—which was what it amounted to from her point of view—just didn't seem to be right in this situation. Even a little white one would have troubled her.

"I do," she admitted. For a moment, as she brought her childhood into focus, she avoided his eyes. "I never knew my dad. He took off before I was born. The story went that he told my mother he wasn't cut out to be a father and that then he proved it by just taking off," she concluded with a shrug that was way too careless to be what it portrayed.

He wanted to put his arms around her, to not just comfort her but to silently offer her protection against the world, as well. Until this moment, those reactions in him had been strictly confined to dealing with creatures in the animal kingdom. This was a whole new turn of events. But even so, he kept his hands at his sides, sensing that he might just scare her off if he did something so personal so early in their acquaintance.

So he restricted his response to a verbal one. "I'm sorry."

"Yes, I was, too—for my mother." Her father had abandoned the person she had loved the most in life— her mother. And for that, she could never forgive the man. "She could have used a little help juggling raising me and paying the bills. Life was a constant struggle for her."

"That's the way I felt, too," he admitted. "But my mother never complained. I don't think I *ever* heard her even say a cross word against anyone. She just plowed through life, doing what she had to do."

"Mine held down two jobs trying to do the same thing." It felt almost eerie the way their lives seemed to mirror each other when it came to family life. She didn't normally seek details, but she did this time. "You have any siblings?"

Christopher shook his head. It was the one area that he wished had been different. "None. You?"

"Same," she answered. "None."

It should have felt eerie to her—but it didn't. Instead, she realized that it made her feel closer to this outgoing man. She knew the danger in that, but for now, she just allowed it to be, taking comfort in the warm feeling that was being generated inside of her.

Chapter Seven

He walked Lily to her car, which was parked not that far from his own.

As he stood to the side and waited for her to coax the Labrador into the backseat, Christopher realized that he wasn't quite ready for their afternoon to come to an end.

His reaction surprised him. He hadn't felt any real interest in maintaining any sort of female companionship since his less-than-amicable breakup with Irene a few months ago. Maybe he was finally ready to move on with his life in every sense.

Watching Lily now, Christopher decided he had nothing to lose by suggesting that perhaps they could just continue with Jonathan's training session in a different setting.

As she turned away from the dog and closed the

rear passenger door, Christopher pretended to glance at his watch.

Looking up again, he said to her, "Listen, I have nothing scheduled for the rest of the day. Why don't I just follow you to your place and we'll get a head start in housebreaking your houseguest?"

"Really?"

"Really," Christopher answered. He didn't, however, want her having any unrealistic expectations about what they were going to accomplish this afternoon. "Remember, though, I did say 'get a head start.' This isn't a relatively quick process, like getting Jonny to come or stay. Or even getting him to do something trickier like rolling over or sitting up and begging. This," he warned her, "is going to take a while. With some luck and a lot of vigilance, best-case scenario, you might be able to get him completely housebroken in two weeks."

"But I work and the hours aren't always regular," she told Christopher. Looking at Jonathan in the backseat, she lamented, "How can I keep up a regular schedule with him?"

"That is a problem," Christopher conceded. "But it's not impossible."

She found herself clinging to those words like a drowning woman to a life preserver. If she was going to wind up actually keeping Jonathan, she would be eternally grateful that Theresa had sent her to this veterinarian. He was a godsend.

"Okay, I'm listening."

"You take him out every hour on the hour when you *are* home. When you're not, you can leave him in a puppy crate."

"A puppy crate?" she repeated, not knowing if she was just stunned or actually horrified by the suggestion. She had to have misunderstood him. "You're telling me to stick Jonathan in a crate?" she asked in disbelief. "That's cruel."

"No, actually, it's not cruel at all. Puppy crates come in different sizes to accommodate the different breeds. They're airy and specifically designed to make the puppy feel safe. Puppies are placed in puppy crates for the same reason that they tightly bundle up newborn babies in a hospital. They actually like small spaces. An added bonus is if they only spend part of their time there each day—such as when you're away at work— they won't mess the crate up because they won't go to the bathroom where they sleep."

"What about in the pet stores?" she countered. She'd seen more than one employee in a pet store having to clean out the cages that the animals were kept in.

"That's because the animals are kept in their cages all the time. They have no choice but to relieve themselves in the same place that they sleep. Those conditions make it harder to train an animal, but not in the case I'm suggesting," he pointed out.

She could tell by his tone when he described conditions in a pet store that the veterinarian didn't really approve of them. Still, the idea of forcing Jonathan to spend part of his time in a crate didn't exactly sit well with her.

"Not that I'm doubting what you just said about puppy crates, but isn't there any other way to housebreak him? I really don't like the idea of sticking Jonathan in a cage—or crate—unless I have no other choice." She looked at the dog, sympathy welling up inside of her. "It just seems too much like making him spend time in prison to me," she confessed.

He liked the fact that despite her attempts at projecting bravado, Lily was a pushover when it came to animals. "Well, there is one other alternative," he told her.

Lily second-guessed him. "Taking him to work with me, the way I did the first day."

"Or you could drop him off at my animal hospital when you go to work and then I could drop him off with you in the evening. Unless you were leaving earlier than I was, and then you could just come and get Jonny. And in between, I can have one of the animal techs make sure our boy here doesn't have any embarrassing 'accidents.'"

That really sounded as if it was the far better choice in her opinion, but again, she felt as if it would definitely be putting him out.

"Wouldn't they mind?" she asked, adding, "Wouldn't *you* mind?"

"No and no," Christopher answered. He leaned against the side of her vehicle as he laid out his new plan for her. "I passed around those pastries you dropped off the other day and if you're willing to supply the staff with them, say once a week or so, I *know* that they'd be more than happy to pitch in and get Jonny here potty trained," he guaranteed.

Since they were still talking, he opened the front passenger door to allow air to circulate through the vehicle for the Labrador. At the same time, he placed his body in the way so that the puppy couldn't come bounding out and escape.

"You're serious?" Lily asked.

She could feel herself growing hopeful again. This

last idea was infinitely appealing—and it meant she wouldn't have to feel guilty about putting the puppy into a cage just to keep her house from turning into one giant puppy latrine.

"Completely," Christopher replied with no reservations.

"Then it's a deal," she declared.

"Great. I'll alert the staff to start looking for new clothes one size larger than they're wearing right now," he said with a straight face. Only his eyes gave him away.

"You don't have to do that," Lily told him, waving away the suggestion.

To which he asked, "You've changed your mind about baking?"

There was no way that was about to happen. She absolutely loved baking, especially for an appreciative audience.

"Oh, no, it's not that," she said, dismissing his suggestion. "But I can duplicate the recipe and make a low-fat version— they'll never notice the difference—and nobody will need bigger clothing."

He appreciated what she was trying to do, but in his opinion, "lighter" was never "better." For that matter, it wasn't even as good as what it was supposed to be substituting.

"You say that now, but I can always tell the 'light' version of anything," he told her. "It never tastes the same."

Lily studied him for a long moment. Her expression was unreadable. And then he saw humor overtaking the corners of her mouth, curving it. "Are you challenging me?"

Christopher took measure of her. She meant well, but as an opponent, she was a lightweight.

"Not in so many words but, well, yes, maybe I am," he conceded.

Lily squared her shoulders. For the first time since she had come into his animal hospital, she looked formidable. It surprised him.

"Okay," Lily said with a nod of her head, "you're on. I'll bake my usual way, and then arbitrarily I'll make a batch of substitutes, and I defy you to definitively say which is which."

"You have a deal," he readily agreed, confident he'd win. He took her hand and shook it.

It was done as a matter of course, without any sort of separate, independent thought devoted to it. But the moment his strong fingers enveloped hers, she could have sworn she felt some sort of current registering, a shot akin to electricity suddenly coursing through her veins from the point of contact.

Her breath caught in her throat for the second time that day.

Out of nowhere, she suddenly caught herself wondering if he was going to kiss her.

The next second, she hastily dismissed the thought, silently asking herself if she was crazy. People didn't kiss after making what amounted to day boarding arrangements for their pet. That wasn't how these situations played themselves out.

Was it?

Clearing her throat, as if that somehow helped her shake off the thoughts swarming through her brain and turning up her body temperature to an almost alarming degree, Lily dropped the veterinarian's hand. She took a step back. She would have taken a few more, but her car was at her back, blocking any further retreat on her part.

"Do you still want to come over?" she heard herself asking in an almost stilted voice. "To start housebreaking him?"

Her mouth had gone completely dry by the end of the sentence.

"Unless you've changed your mind," Christopher qualified. He'd felt it, too, felt the crackle of electricity between them, felt a sudden longing in its wake that had left him a little shaken and unsteady. He was definitely attracted to this woman, but it was more than that. Just what, he wasn't sure.

Yet.

"No, I haven't," Lily heard herself saying.

Her own voice echoed in her head as if it belonged to someone else. Part of her, the part that feared what might be ahead of her, wanted to run and hide, to quickly thank him for his trouble and then jump into her car in order to make a hasty retreat.

But again, that would be the coward's way out.

What was she afraid of? Lily demanded silently. She was a grown woman who had been on her own for a while now, a grown woman who knew how to take care of herself. There was no one else to step up, no one else to take up her cause or fight any of her battles for her, so she had to stick up for herself. She was all she had to rely on and so far, she'd managed just fine—with a little help from Theresa.

Making up her mind, she decided that yes, she did want him to come over. She wanted his help—and if anything else developed along the way, well, she'd face it then and handle it.

"Let me give you my address in case we get separated," Lily said to him, taking a very small notepad out of her purse. Finding a pen took a couple of minutes longer, but she did and then she began to write down her address.

"Separated?" he questioned. "How fast do you intend to be driving?" he couldn't help asking.

"Not that fast," Lily assured him. "But there are always traffic lights turning red at the most inopportune time, impeding progress. I might make it through a light, but you might not, that sort of thing." Finished, she handed the small piece of paper to him. "Can you read it?" she asked. "My handwriting is pretty awful."

He looked down at the paper—and laughed. "You think this is bad? You should see the way some of my friends write—it's enough to make a pharmacist weep," Christopher told her with another laugh.

Glancing one last time at the address she'd written down for him, he folded the paper and put it in his pocket. "Just let me get to my car before you start yours," he told her. "I'll take it from there."

"Okay," Lily answered gamely.

She rounded the back of the vehicle—Jonathan eyeing her every move—and got in behind the steering wheel. Buckling up, she not only remained where she was until Christopher got to his car but waited until he started the vehicle and pulled out of the row where he had been parked, as well.

Only then did she turn her key in the ignition, back out and head for the exit. Within less than a minute, she was on the thoroughfare leading away from the dog park.

Lily glanced in her rearview mirror to make sure that Christopher was following her.

He was.

Meanwhile, Jonathan had taken to pacing back and forth on the seat behind her as she drove them home. Each time she came to a stop at an intersection light, even when she rolled into that stop, Jonathan would suddenly and dramatically pitch forward.

After emitting a high-pitched yelp that sounded like it could have easily doubled for a cry for help, the puppy apparently decided it was safer for him to lie low, which he did. He spread himself out as far as he could on the backseat and seemed to all but make himself one with the cushion.

"It's not far now," Lily promised the Labrador, hoping that if he didn't understand the words, at least the sound of her calm voice would somehow help soothe him.

If it did—and she had her suspicions that it might have because he'd stopped making those strange, whiny noises—the effect only lasted until she pulled up in her driveway some fifteen minutes later.

The second she put the vehicle into Park and got out, Jonathan was up on all fours again, pacing along the backseat—when he wasn't sliding down because of a misstep that sent his paws to the floor.

Since she had kept the windows in the back partially open, she didn't immediately open the rear door to let him out. Instead, she waited for Christopher to pull up alongside of her vehicle. She felt that he could handle the Labrador far better than she could. For one thing, the man was a lot stronger.

The minutes began to slip away, banding together to form a significant block of time.

When Christopher still didn't show up, she began to wonder if he had somehow lost sight of her. She'd stopped looking in the rearview mirror around the time when Jonathan's head was in her direct line of vision, blocking out everything else.

And then she realized that it didn't really matter if Christopher had lost sight of her car or not. She'd given him her address, so even if he had lost sight of her vehicle he still should have been pulling up in her driveway by now.

Since he wasn't, she took it as a sign that he'd changed his mind about coming over.

The more the minutes ticked away, the more certain she became that she was right. Somewhere along the route, he had obviously decided that he had given her enough of his time.

She felt a strange sensation in her stomach, as if it was puckering and twisting.

Why his sudden change of heart left her feeling let down, she didn't know. After all, it wasn't as if this was a date or anything. The man had already been extremely helpful, getting her started on the proper way to train her dog, and she was very grateful for that. No reason to be greedy, Lily silently insisted. The man had already gone over and above the call of duty.

Jonathan began to whine, bringing her back to her driveway and the immediate situation. She was allowing her disappointment to hijack her common sense.

Lily quickly shut down any stray emotions that threatened to overwhelm her.

"Sorry," she apologized to the puppy. She opened the rear passenger door a crack—just wide enough to allow her to grab his leash. She was learning. "I didn't mean to forget about you," she told the dog.

Getting a firm hold of the leash, Lily opened the door all the way.

Jonathan needed no further encouragement. He came bounding out, savoring his freedom like a newly released prisoner after a lengthy incarceration.

"Easy," she cautioned. "Easy now!"

The words had absolutcly no effect on Jonathan, a fact that only managed to frustrate her. And then she remembered what Christopher had taught the dog— and relatedly, what he had taught her.

Grabbing a firmer hold on the leash, she said in the most authoritative-sounding voice she could summon, "Jonathan, stay!"

The dog abruptly stopped trotting toward the house and stood as still as a statuc, waiting for her to "release" him from her verbal hold with the single word Christopher had told her to use.

Getting her bearings, Lily turned toward the front of the house so that the dog wouldn't catch her off guard when he resumed running. Only then did she say, "Okay," in the same authoritative voice.

Just as she'd expected, the very next moment Jonathan was back to bounding toward the front door.

Lily was right on his heels. "Someday, dog, you are just going to have to get a grip on that enthusiasm of yours. But I guess that day isn't going to be today," she said, resigned to having a barely harnessed tiger by the tail—at least for a few more weeks.

The veterinarian's idea of having her drop the dog off at his animal hospital each morning was beginning to sound better and better, she thought as she unlocked her front door.

Once Jonathan had passed over the threshold, she let the leash go and entered the house herself. She locked her front door a moment later. There had been several break-ins in the development in the past couple of months and she was determined that her house was not going to be part of those statistics.

Turning from the door, Lily looked down at the dog. "Looks like we're on our own tonight, Jonathan. But that's okay, we don't need Christopher around. We'll do just fine without him."

The dog whined in response.

Lily sighed, sinking down on the couch. "I know, I know, who am I kidding? We're not really fine on our own, but we just have to make the best of it, right? Glad to hear you agree," she told the dog, pretending to take his silence as agreement.

She thought of the housebreaking lessons that lay ahead of her. No time like the present, right?

"What do you say to having some superearly dinner. We'll fill that tummy of yours and then spend the rest of the evening trying to empty it. Sound like fun to you?" she asked, looking at the puppy. "Me, neither," she agreed. "But what has to be done, has to be done, so we might as well get started. The sooner this sinks in for you, the happier both of us are going to be."

Just then, she heard her cell phone ringing. Her first thought was that Theresa had gotten another booking and wanted to run a few desserts past her to see what she thought of them.

Grabbing her purse, she began to dig through the chaotic interior to locate her phone.

"Why is it always on the bottom?" she asked the dog, who just looked at her as if she was speaking in some foreign language. "You're no help," she murmured. "Ah, here it is." Triumphantly, she pulled the phone out of the depths of her purse.

Just before she pressed "accept" she automatically looked at the caller ID.

The caller's name jumped out at her: Christopher Whitman.

Chapter Eight

Lily pressed the green band labeled "accept" on her cell. "Hello?"

"Lily, hi, it's Chris." The deep voice on the other end of the line seemed to fill the very air around her the moment he began to speak. "I'm afraid there's been a change of plans. I'm not going to be able to make it over to your place."

"I kind of figured that part out already," she told him, trying very hard to sound casual about the whole thing, rather than disappointed, which she was. While she had more or less assumed that he wasn't going to come over, she had to admit that there was still a small part of her that had held out hope when she saw that the incoming call was from him.

Ordinarily, Christopher would have just left it at that, ending the call by saying goodbye with no further explanation.

But he didn't want to, not this time.

He'd always been nothing if not honest with himself and he had to admit that this was *not* an ordinary, run-of-the-mill situation. Not for him. He wasn't sure just what it actually was at this point, but he did know that he wanted to be able to keep all his options open—just in case.

"Rhonda was hit by a car," he told Lily.

"Oh, my God, how awful." Lily's sympathies instantly rushed to the foreground, completely wiping out every other emotion in its path, even though the person's name meant nothing to her. He hadn't mentioned the woman before, but she obviously meant a great deal to him. "Is there anything at all that I can do to help?"

"No, I've got it covered," he told her. "But I'd like to take a rain check on that home training session if it's okay with you."

"Sure, absolutely." Her words came out in a rush. The thought of car accidents always ran a cold chill down her spine. She could relate to loss easily. At times she felt *too* easily. "Don't give it another thought. Go be with Rhonda."

Whoever that was, she added silently.

It occurred to her that she had no idea if Christopher was talking about a friend, a relative, or possibly a girlfriend, or someone more significant to him than that. What she did know was that the event itself sounded absolutely terrible and she really felt for him.

It did cause her to wonder how he could have even spared a single thought about helping her to start housebreaking Jonathan at a time like this. The man either had an exceedingly big heart, or she was missing something here.

"I really hope she pulls through, Christopher," Lily told him in all sincerity.

She heard silence on the other end. Just when she'd decided that the connection had been lost or terminated, she heard Christopher respond.

"Yeah, me, too."

"Let me know how she's doing—if you get a chance," Lily added hastily. The last thing she wanted was for him to think she was being clingy or pushy at a time like this.

It might have been her imagination, but she thought he sounded a little strange, or possibly slightly confused, as he said, "Yeah, sure." And then his voice became more urgent and almost gruff as she heard him tell her, "I have to go."

The line went dead.

She stood looking at her cell phone for a long moment, even though there was no one on the other end anymore.

"Guess it really is just the two of us, Jonathan." The Labrador made a yipping sound, as if in agreement.

Putting her cell phone down on the coffee table, Lily went to the kitchen to see if her landline's answering machine had any incoming calls on it. She hadn't had a chance to check today's messages and wondered if there were any messages on it from a frantic dog owner who had seen one of her posters.

She had a total of three calls waiting to be heard. For a moment, she stood looking at the blinking light, considering erasing the calls without playing them.

Lily reasoned that if she didn't hear the message, she wouldn't be responsible for not returning the call.

C'mon, Lil, since when is ignorance the kind of excuse you want to hide behind? You were eager enough to get rid of Mr. Ball of Fur when you first found him, remember? You wouldn't have posted all those flyers everywhere if you weren't.

While that was true enough then, she'd had a change of heart in these past few hours. Actually, now that she thought of it, her change of heart had been ongoing and gradual.

With all the problems that having this puppy in her life generated, she still found herself reluctant to just hand him over to some stranger, to in effect close her eyes and banish him from her life.

Lily shook her head, looking at the puppy again. It was amazing to her how quickly she could get used to another creature roaming around in her space.

"You're getting attached again, Lil," she reprimanded herself sternly. "You know that was something you didn't want happening."

Well, whether or not she wanted it, Lily thought, looking down at the dog again, it was now official. She *liked* this moving repository of continually falling fur. *Really* liked him.

"So, what do you want to do first?" she asked Jonathan.

And then her eyes widened as she saw his tail go up in that peculiar way he had of making it look like one half of a squared parenthesis. The next moment, she remembered the only time he did that was when he wanted to eliminate wastes from his body.

"Oh, no, no, no, you don't," she insisted.

Grabbing him by his collar—his leash was temporarily missing in action—keeping her fingers as loose as she could within the confining space, she quickly pulled the dog to the rear of the house and ultimately, to the sliding glass back door.

All the while she kept repeating only one order: "Hold it, hold it, hold it!"

She finally stopped saying that the moment she got Jonathan into the backyard. And that was when the energetic puppy let loose. She would have preferred he hadn't made his deposit on the cement patio instead of in the grass just beyond that strip, but in her opinion that was still a whole lot better than having that same thing transpire on the rug or—heaven forbid—the travertine in the kitchen. The latter would become permanently stained if she wasn't extremely quick about cleaning up every last trace of Jonathan's evacuation process.

"You finished?" she asked the dog. As if in response, he trotted back to the sliding glass door, wanting readmittance to the house. "Okay, I'll take that as a yes," she told the animal gamely. "But I want to hear the moment you think you have another overwhelming urge to part company with your breakfast or any of those treats you all but mugged me for in the park."

Acting as if his mistress had lapsed into silence rather than putting him on notice, Jonathan immediately began sniffing around the corners of the room, making no secret of the fact that he was foraging.

He was able to stick his nose in and under all the tight spots, where the cabinets just fell short of meeting the floor. Crumbs had a habit of residing there and

Jonathan was hunting crumbs in lieu of snaring any bigger game.

Lily observed his progress. "You're not going to find anything," she warned the animal. "I keep a very clean house—which means that if you have any further ideas about parting ways with your fur—*don't.* I've got better things to do than vacuum twice a day because you shed 24/7." She turned toward the pantry. "C'mon, I'll give you your dinner—and then I'd appreciate it if you just stretched out over there on the floor by the sofa and went to sleep."

She put Jonathan's food out first, then went to fix something for herself.

The puppy, she noticed out of the corner of her eye, instantly vacuumed up what she'd put into his bowl. Finished, he came over to sit at her feet in the kitchen, waiting for her to either drop something on the floor or pity him enough to share her dinner with him.

"Eye me all you want with those big, sad, puppy eyes of yours," she told him firmly. "It's not happening. While I'm in charge of taking care of you, you're not about to turn into some huge treat-based blimp."

If he understood her—or appreciated her looking out for his health—Jonathan gave her no indication of it. Instead, he seemed to turn into just a massive, needy, walking stomach, ready to desperately sell his little doggie soul for a morsel of food.

Lily had every intention of remaining firm. She held out for as long as she could, looking everywhere but down as she ate. But he got to her. She could *feel* Jonathan pathetically staring at her. And while she knew she was partially responsible inasmuch as she was reading into that expression, she found she couldn't hold out against the canine indefinitely.

With a sigh, she broke off a piece of the sandwich she settled on having and put it on the floor in front of Jonathan. It was gone, disappearing behind his lips faster than she could have executed a double take. She'd barely sat up straight in the chair again.

Looking at the animal, Lily could only shake her head incredulously. "Certainly wouldn't want to be marooned on a deserted island with the likes of you. Two days into it and you'd be eyeing me like I was a pile of raw pork chops—center cut," she added for good measure.

Jonathan barked and she was sure that he was voicing his agreement.

After clearing away the two dishes and the bowl that she had used, Lily found herself way too wound up as well as just too restless to go to bed or even to watch some mundane television program with the hopes that *it* would put her to sleep.

It was Sunday night and as a rule, there was simply nothing worthwhile watching on any of the countless cable channels that she received at that time.

Still, it was far too quiet without the TV, so she switched it on as she washed off the dishes. She kept it on as soothing background noise, glancing at it occasionally just to see if anything interesting turned up.

It never did.

Without anything to watch and with her new four-footed companion sleeping in the corner, Lily did what she always did when she needed to unwind.

She baked.

She started by taking out everything that might lend

itself to baking pastries and lining up the various containers, boxes and jars, large and small, on the far side of the kitchen counter. Seeing what she had to work with, Lily decided what to make.

She was on her third batch of Bavarian-style pastries—low-fat just to prove her point that baking didn't necessarily mean fattening—when she heard the doorbell ring.

The dog's head, she noticed, instantly went up. The dog had gone from zero to sixty in half a second. Jonathan was wide-awake and completely alert.

"Hold that pose, I might need you," she told Jonathan.

Wiping her hands, she went to the front door. Her furry shadow came with her. She didn't bother wasting time by telling him to stay. Having him there beside her generated an aura of safety that had been missing from her life for a while now. Mentally, she crossed her fingers and hoped it wasn't anyone in response to the flyer.

Instead of looking through the peephole, which she found usually distorted the person on the other side of the door, she called out, "Who is it and what are you doing here?"

"Dr. Chris Whitman and I've come to apologize."

Lily's heart ramped up its pace. She fumbled with the lock as she flipped it.

"You already apologized. Don't you remember?" she asked as she opened the door for him. "When you called to tell me you weren't coming, you apologized over the phone."

He remembered, but it hadn't seemed nearly adequate enough to him. And besides, after what he'd just been through, he didn't want to immediately go home to his empty house. He wanted to see a friendly face, talk to a friendly person—and relax in her company. The very fact that he did was a surprise to him since toward the end, he felt nothing but relief to get out of his relationship with Irene.

But then, Lily wasn't Irene. "Then I've come to apologize again," he amended. "And I'm still Dr. Chris Whitman," he added cheerfully, referring to her initial inquiry through the door.

"You didn't have to apologize the first time," she told him. "I mean, it was nice that you thought you had to, but I understand. You had a crisis to handle. By the way, how is she doing?"

He nodded, as if to preface what he was about to say with a visual confirmation. "She's actually doing better than I expected. It looks like she's going to pull through."

It had been touch and go for a while there. It wasn't as if this was the first operation he'd ever performed but it was by far the most demanding and he had done extensive volunteer work at several animal shelters. The five-year-old Irish setter had required a great deal of delicate work.

"That's wonderful news," Lily said, genuinely pleased. She had to raise her voice because Jonathan had decided to become vocal. The animal obviously felt that he was being ignored by the two people in the room, most especially by the man he had taken such a shine to. "But what are you doing here? Shouldn't you be back at the hospital with her?"

Christopher crouched down to scratch the puppy

behind his ears. Jonathan fell over on the floor, clearly in ecstasy.

"Under normal circumstances," Christopher agreed, "I might have stayed the night, but Lara's there. She volunteered to take over this shift. And my number's on speed dial if anything comes up."

That was rather an odd way to put it, Lily thought. Out loud she repeated, "Lara?" Another woman? Just how many women were part of this man's life?

"Yes." He realized that he probably hadn't properly introduced Lily to everyone by name the one time she'd been at his animal hospital. "She's one of the animal techs. You met her the other day when you brought Jonny in to see me."

Lily came to a skidding halt mentally. She put up her hand to stop the flow of his words for a minute. She needed to get her head—not to mention facts—straight.

"You have one of your animal techs watching over Rhonda?" Lily asked incredulously, trying her best to unscramble what Christopher was telling her.

"Yes. Why? What's wrong?" he asked, mystified by the very strange expression that Lily had on her face right now. "It's not like this is her first time."

Well, the only way she was going to clear this up was by asking some very basic questions, Lily decided. "What relation is Rhonda to you? I know it's none of my business, but I'm getting a very strong feeling that we're not on the same page here—"

He'd drink to that, Christopher thought.

"Hold it," he ordered out loud. "Back up." He really wasn't sure he'd heard her correctly. Or had he? "What did you just ask me?"

He was angry because she was prying, Lily thought.

She didn't want to jeopardize her relationship with Christopher. She needed him to help her with the puppy. She just wasn't good at these sorts of things, despite her best intentions.

"Sorry, I stepped over the line, I guess," she told him. "I was just trying to get things straight, but if you don't want to tell me about Lara, or Rhonda, that's your right and I—"

This misunderstanding was getting way out of hand, Christopher realized. The only way to stop this rolling snowflake from becoming a giant, insurmountable snowball to end all snowballs was just to blurt out the truth to Lily, which he did—as fast as possible.

"Rhonda's my neighbor's Irish setter," he explained in as few words as he could. "Josh called me in a panic just as I was driving to your place, said someone driving erratically had hit Rhonda and then just kept on going. She was alive, but had lost a lot of blood. I couldn't turn him down."

Rhonda was a dog? The thought presented itself to her in huge capital letters. The rush of relief that ushered those words in was almost overwhelming. She did her best to refrain from analyzing it. She wasn't equipped for that right now.

"Of course you couldn't." She said the words so fiercely, at first he thought that Lily was putting him on.

But one look into her eyes and he knew she was being completely serious.

And completely lovable while she was at it, he couldn't help thinking.

Christopher only realized much later that his real undoing began at that very minutc.

Just as hers did for her.

For Lily, it was realizing that the man who was helping her discover the right way to train Jonathan wasn't
just someone who was kind when it was convenient for
him to be that way, or because he was trying to score
points with a woman he'd just met and appeared to be
moderately attracted to. The turning point for her, the
moment she discovered that she had absolutely no say
when it came to being able to properly shield her heart
from being breeched, was in finding out that Christopher was selfless across the board, especially when it
came to animals who needed him.

Her heart went up for sale and was simultaneously
taken off the market by that same man in that very
small instant of time.

Instantly distracted, Christopher stopped talking
and took a deep breath. His question was fairly rhetorical because he had a hunch that he knew the answer to
it. "What is that fantastic smell?"

It was very hard to keep her face from splitting in
half; her smile was that wide and it just continued to
widen. It had swiftly reached her eyes when she suggested, "Why don't you come into the kitchen and see
for yourself?"

Turning on her heel, she led the way into her small
kitchen. She didn't realize at the time that there was a
bounce to her step.

But Christopher did.

In keeping with the kitchen's compact size, there
was an island in the middle, but a small one, just large
enough to accommodate two of the three trays she'd
placed in the oven earlier. She had taken the two trays
out while the third one was still baking.

The closer he came, the stronger the aroma seemed to be. His appetite was firmly aroused and Christopher immediately transformed into a kid walking into his favorite candy shop. "Are those the same pastries you made the other day?"

"Some are, some aren't. I like to mix it up," she confessed.

The pastries on the trays were still warm and were most definitely emitting a siren song as he stared at them.

"Are these all for work?" he asked, circling the trays on the island slowly.

"No, they're for me," she corrected. "Not to eat," she explained quickly. "Baking relaxes me. I usually give them away after I finish." Gesturing toward the trays, she asked, "Would you like to sample one?"

She got as far as gesturing before he took her up on the offer he'd assumed she'd been about to make.

Chapter Nine

"You are, without a doubt, an amazingly gifted young woman."

Christopher uttered the unabashed praise the minute he had finished savoring his very first bite of the pastry he had randomly chosen off the nearest tray. The pastry was filled with cream whipped into fluffy peaks and laced with just enough Amaretto to leave a very pleasant impression. It was practically light enough to levitate off the tray.

"I bake," she said, shrugging carelessly. Lily was warmed by his praise, but she didn't want to make it seem as if she was letting his compliment go to her head.

"No," Christopher corrected her. "My late mother, God bless her, 'baked.' Her desserts, when she made them, always tasted of love, but they were predictable,

and while good, they weren't 'special.' Yours are definitely special. You don't just 'bake,' you *create*. There's
a big difference."

Christopher paused as he indulged himself a little
more, managing to eat almost three quarters of the
small pastry before he went on.

"You know, I'm usually one of those people who
eat to live, not live to eat. Nobody could *ever* accuse
me of being a foodie or whatever those people who
love to regale other people with their so-called 'food
adventures' like to call themselves. But if I had access to something like this whenever I felt like indulging in a religious experience, I'd definitely change my
affiliation—not to mention that I'd probably become
grossly overweight. Speaking of which," Christopher
went on, switching subjects as he eyed her, "why aren't
you fat?" he asked.

"I already told you, I don't eat what I make." Then,
before he could say that he had a hard time believing
that, she admitted, "Oh, I sample a little here, a dab
there, to make sure I'm not going to make someone
throw up, but I've just never felt the inclination to pol-
ish off a tray of pastries."

Christopher's expression told her that he was having a hard time reconciling that with his own reaction
to the end product of her culinary efforts.

"If I were you," he told her, "I'd have a serious talk
with myself, because your stubborn half is keeping
you from having nothing short of a love affair with
your taste buds." He licked the last of the whipped
cream from his fingertips, discovering he craved more.
"How *did* you come up with these?" he asked, waving

his hand at the less-than-full tray of pastries that was closest to him on the counter.

Her method was no big secret, either. It was based on a practical approach.

"It's a very simple process, really. I just gather together a bunch of ingredients and see where they'll take me," she told him.

As if to back up her explanation, Lily indicated the containers, bottles and boxes that had been pressed into service and were now all huddled together on the far side of the counter.

He thought that was rather a strange way to phrase it. But creative people had a very different thought process.

"That means what?" he asked her, curious about her process. "You stare at them until they suddenly speak to you?"

"Not in so many words, but yes, maybe. Why?"

He shook his head, still marveling at her stripped-down approach to creating something so heavenly. With very little effort, he could have easily consumed half a dozen pastries until he exploded.

"Just trying to familiarize myself with your creative process," he answered, then added, "I've never been in the presence of a magician before."

"And you aren't now. It's not magic, it's baking. And that, by the way," she said, indicating the pastry he'd just had, "was one of my low-fat pastries."

He stared at her, undecided if she was telling him the truth or putting him on. "You're kidding."

"Not when it comes to calories," she answered with solemnity.

"Low-fat?" he asked again, looking at the rest of the pastries.

"Low-fat," she confirmed. "Told you you couldn't tell the difference."

Christopher shook his head, clearly impressed. "Now that's really *inspired* baking," he told her with just a hint of wonder.

If he wanted to flatter her, who was she to fight it? Lily thought.

"Okay, I'll go with that." She carefully moved around Jonathan, who appeared to be hanging on his hero's every word. "Now, can I fix you some dinner to go with your 'magical' dessert?" she asked.

He shook his head. "I'm good," he told her. When she raised an eyebrow, waiting for him to explain, he said, "I grabbed a burger on the way over here. I didn't want to put you out."

"Did you eat the burger you grabbed?" she asked. "Because I can still make you something a little more edible than a fast-food hamburger."

He liked the way she crinkled her nose in what appeared to be unconscious disdain of the entire fast-food industry. "I'm sure you can, but the burger filled the hole in my stomach for the time being. Besides, that rain check I mentioned earlier was supposed to be for dinner, too. Dinner out," he emphasized.

"You don't have to wait to be seated if we have dinner in," she pointed out gently. Lily viewed all cooking as an outlet for her and she thoroughly enjoyed doing it. She wanted to convince him that this definitely wasn't "putting her out."

"Don't you like being waited on?" he asked Lily.

"Not particularly," she admitted. Then, not wanting

to sound like some sort of a weirdo, she told him, "Although I'm not overly fond of washing dishes."

"Do you?" he asked in surprise. "Wash dishes," he elaborated when he didn't get a response.

"Yes." Why was he asking? She thought she'd just said as much.

He glanced over toward the appliance next to her stove. "Is your dishwasher broken?"

She automatically glanced at it because he had, even though she didn't need to in order to answer his question. "I don't know, I've never used it. There's just me and it doesn't seem right to run all that water just for a few plates."

There was a solution to that. "Then wait until you have enough dishes to fill up the dishwasher," he suggested.

"That seems even less right." Lily suppressed a shiver as she envisioned stacking dirty plates on top of one another.

"Leaving a bunch of dirty dishes lying around until there's enough for a full load sounds awful. Either way is offensive," she said with feeling. "It's a lot easier if I just wash as I go. My mom taught me that," she told him out of the blue. "This was her house—*our* house, as she liked to put it even though I never paid a dime toward its purchase. My mom handled everything," she recalled fondly. "Held down two, sometimes three jobs, just to pay the bills.

"If there was anything extra, she proudly put it toward my college fund. By the time I was set to go to college, there was a lot of money in that little slush fund of hers. Enough to set me on the road to any college I wanted."

Caught up in her reminiscing, Christopher asked, "So where did you go?"

He watched as her smile faded. Sorrow all but radiated from her. "I didn't. That was the year my mother got sick. Really sick. At first, the doctors she went to see all told her it was in her head, that she was just imagining it. And then one doctor decided to run a series of more complex tests on her—which was when Mom found out that she wasn't imagining it. She had brain cancer." She said the diagnosis so quietly, Christopher wouldn't have heard her if he wasn't standing so close to her.

"By the time they found it, it had metastasized to such a degree that it was too hard to cut out and get it all. They went in, did what they could, and then Mom said, 'No more.' She told them that she wanted to die at home, in one piece. And she did," Lily concluded proudly, her voice wavering slightly as she fought back the tears that always insisted on coming whenever she talked about her mother at any length.

"I used the money she had set aside for my college fund to pay off her medical bills." Lily shrugged helplessly, as if paying off the bills had somehow ultimately helped her cope with her loss. "It seemed only right to me."

Lily stopped talking for a second to wipe away the tears that insisted on seeping out from the corners of her eyes.

"Sorry, I get pretty emotional if I talk about my mother for more than two minutes." She attempted to smile and was only partially successful. "I didn't mean to get all dark and somber on you."

"That's okay," he assured her. "I know what it feels

like to lose a mother who's sacrificed everything for you." She looked up at him. "You'd trade every last dime you had just to spend one more day with her. But you can't, so you do the next best thing. You prove to the world that she was right about you. That you *can* do something that counts, to make some sort of a difference. And I have no doubt that somewhere, tucked just out of sight, my mom and yours are watching over us and are pretty satisfied with the people they single-handedly raised," he told her with a comforting smile.

She took in a deep breath, doing her best to get her emotions under control. His words were tremendously comforting to her.

"You think?" she asked.

"I know," he countered. Looking at her, he saw the telltale trail forged by a stray teardrop. "You missed one."

With that, he lifted her chin with the tip of his finger, tilting it slightly. Using just his thumb, Christopher very gently wiped the stray tear away from the corner of her eye.

Their eyes met for one very long moment and her breath felt as if it had become solid in her throat as she held it.

Waiting.

Hoping.

Trying not to.

And then everything else, her surroundings, the kitchen, the pastries, even the overenergized puppy that was responsible for bringing them together in the first place, it just faded into the background like so much inconsequential scenery.

She was acutely aware of her heart and the ramped-up rhythm it had attained.

Christopher lowered his mouth to hers and ever so lightly, like a sunbeam barely touching her skin, he kissed her.

The next moment, he drew back and she thought for a second that the sound of her heart, beating wildly, had driven him back.

"Sorry, I didn't mean to take advantage of you like that," he told her, still cupping her cheek with the palm of his hand.

Her voice felt as if it was going to crack at any second as she told him, "You didn't. And there's nothing to be sorry about, except…"

"Except?" he prodded.

Lily shook her head, not wanting to continue. She was only going to embarrass herself—and him—if she said anything further. "I've said too much."

"No," he contradicted, "you've said too little. 'Except' what?" he coaxed.

Lily wavered. Maybe he did deserve to know. So she told him.

"Except maybe it didn't last long enough," she said, her voice hardly above a whisper, her cheeks burning and threatening to turn a deep pink.

"Maybe it didn't," he agreed. "Let's see if I get it right this time," he murmured just before his mouth came down on hers for a second time.

This time nothing happened in slow motion. This time, she could feel the heat travel through her as if its path had been preset with a thin line of accelerant, a line that ran between the two of them as well as over the length of her.

They'd been sitting at the counter on stools that swiveled and were now turned toward one another. Lily caught herself sliding from the stool, her arms entwined around the back of Christopher's neck.

He stood up at the same moment that she had gotten off the stool.

The length of her body slid against his. His ridges and contours registered with acute details. All the electricity between them crackled with a fierceness that was all but staggering.

He savored the sweetness of her mouth in a far more profound way than he had savored the flour-and-cream creations she'd made. The Amaretto in the pastry had been just the tiniest bit heady. The taste of her lips was far more intoxicating.

So much so that it sent out alarms all throughout his body, warning him that he was walking into something he might not be prepared for. Something he might not be equipped to handle at this juncture of his life, all things considered.

The magnitude of his feelings right at this moment was enough to make Christopher back away, concerned about the consequences that waited for him if he wasn't careful.

It wasn't easy, but he forced himself to draw back again.

"Maybe I better go," he told her, the words that emerged sounding low and almost gravelly.

She needed time to pull herself together. Time to try to understand just what it was that was going on here—aside from her complete undoing. Time to fix the shield around her heart because it had seriously cracked.

"Maybe you'd better," she agreed.

He tried to remember what had brought him here in the first place. It was difficult to get a fix on his thoughts; they were scattered and unfocused. All he was aware of was how much he wanted her.

"I just wanted to tell you in person why I backed out this afternoon," he finally managed to say.

"I appreciate that," she told him, then added belatedly, "I appreciate everything you've done."

Her wits managed to finally come together. The relief she experienced at being able to think again was incredible. She almost felt as if she was in full possession of her mental faculties again. Or at least enough to be able to carry on a normal conversation. Even so, she didn't want to push herself and have it all fall apart on her again.

Something about this man threatened her carefully constructed world and if she wasn't on her guard, all the work she had put in to keeping her heart out of danger's reach would go up in smoke.

"Why don't you take one or two for the road? Or more if you like," Lily suggested, doing her very best to sound casual. It wasn't easy talking with one's heart in one's throat.

"One or two for the road?" he echoed. They'd just been locked in a kiss, so was she talking about those? he wondered, looking at her uncertainly.

"Or more," she repeated again. "I can wrap up as many pastries as you'd like to take home with you. Maybe even give a couple to your poor neighbor for what he's just gone through."

And then it all clicked into place. She was talking about the pastries, not about kissing him again. Christopher laughed—more at himself and at what he had thought she was saying than at what Lily was actually telling him.

"You're being too generous," he said.

She didn't quite see it that way. "I like to spread smiles around and these pastries make people smile."

"That they do," he wholeheartedly agreed. He looked over toward the remaining two and a half trays. "I can completely attest to that."

"Then let me give you some." It was no longer a suggestion but a statement of intent.

She had a total of eight pastries wrapped, placed in a cardboard container and ready to go within a couple of minutes.

"You sure you don't want more?" she asked. He'd stopped her when she had reached for the ninth pastry, saying eight was already too much.

"I want them all," he told her honestly. *And more than just pastries right now, he added silently.* He concentrated, determined to keep even a hint of the latter thought from registering on his face. "But in the spirit of sharing, what you just packed up for me to take with me is more than enough." Not wanting to leave it just at that, he told her, "I can come by tomorrow afternoon if you like—and we can pick up where we left off."

Belatedly, Christopher realized he had worded that last line rather poorly, allowing her to misunderstand his meaning. "Left off training Jonny," he tacked on awkwardly.

He had never been a smooth talker—the type who was able to sell ice cubes to polar bears—but he had never had this much trouble saying what he meant

This woman had definitely scrambled his ability to communicate. Why was that?

He had no hard-and-fast answer—and the one that did suggest itself made him nervous.

"That would be very nice of you," Lily was saying as she walked him to the front door. Jonathan came along, prancing around, all but tripping both of them as he wove in and out between them. "I'll bake you something else next time," she promised with a smile that completely seeped under his skin.

Christopher laughed, shaking his head as he opened the front door. "You do that and I'm going to have to start shopping in the husky-men section of the local department store."

Her eyes swept over him, as if to verify what she already knew. "You have a long way to go before that happens," she assured him.

"Not as long as you think," he replied just before he turned and walked out. He didn't trust himself to stand on the doorstep one second longer.

She made him want things he had no business wanting. Things that, if he recalled correctly—and he did— would only ultimately promise to lead to an unhappy ending sometime in the near future.

Been there, done that, he thought as he got into his car and drove away.

As if to contradict him, the warm scent coming from the pastries seemed to rise up and intensify, filling his car. It made him think of Lily all the way home.

Chapter Ten

There wasn't a single position on her bed that felt comfortable enough for her to fall asleep for more than a few minutes at a time. And when she actually *did* manage to fall asleep, she wound up dreaming about what was keeping her awake, perpetuating her dilemma.

She dreamed about a magnetic pair of blue eyes that pulled her in and thick, dirty-blond hair that curled just enough to make her fingers itchy to run through it.

And at the end of each and every one of these minidreams Lily would experience a deep, dark feeling of bereavement, of being suddenly, irreversibly left behind, to continue on alone.

She felt as if her insides had been hollowed out by a sharp, serrated carving knife. Then she'd bolt upright, awake and damp with perspiration despite the fact that the night air was cool tonight.

Alone in her bedroom, her knees drawn up against her chest as if her body was forming an impenetrable circle, Lily recognized her nightmares for what they were, what they signified: fear. Fear of caring, fear of experiencing the consequences that came from allowing herself to care about someone.

Was she crazy to even *think* that she could have some sort of a relationship without paying the ultimate terrible price that relationship demanded? If you danced, then you were required to pay the piper. She knew that and she desperately didn't want to have anything at all to do with the piper.

Not ever again.

The best thing was just to remain strangers, the way they were now.

Finally, at six in the morning, Lily gave up all attempts of trying to get even a solid hour of uninterrupted sleep.

With a deep sigh, she threw off her covers and got out of her extremely rumpled bed. Glancing at the tangled sheets and bunched-up comforter, it occurred to her that her bed looked as if it had been declared a war zone.

Maybe it had been, she thought ruefully. Except that there had been no winner declared.

She normally never left her bedroom in the morning without first making her bed, but this morning, she abandoned the bed entirely. She just wanted to get out of the house.

Maybe some fresh air would do her some good.

Putting on a pair of jeans and donning a light sweater, she announced to the puppy that had insisted on sleeping on her bedroom floor, "We're going out for a walk, Jonathan."

Fully awake in less than an instant, the Labrador half ran, half slid down the stairs and then darted around until she reached the landing to join him. Picking the leash up where she'd dropped it by the staircase, Lily hooked it onto the dog's collar. At the last minute she remembered to take a bag with her just in case she got lucky and the dog actually relieved himself while they were out.

Taking Jonathan for a walk was yet another exercise in patience. It consisted of all but dashing down one residential street after another, followed by periods of intense sniffing that lasted so long Lily finally had to literally drag the puppy away—at which point he would abruptly dash again.

This theme and variation of extremes went on for close to an hour before Lily finally decided that she'd had enough and wanted to head back to the house.

Just before they reached their destination, Jonathan abruptly stopped dead, nearly causing her to collide with him because of the shift in momentum. When she turned toward the dog to upbraid him for almost tripping her, she saw that the puppy was relieving himself.

She realized that meant she didn't need to be so vigilant for the next few hours. "I guess I'm home free for half the day, right?"

The Labrador had no opinion one way or the other. He was far too busy investigating what he had just parted with. Lily pulled him back before he managed to get too close to it.

This having a dog was going to take some getting

used to, she thought, elbowing the puppy out of the way in order to clean up after him.

A *lot* of getting used to, she amended after she finished with her task.

Lily got back to her house just in time to hear her landline ring. Unlocking the door and hurrying inside, she managed to get to the telephone a scarce heartbeat before it went to voice mail.

Dropping Jonathan's leash, she picked up the receiver. "Hello?"

There was about a second or so delay before someone answered her. She reacted the moment that she heard his voice.

"Lily, hi. I was just getting ready to leave a message on your machine," the deep voice on the other end told her.

She could feel goose bumps forming on her skin. There was something incredibly intimate and, okay, *arousing* about Christopher's voice on the phone. But that still didn't change her resolve about keeping the man at arm's length. If anything, it strengthened it.

"Now you can leave a message with me," she said, forcing herself to sound as cheerful as she possibly could.

When she heard him draw in a long breath, she knew it couldn't be good. "I'm afraid I'm going to have to cancel today."

She had a feeling, a split second before he said the words, that he was going to bow out. Which was fine, because that was what she wanted.

But if that was the case, why was there this vast,

hard lump of disappointment doing a nosedive in the pit of her stomach?

"I didn't know you had the power to do that," she said, still doing her best to sound light and upbeat. "To cancel an entire day." The silence on the other end made her feel like squirming. "Sorry, that was me just trying to be funny. I didn't mean to interrupt you while you were talking."

He did the worst thing he could have done, Lily thought. He was understanding. "You weren't interrupting, you were being humorous."

Maybe he was canceling because he had another emergency, and she was making wisecracks. Lily felt terrible.

"And you're being nice." She apologized in the best way she knew how. She absolved him of any obligation. "It's okay, about canceling," she added since she knew her words sounded vague. "I understand."

"How can you understand?" Christopher asked. "I haven't told you why I'm canceling yet."

He had a point. Her nerves were making her jump to conclusions. She searched for something plausible to use as an excuse, but came up empty. She went with vague. "I'm sure it's for a good reason."

"I wish it wasn't," he told her honestly. Something had made him go in very early this morning, to check on his neighbor's dog. Rhonda hadn't been as responsive as he would have liked. Further investigation had brought him to this conclusion. "Rhonda had some internal bleeding suddenly start up. I have to go back in and cauterize the wound, then sew her up again. When I finish, I want to watch her for a few hours, just to be sure she's on the mend this time. That means I won't be coming over today to work with Jonathan."

That he could even think about that when he had an emergency on his hands made her feel that he was a very exceptional person. She didn't want him to feel as if he was letting her down in any way.

"Well, as it turns out, Jonathan and I went out for a long walk this morning and he decided he couldn't hold it long enough to come back to the house to make a mess, so he went outside."

Tickled at the way she'd narrated her latest adventure with the dog, Christopher laughed. "Congratulations. But you do realize you're not out of the woods yet, right? The process has to be repeated—a lot—before it becomes ingrained. Did you remember to praise him after he finished going?"

Lily pressed her lips together. She *knew* she'd forgotten something. "Is praising him important?" she asked, hoping he'd tell her that it was just a minor detail.

"It is—and I'll take that as a no. Next time Jonny goes, praise him to the hilt and tell him what a wonderful puppy he is. Trust me," he assured her, "it works wonders."

She sighed, glancing at the dog who had plopped down at her feet, apparently content to lie there, at least for the moment. "I'll remember next time."

"Listen, I need to go, but you can still drop Jonny off here on your way to work tomorrow—unless you feel confident enough to leave him alone at your house," he added, not wanting her to think he was talking her into leaving the dog at his clinic for the day.

"I'll drop him off," she said quickly, relieved that he hadn't taken back his offer. She wasn't naive enough to think that one success meant that the puppy's behavior was permanently altered. "And thank you."

"Don't mention it. Now I've really got to go," he told her again.

Christopher hung up before she had a chance to say goodbye.

Mixed feelings scrambled through her as Lily hung up the receiver. She didn't know whether to be relieved that Christopher wasn't coming over—relieved that she wouldn't find herself alone with him—or upset for the very same exact reason.

Jonathan barked and she realized that he was no longer lying down at her feet. The bark sounded rather urgent. She had a feeling that he was asking for his breakfast. Christopher—and her present ambivalent dilemma—wouldn't have been part of her life if Jonathan hadn't been on her doorstep that fateful morning.

"Life was a lot simpler before you came into it, Jonathan," she told the puppy.

Jonathan just went on barking at her until she began walking to the kitchen. Following her, his barking took on a different, almost triumphant intensity.

Lily laughed to herself. Exactly who was training whom here?

She had a sneaking suspicion she knew. Right now, the score was Jonathan one, Lily zero. She took out a can of dog food and popped the top.

The following morning, Lily nearly drove right past the turn she was supposed to make to get to the animal hospital. At the last minute, she slowed down and deliberately made the right-hand turn.

Less than a mile later, she was driving into the

rather busy upscale strip mall where Christopher's animal hospital was located.

Lily had come close to driving past the initial right-hand turn not because she had a poor sense of direction, but because she had a strong sense of survival. The more she interacted with the handsome, sexy veterinarian, the more she was going to *want* to interact with him—and that sort of thing would lead to an attachment she told herself that she ultimately didn't want.

But, as always, stronger still was her utter disdain for behaving like a coward. It didn't matter whether no one knew or not. *She* would know and that was all that really counted. Once she began going off in that direction, there would be no end to the things she would find excuses to run from.

She didn't want to live like that, didn't want fear to get the upper hand over her or to govern any aspect of her life.

If she allowed it to happen once, then it would be sure to happen again. And next time, it would be easier to just back away from something. Before she'd know it, her individuality would be forfeited, buried beneath an ever-growing mountain of things for her to fear and to avoid *because* of that fear.

At that point, she wouldn't be living, merely existing. Life, her mother had always told her, had to be relished and held on to with both hands. It wasn't easy, but it was definitely worth it.

Conquering this fear of involvement because she feared being left alone had to be on the top of her to-do list. Otherwise, she was doomed to be lonely right from the beginning.

* * *

The receptionist, Erika, looked up, a prepasted smile on her lips as she said, "Hello." And then recognition set in. Once it did, the woman's smile became genuine.

"Hi, Dr. Whitman said you might stop by." Coming out from behind the desk, Erika turned her attention to Jonathan. "Hi, boy. Have you come to spend the day with us?"

"I guess I'm boarding him," Lily said, handing over the leash to the receptionist.

"Not technically," Erika told her. "If you were boarding him, there'd be a charge. Dr. Whitman said there'd be no charge, so Jonathan's just visiting," she concluded with a warm smile.

While she was grateful, that didn't sound quite right to Lily. "Do you often have pets come by who are just visiting?"

"Jonathan's our first," the receptionist answered honestly. Then, sensing that the Labrador's owner might be having second thoughts about leaving him for the day, Erika told her, "Don't worry, Jonathan will be just fine here. We could stand to have a mascot hanging around the place. Right, Jonathan?"

The dog responded by wagging his tail so hard it thumped on the floor.

"I'm not worried."

Truthfully, Lily wasn't having second thoughts about leaving Jonathan. The second thoughts involved her running into Christopher. She wondered if he was already here, and if he was, why hadn't he come out?

Maybe it was better if he didn't, she decided in the next moment.

Right, like that's going to change anything about your reaction to the man.

She pressed her lips together and blocked out the little voice in her head that insisted on being logical. It was time for her to say goodbye to the puppy and get going.

Yet for some reason, her feet weren't getting the message. They remained planted exactly where they were, as if they were glued to the spot.

She allowed herself just one question—and then she was going to leave, she insisted. Really.

"How's Rhonda?"

Holding on to Jonathan's leash, Erika looked at her in surprise. "You know Rhonda?"

Serves you right for saying anything.

"Not exactly," Lily admitted. "But Chris—Dr. Whitman," she amended quickly, "mentioned that she was his neighbor's dog and that she'd been hit by a car the other day. I was just wondering if she was doing any better now."

Erika actually beamed.

"Oh, she's doing *much* better. Would you like to see her?"

The response, followed by the question, didn't come from Erika. It came from the veterinarian who had come out of the back of the clinic and was now standing directly behind her.

Lily turned around to face him, trying to act as if her heart hadn't just given up an extra beat—or maybe three.

"Oh, I don't want to put you out any more than I already have—" She saw the puzzled expression on

Christopher's face, so she explained, "By leaving Jonathan here."

"You're not putting anyone out leaving Jonny here," he assured her. He ruffled the dog's head before pushing open the swinging door that led to the back of the clinic. "Rhonda's back here," Christopher told her.

He stood, holding the rear door open with his back, waiting for her to cross the threshold and come follow him.

Lily had no choice but to do as he asked. To do otherwise would have been rude.

Christopher led the way to where the Irish setter was recuperating from her second surgery. The dog was dozing and looked almost peaceful—except for the bandages wrapped around part of her hindquarters. The dog was in a large cage.

"Isn't she cramped, staying in there?" Lily asked, looking at him. Her voice was filled with sympathy.

"Right now, I don't want her moving around too much," he explained. "If I think she's responding properly to the surgery and her stitches are healing well, I'll have her transferred to the run before I have my neighbor take her home with him."

"The run?" Lily echoed.

Rather than explain verbally, Christopher quietly took her by the hand and drew her over to another area of the hospital.

There were three wide enclosures all next to one another. All three were sufficiently wide for a large animal to not just stretch out, but to literally run around if it so chose.

Christopher stood by silently, letting her absorb it

all, then waved his hand at the enclosures. "Hence the term," he explained.

It began making a little more sense, she thought, taking everything in. And then she looked at Christopher again.

"You sure you don't mind my leaving Jonathan here all day?" she asked again.

"I'm sure," he answered. And then he smiled. "Besides, it'll give you a reason to come back."

Why was it that the man could instantly make her heart flutter with just a glance. After all, she wasn't some freshly minted teenager with stars in her eyes. She was an adult who'd endured death and lived life on her own. Heart palpitations over a good-looking man were definitely *not* in keeping with the way she envisioned herself.

There was no one to give her any answers.

Just then, the receptionist popped her head in. Lily noticed that Jonathan was no longer with the woman. "Doctor, Penelope is here for her shots. I put her in Room 3."

"Tell Mrs. Olsen I'll be right in, Erika," he told his receptionist. And then he turned to Lily. "Penelope is a Chihuahua. Giving her injections is a challenge. The needle is almost bigger than she is. Poor thing shakes uncontrollably the minute I walk into the room and she sees me. I hate having any animal afraid of me," he confided as they left the area.

He paused by the swinging door that led to the reception desk. "We're open until six," he told her. "If you need to leave Jonny here longer than that, I'll just take him home with me," he offered.

"Thank you, but that really won't be necessary. I've

got a very understanding boss and she'll let me take off to pick up Jonathan," she told him. "I'll see you before six," she promised.

And with that, Lily hurried out of the animal hospital, moving just a little faster than she might have under normal circumstances.

But even as she reached her vehicle and slid in behind the steering wheel, she had to come to terms with the very basic fact that no matter how quickly she moved, there was no way she was going to come close to outrunning her own thoughts.

Chapter Eleven

Lily felt as if she had never been busier.

Theresa's catering company had not one but two catering events going on, with both taking place that evening.

One event was a fund-raiser for a local charity. It entailed a full seven-course meal and the guest list was for a hundred and fifty-eight people. The other was a celebration on a smaller scale. It was a bridal shower and the only things that were required were champagne and a cake that could feed a group of thirty guests, give or take a few.

Lily worked almost nonstop from the moment she entered the shop until the last dessert was carefully boxed up and sent off on its way.

Without being fully aware of it, she breathed a long sigh of relief. It felt as if she'd been on her feet for at least eighteen hours straight and, although she loved to bake, it was really good to be finished,

"You outdid yourself today," Theresa told her as she oversaw the last of the food being placed in the catering van. Turning from the vehicle, she took a closer look at her pastry chef. "You look really tired, Lily."

Concern elbowed its way to the surface. No matter what else she did or accomplished with her life, Theresa was first and foremost a mother with a mother's sense of priorities. "Do you need someone to drive you home, dear? I don't want you falling asleep behind the wheel. I'd drive you myself but I already have to figure out how to be in two places at once. Three is completely beyond my limit—for now," the older woman added with a twinkle in her eye.

"I'm fine, Theresa," Lily assured the older woman. She didn't want Theresa worrying about her. "Besides, I'm not going straight home."

Halfway out the front door, ready to drive over to the fund raiser first to make sure that all would go well there, Theresa turned back to her. It was obvious that her interest was piqued.

"Oh?" Her bright eyes pinned Lily in place. "Do you have a date?"

"With the dog," Lily quickly informed her boss with a laugh. "I left Jonathan at the animal hospital before coming here this morning."

"Oh, is he sick?" Since this was partially her idea, to unite Lily with the puppy, she couldn't help feeling responsible for this turn of events.

Lily immediately set her straight. "Oh, no, nothing like that. Christopher, um, Dr. Whitman," she quickly amended, "said I could drop Jonathan off at his office so that he'd be properly looked after while I was gone. Otherwise, he might cause havoc in the house and I really didn't have the heart to stick him into one of those crates."

Theresa cocked her head, still regarding her intently. "You *are* talking about the dog and not the veterinarian, right?" the catering company owner wanted to verify.

Lily couldn't help laughing. Thanks to that, she felt close to rejuvenated as she answered, "Yes, but just for the record, I wouldn't want to put Dr. Whitman into a crate, either."

Theresa inclined her head, agreeing. "I'm sure that he'll be happy to hear that. And now," she announced as the catering van's driver honked to remind her that she had to get going, "I'm overdue getting out of here and have to fly. Enjoy yourself."

Lily felt the instruction was completely misplaced. "I'm only picking up my dog."

A rather ambiguous, mysterious smile graced Theresa's lips. "No reason you can't enjoy that," the older woman tossed over her shoulder just before she finally hurried out the door.

That was definitely a very odd thing to say, Lily thought, staring at the closed door.

But she didn't have any time to puzzle it out. She had a dog to pick up and—Lily glanced at her watch— only half an hour to do it in. The animal hospital closed at six o'clock.

She could make it there in twenty, Lily thought confidently.

She didn't.

Under ordinary circumstances, she could have easily made it to the animal hospital in the allotted amount of time left. However, ordinary circumstances did *not* involve a three-car collision that caused several blocks to be shut down to through traffic as two ambulances and three tow trucks were dispatched and made their way through the completely clogged area.

Utterly stressed out, the last of her patience all but stripped from her, Lily finally arrived at the Bedford Animal Hospital sixteen minutes after its doors had closed for the evening.

Even so, ever hopeful, Lily parked in the first space she could find, jumped out of her vehicle and ran to the animal hospital's front door. Lily tried turning the knob, but it was securely locked and the lights inside the office were turned off.

Everything was dark.

Now what? Christopher was going to think that she deliberately left the dog with him and wasn't coming back for Jonathan.

That was when she finally saw it.

There was a business envelope with the hospital's return address in the corner taped to the side of the doorjamb. Her name was written across the front in bold block letters.

She lost no time in pulling off the tape and opening the envelope. Inside was a single sheet of paper.

It read: "Lily, had to close up. Couldn't reach you by phone so I'm taking Jonny home with me. If you want to pick him up tonight, here's the address."

Just like the rest of the note, the address on the bottom was printed in block letters, but even bigger than the previous part so that there was no chance that she would have trouble reading it.

Staring at it, she realized that the address was close to her own house. If she wasn't mistaken, the veterinarian's house was just two developments away.

It really was a small world.

With her GPS turned on and engaged to make sure she didn't accidentally go off in the wrong direction, Lily lost no time in driving over to the address in Christopher's note.

She didn't know why, maybe because of his practice, but she had just naturally assumed that Christopher would be living in one of the newer homes that had recently gone up in the area. Once a homey small town built around a state university, Bedford had grown and was still continuing to grow. A thriving city now, it still managed to maintain its small-town feel.

Her GPS brought her to one of the older, more mature neighborhoods. Looking at the address that matched the one in the note, she judged that the house had to be around the same age as the one she lived in. That made the building approximately thirty years old.

After her mother had died, Lily found that she couldn't bear to sell the house. The thought of having another family move in and change everything around had just been too hard for her to cope with at the time. There were just too many memories there for her to part with so easily.

As she slowed down and approached the house, she saw Christopher's car in the driveway. Parking at the curb, Lily got out and made her way to the massive double front doors. The moment she rang the doorbell, she heard barking.

Jonathan.

But the very next moment Lily thought she made

out two distinct barks—or was that three? There was definitely another dog there besides Jonathan. Had her dog learned to play with other dogs? The thought raised other questions in her mind, all having to do with the energetic puppy's safety.

Worried, Lily was about to ring the doorbell a second time when the door suddenly swung open. Christopher was standing inside, one hand on the door, the other holding off not one dog, but three.

The second he realized it was her, he grinned. "So you made it." The way he said it sounded as though congratulations were implied. "I wasn't sure if you'd see the note."

He shouldn't have had to post the note, Lily thought, feeling guilty that he'd had to go to extra trouble on her account. She should have been at the hospital to collect her pet before he'd ever left the place.

Her apology came out in a rush. "I'm sorry. We had two big events going on at the same time then there was a three-car collision and—"

Somewhat overwhelmed by the words and her speed in offering them, Christopher held his hand up as if to physically stop the flow of explanation.

"That's okay, no harm. I would have kept him here overnight if you couldn't come to pick him up for some reason. I did try reaching you before we closed up," he told her. All three attempts went directly to voice mail. Usually there was only one reason for that. "Is your phone off?"

She would have been the first to admit that this had not been her best day. "My cell phone battery died," she said, chagrinned but owning up to her oversight. "I left it on overnight and forgot to charge it."

Christopher looked amused rather than fazed. "I do the same thing," he told her.

Lily doubted it. She had a feeling the man was only saying that to make her feel better, and he had a tiny bit.

"Jonathan's been making friends with Leopold and Max," he told her, gesturing toward the two Great Danes that were on either side of her puppy like two huge, somewhat messy bookends. "I think they think he's a toy I brought home for them."

"As long as they don't think he's a chew toy or try to bury him in the backyard," Lily quipped, then became serious. "I don't know how to thank you," she began. "Except to just grab his leash and get out of your way."

"No need to hurry off," he countered. His eyes swept over her, backing up his statement. "I'm having pizza delivered. You can stay and have some if you like. There's more than enough to share."

"Pizza?" Lily repeated.

He wasn't quite sure why she looked at him uncertainly. "Yes. You know, that round thing with sauce and cheese. People usually have more things put on top of it."

"I know what pizza is." She looked around at the towering boxes that seemed to be just about everywhere. "Are you having that for dinner because you're busy packing up to move?"

"I'm not packing up," he told her, then asked, "What makes you think I'm moving?"

"There are boxes stacked up all over the place," she said, gesturing toward the nearest cardboard tower. "You're not moving?" she questioned. Then why were all these boxes here?

"I'm not moving *out*," he corrected. "I'm moving

in. This is—was," he amended, "my mother's house. I thought I'd stay here instead of renting an apartment until I decide if I want to sell the place or not."

She could more than understand how he felt. "So you lost your mother recently." It wasn't a question so much as a conclusion, one voiced with all due sympathy since she vividly recalled how she had felt at the time of her mother's death.

"Feels like it," he admitted. Still, he didn't want the facts getting lost. "But it's been close to five months."

Her eyes swept around the area. The boxes almost made her claustrophobic. In his place, she didn't think she could rest until she got everything put away and the boxes stashed in some recycling bin.

"When did you move in?" she asked him, curious.

"Close to three months," he answered.

He was kidding, she thought. But one look at his chiseled face told her that he was being serious. How could he *stand* it like this?

"Three months? And you haven't unpacked?" she questioned, staring at him.

"Not all of it," he answered vaguely, hoping she didn't want any more details than that.

The truth was, except for some of his clothes, he hadn't unpacked at all. A reluctance had taken hold of him. If he didn't actually unpack his things, he could pretend that somewhere, on some plane, his old life was still intact, maybe also that his mother was still alive. He knew that was far-fetched but the mind didn't always work in a logical, linear fashion.

"I'm doing it slowly. I'm really not much on unpacking," he admitted.

Lily ventured into the next room, which looked a great deal like the room she had initially entered.

"Really? I would have never guessed," she told him, raising her voice so that he could hear her. Coming out again, she made him an offer. "How would you like some help? It goes faster if there're two people unpacking instead of one."

He didn't want to put her out and, if he read that look in her eyes correctly, he definitely didn't want her pity.

"Thanks, but I can handle it."

"No offense, Christopher, but I don't think you can. Besides, it would make me feel that in a way, I'm paying you back for taking care of Jonathan."

The doorbell rang. "Hold that thought," he instructed as he went to answer the door. "Does that mean you'll have some pizza with me?" he asked as he reached for the doorknob.

"Okay, if that's the package deal, then yes, I'll have a slice of pizza—and then get to work," she specified.

Christopher paid the delivery boy, handing him a twenty and telling him to keep the change. Closing the door with his back, he held on to the oversize box with both hands. The pizza inside was still very warm and the aroma that wafted out was mouthwatering.

Lily couldn't take her eyes off the box he was holding.

"That box is huge," she couldn't help commenting.

He glanced down as if seeing it for the first time. It *was* rather large at that. "I thought while I was at it, I might as well get enough to last until tomorrow night, too."

Lily shook her head. "Oh, no, tomorrow night you're having a hot meal," she contradicted.

"This is hot," he told her.

"A *real* hot meal," she emphasized. Since he seemed to be resisting her suggestion, one she was making for the purest of reasons, she further said, "You don't even have to go out of your way to get it. I'll bring it here to you." Once out of her mouth, she found she liked what she'd just come up with. "That way, we can eat as we unpack."

He didn't remember this becoming a two-day joint project. And while he liked the idea of having her come over and sharing another meal with him, he didn't want her to feel that this was some sort of a two-for-one deal. "You don't have to do that," he insisted.

"You didn't have to offer to watch Jonathan for me, or teach him—and me—a few of the basic commands," she countered.

Christopher could see that arguing with her was futile. She certainly didn't look stubborn, but she obviously was.

"Point taken," he allowed, "but this—" he gestured around "—is a lot more than just having a pet take up a little space."

"Potato, po*ta*to." She sniffed. "Those are my terms, take them or leave them."

He didn't quite comprehend the connection and said as much. "Not quite sure what you're getting at, but all right," he agreed, knowing when to surrender and when to dig in and fight. This was not the time for the latter. "I guess I could stand the help."

Lily smiled her approval at him. "Good, because I was going to help you whether you wanted me to or not," she told him.

"And just how were you going to do that?" Chris-

topher asked, curious. "You don't know where anything goes."

"Granted," she allowed. "But I'm good at making
educated guesses, and besides, I'm pretty sure you'd
break down eventually and tell me."

"Can we eat first?" Christopher suggested, nodding
at the pizza box, which was now on the coffee table,
awaiting their pleasure. "After all, the boxes aren't
going anywhere."

"True, but they also aren't going to unpack themselves," Lily countered.

"How about a compromise?" he asked.

Lily had always believed in compromise. And, in
any event, she didn't want the man thinking she was
some sort of a fanatic who picked up all the marbles
and went home if she couldn't have her way.

"Go ahead," she urged, "I'm listening."

"We each have a slice first, *then* we get started," he
suggested, shifting the box so that it seemed closer to
her. "I don't know about you, but I had a nonstop day
and I'm starving. If I don't eat something soon, I'm not
going to have enough energy to *open* a box, much less
put whatever's in the box away."

That just about described her day as well, she
thought. But before she could say as much, or agree
with him, her stomach rumbled, as if to remind her
that it was running on empty. She'd worked through
lunch, grabbing a handful of cherry tomatoes to try to
appease her hunger. Cherry tomatoes only went so far.

"I'll take that as a yes," Christopher concluded with
a satisfied grin. To cinch his argument, he raised the
lid on the pizza box and inhaled deeply. The aroma

was damn near seductive. "Right now, that smells almost as good to me as your pastries did the other day."

"Okay, one slice apiece and then we work. If you point me in the right direction, I'll get a couple of plates and napkins," she offered.

Christopher laughed. "Thanks, but it would probably take me more time to explain where to find them than it would take for me to get them myself." He began to cross to the kitchen, then abruptly stopped as one of the dogs sashayed around him. "Guard the pizza," he told Lily. "And look fierce," he added. "If either Leopold or Max detect the slightest weakness, they'll tag team you and get that box away from you before you even know what's going on."

She looked at him, utterly stunned. "Tag team?" Lily repeated. "You mean like in wrestling?"

That seemed rather unbelievable to her. After all, Christopher was talking about dogs, and while this was still pretty unfamiliar territory to her, she wasn't about to endow four-footed animals with a humanlike thought process.

He had to be pulling her leg.

But Christopher seemed dead serious. "Exactly like in wrestling." He looked rather surprised and then pleased that she was familiar with the term he'd used. "Don't let those faces fool you. They're a cunning duo."

"Apparently," she murmured.

She wasn't sure if she believed Christopher, but she focused her attention on the two Great Danes just to be on the safe side.

Meanwhile, Jonathan had gotten tired trying to get the best of the two older, larger dogs and had fallen back on the familiar. He had plopped down at her feet where he remained, lying there like a panting rug. He continued to stay there even after Christopher returned with a handful of napkins as well as a couple of plates.

The second Christopher offered her the first slice, Leopold and Max both raised their heads, their interests completely engaged.

"Down, boys," Christopher ordered. "You're not being polite to our guest." When the two dogs continued to stare at Lily's plate and drool, he said the command a second time, this time with more force.

Moving as one, the two Great Danes dropped their heads, sank down on the floor simultaneously and stretched out. Within seconds, their eyelids had drooped—along with their heads.

She could have sworn the two dogs had instantaneously fallen asleep.

Chapter Twelve

She stared at the two Great Danes for another few seconds. The sound of even breathing was evident. They really *were* asleep, she marveled.

"Nice trick," she said to Christopher, greatly impressed by the way his pets had responded to him. He had a gift, no two ways about it, she thought.

"Training," he corrected.

Lily supposed it was all in the way someone looked at it. But he did have a point. She could see how there would be no living with animals as large as these two dogs were if he hadn't succeeded in rigorously training them to respond to his commands.

"That, too," she allowed.

"Want another one?" he asked her.

Lily turned around to face him. She wasn't sure what the veterinarian was referring to. "Training trick?" she asked uncertainly.

He laughed. "No, pizza slice." He moved the opened box closer to her side of the coffee table. "You finished the slice I gave you, but there's still three quarters of a box to go."

"No, thank you, not right now." She had more than enough room for another slice, but she really wanted to make at least a slight dent in this box city that was invading his house. The aroma from the pizza teased her senses. She would have given in if she'd been less disciplined. "Although I can see the attraction," she admitted.

Christopher's eyes skimmed over her a little slower than they might have. "Yes, me, too."

Her mouth curved, silently accepting the compliment he was giving her. "I'm talking about the pizza," she told him pointedly.

"I know. Me, too," he replied whimsically. He still wasn't looking at the slices inside the pizza box.

Lily felt herself growing warmer, her mind filling with thoughts that had nothing to do with restoring order to his house, or eating pizza, or training unruly puppies. The way he watched her made her feel desirable; moreover, it made her imagination take flight.

Right, because you're so irresistible, just like veritable catnip to the man, the little voice in her head mocked.

Straighten up and fly right, she silently lectured. Out loud, she laid out terms that she felt would satisfy both of them.

"We can both have another slice after we each unpack two boxes," she told him. When he gave her a rather amused, dubious look, she amended her terms. "Okay, one box for you, two for me." Then, in case he thought she was saying she was faster than he was, she explained, "I've had practice at packing and un-packing."

He got started opening the large box next to the sofa. "You moved around often?"

She laughed softly, shaking her head. The house she lived in was the house she'd been born in. "Not even once."

For a second, he seemed slightly lost. "Then why—?"

"—did I say I've had practice?" She filled in the rest of his question and continued, "Because I have. I pack pastries before they're transported to their destination and once they get there, I have to unpack them, making sure that they make it to the table in perfect condition, the way the customer expected when they paid the catering bill. Making sure the pastries are displayed to their best advantage requires a delicate touch," she pointed out. "There's nothing worse-looking than a squashed or lopsided pastry or cake at a party."

"If they taste anywhere near as good as what I've sampled from your oven so far, I'd be willing to scrape them off the inside of a cardboard box just to be able to eat them."

She laughed. "That's very nice of you, but it doesn't change my point, which is that I can unpack things quickly, whereupon it looks as if you're willing to latch on to any excuse, any port in a storm no matter how flimsy it might be, just as long as you don't have to tackle what's inside those boxes."

"Busted," Christopher freely admitted, then in his defense, he added, "I'm pretty much the same way about groceries, which is why I don't have any and

I'm on a first-name basis with a lot of take-out places around here."

Pushing up her sleeves, Lily turned her attention to the closest large carton. "I wouldn't have pegged you as a procrastinator."

On the contrary, she would have said that he seemed like the type that tackled whatever was in front of him rather than putting it off till another time. Looks could be deceptive.

His were also very distracting, she couldn't help noticing.

"I guess that makes me a man of mystery—someone you *can't* read like an open book," he said, amusement highlighting his face.

"What that makes you," she corrected, "is a man who needs to be prodded. Now, do you have a utility knife—or if you don't, just a plain knife will do," she told him. She'd tried pulling the carton apart and the top just wouldn't give. "I just need something I can open the boxes with. If I keep trying to do it with my bare hands, I'm going to wind up breaking off all my nails in the process."

"I wouldn't want you to do that," he told her, going back to the kitchen to get a knife out of one of the drawers.

When he gave it to her, hilt first, she nodded toward the utensils that were in the drawer. "So you did put some things away."

He glanced over his shoulder, back at the drawer, which hadn't closed properly and had subsequently rolled back open again. He crossed to it to reclose it.

"Much as I'd like to take the credit," he answered, "no, I didn't."

"The drawer's full, and from what I could see those were all utensils in it. In other words, it's not just a junk drawer that you tossed things into as you came cross them. That's organization."

"No," he corrected, "that's my mother. Those were her utensils. After she died, I just couldn't get myself to throw any of her things away."

Not to mention the fact that hers had been a better quality than the ones he'd picked up when he'd lived off campus while attending school back East. When things had blown up on him so suddenly with Irene, he'd just told the movers to throw everything into boxes and move the lot to his mother's house in California.

She understood where he was coming from. But right now, the issue was a practical one of two things not being able to occupy the same space.

"There are always charities you can donate things to," she told him gently.

Christopher nodded. He knew she was right. "Soon—but not yet."

Lily didn't want him to think she was being insensitive—or pushy, especially not in this instance. "Actually, I understand exactly how you feel. When my mother passed away, I couldn't get myself to give anything of hers away, either. But after a while, I decided I was being selfish. My mother had a lot of nice things that still had a lot of life left in them. There were women out there who were—and are—needy, who could use one nice pair of shoes, or one nice dress, to lift their spirits, to maybe even turn them around and start them back toward a positive feeling of self-worth."

Lily went on talking as she methodically emptied

the first box, arranging its contents on the coffee table and the floor next to it.

"My mother was the type that liked helping people, even when she barely had anything herself. I know she would have wanted me to give her things away, so I picked a few special things to keep, things that really reminded me of her, and then I distributed the rest between a handful of charities. But it took me a long time before I could do that," she emphasized. "So I really do understand exactly what you're feeling."

Lily was coming to the bottom of the box and she felt that she had to comment on what she'd found while unpacking.

"You know, for a man who doesn't like to unpack, you certainly pack well."

Christopher thought of letting her comment go and just accepting it as a compliment. But not saying anything was practically like lying—or at least allowing a lie to be established. He couldn't do that, seeing as how she was really putting herself out for him—as well as the fact that he was giving serious thought to having a relationship with this unique woman.

"Not me," he told her. She looked at him in surprise. "It was the movers I hired, they did the packing for me. Unfortunately, while they obviously could pack extremely efficiently, they couldn't be bribed to unpack once they reached their destination."

"You actually tried to bribe them?" she asked, trying not to laugh at him.

"No," he admitted, "but looking back, I should have. I honestly didn't think that I would be putting it off as long as I have. But each day I found a reason not to get started—and Leopold and Max didn't seem to mind," he added, spreading the blame around. "I actually think they kind of like having all these boxes scattered throughout the house. For them it's like having their own private jungle gym."

This time she did laugh. "No offense, but I don't think dogs care about a jungle gym. In any case, even if they do, they're going to have to adjust," she informed him.

For the time being, she set the now-empty box to one side. She intended to break the carton down for easier transport and recycling later.

Christopher looked at her a little uncertainly. "Are you telling me that you intend to stay here until all these boxes are unpacked and taken apart?"

She couldn't tell if he was just surprised—or if the idea of her being here like that put him off. "No—but I do intend to keep coming back until they are."

Curiosity got the better of him. None of his old friends from high school had ever volunteered to help him conquer this cardboard kingdom of his. "Why would you do that?"

There was no hesitation on her part. "Call it repaying one favor with another—besides, my mother taught me to never leave something half-done. The job's done when the job's done," she told the veterinarian, reciting an old axiom.

She'd amused him—again. "That sounds like something out of Yogi Berra's playbook," he said, referring to the famous Yankees catcher.

The smile she gave him told Christopher that she was familiar with baseball history. Something else they had in common, he couldn't help thinking.

"Wise man, Yogi Berra," Lily commented with a smile as she went back to work.

By the end of the evening, they had managed to unpack a total of five boxes and they had put away the contents of three of them—not to mention all but polishing off the pizza he had ordered. There were only two slices left, which Christopher earmarked for his breakfast for the following morning.

Tired, Lily rotated her shoulders to loosen them a little.

"Well, I've got an early day tomorrow," she told Christopher, "so I'd better be going home."

He wanted to ask her to stay a little longer. Not to unpack, but just to talk.

Just to *be*.

He found that he liked Lily's company, liked her sense of humor and her determination, as well. Liked, too, the way her presence seemed to fill up his house far more than the towering boxes she had them tackling ever had.

But asking her to stay when she had to be up early would be selfish of him. So he let the moment pass—except to voice his thanks for her help as he walked her and Jonathan to the door.

"You know, this has to be one of the most unique evenings I've ever spent," he confessed, then added, "I enjoyed it."

The dimpled smile on his face seemed to work its way into every single nook and corner of her being. Lily returned his smile and replied, "So did I."

He wanted to be sure that, despite what she'd said, having her work like this, putting his things away, wasn't going to ultimately scare her off. So he asked, "And you'll be dropping Jonny off at the animal hospital tomorrow?"

She wanted to, but there was a problem. "I've got to be at work at seven," she told him, knowing the clinic opened at eight.

If she needed to leave the dog at seven, then he was going to be there at seven. He found himself *wanting* to be there for her. "Funny, so do I."

"No, you don't," she countered, seeing through his lie. She didn't want to put him out and he'd already been so helpful to her.

He pretended to narrow his eyes, giving her a reproving look. "It's not nice to call your pet's doctor a liar."

Her heart felt as if it was under assault. Her mouth curved again as she shook her head. "I'm not calling you a liar—" Then, whimsically, she made a suggestion. "How about a stretcher of truth?"

"I'll take that under consideration," he told her. His tone changed as he told her fondly, "Now go home and get some sleep."

That was the plan. Whether or not it worked was going to be another story, she thought, looking at Christopher. "Thanks for the pizza."

"Thanks for the help," he countered. "And for the kick in the pants."

That sounded so callous when he said it that way. "I didn't kick, I prodded," she amended politely.

He laughed as he inclined his head, playing along. "I stand corrected." Reaching the door, he paused, his brain engaged in a verbal tennis match. He decided to leave the decision up to her—sort of.

"Lily—"

There was something in his voice that put her on alert. "Yes?"

His eyes held hers for a full moment before Christopher put his question to her. "Would you mind if I kissed you?"

This time, the smile she offered began in her eyes. "Actually," Lily admitted, "I think I'd mind if you didn't."

"I definitely wouldn't want that," Christopher confessed as he framed her face with his hands. The next moment he brought his lips down to hers.

It began lightly, politely, but almost instantly took on a life and breadth of its own, escalating quickly. Along with that escalation, it brought with it a whole host of emotions.

She didn't quite recall wrapping her arms around Christopher's neck, didn't remember, once anchored to him this way, tilting her body into his. What she did remember was the wild burst of energy that seemed to spring out of nowhere and wrapped itself around her tightly for the duration of that intense kiss.

Lily's mouth tasted of every forbidden fruit he'd ever fantasized about. It made him want more.

Made him want her.

He struggled to hold himself in check, to only go so far and no further. It was far from easy, but he was not about to pay this woman back for her help, for her providing him with his first decent evening since his breakup with Irene, for giving him his first shot at feeling *human* since Irene had taken a two-by-four to his life—and his pride—he was not going to pay her back for all that by overpowering Lily and forcing himself on her.

So, with a wave of what he felt was close to super-human control, Christopher forced himself to back away from what could have easily become his with just the right moves.

He wasn't about "moves," he reminded himself, he was about sincerity, no matter *what* his body was attempting to dictate to him.

Drawing back, he paused to take a couple of discreet, very deep breaths, doing his best to regulate the timbre of his voice.

"Thank you again," he murmured.

She knew he wasn't thanking her for helping him to unpack those few boxes. She struggled to stifle the blush that wanted so badly to take root. But she didn't seem to have a say in that. Her body seemed to be on its own timetable, one that had little to do with anything she might have dictated.

After a beat, Lily cleared her throat, managed to murmur something that sounded like "Don't mention it," and then left quickly with her puppy.

She wasn't sure just how long it had taken for her heartbeat to settle down and return to normal. All she was aware of was that it had remained rather erratic for the entire trip home, and even for a few minutes after she'd walked into her house.

She was also aware of the happy glow that had taken hold of her.

This, she felt rather certain, was the very first leg of the journey that ultimately led to genuine affection. Lily stubbornly refused to use the *L* word to describe what she might wind up achieving since she felt if she did, she might just jinx what was happening.

Deep down, though she wasn't a superstitious person by nature, she was afraid that thinking about falling in love with this man would almost assuredly guarantee that there would be no happily ever after waiting for her at the finish line.

Besides, she hardy knew anything about the man except that he hated unpacking—and he had a killer smile. The really safe, smart thing to do, Lily told herself as she unlocked the front door and Jonathan pushed the door opened with his shoulder, walking right in, would be for her to find Jonathan another veterinarian.

If she went that route, it would guarantee that she would have no entanglements with the man whose house she'd just left, no further temptation to wander down the wrong road someday soon.

Oh, who are you kidding? she scolded herself.

She had never been one to automatically opt for doing things the "smart way," especially if that "smart way" promised just more of the same.

More dullness, more playing it safe.

And that in turn meant that there wouldn't be anything to light up her life. Nothing would cause her fingertips to tingle and her imagination to take flight, going to places she would have never admitted to yearning for, at least not out loud.

"You continue torturing yourself like this and you are not going to get any sleep no matter what you try. Turn off your brain, change into your pj's and for God's sake, get some rest before you wind up dropping from exhaustion."

Easier said than done.

Oh, she could certainly change into her pajamas and crawl into bed. The next-to-impossible part of the equation was the part about turning off her brain.

Her brain, it seemed, wanted only to vividly relive that last kiss and play it over and over again in her mind's eye, heightening every last nuance to its uppermost limit.

She was doomed and she knew it.

Resigned, Lily went up the stairs to her bedroom, her four-footed black shadow following right behind her, barking happily.

Chapter Thirteen

Christopher knew it would make a difference, but until the job was almost completed, he hadn't realized just how *much* of a difference the undertaking would actually make.

Each time he looked around, the amount of space surprised him all over again. Without fully being conscious of it, he'd gotten accustomed to weaving his way in and out between the boxes, accepting the clutter that existed as a given. With Lily insisting on helping him unpack the countless boxes, large and small, that had been here for months, the house gradually returned to looking like the place he'd known during his childhood, growing up with a single mom. Lily had not only gotten him to organize and clear away the physical clutter, but through doing that he had also wound up clearing away some emotional clutter, as well.

Without boxes being everywhere he turned, Christopher felt as if his ability to think clearly had vastly improved, allowing him to finally move forward in his private life.

It was almost as if his brain was like a hard drive that had been defragmented. The analogy wasn't his. Lily had tossed the comparison his way when he'd commented that he felt less oppressed, more able to think these past few days. He thought her analogy seemed to hit the nail right on the head.

As they worked together, he discovered that Lily had an uncanny ability to simplify things. She seemed to see into his very soul.

Without discussing it or even being fully conscious of it, he and Lily had settled into a routine that was beneficial to both of them. Weekday mornings she would swing by with Jonathan, dropping the Labrador off at the animal hospital, and then in the evenings she would collect her pet and then follow Christopher to his home. Once there they would both tackle emptying out and breaking down at least one of the boxes, if not more.

They also ate dinner together, usually one she had prepared in his kitchen. It was just something she had gotten into the habit of doing. While he continued to tell her that she really didn't have to go out of her way like this, Christopher made no secret of his enjoyment of each and every meal she prepared.

As much as he appreciated her help de-cluttering his house and looked forward to exhibits of her stellar culinary abilities, what he looked forward to most of all were the conversations they had. Each evening while they worked and ate, they talked and got to know one another a little better than before.

It definitely made Christopher anticipate each evening.

Oh, he loved being a veterinarian, loved being able to improve the lives of almost all the animals who were brought to his hospital.

He was lucky enough to treat a larger variety of pets than most, everything from mice, hamsters and rabbits to dogs and cats and birds, as well as several other types of pets who fell somewhere in between. He couldn't remember a time when he hadn't wanted to be a veterinarian, and if he hadn't become one he honestly didn't know what he would be doing these days.

But Lily, well, she represented a completely different path in his life, a path he was both familiar with in a distant, cursory fashion, and one different enough for him to feel that he hadn't actually traveled it before.

She very quickly had become an integral part of his life. Being around her made him feel alive, with an endless font of possibilities before him. It was akin to being brought back from the dead after having attended his own funeral. He'd never thought he could feel like this again—and it was all because of Lily.

"We're almost done, you know," Lily said one evening, pointing out what she knew was the obvious. But it felt good to say it nonetheless. "There are just a few boxes left. When they're gone, I really won't have a reason to stop by here after work each night." She held her breath, waiting to see if Christopher would express regret or relief over what she'd just said.

His answer more than pleased her—and put her mind at ease. "I could try rustling up some more boxes, maybe steal some from the local UPS office or from FedEx, or the post office on Murphy if all else fails."

She laughed at the very thought of his contemplating hijacking boxes. He was nothing if not exceedingly upstanding. "It's not the same thing."

He stopped working and looked at Lily seriously. She had become part of his life so quickly that it all but took his breath away.

Just like she did.

"I'd still do it if it meant that it would keep you coming over every evening. Besides, as selfish as this might sound, you've gotten me hooked on your cooking. I find myself expecting it by the end of the day," he freely admitted. "You wouldn't want to deprive me of it, now, would you?"

She turned away from the box she'd almost finished emptying and gazed at him, a hint of a pleased smile playing on her lips. "Just so I'm clear on this, let me get this straight. You want me to keep coming over so I can continue unpacking your boxes and cooking your dinner, is that right?"

"What I want," he told her, crossing over to Lily and taking the book that she'd just removed from the last box out of her hands, "is to continue having *you* to look forward to each evening."

His eyes on hers, Christopher let the book he'd just taken out of her hands fall to the floor.

He realized that he was risking a great deal, crawling out on a limb that had no safety net beneath it. But if he didn't, if he didn't *say* something, he ran the very real risk of losing her, of having her just walk away from his life.

This, he knew, was a crossroads for them, for although they had shared an occasional heated moment, an occasional kiss, they had each always returned to their corners, respectful of the other's barriers and limits. They pushed no boundaries, leaving envelopes exactly where they lay.

Risk nothing, gain nothing.

Or, in this case, Christopher thought, risk nothing, lose everything.

He didn't want to lose everything.

"I'd still be stopping by the animal hospital to pick up Jonathan," Lily reminded him. "That is, if, once we're finished here, you'd still be willing to have me drop him off with you in the morning."

"Sure, that goes without saying," he assured her. Jonathan barked as if he knew he was being talked about, but Christopher continued focusing on her. "Everyone looks forward to having Jonny around during the day. But that still leaves a large chunk of my evening empty. I'm not sure I'd know how to deal with that," he told her in a voice that had become hardly louder than a whisper.

As she listened, giving him her undivided attention, that whisper seemed to feather along her lips, softly seducing her, causing havoc to every single nerve ending within her body.

"Why don't we talk about it later?" Christopher suggested in between light, arousing passes along her lips.

"I know what you're doing," she said. It was an effort for her to think straight. "You're just trying to get me to stop unpacking the last boxes."

She saw his mouth curve in amusement, *felt* his smile seeping into her soul.

"I always said you were a very smart lady," Christopher told her.

"And you are exceedingly tricky. Lucky I majored in seeing through tricky," she quipped.

"Maybe lucky for you, not so much me," he told her in a low, unsettling voice.

He was still playing his ace card, Lily thought. Still managing to reduce her to a pliable, warmed-over puddle. And she'd discovered something just now, in this moment of truth. Christopher wasn't just hard to resist. When he got going, moving full steam ahead, the man was damn near *impossible* to resist.

Even so, she did her best to try.

Her best wasn't good enough.

Gladly taking the excuse that Christopher had so willingly handed her, she completely abandoned the box she'd been emptying, leaving it to be tackled on some other day. She certainly wasn't up to doing that this evening.

Tonight had suddenly become earmarked for something else entirely. Tonight she was finally going to give in to all the demands that had been mounting within her, all the demands that were vibrating within her.

She had given herself endless pep talks against taking the step she was contemplating, mentally listing all the reasons she would regret crossing this final line in the sand. The line separating flirtation from something a great deal more serious.

And possibly a great deal more fulfilling.

Commitment and, yes, possibly even love were on the other side of that line.

But just because she was willing to cross that line,

Lily reminded herself, that did not necessarily mean that he did or would.

Even if Christopher said it, said that he *wanted* to cross the line and made a show of embracing both concepts—commitment *and* love—that wouldn't really make it a reality. She wasn't naive enough to believe that just because someone said something meant that there had to be even an iota of truth to it.

That was the part where a leap of faith would need to come in.

She knew that. Logically, she knew that. But right now, logic had been left standing somewhere at a door far away. She would have to deal with this later, one way or another.

Right now, at this burning moment in time, Lily realized that what she wanted, what she *needed,* was to have him make her feel wanted, make her feel that she was special to him.

Never mind whether or not it was true. She would pretend it was true.

And maybe, just maybe, if wishing hard enough could make it so, it *would* be true. But again, that was a struggle, a battle to be undertaken later.

Right now, every fiber of her being wanted to be made love to—make love with—Christopher.

So rather than resist, or coyly move just out of his reach, gravitating toward another excuse, another road-block to get in the way of what she knew they both wanted, Lily remained in his arms, kissed him back the way he had kissed her and, just like that, effectively brought down every single barrier, every make-shift fence, every concrete wall they had each put up to protect the most frail thing they each possessed: their hearts.

This was different, Christopher realized. She wasn't kissing him back with feeling, she was kissing him back with fire. He could feel the passion igniting, could feel it being passed back and forth between them and growing sharply in intensity by the nanosecond.

He kissed Lily over and over again and with each kiss he only craved more. He made love to her with his mouth, first to her lips, then to her throat, sliding down to the tender hollow between her breasts.

Her moan only served to inflame him more. It increased the tempo, inciting a riot right there within his veins.

Christopher was afraid of letting loose. And equally afraid not to.

To contain this amount of passion would bring about his own self-destruction. Not someday but before the evening's end.

Her hands passed over his chest, possessing him even before her fingertips dove beneath his shirt, sliding along the hard ridges of his pectorals, hardening him at the same time that she was reducing him to a mass of fluid flames and desires.

He had to hold back to keep from ripping off her clothes. But even as he tried to keep himself in check, he felt Lily's quick, urgent movements all but tearing away his shirt and slacks.

It was the proverbial straw, unleashing the passionate creature caged within.

His hands, sturdy and capable yet so gentle, were everywhere, touching, caressing, possessing.

Worshipping.

He just couldn't seem to get enough of her. He felt himself feeding on her softness; feeding on her frenzy as if it comprised the very substance of his existence.

As if Lily and only Lily could sustain his very life force.

Christopher was making her crazy, playing her body as if it was a highly tuned musical instrument that would only—*could* only—sing for him, because only he knew just how to unlock the melody that existed just beneath the surface.

Lily ached to feel his touch—to feel *him* along her body.

She arched her back, pressing herself against him as he made the fire inside of her rise to greater and greater heights.

There hadn't been all that many lovers and she knew she wasn't exactly all that experienced before tonight, but Lily honestly thought that she'd been to the table before. It was only now that she realized she had only had her nose pressed up against the glass window, aware of the existence of these sensations, but never really *feeling* any of them.

Certainly not like this.

She felt things now, responded to things now. Did things now, things that had never even crossed her mind to consider doing before tonight.

But suddenly, she wanted to pleasure this man who had utterly lit up her entire world. She wanted to give him back a little in kind of what he had so generously given her.

With the feel of his breath trailing along the more sensitive areas of her skin still incredibly, indelibly fresh along her body, Lily arched and wrapped her legs around his torso, teasing him, urging him to cross the final line.

To form the final union.

Her body urgently moving beneath his, Christopher discovered that he hadn't the strength to hold off any longer. His goal had been to bring her up and over to a climax a handful of times before he claimed the irresistible, but he was only so strong, could only hold out for so long and no more.

That time was now.

With a moan that echoed of surrender, Christopher proceeded to take what she so willingly offered him. Shifting seductively, Lily opened for him.

His mouth sealed to hers and, balancing his weight as best he could, he entered her.

Her sharp intake of breath almost drove him over the brink. At the last moment, he did his best to be gentle, to rein himself in before the ultimate ride took hold and control was all but yanked away from him, no matter how good his intentions.

The more she moved, the more he wanted her.

Wanting her became his only reality.

His heart pounding hard, Christopher stepped up his pace until the ride became dizzying for both of them.

By the end, just before the heat exploded, embracing them fiercely a beat before the inevitable descent began, he felt confident that he had been granted every wish he'd ever made in life.

The feeling was so intense, he tightened his arms around her to the point that he almost found himself merging with her very flesh.

Somehow, they remained two very distinct, if two very exhausted people. Two people clinging to one an other, forming their own human life raft in the rough sea of reality as it gradually descended upon them and came back into focus.

When Christopher could finally draw enough air into his lungs to enable him to form a sentence, albeit a softly worded one, he kissed the top of her head and said, "I am definitely hijacking a moving van and having more boxes delivered."

She laughed and her warm breath both tickled him and somehow managed to begin to arouse him again. He didn't understand how that was possible, but there was a magic to this woman that seemed to make all things possible.

After all, he had been so sure, after what Irene had done to him, that he could never feel again, never *want* to feel again, and yet here he was, feeling and grateful to be doing it.

"I think," she said as she lay her head on his chest, "that we've gotten past that stage—needing boxes as an excuse."

Christopher managed to kiss the top of her head again before he fell back, almost exhausted by the effort as well as insanely happy.

"Can't argue with that," he said, the words straggling out one after the other in an erratic fashion. "Even if I wanted to," he added, "I can't argue. Not enough air in my lungs to argue and win."

He felt her smile against his chest. "Then I win by default."

They both laughed at the absurd way that sounded. And they laughed mainly because just hearing the sound of laughter felt so good and so satisfying, as well as oddly soothing at the same time.

Christopher's arms tightened around her.

Feeling Lily's heart beat against his felt as if it was the answer to everything that was important in his life.

He knew that he had never been happier than right at this very moment.

Chapter Fourteen

Lily very quickly came to the conclusion that there really was no graceful way to go from making mind-blowing love with a man to getting dressed and slipping back into the everyday world that she had temporarily stepped away from.

It would have been a great deal easier to get dressed and make her getaway if Christopher had been asleep. But the man who had lit up her entire world, complete with skyrockets and fireworks, was lying right beside her and he was very much awake.

Even if he was asleep, there was still the small matter of actually making a soundless getaway with her Labrador in tow *and* getting by Christopher's two Great Danes, Leopold and Max. She'd made friends with them over the past few weeks so she was fairly confident that the dogs wouldn't immediately begin barking the moment she stirred. But she had a feeling that they wouldn't turn into two docile statues, silently watching her slip out of the house with Jonathan in her arms.

Any attempt to see if she was right went up in smoke the very next moment.

"Going somewhere?" Christopher asked as she tried to sit up on the sofa, ready to begin the taxing hunt for her clothes—*any* of her clothes.

He slipped his arm around her waist, firmly holding her in place as he waited for her to come up with an answer.

"I thought I'd finish tidying up the family room, break down the empty boxes we left behind, little things like that," she told him innocently.

"In the nude?" Christopher sounded both amused and intrigued. "Glad I didn't doze off like you did. This I have to see."

She looked at him over her shoulder and protested, "I didn't doze off."

"Yes, you did, but that's okay," he told her. "It was only for a few minutes." He drew her in a little closer, his arm still around her waist. "Besides, you look cute when you sleep. Your face gets all soft."

Lily turned her body toward him and gazed down at his face. "As opposed to what? Being rock hard when I'm awake?"

"Not rock hard, but let's just say…guarded," he concluded, finally deciding upon a word. Once he said it out loud, it seemed to fit perfectly. "You know, kind of like a night watchman at an art museum who's afraid someone's going to steal a painting the second he lets his guard down."

Lily frowned. "Not exactly a very romantic image," she commented.

"But an accurate one," he pointed out. His intention hadn't been to insult her or scare her away. He was just being observant. "You don't have to go, you know."

Oh, yes I do. I can't think around you, especially after this.

"I know," she said out loud. "But I'm thinking that a little space between us might not be a bad thing, so I can get my bearings."

He wasn't about to keep her against her will if it came down to that, but he wasn't going to just give up without a word, either.

"A GPS can give you the exact latitude and longitude, but it can't give you a secure feeling. That kind of thing only happens between people," he told Lily, lightly brushing her hair away from her face.

She felt herself tensing. Reacting. "Don't do that," she told him, moving her head back, away from him. "I can't think when you do that."

"Good, I was hoping you'd say that."

Lying back against the sofa again, Christopher pulled her down to him. Before she could make a half-hearted protest, his lips brushed hers.

In less than a moment, she lost the desire to speak, as well. He had relit her fire and they began making love all over again.

There were still a few boxes left scattered around his house. It was a definite improvement over the first time she'd walked into the older home, but the fact that there were any left at all bothered her.

But each time she thought they were going to spend

a quiet evening going through the last of moving cartons, something came up. The first time he'd had another emergency surgery to perform, this time on a mixed-breed dog that had been left on the animal shelter's doorstep. The poor dog had been more dead than alive and, he'd explained to Lily, he was one of the vets who volunteered their services at the shelter. He couldn't find it in his heart to say no when they called. One look at the sad mutt—a photo had been sent to his smart phone—and neither could Lily.

She'd insisted on coming with him to help in any way she could. As sometimes happened, she had made extra pastries for the event that Theresa's company had been catering that day, and Lily brought some of the overage with her to share with Christopher and the other volunteers who were at the shelter.

In the end, the surgery had been a success—and so had her pastries.

"I think they want to permanently adopt you," he told Lily as they left the shelter several hours later. He smiled at her, lingering in the all-but-deserted parking lot. "Those pastries you brought with you were certainly a hit. Thanks."

She looked at him a bit uncertainly. "For what?"

"For coming along. For being so understanding. For being you." He took her into his arms, something he had gotten very used to doing. "It's pretty late, but we can curl up in front of the TV and not pay attention to whatever's on cable. I can order in."

"You need your rest," she told him, amused.

He kissed the top of her head. "What makes you think I won't be resting?"

Amusement highlighted her face. "I'm beginning to know you."

"Damn, foiled again. I'll make it up to you tomorrow," he promised.

She paused for a moment, tilted her head back and, grabbing the front of his shirt, pulled him down slightly to her level. Lily pressed her lips against his, kissing him with feeling.

Before either of them could get carried away, she moved her head back and told him, "There's nothing to make up for. I like watching you come to the rescue like that. You're like a knight in shining armor, except that instead of a lance, you're wielding a scalpel." Stepping away from him, she unlocked her car. The second she opened up the rear passenger door, Jonathan bounded inside. "Now go home."

"Yes, ma'am," he answered obediently, then repeated, "Tomorrow."

"Tomorrow," she echoed.

Despite occasional detours like that, she had expected that they would be back on track the next evening, spending it at his place, unpacking the last of the boxes that were upstairs in his bedroom. Dinner would consist of something she'd prepared.

But when Christopher closed up the hospital for the evening, he informed her that he had a surprise for her.

"What kind of surprise?" she asked suspiciously.

"The kind you'll find out about when we get there," he said mysteriously.

"We're going somewhere?"

"Good deduction," he applauded.

"Shouldn't we drop Jonathan off first?"

"No. He's coming along with us."

"Then we're not going out to eat?" That would have been her first guess at the kind of surprise he was taking her to.

Instead of answering, he merely smiled at her and told her to follow him.

She was intrigued. He had succeeded in capturing her complete attention.

"This is a restaurant," she noted when, fifteen minutes later, she had pulled her vehicle up next to his in a semicrowded parking lot. She was standing beside her car, looking at the squat building that was obviously Christopher's intended destination.

"It is," he confirmed cheerfully.

"We can't leave Jonathan in the car while we eat."

"We're not going to," he informed her, taking the leash from her hand.

"But—"

"Ruff's is a restaurant where people can go to dine out with their pets," he told her. "I thought you might get a kick out of it.

She didn't get a kick out of it, she *loved* it and told him as much over dinner, and continued to do so when they got back to his place.

"How did you find it?" she asked.

"One of my patients' owners opened it up not too long ago. I thought it was an idea whose time has come. I'm one of the investors," he confided to her.

"Really?" The idea excited her—just as the man did, she thought as she felt him trail his fingertips along the hollow of her throat.

"Really," he confirmed. "I'd never lie to a beautiful woman."

"But I'm the only one in the room."

He laughed. "Fishing for compliments, are we?"

She put her hand to her breast. "Me?"

"You," he said, nipping her lower lip.

That was the last of the conversation for quite a while.

"Who's this?" Lily asked, pulling a framed photograph out of the last carton that was still only semi-unpacked in his bedroom.

Time had gotten away from her and she'd wound up spending the night. Which meant she needed to hurry getting dressed so she could swing by her place and get a fresh change of clothing before proceeding on to work.

They had already decided, sometime during the night, that Jonathan would remain here and Christopher would take the dog with him when he went in to the animal hospital.

The framed photograph—Christopher posing with an aristocratic-looking brunette, his arm around her waist in the exact same fashion that it had been around hers that first time she'd tried to slip out of his bed— had all but fallen at her feet when she'd bumped into the open box. It had fallen over, spilling out its contents. The framed photograph was the first thing she saw.

"Who's who?" Christopher asked, preoccupied.

He was searching the immediate area for his keys. He assumed they had fallen somewhere as he and Lily had made love last night. Rather than settling into a certain predictability, their lovemaking only seemed to get better each time.

Instead of answering, she turned toward Christopher holding up the framed photograph. "This woman you've got your arm around," she told him. Even as the words came out, she had a sinking feeling she wasn't going to like his answer.

Christopher's mind went temporarily blank as he saw the frame she had in her hands. "Where did you get that?" he asked, his throat drier than he could ever recall it being.

"It fell out of that box when I accidentally knocked it over," she told him, nodding her head toward the carton that was still on in its side. "Who is she, Chris?" Lily repeated. With each word, the deadness inside of her seemed to grow a little larger, a little more threatening. "She has to be someone because you wouldn't have packed up this photograph if she wasn't."

"I didn't do any of the packing," he reminded her. "The movers did."

The point was that it had been there, at his residence, for them to pack. The fact that he was being evasive right now just made her more anxious.

"Well, it has to be yours," she insisted. "The movers wouldn't have packed up a stranger's things and put them into your moving van—besides, you're *in* the picture and that's your arm around her waist." Each word tasted more bitter than the last. "Who *is* she, Chris?" Lily asked for a third time, growing impatient. It wasn't as if they didn't both have pasts, but she didn't like the idea of not knowing enough about him—and his having secrets.

"She's nobody," he told her, taking the frame out of her hand and tossing it facedown on his rumpled bed.

Lily squared her shoulders defiantly. "If she was nobody, you would have said that right away. You don't take a picture with nobody and then have it framed," she pointed out. "Why won't you tell me who she is?"

Christopher blew out a breath. He'd honestly thought he'd thrown that photograph—all the photographs of her—out. "Because she doesn't matter anymore."

Lily heard what wasn't being said. "But she did once, right?"

"Once," he admitted because to say otherwise would really be lying.

Lily's voice became very quiet. "How much did she matter?"

Because he knew he had to, Christopher gave her the briefest summary of the time he had spent with Irene. "Her name was Irene Masterson and we were engaged—but we're not anymore," he emphasized. "We haven't been for three months."

Three months. The words echoed in her brain. She had him on the rebound. There was no other way to interpret this. She was a filler, a placeholder until he got his act together. How could she have been so stupid as to think this was going somewhere? Things didn't go anywhere except into some dark abyss.

For a moment, Lily stared at him, speechless. She felt her very fragile world shattering and crumbling. "And you didn't think that was important enough to tell me?"

He told her the only thing he could in his own defense. "The topic never came up."

Was he saying it was her fault because she hadn't interrogated him?

"Maybe it should have," she countered, feeling hurt beyond words. "Preferably before things got too hot and heavy between us." At the last moment, she had stopped herself from saying "serious between us" because it wasn't. How could it be if he had kept something so important from her? She'd been deluding herself about his feelings for her. It was painfully obvious now that she had read far too much into ther relationship. There wasn't a "relationship," it was just a matter of killing time for him, nothing more.

"I don't remember a single place where I could have segued into that. When was I supposed to say something?" he asked. "Just before we came together? 'Excuse me, Lily, but in the interest of full disclosure, I think you should know that I had a serious girlfriend for a few years and we were engaged for five months.'"

Five months. The woman in the photograph had had a claim on him for five months—longer than they had known each other. Plus, it had only ended recently, which made her presence in his life shaky at best. The very thought twisted in her stomach, stealing the air out of her lungs.

"Yes," she retorted. "You should have told me, should have said something."

Trying to get hold of herself, Lily took a deep breath. This was her fault, not his. Her fault because she'd given in to the longing, the loneliness she'd felt, thinking that she'd finally found a steady, decent man, someone she could love and go through life with. But Christopher wasn't the guy. He couldn't be with what he'd just gone through. She didn't want to be the girl who picked up other people's messes, a placeholder while the injured party healed.

Her voice was emotionless as she said, "Why aren't you still engaged?"

Christopher lifted a shoulder and let it fall in a careless shrug. "We wanted different things. She wanted me to change, to be someone else, someone who fit into her blue-blooded world. I didn't want to change."

Lily was struggling to understand, to come to grips with what she'd just stumbled across. Trying to tell herself that it didn't matter when every fiber of her being told her that it did.

"Did the engagement just disintegrate on its own?" she asked.

What could he say to make this right? To fix what he seemed to have broken? "It probably would have in time."

Her eyes held his. "But?"

He had no choice. He had to tell her the truth and pray that he wasn't going to regret it. "But with everything going on, losing my mother, I just wanted to get away and be done with it."

Her expression gave him no indication what she was thinking. "So you broke it off?"

Christopher nodded. "Yes."

She needed to get this absolutely straight in her mind. "You made a commitment to someone you loved and then you broke it off?" she pressed.

He wanted to deny it, to deny that he had ever loved Irene. But he *had* loved her, and if he lied about it he knew it would backfire on him, if not now then someday. That damage would be irreparable.

"Yes."

The sadness that washed over her with that single word was almost overwhelming. She couldn't stay here any longer, not without breaking down. "I have to go," she said abruptly. "Jonathan!" she called, her voice growing edgy. "Jonathan, come!"

After a moment, the Labrador appeared at the bottom of the stairs, barking at her. Lily practically ran down the stairs. Not wanting to waste time looking for his leash, she grabbed the dog's collar and as quickly as possible guided him toward the front door.

Christopher flew down the stairs right behind her. "Wait, I thought we agreed that I'd take him to the animal hospital for you this morning."

Lily didn't even turn around. "There's no need. He's coming with me."

"Lily—" Her name echoed of all the hurt, the concern that was ricocheting through him.

"I've change my mind, okay?" she snapped, afraid that she would start to cry at any second. She had to get out of there before it happened. "You changed yours, right? Why can't I change mine?"

Wanting to sweep her into his arms, to hold her against him until she calmed down, Christopher took a step back instead. His instincts told him not to press. "Sure, you can change your mind," he told her quietly. "Will I still see you tonight?"

"I don't think that's a good idea," she told him crisply.

Lily found she had to all but drag Jonathan away— the Labrador seemed reluctant to leave both his canine friends and the man who had treated him so nicely. When he resisted, Lily pulled his collar harder, said his name in a very authoritative voice followed by a command that Christopher had taught her. After a second, Jonathan followed her.

The training had worked out well, she thought, fighting back tears as she crossed the threshold. The trainer, however, had not.

"Lily," Christopher called after her. "I don't want you to leave."

It took a great deal for him to put himself out there like that after he had promised himself not to even think about having a relationship with a woman until he had gotten over his grieving period. Telling himself that his mother would have really liked Lily hadn't exactly tipped the scales in Lily's favor—but it hadn't hurt, either.

"Now," she said, aiming the words over her shoulder as she hurried to her car. "You don't want me to leave *now*. But you'll change your mind soon enough," she said between clenched teeth. She had to clench them or risk beginning to sob.

Served her right for allowing herself to connect with a man so quickly. Lily could feel tears aching in her throat.

Two weeks passed.

Two weeks that moved with the torturous pace of a crippled turtle. Every minute of every day seemed to register as time dragged itself from one end of the day to the other. He felt as if he was going crazy. His work, rather than being his haven, became his trial instead.

He had trouble concentrating.

He tried to move on, he really did. Following his breakup with Irene, after the initial hurt subsided and after he stopped feeling as if he'd been a colossal fool for missing all the signs that had been right there in front of him, Christopher had actually experienced a sense of relief. The kind of relief survivors experienced after learning that they had just narrowly managed to dodge a bullet. The young woman he had thought he had fallen in love with wouldn't have been the woman that he was supposed to end up marrying. Avoiding that was the part where the relief came in.

But in this case, with Lily, there was no sense of relief. There was only a sense of loss, a sense that something very special had somehow managed to slip right through his fingers and he was never going to be able to recover what he had lost.

Consequently, life had progressively become darker for him. It felt as if the light had gone out of his world and he had no way to turn it back on. Resigned to this new, grimmer view of life, he found his whole demeanor changing.

Theresa had alerted her that something was definitely up. She'd said that Lily had become very quiet and withdrawn these past two weeks and that the young woman had taken to bringing the puppy to work with her instead of leaving Jonathan with Christopher. But atypically, Theresa had added, Lily wasn't talking. The pastry chef had told her that everything was "fine" every time she'd asked if something was wrong.

Maizie decided to find out some things for herself.

Which was why she popped into the animal clinic the following Tuesday, when things had slowed down in her own real estate office.

She came armed with one of Cecilia's remaining puppies, telling the receptionist that she had recently acquired this pet and was going to give it to her grand-daughter as a gift. Erika had managed to fit her in be-tween scheduled appointments.

"Hi," Maizie said cheerfully, popping into the last exam room where she'd been told she'd find the object of her visit. "Your receptionist—lovely girl, Erika," she commented before continuing, "said you were back here and that it was all right for me to bring Walter to you. I hope you don't mind my just dropping by. But Walter's going to be a gift for my granddaughter and I just want to be sure he's healthy before I give him to her," she said.

Christopher stared at the puppy. It looked almost exactly like Jonathan. But it couldn't be—could it?

"Where did you get him?" he asked Maizie.

"I know a breeder up north, around Santa Barbara," Maizie replied innocently. "Why do you ask?"

Christopher tried to sound casual as he explained, but just the thought of Lily put longing in his voice. "Someone I know has a dog just like that. She said he just turned up on her doorstep a couple of months ago."

Maizie pretended to take the story in stride. "I hear that Labradors are popular these days because they're so friendly. That's why I got one for my granddaugh-ter." She looked closely at Christopher as he proceeded to examine the puppy. "Is something wrong, dear?"

"The puppy seems to be fine," he said as he contin-ued with his exam.

"I was talking about you, Christopher," Maizie said gently.

He shrugged, wishing the woman would just focus on the puppy she'd brought in and not ask him any per-sonal questions. He couldn't deal with them right now.

He'd left numerous messages on Lily's phone. She hadn't called back once. When he went by her house, there were never any lights on and she didn't answer the door when he rang the bell.

"I'm fine," he told Maizie again.

Maizie placed her hand on his shoulder—she had to reach up a little in order to do it. "You know, Christopher, I feel that I owe it to your mother to tell you that as an actor, you're not very convincing. What's bothering you?" she asked. "I might not be able to help, but I can certainly give you a sympathetic ear."

He didn't want to talk about it. Concluding his exam, he looked at her. "Walter's very healthy. And as for me... Mrs. Connors, I know you mean well—"

Maizie took the puppy off the exam table and placed him on the floor. "You can call me Maizie at this point and hell, yes, I mean well." Her eyes locked with the young veterinarian's. "When my daughter looked like you do right now, it was because something in her relationship with the man she eventually married — wonderful son-in-law, by the way—had gone wrong. Now, out with it. You need an impartial third party to tell you if you're overreacting or if you should give up—and since your mother's not here to listen, I'll be that party in her memory."

Crossing her arms before her, Maizie gave him a very penetrating look that all but declared she was *not* about to budge on this. "Now, you might as well talk to me because I'm not leaving until you do. If you plan on seeing any more patients today, you had better start talking, young man."

Chapter Fifteen

He wound up telling her everything.

It was against his better judgment, against anything he'd ever done, but he gave Maizie a condensed version of what had transpired, right up to Lily discovering the photograph of Irene and him, the one he had since thrown out.

Christopher secretly hoped that, in saying the words out loud, it would somehow help him purge himself of this awful deadness he was experiencing and *had* been experiencing ever since Lily had walked out.

It didn't. It just made it feel worse, if that was possible.

Desperate, he tried to describe to Maizie what he was feeling.

"It's like someone just sucked the very life force out of me." He shrugged, embarrassed. He was being weak and that just wasn't like him. "I'm sorry, I'm not explaining this very well and you didn't come here to hear me carry on like some twelve-year-old school-boy, lamenting about his first crush." He sighed, re-signed to his present state as he squatted down to the puppy's level to scratch the animal behind his ear. "I suppose you do remind me of my mother and I guess I just needed a sympathetic ear."

"Well, I'm very flattered to be compared to Fran-ces, Christopher," Maizie assured him. "Your mother was a very warm, wonderful lady." Touching his arm, she coaxed him back up to his feet. "You know what she'd say to you if she were here?"

He doubted that the woman had the inside track on his late mother's thoughts, but since he'd unburdened himself to Maizie, he did owe her the courtesy of lis-tening to what she had to say. Besides, he really did like the woman.

"What?"

"She'd ask you if you really cared about this Lily you just talked about and then, if your answer was yes, she'd tell you to not just stand there and grieve, but *do* something about it."

The laugh that Christopher blew out had no humor to it. "I think they call that stalking these days, Mrs. Connors."

In contrast, Maizie's laugh was light, airy and com-passionate. "I'm not talking about standing beneath this young woman's bedroom window, reciting lines from *Romeo and Juliet* or *Cyrano*. I'm suggesting doing something creative that would allow your two paths to cross—initially in public," she added for good measure.

Maybe the woman did have something up her sleeve.

At this point, he was willing to try anything. He felt he had nothing to lose and everything to gain.

"Go on," he urged.

"What does your young lady do for a living?" Maizie asked innocently as she stroked the Labrador. "Is she an accountant, or a lawyer, or—"

"She works for a catering company."

"A catering company," Maizie repeated, seeming very intrigued. "In what capacity?" she pressed, knowing very well that Lily was Theresa's pastry chef. "Cooking? Serving?"

"Lily bakes," he answered, although the word was hardly adequate to describe just what she could do. "Creating delicacies" was closer to the actual description, he thought.

Maizie made sure she appeared properly delighted. "Ah, perfect."

Christopher didn't understand. At his feet, the puppy who was Maizie's accomplice in this was beginning to chew the bottom of the exam table. Christopher took out a hard rubber bone and offered it to the teething puppy.

Walter took the bait.

"Perfect?" he asked Maizie.

"Yes, because I just thought of a plan. Every so often, the Bedford animal shelter has Adopt a Best Friend Day. The local businesses contribute donations or their time to help out."

Since he volunteered at the shelter, they had taken to sending him their newsletters. "I'm aware of those events, but I don't see—"

He never knew what hit him as Maizie went into automatic high gear. "I could pull a few strings, make a few suggestions, get this event up and running in, say, a week—two, tops—but probably a week."

How was this supposed to get Lily back into his life? "I still don't see how this has anything to do—"

Maizie held up a finger, about to make a crucial point. "Think how many more people might be attracted to come see the animals in the shelter if they knew that there were pastries being offered, the proceeds all going to keep the shelter operational? 'Come sample the pastries and go home with a best friend,'" Maizie said, coming up with a slogan right on the spot.

Then she eyed Christopher thoughtfully. "Didn't you say that you sometimes volunteer at the shelter, check out the animals, make sure they're healthy?" She knew the answer to that, as well.

His face lit up as his mind filled in the blanks, padding out what his mother's friend was telling him. "You know, that's just crazy enough to work," he agreed. "And Lily makes the most exquisite pastries." Christopher stopped short. He looked at her, slightly puzzled. "How did you know that?" he asked. "How did you know that Lily makes pastries?"

That had been a slip, but one that Maizie was quick to remedy. "I didn't. It was just a lucky guess," she told him. "I have a weakness for pastries."

"Well, if this gets her talking to me, Mrs. Connors, I'll make sure you get a pastry every day for the rest of your life," he promised, getting into the spirit of the thing.

"Which is guaranteed to be short if I start indulging like that," she told him with a laugh. Bending down, she picked up the puppy she had brought as a prop. "So, you're sure that Walter here is healthy?"

"Absolutely in top condition," he assured her. Christopher paused and regarded the Labrador thoughtfully as he scratched the dog's head. "He really does look like Lily's puppy," he told her.

"Then this Lily's puppy must be a very fine-looking dog," Maizie speculated with a wink.

She was quick to turn away and walk out before Christopher had a chance to see how broad her smile had become.

When she first heard about it, Lily's first inclination was to beg off. She knew that if she gave Theresa some excuse as to why she couldn't go to the catering event to serve her pastries, the woman would believe her and say it was all right.

But that would mean lying to someone who had been like a second mother to her. Not only that, it would be putting Theresa in a bind since she already found herself shorthanded. At the last minute, two of her regular servers, Theresa told her, had both come down with really bad colds, making them unable to work.

Lily didn't mind working, didn't mind being in the middle of things and hearing people rave about her desserts. But this particular event had to do with an adoption fair for the city's animal shelter. And that meant that Christopher might be there.

She knew that he volunteered his services at the shelter, that he periodically treated some of the animals that were left there. Funny how the very same thing that had made her love him now just made her feel uneasy.

It had been over two weeks since she'd walked out. Two weeks she'd been functioning—more or less—

without a heart. She hadn't taken any of his calls since that night.

The night that had been by turns one of the best and then worst nights of her life.

For a brief, shining moment, she had thought that she'd finally found the man she'd been looking for all her life. She and Christopher seemed to be of one mind when it came to so many things.

She had wound up running toward him when what she should have done was walked—slowly. Walked slowly and gotten to know the man.

But she hadn't, and then that bombshell had dropped, shattering her world.

Not only hadn't he told her that he'd been engaged, but he'd been the one to break off the engagement—and so recently. That meant he wasn't serious enough about his commitment. If he could break an engagement, walk out on a promise once, well, what was to keep him from doing it again? From bringing her up to the heights of joy only to let her fall onto the rocks of bitter disappointment somewhere down the line? Even if he could put all that behind him and change, that would take time for him to work out. He couldn't be ready for something so solid so soon after breaking off his engagement. He had to see that and once he did, he'd back away from her on his own.

She wasn't going to risk that, risk having her heart ripped out of her chest, risk tumbling down into the abyss of loneliness and despair. She just wasn't built like that. It was better not to dream than to have those dreams ripped up to pieces.

She hurt now, but she would hurt so much more later

if she continued seeing Christopher—continued loving him—only to be abandoned in the end.

"You are a lifesaver," Theresa was saying to her, the woman's very words of praise sabotaging any hope of remaining behind. "I am so shorthanded for this event, I might just have to put out a call to my children to have them come and help. This Adoption Fair promises to be huge." Theresa slanted a look at her protégée. "You are all right with doing this, aren't you, Lily?"

Lily forced a smile to her lips. There was no way she was going to let Theresa down—even if she spent the whole time there looking over her shoulder.

"I'm fine."

"This is for a good cause," Theresa said by way of a reminder. "But I don't have to tell you that. Once you take a pet into your home and into your heart, you see the other homeless animals in a completely different light. You outdid yourself, by the way." Theresa looked over to the boxed-up pastries that were all set to be transported. "Everything smells just heavenly, even through the boxes." Theresa beamed, then asked, "Are you ready?"

Lily snapped out of her mental wanderings. "You mean to go? Sure," she answered a bit too cheerfully.

She was ready to transport the pastries she'd made, ready to do her job. But as far as being ready to see Christopher again, the answer to that was a resounding no.

The best she could hope for was that he didn't show up. After all, it wasn't as if there were going to be any sick animals at the event. The object of this fair was to get as many of the shelter's residents adopted as possible. That guaranteed that only the healthy ones would be on display.

He probably wouldn't be there.

Lily was still telling herself that more than an hour later.

The adoption fair had gotten underway and it seemed as if at least a quarter of Bedford's citizens had turned out to check on the available animals and, as an afterthought, the food, as well.

Her pastries were going fast. She could only hope that some of the people doing all that eating were also seriously considering going home with one of the cats, dogs, rabbits, hamsters and various other species the shelter had on display.

"Your pastries are certainly a major attraction," Theresa said as she passed by the table where Lily was set up. "I think that by the end of the day, your 'contribution' will have raised the biggest amount of money for the animal shelter," Theresa told her with warm approval. In keeping with it being a charitable event, Theresa had charged only half her regular fee. "You should be very proud of yourself."

Although Lily did like receiving compliments, they always made her feel somewhat uncomfortable. She never knew what to say, how to respond, so she usually said nothing, only smiled. This time was no different. After smiling her thanks, Lily pretended to look off toward a group of children who were having fun with a litter of half Siamese, half Burmese kittens that had been born at the shelter. The mother, she'd been told, had been left at the shelter already pregnant.

Patting her hand, Theresa murmured something

about seeing how the others were doing and wove her way into the crowd.

No sooner had she left than Lily heard a voice behind her. "How much for that raspberry pastry?"

Lily stiffened. She would have recognized that voice anywhere. It was the voice that still infiltrated her dreams almost every night. The voice that made her ache and wake up close to tears almost every morning.

"Two dollars," she replied formally.

"Very reasonable." Christopher came around the table to face her. He handed her the two dollar bills and she pushed the paper plate with the aforementioned raspberry pastry toward him. Christopher raised his eyes to hers. "How much for five minutes of your time?"

"You haven't got that much money," she told him crisply.

More than anything, she wanted to flee the premises, to just take off and leave him far behind in her wake. But there was no one to cover for her and she couldn't let Theresa down after she'd agreed to be here.

She was just going to have to tough it out, she thought, hoping that she could.

"I've called you every day, Lily," he told her in a low voice so that they wouldn't be overheard. "You haven't returned any of my calls."

She looked at him sharply. Ignoring each call had been agony for her, especially the ones that came while she was home. The sound of his voice, leaving a message on her answering machine, would fill her house. Fill her head. He made it so hard for her to maintain her stand.

"I didn't see the point, Christopher. It wasn't going

to work anyway. Please just accept that," she told him as calmly as she could.

Now that he had her in front of him, he wasn't about to let this opportunity get away. "Lily, I'm sorry I didn't tell you about Irene, especially since it happened not too long ago. You have every right to be angry about that. I shouldn't have kept it from you."

"I'm not angry that you didn't tell me. I'm not denying that it didn't hurt, finding out that way, but that's not why I haven't returned your calls."

He looked at her, completely at a loss. "Then I don't understand," he confessed.

"*You're* the one who broke off the engagement. And how could you be ready to be with anyone yet?" she asked. "You made a commitment, Christopher. A *lifelong* commitment," she stressed. "And then you backed out of it just like that. Suddenly I come along, and who's to say you wouldn't drop me, just like that, too?" She snapped her fingers to underscore her point.

Unable to remain in the same space as Christopher any longer, she threw up her hands in despair and started to walk away. But she couldn't outpace him and she had a feeling that if she began to run, he'd only catch up. She didn't want to cause a scene, so she stopped moving. Maybe if she heard him out, *then* he'd go away.

"It wasn't 'just like that,'" Christopher contradicted, angry and frustrated by the accusation. "You didn't give me a chance to explain what happened. I wasn't just engaged to Irene for a day or a week, it was for five months—and during that time, she began to change from the person I thought I was going to marry to a completely different woman. Not only that, but she made it clear that she expected me to change as well, to transform into what she, and her family, felt was a suitable match for her and her world.

"I realized that our marriage wasn't going to be a happy one. What I'd pictured was going to be our life together just wasn't going to happen. She wanted me to give up being a veterinarian and go to work for her father's investment firm. In essence, she wanted me to give up being me and I couldn't do that.

"So I broke off the engagement, hired a moving company to pack up all my things and I came back to a place I always considered to be my home."

His eyes on hers, Christopher took her hand in his, in part to make a connection, in part to keep her from running off until he was finished. He still wasn't sure just what she was capable of doing in the heat of the moment.

"After the breakup, I was certain that the last thing I wanted was to be involved in another relationship, but I hadn't counted on meeting someone as special as you. You brought out all the good things I was trying so hard to bury," he confessed. "You made me feel useful and whole and you made me want to protect you, as well.

"I honestly didn't think I could feel this alive again, but I did and it was all because of you. I know how I feel about you." He tried to make her understand, to see what was in his soul—and to see how much she mattered to him. "I don't want to go back into the darkness, Lily. Please don't make me." His hands tightened ever so slightly on hers and he was relieved when she didn't pull them away. "I haven't been able to concentrate, to think straight since you walked out that morning. And frankly," he confided, his expression even more solemn than before, "the animals are beginning to notice that something's very off with me."

He made her laugh. Lily realized that it was the first time she had laughed since before she'd run out of his house.

"Let's just say—for the sake of argument," she qualified, "that I believe you—"

He jumped the gun and asked, "So you'll let me have a second chance?"

"If you did have a second chance at this relationship, what would you do with it?"

There was absolutely no hesitation, no momentary pause to think. He already knew what his answer would be. "I'd ask you to marry me."

She lifted her chin. He knew that meant she was preparing for a confrontation. "The way you asked Irene," she concluded.

"No, because I know now that the Irenes of this world are to be avoided if at all possible," he told her. "They don't want a husband, they want a do-it-yourself project. I want someone who loves me—who *likes* me for who I am and what I have to offer. More than that," he amended, looking into her eyes with a sincerity that almost made her ache inside, "I want you."

"For how long?" she challenged, even though she felt herself really weakening.

"I have no idea how long I have to live," he told Lily honestly, rather than resorting to fancy platitudes, "but for however long it is, I want to be able to open my eyes each morning and see you there beside me. These past two weeks without you have been pure hell and I will do anything, *anything,*" Christopher stressed, "for a second chance."

"Anything?" she asked, cocking her head as she regarded him.

"Anything," he repeated with feeling.

"Well," she began philosophically, "you could start by kissing me."

He immediately swept her into his arms and cried, "Done!"

And it was.

Epilogue

"Well, ladies, I believe we can happily chalk up another successful venture," Maizie whispered to Theresa and Cecilia.

All three women were seated together in the third pew of St. Elizabeth Ann Seton Church. It was six months since the animal shelter adoption fair had taken place, resulting in more than one happy ending.

Maizie beamed with no small pride as she watched the young man standing up at the altar. He was facing the back of the church, anxiously waiting for the doors to open, and for the rest of his life to finally begin.

He looked very handsome in his tuxedo, Maizie couldn't help noticing.

Theresa dabbed at her eyes. No matter how many weddings she attended—and there had been many in the past few years—hearing the strains of "Here

Comes the Bride" never failed to cause tears to spring to her eyes.

"Frances should be here," Theresa told her two friends wistfully.

Cecilia leaned in so that both Theresa and Maizie could hear her. "What makes you think she isn't?" she asked in all seriousness.

Neither of her two friends offered a rebuttal to her question. The thought of their friend looking down on her son with approval as the ceremony unfolded was a comforting one.

"Oh, isn't she just spectacularly beautiful?" Theresa said in awe as they watched Lily slowly make her way down the aisle, each step bringing her closer to the man she was going to spend forever with.

"Every bride is beautiful," Maizie whispered to her friend.

"But some are just more beautiful than others," Theresa maintained stubbornly. Lily had become very special to her in the past year.

"Do you think she ever figured out how Jonathan just 'happened' to appear on her doorstep that morning?" Cecilia asked the others.

"I'm pretty sure she didn't. But I think that Chris might have a few suspicions about that," Maizie whispered back, thinking back to her impromptu visit to his office. He was, after all, a very intelligent young man.

"I told you that you should have used a different dog than one of Jolene's puppies," Cecilia reminded her.

Maizie shrugged. "Water under the bridge," she answered carelessly. "Besides," she went on with a grin her friends had always referred to as mischievous, "it did the trick, didn't it?"

"Shh, it's about to start." Theresa waved a silencing hand at her friends as she nodded toward the priest, who was standing at the front of the altar.

"Not yet," Maizie pointed out as she glanced over her shoulder to the rear of the church. Just before the doors closed, one more wedding participant had to make his way through the narrow opening.

A buzz went up in the church as guests nudged one another, each turning to look at the last member of the wedding party.

"Well, would you look at that."

"Certainly isn't your everyday member of a wedding, is it?"

"Aren't they afraid he's going to swallow the rings?"

The last comment had come from the man in the pew directly in front of the trio.

Unable to hold her tongue any longer, Maizie tapped him on the shoulder. When he turned around to look at her quizzically, she said, "They're not worried about the rings because that's the bride's dog and the groom did an excellent job training him. Besides, if you look very closely, both the rings are secured to that satin pillow in his mouth."

"Why would they include a dog in their wedding?" someone else asked.

The person's companion explained in a voice that said he was the final authority on the subject, "The way I hear it, if it hadn't been for that dog, the two of them would have never met and gotten together."

"Imagine that," Maizie murmured.

She slanted a glance toward Theresa and Cecilia, her eyes shining with amusement. What the young man had just said was the way Lily and Christopher might have viewed how their meeting had come about, but she, Theresa and Cecilia knew the whole story.

Maizie sat back in the pew, paying close attention to what was being said by the couple at the altar. She never tired of hearing vows being exchanged, sealing two people's commitment to one another.

This one, Frances, is for you, Maizie declared silently.

And then, just as with her two friends, her eyes began to tear.

* * * * *

*Don't miss Marie Ferrarella's next romance,
COWBOY FOR HIRE,
available November 2014!*

14_PROMO

MILLS & BOON®

Why not subscribe?
Never miss a title and save money too!

Here's what's available to you if you join the
exclusive **Mills & Boon Book Club** today:

✦ *Titles up to a month ahead of the shops*
✦ *Amazing discounts*
✦ *Free P&P*
✦ *Earn Bonus Book points that can be redeemed
   against other titles and gifts*
✦ *Choose from monthly or pre-paid plans*

Still want more?
Well, if you join today we'll even give you
50% OFF your first parcel!

So visit **www.millsandboon.co.uk/subs**
or call Customer Relations on 020 8288 2888
to be a part of this exclusive Book Club!

SUBS_2014

MILLS & BOON®

Why shop at millsandboon.co.uk?

Each year, thousands of romance readers find their perfect read at millsandboon.co.uk. That's because we're passionate about bringing you the very best romantic fiction. Here are some of the advantages of shopping at www.millsandboon.co.uk:

* **Get new books first**—you'll be able to buy your favourite books one month before they hit the shops

* **Get exclusive discounts**—you'll also be able to buy our specially created monthly collections, with up to 50% off the RRP

* **Find your favourite authors**—latest news, interviews and new releases for all your favourite authors and series on our website, plus ideas for what to try next

* **Join in**—once you've bought your favourite books, don't forget to register with us to rate, review and join in the discussions

Visit **www.millsandboon.co.uk**
for all this and more today!